RAY HOGAN, author of the bestselling
Shawn Starbuck series, was born in Mis-
souri in 1918. Married, with two children,
he has lived most of his life in New Mexico. His father was an early Western
marshal and lawman, and Hogan himself
has spent a lifetime researching the West.
In the last 30 years he has written over
50 books, the majority dealing with the
American West. His work has been filmed,
televised, and translated into 6 languages.

 Signet Brand Double Western

SIGNET Westerns You'll Want to Read

The
RIMROCKER

and

The
OUTLAWED

Shawn Starbuck Westerns

by RAY HOGAN

A SIGNET BOOK
NEW AMERICAN LIBRARY
TIMES MIRROR

Originally appeared in paperback as separate volumes published
by The New American Library.

SIGNET TRADEMARK REG. U.S. PAT. OFF. AND FOREIGN COUNTRIES
REGISTERED TRADEMARK—MARCA REGISTRADA
HECHO EN CHICAGO, U.S.A.

SIGNET, SIGNET CLASSICS, MENTOR, PLUME AND MERIDIAN BOOKS
are published by The New American Library, Inc.,
1301 Avenue of the Americas, New York, New York 10019

FIRST PRINTING (DOUBLE WESTERN EDITION), JANUARY, 1978

1 2 3 4 5 6 7 8 9

PRINTED IN THE UNITED STATES OF AMERICA

The
RIMROCKER

◎ 1 ◎

Shawn Starbuck halted in the shadowy depths of an oak thicket and studied the men. They were in a small clearing, and although it was not yet dark, had built a fire and begun preparations for the evening meal.

Three in the party. He looked beyond them, located their horses. Three also. That meant everyone was accounted for—not that it mattered particularly, but caution was a necessary ally in the world where a loner was always suspect.

Lean, much younger than his brow-hooded gray eyes indicated, he watched the men moving about their chores. For well over a year he had pursued his solitary quest, asking his question of every person encountered on the numberless trails, in the dusty, sunbaked towns, at desolate huts and at sprawling prosperous ranches. Here was another opportunity.

Thoughtful in the fading summer afternoon of the towering, hushed hills, he considered the party. Hard cases, all of them. No doubt of that. One, a ruddy-faced redhaired man, stood slightly apart, taking no hand in the camp chores as if above such menial tasks.

The second, at that moment hunkered before the fire slicing chunks of dried meat into a spider, appeared to be the youngest. He was thick-shouldered with dark, curly hair and a full moustache. The last was a much larger man than the others, fully six feet tall, of heavy build and with big, hamlike hands. All were dusty, travelworn—and armed.

It was difficult to think of his brother running with the likes of these, but then he really didn't know Ben—so he had no measure to go by. As in times before he had but one choice—ask.

"Ev'nin'."

At his bid for recognition, the men came to quick alert,

5

hands dropping to the pistols at their hips. Prodding his horse lightly, Shawn rode forward, elbows up, palms cupped on the horn of his saddle.

"Saw your fire. Figured I could bum a cup of coffee."

The men relaxed. Curlyhair resumed his slicing. The big one spat and settled back on his heels, evidently dismissing the newcomer as of no consequence. The redhead didn't stir, simply waited, watching with suspicious eyes as Shawn rode to the edge of the clearing and halted.

"Man could get himself shot sneaking up like that," the big one said, irritated.

"Been coming down that slope for ten minutes," Starbuck replied evenly. "You heard. All right if I get down?"

The two near the fire glanced at the redhead. He shrugged indifferently, nodded. "Suit yourself."

Shawn dismounted the chestnut and grunted wearily as his heels hit the ground. It had been a long day. "Name's Starbuck," he said, making an invitation of it. Sometimes the approach met introductions all around, other times silence or an outright snub.

"Names don't mean nothing," the big man said, "seeing as you ain't staying long." He reached for a tin cup, poured it full of steaming liquid from a blackened pot, and handed it to Shawn. "Here's yours. Slop it down and move on."

Temper stirred through Starbuck, hardened the line of his jaw as he accepted the cup.

"Obliged," he said quietly. "Except I can dig up a nickel to pay for the coffee if that'll help. Never like to put folks out any."

Curlyhair laughed. The big one stiffened angrily. "Keep your goddam nickel!" he snapped. "And don't you get smart with me, boy! I'll slap you around some."

"Simmer down, Rufe," the redhead murmured. He shifted his small, deep-set eyes to Shawn. "Where you riding, cowboy?"

"Little bit of everywhere. On the move most of the time —looking."

"For what?"

"M'brother. Thought maybe you might know him."

"Might," the redhead said. "He got a name?"

"Ben Starbuck," Shawn said, finishing off the coffee and setting the cup on the rocks near the fire. "Likely not going by that handle, though."

The redhead studied him in silence. Then, "What's he look like?"

"Not sure about that either. Been more'n ten years since

6

I saw him. Probably won't be as tall as me. Had dark hair and sort of blue eyes. Scar over the left one, but a man would have to look close to see it."

Rufe laughed. Curlyhair glanced up. "Hunting for somebody you don't know the name of or what he looks like. What kind of a yarn you handing us?"

"The truth," Shawn said. "Been combing this country for a long time. Important I find him."

Rufe cocked his head to one side slyly. "Take a right smart amount of cash to just go traipsing around here and there, looking and not working. . . . You must be one of then rich galoots from the east."

"Not me! Go busted pretty often and have to scare myself up a job, work for a spell. About to do that right now."

"We're busted flat and hunting work, too," the redhead said quickly, as if to ward off any hint that Starbuck throw in with them.

The man at the fire raised an arm, pointed to Shawn's belt buckle. "You ain't never going clear broke while you've got that."

Starbuck's hand dropped to his ornate, beautifully scrolled oblong silver buckle on which was mounted in carved ivory the figure of a man posed in the celebrated, crooked arm boxer's stance. Once it had been worn by Hiram Starbuck, the gift of admirers who appreciated his fighting skill.

"Reckon not, but I'd never part with it. Belonged to my pa. Came to me when he died."

"Sure mighty fancy," Curlyhair said. "This pa of yours —he a champion or something?"

"Was a farmer but he learned to be a boxer from an Englishman friend of his. Was never beat at it."

"You learn from him?"

"Some. . . . You sure you never run into anybody that could've been my brother?"

Rufe and Curlyhair shook their heads. The third man shrugged. "No more'n you've told us, we could've a hundred times. Description fits half the men in the country. There some extra special reason why you're so set on finding him?"

A most important reason, Shawn thought. As an heir of Hiram's, he must locate his brother or produce incontestable proof of his death. Otherwise the thirty thousand dollars lying in the vaults of an Ohio bank would go to charity, and his legacy of half would be lost.

It was a provision in Hiram Starbuck's will. Ben, who

ran away from home at sixteen rather than live under the iron-fisted rule of his father, had to be found so that he might receive his rightful share of the estate. It was the old man's way of saying he was sorry, and the lawyer had told Shawn there was no way of getting around it. But this was no matter for strangers' ears.

"Him being my brother—guess that's special enough. Folks are both dead now. He's all the kin I got."

"And you just aim to keep looking till you find him," Curlyhair said, eyes again on Shawn's buckle.

Starbuck nodded. "I'll find him."

Rufe grunted. "Plain loco, I'd say. No more'n you got to go on, you can hunt till you got a beard three foot long, and you probably won't run into him."

Again the redhead shrugged. "Luck," he murmured and turned to Curlyhair. "Pete, how's that stew coming?"

"Pretty soon," the younger man replied irritably. "Got to let it boil for a spell." He glanced at Rufe. "Would help some was you to get some more dry wood. . . . You know—I don't recollect ever signing up to be cook for this outfit!"

Rufe walked to the edge of the clearing and dragged back a fair-sized dead limb. Dropping it, he began to stomp the limbs, breaking them into short sticks. Scooping up an armload, he tossed them to Pete's side.

"That make you happy, Mister Brock?"

Curlyhair made no answer, but simply fed a handful of the wood to the flames and swung his attention to the redhead. "Starbuck eating with us? Have to add some water if—"

"Nope, best I be moving on," Shawn cut in before the man could reply. "Obliged just the same."

Whatever it was cooking didn't smell particularly appetizing. Besides, if he expected to reach the Underwood ranch sometime the next day, he'd best keep moving until full dark before halting for the night.

"Might as well hang around," Brock said. "We'll have plenty."

Starbuck shook his head, turned toward his horse. Pete's voice, almost insistent, reached him.

"We got us a pretty nice camping spot here, and you're sure welcome. Don't mind us none if we ain't been too polite. And Rufe ain't half bad, once you know him. Neither is Rutter. Just act that way to fool folks."

Shawn was conscious of Rutter's eyes upon him, sharp, suspicious. "Something about me bother you?"

"That gun you're packing," the other replied. "Don't look like no farmer's iron to me."

8

"Wasn't my pa's. Bought it myself, brand new, when I started hunting for Ben."

"From the looks of the handle, I'd say you've been using it right often," Rutter observed drily.

"Man learns," Starbuck said, equally dry.

Rufe slapped at his leg. "Man! Why, you ain't much more'n a slick-eared kid! I bet you ain't even eighteen yet."

"Old enough to wipe my own nose—and pick my friends," Shawn said, swinging into the saddle.

"And I'll bet you're sharp with that hogleg, too! Even wearing it left-handed! Whooo—ee! Boys, them's the worst kind—them killers that wears their iron on the left side!"

Pete Brock lifted his hands in mock alarm. "You think there's a chance he might be Billy the Kid or somebody 'stead of who he claims? Rufe, you sure better button your lip! Could get yourself in a peck of trouble—killed maybe."

"That's a fact," Rufe grinned. "I ain't saying no more."

Starbuck, only faintly stirred by the razzing, nodded. "Thanks for the coffee. You run into anybody who might be my brother, appreciate your mentioning that I'm looking for him."

Rutter's expression did not change. "Sure," he murmured. "We'll do that."

◎ 2 ◎

Starbuck never placed much confidence in such assurances, even those more convincing than Rutter's. Men forget when no personal interest is involved; Rutter and his two friends could come face to face with Ben that next day and likely make no connection unless, of course, the name Starbuck came up—and that was unlikely. Ben had long ago made it plain he was through with the family name.

Riding slowly down the slope, Shawn again relived the stormy scene that had taken place so far back now in the past. He recalled vividly the large kitchen of the farmhouse near the Muskingum River in Ohio; the squat, powerful figure and glowering features of his father; the tight, drawn face of Ben, fearful yet stubbornly defiant, like a young wolf at bay crouching near the doorway.

"I'm leaving, Pa! And I'm never coming back. Changing my name, too! Don't want anybody knowing you're my kin!"

"You ain't going nowhere, boy," the elder Starbuck had replied. "That licking was for your own good—what you earned for not doing what you was told."

"You always say that, and I'm tired of hearing it. You're not ever getting the chance to beat me again!"

Had their mother been alive there wouldn't have been that final confrontation, Shawn realized years later. Hiram Starbuck, despite his tough, brutal way, displayed a strange, almost childlike reverence for his wife, and while she lived he was not too hard on Ben.

Clare Starbuck had been a schoolteacher, and although her husband had had little patience with books, considering them a waste of good time that might be better spent working in the fields, he had deferred even to her wish that their sons acquire an education. And they did so;

partly in the schoolhouse in Muskingum, and partly through Clare's own efforts.

But when Clare died one winter, a victim of lung fever, a change came over Hiram and brought with it a deep bitterness that for some inexplicable reason focused upon the elder of the two sons. Ben accepted it stolidly for two years, and then rebelled.

As is often the case, the cause was minor: a hayrick that Ben had been told to cover before an impending rain storm. He had gotten busy at another chore and forgotten. Hiram, driving into the yard after a trip to town, noted the rick, and even though the rain had not arrived, flew into a rage, whipped Ben mercilessly.

And so the break came. Hiram never really believed that his son would leave, but he had been wrong. Ben, filled with grim outrage, had turned through the doorway and strode off down the road.

"He'll be coming back," Hiram had said. "And it'll be before morning."

But Ben didn't come back, and as the days passed into weeks, and the weeks changed into months, Shawn knew his brother never would. Ben had been that way: steadfast and determined like their mother, but equally strong and stubborn like their father. He'd cut his rope, and be it too short or too long, he'd make the best of it.

Things changed slightly after Ben's departure. Hiram, who had more or less ignored Shawn before, now turned his thoughts to the younger boy. But it was a less violent, less demanding attention; he actually became somewhat considerate and understanding, either because he had a deep fear of losing him also, or because he saw in Shawn a strong likeness to the woman he'd worshipped. Accordingly, life on the farm was somewhat easier for the boy.

Education, of course, had stopped that spring after Clare Starbuck's death, but Shawn had been quick to learn and accrued more in the way of formal knowledge than the average student; thus he felt no great heartache when he put aside his books for the last time.

Moreover, Hiram seemed to lose some of his zest for working. He hired two men to work the farm; and giving up his weekly boxing exhibitions in the ring they had built behind the general store in town, devoted those hours to instructing Shawn.

"Want you able to take care of yourself," he said once after they had completed a lengthy boxing lesson. "Reckon you'll do that, too. You're quick moving, like your ma. And you got strength, like me."

Praise from Hiram Starbuck was something seldom heard, a jewel to be cherished; but the glitter dulled in the succeeding moment.

"You'll never be real good like Ben, though. He was a natural, that boy. An honest-to-God fighter."

Shawn had said nothing. Ben had always come first with their father; he guessed Ben always would.

That same day as they were washing up on the back porch of the house, Hiram had paused and looked at Shawn keenly.

"You figure he'll ever come home?"

"No, Pa," Shawn had answered. "He never will."

Hiram's square-jawed face, only slightly marked from all the years of bare knuckle contact, had remained intent as he studied his younger son.

"How about you? Aiming to follow him?"

Shawn had scrubbed thoughtfully at the dirt clinging to his arms—dirt ground into his hide when he had been knocked sprawling by one of his father's accurate blows. He'd have no trouble locating Ben if he wanted to leave, join up with him. Several times in the few weeks before his departure Ben had talked to Shawn about going west, to Texas and a town on the Mexican border called Laredo. He'd learned of it from a family named Yawkey who'd camped in the grove below the farm for several days. They had pulled up stakes in Pennsylvania and were heading southwest. Fortunes were being made by bringing cattle across the Mexican border and driving them north to Kansas markets. If a man didn't want to get in business for himself, he could always find a good job working for one of the big outfits. That's where Ben would be—with one of the big cattle companies.

But Shawn had never given much thought to leaving, perhaps because Hiram had not been too hard on him, and he looked upon the man more in awe than in fear; and very possibly, too, an unrecognized, deep-seated sense of loyalty was working below the surface.

"Reckon I'll stay, Pa," he'd replied. "Leastwise till I'm full grown and ready to strike out for myself."

"Which ain't going to be long. You're more'n most men now through the shoulders and arms. And you're talling up. Expect you'll reach six foot. Let's see, you'd be fifteen, maybe sixteen year now."

"Sixteen—almost."

"Sixteen. Sort of lost track of things, seems, since I lost

12

your ma. Well, you're old enough if you take the notion. And I reckon you're man enough—but you'd be a fool. I've got a fine place here. Worth a plenty of money, figuring what's laid aside in the bank."

"Wasn't thinking about that. Just aimed to stay around long as you needed—wanted me."

"Ben was a fool," Hiram went on, murmuring, not hearing. "Could all have been his."

"Only half, Pa," Shawn had said at once in one of the rare times he had contradicted. "Half's rightfully mine."

"Sure—that's what I mean. It'll be split between you two."

Hiram Starbuck hadn't meant it exactly that way, Shawn knew, but the knowledge hadn't bothered him.

A year later Hiram was dead, and with the approaching end he evidently still had Ben uppermost in his mind. His will directed the farm be sold and the money added to his savings.

This was then to be divided equally between his two sons. Shawn's responsibility would be to find his brother and bring him back to Muskingum where the lawyer handling the matter could be satisfied as to his identity. Should Ben be dead, legal proof would have to be produced.

Thus Hiram would have his way. Ben would return home, and the elder Starbuck, who had never learned how to lose at anything, would win again. It would seem, however, that Hiram was so busy being clever that he paid little attention to reality. For one thing Ben undoubtedly had stood by his threat and changed his name. Also, he had been gone well over ten years and his appearance would have altered considerably. He could have grown taller or thinner, or, as time matured him, even have come to take on his father's blocky physique. And as for identification marks, a small scar over one eye was really the only definite one Shawn had to go on. And Ben's present whereabouts? He knew that a family named Yawkey had been headed for a town called Laredo on the Texas-Mexico border, more than a thousand miles away—and that Ben had indicated he would be joining them.

And to compound the difficulties Hiram Starbuck had not thought to provide funds for the search. Possibly it was an oversight and unintentional. At any rate, the lawyer saw it that way and advanced two hundred dollars of Shawn's share of thirty thousand to outfit himself with.

And so Shawn had set out for Laredo where he encountered the first of his disappointments. The Yawkeys were still there—at least some of them. Yes, they remembered a young fellow; name of Ben, seems—or was it Jim? Anyway, he was the one they'd got acquainted with up in Ohio. . . .

Where was he? Lord only knowed! Folks moved around so a body just plain couldn't keep track of nothing. But he'd hung around for a spell and then gone on to California. Come back a year or so later, was on his way to Colorado—place he called Cripple Creek. Was going up there and try his hand at digging gold. Might still be there, too. Heard tell folks had done right well in that part of Colorado.

But Ben wasn't at Cripple Creek either. Shawn was told there was a man who sort of fit the description who'd done a little mining back in the hills. Had no luck and one day up and pulled out for Wyoming; said he was going back to cowpunching. . . . He was a plain fool, though; once or twice he put on a fist fight—"boxing exhibitions" he called them—in one of the saloons so's to raise a little eating money. Was a caution the way he danced around and beat up them other birds—some of them a lot bigger'n him, too! Could have made himself a living putting on them shows and not fooled around with punching cows. . . . Whereabouts in Wyoming? Rock Springs. . . .

It could have been Ben—it probably was; but Shawn was six days late. The fellow he was asking about worked for the Haycox outfit, the town marshal informed him. Gone now, about a week. Got in a fight with the ranch foreman and damn near beat him to death. Fellow was in the right, too, but the foreman was Haycox's brother-in-law, so there just wasn't nothing for the fellow to do but ride on.

The marshal couldn't recall his name. Could've been Ben, or Dan, and the men at Haycox's knew him as Tex, but the lawman was pretty sure it was the right man; he did have a scar over one eye. . . . Was *he* looking for him he'd head for Dodge City. . . . Punchers on the loose all seem to light out for there. . . . But Ben wasn't in Dodge. There was a rider, though, who—

So it began, and so it went; often close, but always not quite, and during those passing months Shawn grew taller, leaned out into a big-shouldered man with cool, blue eyes that belied the youthfulness of his features and his years. He changed inwardly and a remoteness born of patience grew in him; and while there was friendliness for those who were congenial, there was also a quiet reserve that no one ever succeeded in penetrating.

14

He became a wanderer, drifting ceaselessly, halting only when he ran out of money and was forced to take employment. He learned as he went, acquiring knowledge and experience, but never losing sight of purpose: find Ben.

It was a disheartening, discouraging task made endurable only by the restlessness of youth; but Shawn Starbuck never thought of that: he thought only of the day when he would encounter his brother and the quest would end.

He'd take his share and build himself a ranch, he had decided. At first he had made no plans, being unsure just what he did want to do with his half of the money. But now he knew; a ranch—a fine one. Maybe Ben would want to throw in with him. Together, cash pooled, they could have one of the best. He knew where there was good land to be had, land where grass stood knee high the year around and there was always plenty of water—

But first: find Ben.

A practical streak inherited from his schoolteacher mother always interrupted such dreams when they began to captivate him, set his pulse to racing. . . . Find Ben. . . . That came first—

He glanced to the undulating horizon in the west. The sun was well below it now, and darkness was closing in fast. Time to be looking for a suitable camp site. Raising himself in the stirrups, he glanced around. He was about midway on a long hillside.

Everywhere was scrub oak, twisted cedars, an occasional pinon laden with sticky, nut-filled cones. No darker green band of growth indicated the presence of a stream or spring. It would have to be a dry camp, but that was not unusual, nor was it a problem. He had learned to carry an ample supply of water in two canteens in his passage across the arid west, and both were still well-filled from his last stop. He'd see to the chestnut's needs from one of them.

A small break in the brush appeared before him. He rode his horse into the clearing and swung down. For a time he stood in silence, listening into the falling night, alert for any sounds that would warn him of the presence of others. There was only the clicking of insects, the faraway mourning of a dove. Satisfied, he began to pull his gear off the gelding, lay it aside. The big, red horse was in fine condition, just as he always seemed at the end of a day. Shawn had made a smart trade that day in Abilene when he'd swapped the old mare he'd started out on for the chestnut—even if it had taken his last dollar.

"Ain't the fastest thing on legs," the down-on-his-luck

cowpuncher who owned him had said. "But you ain't never coming across one with more bottom."

It had been true. Parting with the mare, last tangible symbol of home on the Muskingum, had not been easy, but Shawn knew a long, hard trail lay ahead—all in a country where a good horse was a man's most important possession, and thus the exchange was made. The tall, white-stockinged gelding had never given him cause to regret it.

When the animal had been picketed outside the clearing, watered, and given the last of the grain carried as reserve against the all too many times when no natural feed was available, Starbuck got down to preparing his own meal. He was low on grub, too, and if things had felt right back in the camp with Rutter, Pete Brock, and the big one called Rufe, he would have put in the night there, contributing what he had in food to make the meal complete. But he'd learned to judge men well, and there was something about the trio that hadn't set right with him.

It mattered little, anyway. Tomorrow he'd locate the Underwood ranch and there restock his supplies if he discovered he'd reached another dead end.

Dead end. . . . How many had there been since he'd ridden out to find Ben? How many false leads? How many times had he pulled hopefully into a town or a ranch or a homestead, certain that he'd reached the end of his quest, only to meet with disappointment?

So many times that surging expectancy and soaring anticipation no longer moved him. Now, when he reached a goal where his brother might be, he approached with a quiet caution, almost a reluctance, and always with the thought: *don't get all fired up—wait and see,* uppermost in his mind. He'd learned it was better that way. Somehow the keen edge of disappointment was blunted.

Underwood's could prove to be like all the others. A cattle buyer in Wichita had heard Shawn ask his question of a bartender in a saloon and had spoken up: the trail boss for a rancher named Underwood sort of matched the description, such as it was, of Ben. Underwood's spread was over New Mexico way, up in the northeastern part. Somewhere near the South Canadian River. . . .

Big place, the cattle buyer had assured him. Be no trouble locating it. . . . Underwood used the Sunrise brand—a circle with four bars sticking up from the top. . . . Man could spot his cattle anywhere. . . . Might pay to have a look—talk with the trail boss, if he didn't mind the long ride. . . .

16

Shawn didn't. He never turned away from a possibility, even if it meant backtracking over trails he'd just traveled. There was always the chance—and this time it was better than a good possibility. Ben had been good with livestock, and likely had developed into pretty much of a leader where men were concerned. Starbuck had headed west that next day—and now, tomorrow, he'd know he'd either find the end of the trail, or the beginning of another one.

After his meal of bacon, fried potatoes, grease-soaked hardtack and black coffee, Shawn stretched out on his blankets and stared up into the star-littered, velvet sky. The dove was mourning again, and from somewhere close by an owl hooted peevishly.

Sometimes the weariness of the search, the loneliness of the trails, drilled deep into his bones. . . . Sometimes it all seemed so hopeless. Ben was everywhere—nowhere; Ben could be dead, buried under another name. . . . And, wanderer, drifter that Shawn had become, he could waste an entire lifetime—end up with nothing.

Not entirely. . . . He'd been a lot of places, met a lot of people—some good, some bad, and from all of them he'd learned something. That had value. Like the gunslinger he'd helped out of a jam. He'd really found out how to use a pistol from him—how to bring it up fast and smooth and at the same time preserve accuracy. *Left-handed man's got an edge*, Allison—the gunslinger—had told him. . . . And then there was that lawman in Wyoming who had befriended him. . . .

The dry crack of a dead branch brought Starbuck from a sound sleep. Motionless, eyelids only slightly cracked to give the impression he was not yet awake, he strained to locate the intruder. It was near first light, still too dark to distinguish much in the shadows. He could see nothing.

But there *was* something—someone out there. Indians? He discarded the thought. In this area there were only pueblo tribes, mostly farmers. No, it wouldn't be Indians.

Abruptly he tensed. A figure stepped from the fringe of brush directly opposite into the clearing. Pete Brock. Shawn's fingers sought and found the pistol lying beside him under his blanket. Continuing to hold himself rigid, he watched Brock, curly hair straggling down over his forehead, cross and halt before him. A hard grin was on the man's lips as he drew back his leg and delivered a kick to Starbuck's feet.

Shawn raised himself to a sitting position. Being awake, Brock's actions did not startle him.

"What the hell do you want?" he asked coldly.

17

Pete's grin widened. "Why, I just dropped by for that there buckle you're wearing. Took a real fancy to it."

Starbuck swept the blanket aside, sprang upright in a single motion. Right fist cocked, left hand holding his pistol, he faced Brock.

"Move on," he said in a low voice. "Only thing you'll get from me is trouble."

In that same instant Shawn heard the rustle of brush behind him. Alarm shot through him. He started to jerk to one side, wheel. In the next fragment of time he felt himself falling as solid pain and exploding lights overpowered his consciousness.

◎ 3 ◎

Starbuck fought his way back from what seemed a deep pit. Sharp knives stabbed at his brain and a mist swirled about him in thick layers. He stirred, shook his head. The mist began to fade but there was no lessening of the pain. Somebody—either Rutter or Rufe—had handed him one hell of a wallop from behind with a pistol butt or a club while Pete Brock held his attention.

He swore angrily, rolled over, sat up. The abrupt motion sent a wave of giddiness rushing through him. Fixed, eyes closed, he hung there, waited for it to pass. The world stopped spinning; slowly, he raised his head, looked around.

Two lean, gray wolves waiting stolidly at the edge of the clearing came warily to their feet. Tails drooped, heads slung low, they considered him through agatehard yellow eyes and then slunk off into the brush.

Starbuck grinned humorlessly, muttered: "Not this time, damn you," and pulled himself to his feet.

He stood there, a tall, swaying shape in the clear, raw light of early dawn, until his senses once more ceased their gyrations, and then took stock. The buckle—belt with it —was gone. His pockets had been turned inside out. Except for the clasp knife he'd carried since a small boy, he'd been picked clean.

Not entirely. . . . He saw his forty-five then. It lay under the edge of his blanket, only a part of the butt visible. And he wasn't broke. The twenty-dollar gold piece he carried as reserve was in its secret pocket sewed inside his shirt.

That wasn't important—the buckle was, along with the fact that he'd been set upon, slugged, and left for dead on the mountainside.

Grim, he retrieved the pistol, thrust it under the waistband of his pants. Walking quickly, he crossed to where

19

the chestnut waited in the brush and led him back into the clearing. Saddling and bridling the horse, he collected his possessions (he had found his holster in a clump of rabbit brush where it had been tossed after being removed from the belt) and stowed them in their customary places; he mounted and rode out. Breakfast could wait. He was too worked up to delay.

Circling the clearing, he located the spot where their horses—at least two of them—had been hidden, and later where they had moved off, striking due west. That brought a grunt of satisfaction from Starbuck's set lips and he cut the chestnut onto the outlaws' trail. They had an hour, perhaps two, on him, but that meant nothing; he'd run them down if it meant tracking them all the way to Mexico.

They had left an open trail, making no effort to conceal hoofprints. Probably figured him dead, or else that he wouldn't be fool enough to come after them—one against three: a slick-eared kid, as Rufe had put it, taking on three hardened men. The corners of his mouth tightened. Rufe would learn—the odds meant nothing.

He rode steadily down. Soon the sun broke over the rim of hills behind him, and began to spread its light and warmness through the brush, across the flats, into the deep washes and sandy-bottomed arroyos. Rocks began to gleam dully under the brightening rays, prepared to resume their endless chore of gathering heat during the day only to surrender it when night again fell.

A brown and gray cottontail scampered out from beneath the chestnut's hooves, causing the big horse to throw back his head and shy to the side. Shawn had a second glimpse of the wolf pair, still lurking about, not entirely ready to give up on what had appeared to be an easy prey.

He reached the foot of the slope, halted, and looked out upon the wide mesa lying before him. It was almost level with only a short rise lifting here and there to break the grass-covered, tablelike expanse. No riders were in sight. Impatiently Starbuck swore. He hadn't thought he was that far behind the three men. Evidently he'd been unconscious longer than he figured.

Spurring the gelding, he broke out of the fringe of mountain mahogany in which he had paused, moved onto the flat, eyes once more on the ground as he searched for tracks. It wasn't going to be easy here; the country had enjoyed a wet spring and the grass was thick, spongy. Hoofprints would be hard to spot, harder yet to follow.

But eventually he found where three riders had descended the slope, still heading west, and assuming they would continue to follow such course at least until they reached the dark green band of trees on the far side, he urged the gelding to a lope and headed for that distant point.

An hour later he rode up to the trees, found them bordering a small stream that wound off north and south in an aimless, carefree fashion. He located the tracks of the outlaw's horses some time after that, having had to search both up and down stream before discovering what he sought. They had entered the water, and Starbuck, in almost their exact marks, followed, crossed over. There he halted, puzzled, a deep frown on his face. There were no signs indicating where the men had emerged. And then the answer came to him: the riders were keeping their horses in the stream, were now deliberately wiping out their trail. That could mean only one thing; they had spotted him.

Silent and simmering, he studied the soft ground along the stream. Which way had they gone—up or down? It was anybody's guess. Keeping close to the edge of the creek, he rode against the current for a mile or so, found no trace. Reversing, he headed the gelding back with the flow. After a similar distance below his original starting point, he once again halted. He'd met with no better success.

Hooking a leg over the saddlehorn, he stared out over the land now beginning to shimmer with the steadily rising heat. There was no doubt in his mind: they had seen him, and they were doing everything possible to lose him. Something had forced them to change their minds.

He wasted no effort endeavoring to figure out what such might be, gave his consideration instead to wondering where they could have gone. Had they mentioned any destination during the time he was in their camp? He could recall none. They had been low on grub. . . . It was logical to assume they'd head for the nearest town.

Shawn picked his mind for some knowledge of the country. Was Taos near? He seemed to recall that it was pretty far north and somewhat west of that particular area. Santa Fe? The old settlement that marked the end of the Trail was due west, he was certain. . . . They could be going there.

Las Vegas. It dawned on him suddenly. Las Vegas was a good, live town, he'd heard, and it lay well this side of Santa Fe. Since it was closer, they undoubtedly would make for it. Immediately he settled into his saddle and pulled away from the creek, aiming the chestnut for a long bank of low buttes in the distance. He had no idea how far away the town would be—sixty, seventy miles, possibly more. But it didn't matter; that's where the outlaws would go.

He'd have to ignore Underwood's ranch and the possibility of finding Ben there, for the time being. Starbuck shook his head in irritation. He didn't like the thought of passing up the opportunity, but on the other hand another day or two could hardly make any difference. Underwood's trail boss was not likely to disappear in that short a time.

He reached the bluffs and began a slow climb up a steep wash to the crest. No grass grew here. The sterile, rock-studded ground afforded life only for a scattering of globular clumps of snakeweed and yellow-flowered groundsel, little else.

The chestnut found the grade difficult. Halfway up Shawn dismounted and went on foot, leading the big horse with a slack rein so that he could pick his own way. They crested the rugged formation, came onto a flat, halted. A dozen yards back from the rim, a rider slouched in his saddle, sweat-stained hat brushed to the back of his head, watching their arrival with lazy interest.

"Howdy," he said, shifting to one side. "All that racket you was making, I figured maybe a whole passel of mustangs was coming up the draw."

Starbuck swung onto the gelding, rode forward. "Hard climb," he commented.

"Can't fault you there. . . . You know where you're at, friend?"

"New Mexico—not much else. It make a difference?"

"Some. This here's Underwood range. We're a mite touchy about strangers riding across it, and plenty interested in where they're going."

A stir of surprise moved Shawn. "Was looking for the Underwood place. Didn't know I found it."

The old puncher plucked at his tobacco-stained moustache. "You got business with Sam?"

"In a way. Aim to ask about a man working for him. First off, however, I've got to catch up with three jaspers who owe me. Figure they came this direction. You see them?"

The older man eyed Starbuck shrewdly. "Owe you, eh? No, ain't seen nobody this morning but you."

"Likely heading for Las Vegas. It on west of us?"

"Vegas? Well, sort of. A bit south, maybe. . . . This

22

fellow you're aiming to ask Sam Underwood about—what's his name?"

"Ben Starbuck, but he'll be going by something else."

"Starbuck sure ain't familiar. Best thing you can do is forget Sam, talk to Tom Gage. He's ramrodding the outfit. Does all the hiring and firing."

Shawn nodded. "Obliged. I'll drop back and see him after I've taken care of this other business in—"

"If you're aiming to go to Vegas, you'll be riding right by the ranch. Road cuts across Underwood's property."

That was a bit of good luck. Starbuck said: "Fine. How's the quickest way to get there?"

The puncher twisted around, spat a stream of brown juice at a nearby rock, and pointed to a dark, cone-shaped hill in the distance.

"Just you set your sights on that. You'll run smack-dab into Underwood's."

Shawn thanked the man and rode on. He was beginning to feel hunger now and considered briefly the idea of halting, brewing himself some coffee and eating the last of his supplies. But the prospect of soon reaching the Underwood ranch, meeting with the man who could be Ben, washed all thought of that away. He could hold out.

Close onto midday, with the sun bearing down full strength, he reached the end of the mesa across which he was riding and looked down into a broad, green swale. A cluster of well-kept buildings surrounded by large trees lay in exact center. This would be Underwood's.

Spurring the chestnut, he came off the plateau, followed out a narrow arroyo and entered a clearly defined road that led up to the gate. He cut into the yard, angling toward a long, barracks-type structure that lay to the right and somewhat beyond the main house. That would be the crew's quarters, and if Gage, the foreman, was around and not on the range, he most likely would be found there.

Passing to the right of the first building, Shawn glanced to the corrals ahead, noted the several horses lazing in the sun. At that moment a door slammed, drew his attention. A thin, elderly man stiffly erect, with a sharp face and thick moustache, came from a side entrance of the house, advanced to the center of the yard, and halted. Either Underwood or Tom Gage, Shawn guessed.

Veering the chestnut, Starbuck angled toward the older man, conscious of a cold, hostile scrutiny from small, intensely blue eyes. Pulling to a halt before him, Shawn started to speak but was silenced by a question.

"You another one of them looking for Sam?"

There was impatience in the voice. This would be Gage, Shawn decided, and irritated for some reason.

"Looking mostly for you," he began, and then his jaw clamped shut as the bunkhouse screen door opened and three men moved into the yard. He forgot everything else in a sudden surge of anger as he instantly spurred the gelding forward; he leaped from the saddle in a low dive for the man in the center of the trio—Brock.

◎ 4 ◎

Starbuck's outstretched arms wrapped around Brock while he was still in mid-air. They went down in a driving wedge, bowling Rufe over as they collided with him. Rutter shouted a curse, springing back beyond reach of the struggling men.

Brock, on the bottom, took the brunt of the fall. Wind gushed from his mouth and his eyes rolled wildly. Shawn, jerking aside, bounded to his feet. Seizing the gasping man by the shirt front, he yanked him upright, knocked him sprawling with a hard blow to the chin.

Rufe muttered something, closed in from behind. Shawn pivoted fast, fell into a cocked stance. He jabbed with his left, rocked the big man off balance, and then in the smooth, lightning-fast manner that Hiram Starbuck had taught him, crossed with a whistling right.

Starbuck's balled fist caught the outlaw flush on the jaw. Rufe stalled, a surprised look filling his eyes while the muscles of his face sagged. His mouth fell open, and taking an uncertain step backwards, he went down.

Shawn spun back to Pete. A fist met him before he had completely turned, jarred him to his heels. He shook off the effects of the blow, lowered his head and moved into the spinning dust stirred up by their scuffling boots. Pete Brock was a confidently grinning, half-crouched shape awaiting him.

Almost instinctively Shawn dropped into the stance he'd been taught: arms forward and crooked at the elbows, fists knotted. Pete's grin widened.

"A real fancy Dan, eh!" he said, and lunged through the haze.

Starbuck took a slanting step forward, met the rush with a stiff left, again brought over a hard right. Both blows landed high on the outlaw's head, had little good results. Pete, still grinning, turned, moved in, arms churning.

25

Shawn ignored the obvious attempt at confusing him, feinted left, dodged to the right and suddenly hammered two stinging blows to the man's face.

Brock hesitated, frowned. He appeared puzzled, as if he couldn't understand where the hard-knuckled fists had come from. Shawn watched him narrowly, circled slowly. He slid a glance at Rufe, on his feet, sagged against the wall of the bunkhouse; the man was rubbing at his jaw in a dazed fashion. It was clear he no longer had any interest in the proceedings.

Rutter stood back well out of the way, watching it all with cold, speculative eyes. A bit to his left Tom Gage, hanging onto the reins of the chestnut, was looking on with frank pleasure.

Starbuck, the anger within him now satisfied in pure physical violence, abruptly danced in and flicked Brock on the face with a sliding blow that drew blood. He tapped the outlaw again, lightly, below an eye, brought an immediate welt, followed that with a cross that cracked like a mule skinner's whip when it landed. Pete yelled in rage and lunged forward.

Shawn blocked the charge with an outstretched left, swiftly complemented that with a solid right. Pete halted abruptly, eyes rolling to the back of his head. He caught himself, raised his arms, came on. Again Shawn landed that vicious combination. The other man's knees quivered. His hands dropped heavily to his sides. His head sagged forward, and sinking quietly, he sprawled full length in the dust.

Breathing hard, Starbuck threw a look to Rufe and then to Rutter. Neither seemed inclined to pursue the fight. Stepping back, he recovered his pistol from where it had dropped, thrust it into his waistband. Again touching Rutter and Rufe with his eyes, he crossed to where Brock lay.

Nudging Brock with his toe, he straightened him out to where he was flat on his back. Reaching down, Shawn tripped the tongue of the buckle, and pulled the belt free. Hanging it over his shoulder, he dug into Brock's pockets, drew out a handful of loose coins. Assuming that all belonged to him, he thrust them into his own pocket and turned to face Rutter and Rufe.

"Which one of you slugged me from behind?"

Rutter's eyes narrowed. "You got your goddam belt back—and your money. Don't press your luck—leave it at that."

"Not about to," Starbuck said tightly. "It you?"

26

The redhaired man shook his head. "Wasn't even there," he murmured.

Shawn's pressing gaze shifted to Rufe. "Leaves you."

"Leaves me," the big man said, and reached for his pistol.

In a single stride Starbuck was on him. With a sweep of his right hand he knocked the weapon to the ground. He caught the man by the arm, swung him half about, smashed a balled fist into his belly. Rufe grunted, doubled over. Instantly a fist thudded into his chin. He straightened up, fell back against the side of the bunkhouse.

From the tail of his eye Shawn saw Rutter drop into a crouch as his hand darted for the pistol on his hip. With a quick, half-turn Starbuck came about, his left hand gripping the forty-five, holding it level on his opponent.

Rutter's fingers had closed about his weapon, stalled. Somewhere a door opened and closed in the heat-filled hush. Starbuck, his gaze never shifting from Rutter, rode out the dragging moments.

"What's it to be?" he asked, finally.

Rutter shrugged, allowed his hand to slide off the butt of his pistol. Shawn relaxed slowly, aware now that there were others in the yard watching besides Tom Gage. A well-dressed man was approaching in short, quick strides. Two of the hired help had paused near a corral, and another, pitchfork across his shoulder, was standing in the doorway of the barn. The faces of two women, one young, were at a window of the main house. . . .

"Supposing you both forget about them irons," the old foreman drawled. "You got some shooting to do, get off the place."

Rutter swung his attention to Gage, raked him with a contemptuous glance, and moved toward Rufe. Starbuck, breathing easier, shook off the tension that gripped him with a stir of his shoulders, crossed to the chestnut. He nodded crisply to the older man.

"Obliged," he said, taking the gelding's leathers. "Didn't aim to start a—"

"Just what the hell's going on here?"

It was the well-dressed man who had apparently come from the main house. He was slim, business-like, somewhere in his forties. He had graying hair and close-set, dark eyes. This would be Sam Underwood.

Gage nodded genially. "Well, Sam, seems that them friends of your'n must've jumped this young fellow, took some of his belongings—that belt he's holding and a bit of cash. He was just getting it back."

27

The rancher frowned. "You know I don't stand for brawling on my place, Tom—"

"Sure, I know it. But that young rimrocker's sort of all-of-a-sudden-like in his acting. Wasn't nothing I could do about it."

"He a friend of yours?"

"Ain't never seen him before."

Underwood's eyes swept Shawn coolly, appraisingly, and moved on to Rutter and Rufe who were now helping Pete Brock to his feet.

"Mr. Underwood," Shawn said, "my name's Starbuck. Fight was no fault of your foreman's. . . . Rode in to ask—"

The rancher lifted his hand, brushed Shawn aside and moved toward the three defeated men. He pointed to a horse trough near the corrals, and then with a jerk of his head to Rutter, strode across the yard to where a circular bench had been built around the trunk of a large cottonwood tree.

Starbuck watched the man for a moment, and then drawing his pistol, brushed the dust from it, tested its action. Digging into his saddlebags, he withdrew the holster, slid the belt into the fold, and strapped it about his waist. Dropping the weapon into its leather pocket, he again looked to Gage.

"Sorry about the ruckus. When I rode in had other things on my mind—then I saw them."

"Forget it. Was what I told Sam somewheres close to the truth?"

"Is the truth. Ran into them back in the hills late yesterday. They came at me later in the night—when I was asleep. Rufe—the big one—hit me from behind while I was talking to Brock. Then they robbed me."

"Expect you've cured them of trying that again—on you, anyway," Gage observed drily, and then shook his head. "Seeing you take on all them three at once, put me in mind of a mustang I roped up Montana way—big and strong and feared of nothing—a real rimrocker, he was."

Shawn grinned. "Reckon this is the first time I've ever been called a horse, but I take it you mean it kindly." He glanced toward the bench. Rufe and Pete, both dripping from dousing themselves in the trough, had joined Underwood and Rutter.

"They work here?"

"No, sir!" Gage snapped. "Strangers to me. Rode in a couple hours back, looking for Sam. Friends of his, they claimed, and I guess they are from the way they're talking.

28

Say—that there was about the fanciest job of cutting a man down to size I ever seen! Where'd you learn to use your fists like that?"

"My pa," Shawn replied, taking the edge of the belt buckle between his fingers and tipping it so the older man could see it better. "He was real good at it. Could have been a champion, I guess if my ma had let him."

"Well, he sure taught you good. Once seen one of them boxing matches. Over in Fort Worth. Black fellow and his manager, touring the country. From England, they was. Picked himself out the biggest man in the saloon and dang nigh beat him to death."

Starbuck nodded. "Pa always said a man's fists could be deadlier than a gun, if they were used right."

"Amen," Gage said. He cocked his head to one side. "Appears to me you've learned how to use both."

Shawn's thick brows pulled together in a frown. "I'm no gunhawk, if that's what you're thinking. But you move around a lot, you learn a lot. Things sort of happen to you and you measure up, or run. Don't like running."

"See what you mean," Gage said thoughtfully. "Just riding through?"

"Not exactly. Was trying to explain that to Mr. Underwood when he walked off. Came here looking for a man —one working for you."

"There's a plenty of them doing that. What's his name?"

Shawn Starbuck grinned wryly, knowing beforehand the reaction he would get when he answered the question. It was an old, familiar procedure.

"I don't rightly know," he said.

◎ 5 ◎

Sam Underwood had been gone when Rutter and the others had arrived. He'd ridden out early that morning to have a look at his south range and, incidentally, to drop by for a few minutes' chat with Greg Cryden who owned the spread below him. Cryden had been in the country for a long time, was well thought of and his influence in political matters was extensive.

Amy Underwood had met Sam at the door when he returned. Her flaccid, colorless features were drawn with concern and there was a troubled look in her eyes. They were her sole claim to beauty, large, dark and soft as those of a deer—and they were the only thing about her that hadn't changed since the day of their marriage.

"They came after you rode off," she had said. "Told me they were old friends of yours from the war. They acted as though I should invite them in, but I didn't like their looks and told them to wait in the bunkhouse. Who are they, Samuel? Something about them gives me the chills."

He had shrugged off her distress, but within him a dread had sprung alive as facets of his past stirred in the shadowy recesses of his mind. Was it Guy Rutter and Brock and Rufe Mysak—and Billy Gault? Three men, Amy had said. Someone was missing. Which one? What did they want?

But he had smiled, assured Amy that everything was all right. It wouldn't do to show alarm in her presence. She never dreamed he could be other than what he had always professed to be—an honest, hard-working, successful rancher well on his way to becoming governor of the Territory.

The same applied to Holly. In the eyes of his stepdaughter, he represented the utmost, a man who could do no wrong—the epitome of what a husband and father should be. To shatter her illusions would break her heart.

Maybe he was upsetting himself over nothing, if, indeed, it was Rutter and the rest of the bunch from the Old Fifth Ohio—and he couldn't be sure of that until he got a look at them. Even if it were them, they could just be riding through, heard he was there, stopped to pass the time of day. Hope rose within him.

"Where'd you send them?" he had asked.

"The bunkhouse," Amy had replied. "I saw them go in."

He had walked to the window, glanced out just in time to see the men coming out of the crew's quarters. His spirits had sagged once more as all the harsh fears lifted again within him, began to claw at his guts.

He had guessed right. Guy Rutter—Pete Brock—Rufe Mysak. All of the bunch who'd been with him that day at Medford's Crossing, all but Billy Gault.

"Do you know them?" Amy had asked.

"Know who?" Holly, entering the room at that moment, had broken in.

"Some men to see your father, honey," Amy had answered. "No one you should meet."

An instant later everything in the yard was in confusion as some stranger, who had been talking to Tom Gage, suddenly tore from his horse and took on Brock and Rufe Mysak, knocking them about like dummies.

Sam Underwood had watched briefly, marveling at the stranger's ability and deriving some enjoyment from the punishment being meted out to Mysak and Brock; and then he had turned away from the window to the door.

"I'll take care of this," he had said in a firm, decisive way, and gone out into the yard to meet the specters from his past.

Now, facing the three men in the cooling shadow of the cottonwood—one he'd hauled in from the river bottom and planted with his own hands ten long years ago—he looked each one over, masking his apprehension with an impersonal smile.

"What brings you men here?"

Rutter's reddish hair was much thinner than it once was, but his small, mean eyes had not changed; the blue was colder, if anything.

"You," Guy Rutter said.

"And I can't say you seem real pleased to see your old army pals again," Mysak, much heavier than in previous years, observed. "Does he, boys?"

Brock, still somewhat dazed, shook his head woodenly. Rutter shrugged, spat.

"All right," Underwood snapped. "I'm glad to see you." And then in an effort to further prove his words, he added, "Where's Gault?"

"Billy? Hell, he's dead," Mysak answered. "Got his fool head shot off in a poker game. About a year after he was mustered out."

"Too bad," Underwood murmured. "Figured you'd all be living back east somewhere. Surprised to see you in this part of the country. Where you headed?"

"Right here," Rutter said in his flat, emotionless way.

The rancher's head lifted in surprise. "You came on purpose to see me? Didn't think anybody—that is—any of the old bunch knew—I—"

"We heard," Rutter said blandly. "Heard all about how you had yourself a big ranch and was doing fine—and how you were in the banking business—was even about to become governor. Told ourselves you'd be real happy to help us with a job we've got in mind."

"Of course. Be happy to do what I can for you," Underwood said, relief in his voice. "Have some influence around the Territory, if I do say so myself. Just what is it you're planning?"

"We're robbing the bank in Las Vegas," Rutter said, and smiled.

Sam Underwood's jaw sagged. "You're *what?*"

"Your hearing's good. Was up in Denver, learned about this bank in Las Vegas—how all the big cattle growers kept their cash in it, same as the army at Fort Union does with its payroll. Sounded real good. We'd been looking for something easy for quite a spell."

"But—you—"

"Sounded even better when we found out one of the owners was an old friend of ours—Sam Underwood."

"Wasn't real sure it was our Sam, not at first anyway," Mysak said. "Then we took us a little trip to Las Vegas and hung around till we got a look at you. Sure enough, it was our Sam—but we was betting it would be all the time. Be like old Sam, we told ourselves, to take his share of that payroll and set himself up in business."

The blood in Underwood's veins had been turning slowly to ice. "That money—share—always intended to send it back, not keep it. . . ."

"But you didn't," Rutter said drily. "Even if you did you got some way of bringing life back into them guards we killed taking it?"

The rancher looked down and shook his head helplessly.

32

"That was a mistake—a big mistake. I was a fool to throw in with you."

"But you did—and you're coming in with us again or—"

Underwood's eyes, unseeing, were on Pete Brock, now finally recovered and gingerly probing his bruised, discolored face with careful fingers.

"Or—" he prompted halfheartedly.

"This whole country's going to know right quick about the real Sam Underwood—about how he was in on robbing an army paymaster during the war, and how three soldiers got killed trying to stop it."

"But I—"

"How's that going to sound to all those folks who're backing you for governor? How's that fine wife of yours going to take it? Hear she cuts quite a figure with all the high society muckity-mucks in Santa Fe—Denver, even! And you got yourself a daughter who—"

The mention of his family stiffened Sam Underwood. His features hardened and a sternness came into his eyes.

"You'll find it won't be so easy—not with me—"

"Oh, it'll be easy, all right," Rutter cut in. "About the easiest thing a man could imagine. We just haven't worked this deal up overnight, Sam. We've been planning it out for better'n a month."

"Ever since we run out of cash," Pete Brock volunteered.

"Last little job we done over Kansas way didn't pay off so good," Mysak added.

Guy Rutter waited in sullen patience for the two men to speak, and then again turned to Underwood.

"We got a good look at your bank, know just how to handle it. Vault ain't much. Rufe can blow it with no problems. And if you're getting an idea about tipping off the sheriff or somebody, you better forget it damn quick."

"You don't think—"

"That part's all covered, too. We brought us a lady friend who's sort of been running with us the last couple of years. She got herself a job in that Gold Dollar Saloon in Las Vegas. She's keeping a letter for us."

Underwood said, "A letter?"

"A real important one. It's made out to the U.S. Marshal, and it tells all about that payroll robbery and killing at Medford's Crossing. Gives all our names. I even dug up some of the newspaper stories about it, put them in the envelope. If anything happens to us while we're cleaning out your bank—or after—she hands that letter over to the first lawman she can get to."

The rancher's features had drained of all color. "Then she knows—"

"All she knows is what she's to do with the envelope if you double-cross us."

"Guy's fixed things up plenty good," Mysak said. "Guess you can see that, so it's up to you to make sure everything goes off all right."

Underwood mopped at the sweat covering his face. "But—I'm half owner of that bank. Some of the money in it is mine—"

Rutter shrugged. "Make you feel any better, we'll give you a little cut of what we get. Maybe it'll be enough to cover your losses."

The rancher wagged his head. "No—I won't touch it! I'm not going through again what I did after that payroll robbery—and killing."

"Up to you. But you figure yourself in, clean up to the collarbone. Now, first thing we want is a key to the back door of that bank building. Never mind the safe. Rufe'll take care of it. And we want a place to hang out. Just won't be smart for us to lay around the town for the next couple of days. Somebody might get nosy."

"You can hire us on as cowhands," Mysak suggested. "We'll make real good ones—doing nothing."

Rutter nodded. "Gives us an alibi, too, in case somebody gets lucky and sees us coming out of the bank. Be up to you to speak up and say it couldn't have been us because we work for you, and we were all here together on the ranch the night of the robbery. Nobody will dispute the word of Sam Underwood."

"I can't do it," the rancher mumbled uncertainly. "I can't get mixed up—"

"You're already mixed up in it," Guy Rutter snarled. "Don't you forget that—not for a minute! Now, if you don't want your share of the cash we'll be taking, all right. Makes more for us. Thing is—just don't get in our way and be goddamned sure you do what you're told and that you keep your mouth shut."

"Yessir," Mysak said. "You don't, everything's going to blow right up in your face—and the next thing you know you'll be peeking through the bars of a cell in the Federal pen!"

"But—I—well, I've got to think—"

"Think—nothing!" Rutter snapped. "You've got that

34

done for you. You're in this deal whether you like it or not."

"And since we're working for you and we're all flat busted," Pete Brock said, managing a grin, "we'll take a little of our wages ahead of time. Maybe fifty apiece."

"Now, that's a smart idea!" Mysak exclaimed, rubbing his big hands together. "I recollect a little yellow-haired gal back there in the Gold Dollar that I got me some unfinished business with. . . . Supposing you make that a even hundred dollars a piece, Sam."

Underwood's shoulders settled into a helpless slump. "Don't carry that kind of money on me."

"But I'm betting a big man like you'll easy have that much in the house—maybe in a tin box or a safe. You want us to have a look?"

"I'll get it," the rancher said heavily.

"Make it a hundred flat, like Rufe said." Rutter's words came as an order, uncompromising.

Underwood nodded, started to turn away when Rutter caught him by the arm.

"Better tell that foreman of yours about us working for you. He don't cotton to us much."

"I'll tell him," the rancher said, "but if you're planning on hanging around here, you'd better play it smart and get along with him."

◎ 6 ◎

Tom Gage pulled off his hat and rubbed at his balding head while a puzzled expression covered his weather-seamed face.

"That sure does kind of put us in a fix, don't it?" he drawled. "You're a-looking for somebody but you don't know who."

"Guess that's the way it sounds," Shawn replied with a smile. "Fact is, it's my brother Ben. . . . Ben Starbuck. Pretty sure he's not using that name nowadays."

The old foreman pursed his lips. "I see. . . . What's he look like?"

"Can't tell you much about that either. Been ten years since I last saw him—and I was just a kid. Likely he'll be dark, on the stocky side. He had blue eyes."

"You sure don't give a man much to go on," Gage murmured.

"Only thing I know for sure is he's got a scar just above the left eye. Only about an inch long and it's kind of hard to notice."

Tom Gage studied his gnarled hands. "Just don't right off recollect anybody around here with a mark like that. Somebody say we had a man who did?"

"Ran into a cattle buyer up Kansas way. Was asking for Ben. He said your trail boss sort of fit the description."

"Henry Smith?"

"Buyer didn't know his name, only that he bossed Underwood's trail drives—and been doing it last three or four years."

"That's Henry, all right. It's where he's at right now. . . . Come to think on it, he does kind of match up to the man you're looking for. Don't remember the scar, though."

"You'd have to look close for it. He got it when we

were kids playing in the rocks back of the farm. You say he's on a drive now?"

"Drive's over. Likely on his way back. Ought to be showing up next day or two."

Shawn glanced at the four men gathered under the cottonwood. The rancher appeared strained, upset. Rutter and the two others were half smiling, joking in a smug sort of way.

"Hate to hear that," he said, touching his jaw with a fingertip. Pete Brock had got in one good blow during the fight, and the spot was tender. "Was hoping I could find out one way or another today—know if I'd made another long ride for nothing."

"It real important you find him, that it?"

Starbuck nodded. "Guess I could ride on to Las Vegas, put up there a couple of days, then drop back. How far is it?"

"Half a day—less if you get right along. But there ain't no sense in your doing that. Henry'll be here tomorrow most likely—for sure the next day—all depending on how drunk him and the rest of the drovers get after the settling-up's done. You can wait here."

Shawn ducked his head at Underwood. "What about *him?* Don't think he's going to feel very kindly toward me after the ruckus I had with his friends."

Gage shrugged. "You know what, I ain't so sure they're all that much friends. But don't let it bother you none—Sam, I mean. He leaves running this ranch up to me, him being busy politicking and banking and squiring his missus around to all the high-toned shindigs going on."

"I understand. It'd be a favor if you'd let me pull off in those trees back of the corrals, set myself up a camp there, and wait—"

"I'm damned if you'll do any such thing!" Gage snapped indignantly. "Long as I'm around any decent man's welcome to stop over, stick his legs under the crew's vittle table, and use an empty bunk. Been that way since I can recollect, and I ain't about to let it change."

Starbuck smiled. "Appreciate that—and I'll be glad to lend a hand. Worked cows and horses aplenty, all over the country. And I'm not above doing yard chores."

"Help's something we sure don't need. Sam's maybe kind of got big ideas for hisself, but he's square when it comes to dealing with the hired hands. Never lays a man off when things get slack the way most ranchers do. Just keeps them on, paying regular wages every month."

"Shows it," Shawn said, glancing around. "Can see the

37

men take pride in the place and keep it looking fine. One way of them saying thanks, I guess."

"There's them that likes to stay busy doing things," Gage said drily, "and there's them that don't."

"Man's lucky to ride for an outfit like this."

The old foreman stroked his moustache. "Cows is cows. Makes no difference what kind of a place they're on, they're still plain ornery, mean, cantankerous critters that can drive a man to plucking out his eyeballs. But there ain't no sense us standing here in the hot sun jawing. Expect you'd like to wash off some of that dust, and then—"

"Tom—"

Gage turned, faced Underwood who was approaching with his friends trailing slightly behind.

"I'm hiring these men."

"Hiring—to do what?"

"Whatever you can figure out for them," Underwood snapped, nettled at the foreman's belligerence. "Names are Guy Rutter, Pete Brock, and Rufe Mysak. We were in the war together."

"So they was telling me. . . . Hell, Sam, hired help's so thick around here now you can't stir them with a stick—"

"Realize that, but I want them put on anyway. They can do range riding."

"We're real good at doing that," Mysak said with a broad wink at Pete Brock.

Gage sighed resignedly. "All right, Sam, it's your money. I'll fix them up."

Starbuck, waiting off to one side, felt the rancher's eyes upon him.

"You waiting to see me?"

"Waiting to see Hank Smith," the foreman replied before Shawn could answer. "I'm inviting him to bunk in with me."

The rancher studied Starbuck speculatively. "You an old friend of Hank's?"

"Maybe. Not sure yet."

Underwood looked puzzled, then shrugged, said, "You're mighty fancy with those fists of yours. . . . That gun, too. It your line of work?"

"Cowhand, mostly," Shawn said.

"I see," the rancher murmured, and turning, strode for the house.

Starbuck watched him briefly, and then, arms folded across his chest, faced Rutter and his two shadows. All were considering him intently.

"We take things up where we left off?" he asked in a quiet voice.

Guy Rutter's features hardened fleetingly, and then he produced a forced smile. "All forgot, far as I'm concerned. Same with you boys?" he added, glancing to Brock and Mysak.

Rufe nodded. Pete Brock made no answer, but continued to stare sullenly at Shawn. Rutter's small eyes glittered.

"What about it, Pete?"

"I ain't making no promises," Brock answered. "I figure I got me a few good licks coming."

"Any time you say," Starbuck countered. "Everything's settled and I'm holding no grudge. Got my stuff back. That's the main thing I was interested in."

"And you'll forget it, too, Pete!" Rutter snapped. "Told you we didn't have no time to be messing around with a penny-ante thing like that belt. Forget it, hear? We can't afford—"

Guy Rutter's words ended abruptly. He looked away as if regretting what he had said, and then, after a moment, came back to Tom Gage.

"All right, Grandpa, where you want us to put up?"

The foreman bristled. "My name ain't grandpa—it's Tom Gage—and you can roost with the crows far as I'm concerned. But Sam said I was to take you on, so I reckon that mean's you'll bed down with the crew."

"In there?" Rutter asked, thumbing at the bunkhouse.

Gage nodded. "In there. You'll find some extra bunks. Pick some."

Guy Rutter turned away. "Pity we ain't friends of yours instead of the man that owns the place, then maybe we could have a special place to stay."

The foreman grinned maliciously. "Yeh, a real pity, ain't it?"

Brock and Rufe Mysak wheeled to follow Rutter. Pete glanced back over his shoulder. "Grandpa, you be sure and call us when supper's ready, hear?"

"I ain't calling nobody. When grub's ready, the cook'll hammer on his bar. If you don't come, then go without."

"Sure don't want that to happen," Mysak said, shaking his head. "Boys, we'd better keep our ears open."

Gage watched them until they had reached the crew's quarters and entered and then looked at Shawn. "If them three are what Sam calls his friends, I figure he's a lot better off with his enemies."

"Could cause you a lot of worry," Starbuck admitted. "Don't let them get under your hide."

"Well, Sam or no Sam, I don't aim to take no sass off them. . . . Now, what I was about to say—you're wanting to clean up a mite—"

"Horse trough will do me fine."

"Horse trough, hell! There's a sink and a pump in my cabin. Use it. Bring your gear along, too, since you'll be bunking with me."

Restless, unable to sleep despite his weariness, Starbuck sat up, swung his legs over the side of the bed. An arm's length away, Tom Gage snored in deep cadence. He guessed it was because Henry Smith could be Ben that he was finding it difficult to settle down. But it was always like that—the waiting, the not knowing, was hard.

Slipping into pants and boots, he rose, crossed to the door and stepped out into the cool night. One window showed light in the main house; over everything lay a heavy silence. The smell of sage was strong in the air and far off a coyote gave voice to his loneliness.

Almost at once an ease began to fill Shawn Starbuck, release the tautness, soothe the raw ends of his nerves. A serene patience came over him bringing contentment.

Maybe this was where the search would end—here on Sam Underwood's ranch. Gage had seemed to think Henry Smith fit what little description he had given of his brother; and there was the fact that the name—Henry Smith—in itself, didn't exactly ring true. Men, wishing to hide their real identities, usually adopted the simplest, most commonplace designation they could think of.

It was as good as any lead he'd had yet, Shawn thought as he strolled toward the corral into which he'd turned the chestnut. The cattle buyer and Tom Gage had both given him cause for hope.

He halted, suddenly aware of three figures standing in the half dark to his left. Rufe Mysak's voice came to him.

"Doing some spying on us, cowboy?"

Starbuck's muscles tightened. He hadn't expected to meet anyone at that hour of the night, much less these three.

"Getting some air," he replied.

Rutter's comment was dry. "Sure, and you just happened to come after that air on this side of the yard."

The solitary light in the main house blinked out. The thought came to Shawn that Rutter and the others had been visiting with Underwood. Probably hashing over old

40

times in the army. He failed to understand what difference it made whether he had seen them or not. Spying?

Vaguely irked, he said, "Suit yourself. That's the way it is."

"I've got a hunch," Rutter continued in that same, level voice, "that you're going to step out in front of us once too often. Might be a real smart thing for you to get your belongings, saddle up, and ride on—now."

Starbuck came about slowly until his back was against the pole bars of the corral. He'd been a fool to come out without his gun, but then he doubted if they'd try using theirs. . . . And if it came to fists again. . . .

"Best you overlook that hunch," he said. "Happens I'm not ready to pull out. Expect I'll be around a couple a days or so—more if need be. After I've done what I came for, I'll move on."

"Could be we'll do a little persuading," Mysak said insinuatingly. "Now, Pete here feels he's got a call coming. Was we to step in, give him a hand—"

"And raise the whole damned place!" Rutter finished in disgust. "Show some sense, Rufe."

"Then let's herd him off into the brush," Brock said eagerly. "He ain't packing no gun—and nobody'll hear."

"Then what? Comes daylight and somebody finds him—"

"What difference that make?"

"Plenty, goddammit! Get it in your head—we don't want to stir up trouble around here. Draw too much attention. We'll leave it up to him—give him till noon tomorrow. If he ain't gone by then, well, there's plenty of open country we can bank on. You savvy what I'm driving at, Starbuck?"

"Plain enough," Shawn answered. "Only it doesn't mean anything. I'll pull out when I'm ready—and that'll be after I've had a talk with the man I'm waiting for."

"I ain't buying that," Rutter said flatly.

Mysak's bulk shifted in the shadows as he turned to face the redhead. "You mean he ain't hunting for no brother, like he claims?"

"Just what I mean. I figure that's a lot of bull, a way to hide what he really is."

Brock said, "What's that?"

"Let him tell you," Rutter replied. "Talk up, Starbuck. You ain't no plain cow-nurse. You don't act like it and you don't look like it. I'd say you was a *lawman* of some kind."

Shawn smiled into the darkness. "Done a lot of things

41

moving round, looking for my brother. Never happened to take on a lawman's job, though."

"More'n likely he's some kind of hired gun," Mysak said.

"Wrong again."

A silence followed that, broken finally when Rutter said, "Anyway, can't see as it matters none, one way or other. You got till noon tomorrow to haul freight, mister. If you're still around then—well, you'd best start watching your back trail."

"I'll be here," Starbuck said in a soft voice, "unless I've finished with my business."

"Take my advice," Rutter said. "Be finished."

◎ 7 ◎

Starbuck said nothing to Tom Gage about his encounter with Rutter and his friends that next morning. The foreman was riled enough at being forced to add them to his already overloaded crew, and Shawn could see where little could be gained.

As far as Rutter's threats went, they meant nothing to him. He would stay, as he had declared, until Henry Smith returned and he was satisfied that the trail boss was or was not Ben.

At the crew table in a room off the kitchen for the early meal, he sat next to Gage, acknowledged the introductions the older man felt inclined to make, and paid no attention to Guy Rutter, Brock, or Mysak who sat on the opposite side of the long counter. Gage introduced them also to the hands present grudgingly, and only out of necessity. As on most ranches, strangers riding across the open range were always suspect and required to identify themselves. It wouldn't do to have Sam Underwood's three army chums roped and ridden off the land by punchers bent only on doing their duty.

Rutter finished the meal before Brock and Rufe. Rising, he sauntered over to where Gage and Starbuck were dawdling over a last cup of coffee. Most of the men had already moved on and were in the yard mounting up and heading out in the early morning light to assume their various jobs.

"You got something special for us to do?" Rutter asked, picking at his teeth.

Gage twisted half about on his chair. "Sure have. There's a brake—four, maybe five miles south of here. Some of the boys are down there chasing strays out of the brush. Go down and give them a hand."

Brock and Mysak, finally through with their plates also, rose and moved to Rutter's side. Brock assumed a pained expression, and said, "Now, that sounds like real hard work! I don't calculate old Sam figured on us doing something like that."

Mysak grinned his wide, toothy grin. "Not us, no sir. We're mighty close friends of his'n."

"I don't give a hoot in hell who you are!" Gage roared, eyes blazing. "That's what I'm telling you to do, and if you don't aim——"

"What's the trouble here?" Underwood's voice came from the doorway.

Gage jumped to his feet. "These here hands you hired——"

"Never mind, Tom," the rancher cut in soothingly. "I'll see to them myself." He hesitated and a forced smile came to his lips. "Don't mind them, now. They always were great ones for joshing a man."

The old foreman stood in silence. Rutter and Brock wheeled, swaggered toward the waiting Underwood. Mysak nodded, said, "Sure, don't you mind us none," and followed his friends and the rancher into the yard.

Gage, his face flushed to a bright red, swore deeply. "If that's the way Sam Underwood wants this here ranch run, then, by damn, he can run it hisself," he said, and started for the door.

Starbuck caught him by the arm. "Don't fly off the handle," he murmured. "Just what they're trying to do—get your goat. Let it ride. Underwood acts to me like a man who's got himself some trouble. Worst favor you could do him is quit now."

The foreman relented, his gaze on the four men swinging to the saddle. After a moment he wheeled.

"You know something I don't?"

Starbuck downed the last of his coffee, rose to his feet. "Nope, only that it's not hard to spot a man who's got a cougar by the tail."

Gage nodded slowly. "Kind of got that idea about Sam myself. Ain't never seen him act like this."

"It'll blow over. Everything always does. . . . You want me to ride down, help with those strays in the brake?"

"Hell no, I don't!" Gage barked testily. "Was sending them there just to rid myself of them, not because I was needing them. . . . You do what you please. Maybe I can think up a chore or two later."

"Sing out when you do," Starbuck said. "Like to pay for my keep. I'll be at the corral. Think I'll rub down my horse. Haven't given him a good going over in quite a spell."

The foreman bobbed his head. "Get anything you need

from Manuel, in the stable. He looks after the boss's horses. Be seeing you later. There's a few things I got to do."

Shawn moved into the yard with Gage, turned off to the corral where he had put the chestnut. Slipping a halter on the big gelding, he led him to a hitchrack near the barn, sought out the hostler, and obtained a steel comb and a stiff brush.

The gelding was still a bit shaggy from his winter coat, and there was considerable mud caked on his shanks and fetlocks, accumulated during their passage along the several creeks they'd encountered. His tail also nested more than a fair share of cockleburs.

Shawn set to work and kept at it steadily for better than an hour. Soon the chestnut began to take on a new look; his reddish coat glowed sleekly in the sunlight while his white-stockinged legs became trim and clean. However, the burrs were hard to pick out. Many were deeply entwined in the coarse hair and Starbuck worked at them diligently, not wanting to cut away any more of the black strands than necessary, but knowing the troublesome burrs had to be removed.

"You're going to a lot of bother. . . ."

At the sound of the voice Shawn looked up. A girl of perhaps seventeen or eighteen, blond, with dark brown eyes, was standing at the end of the rack. She was nicely shaped and dressed in a white shirtwaist, corduroy riding skirt and soft, black boots. A bright blue scarf was around her head.

Starbuck grinned. "If I don't get them out he'll be mad at me all the rest of summer."

The girl laughed, moved closer. "I'm Holly Underwood. Are you going to work for my father?"

Shawn shook his head. "Just passing through. Stopped by to see a fellow."

"Oh—a drifter," she murmured, a thread of scorn underlying her tone.

"Not exactly," Starbuck replied, his own voice somewhat stiff.

Holly took an impulsive step toward him. "Oh, I don't mean anything bad by that! It's only—well—I think a man should be like my father—settle down, work hard, make something big of his life. You can't do that wandering around, going nowhere—doing nothing. . . . Can I help?"

Without waiting for him to answer, she grasped a thick

45

strand of the chestnut's tail in her hands and began to pick at the burrs.

"Not always easy for a man to be like your pa—father."

She nodded, said frankly, "He's different from most men. Real smart. A fine person—good to everybody." Holly broke off, smiled disarmingly. "I don't mean that you're not, Mr.—"

"Starbuck. Shawn's my first name—without the mister."

"All right, Shawn. I—I'm sorry for how I said that. I guess my father means so much to me that I'm always comparing him to other men without thinking." She glanced toward the barn, called, "Manuel—will you get my horse, please?"

Starbuck worked out the last of the burrs.

"He's certainly a beautiful horse," the girl said admiringly. "How old is he?"

"Around four. We've covered a lot of territory together. Never let me down yet."

"That's because you take good care of him," she said approvingly. "I like that. Show's you're not one of the ordinary cowhand kind."

"Reason for that maybe. Man puts in a full day's work on the range, he doesn't feel much like playing nursemaid to a horse when he comes in."

She was studying him closely. "You don't talk like a cowhand, either."

"My mother was a schoolteacher. Took a lot of pains to see that I got some teaching. Guess a little of it stuck."

Holly glanced to the barn. The hostler was leading out a tall sorrel. "I'm going for a ride," she said. "Why don't you come along? I could show you some of the ranch, that is—if you've nothing better to do."

He had nothing better to do, Shawn decided quickly. "Be my pleasure. Just give me time to saddle up and we'll be on our way."

◎ 8 ◎

They rode south out of the yard, meeting Tom Gage a short distance from the ranch buildings. The foreman smiled, raised his hand in salutation, but did not stop.

"It's a fine place," Shawn said some time later when they had topped a small rise and were looking out onto a vast, rolling plain green with grass.

"Seventy thousand acres," Holly said proudly. "Most of it just like that. There's no better ranch in the whole Territory."

"Man would have no trouble raising prime beef here," Starbuck admitted, and then pointed to a distant mound of dark earth and rock. "What's that?"

"An old Indian ruin. I used to go there a lot before I went away. I'd dig for arrowheads, things like that."

"Away? Where?"

"Only to Santa Fe. I attended the Academy there. Graduated last year. . . . I sort of had ideas about being a schoolteacher, too—like your mother."

"But you changed your mind."

"Yes—or maybe it was my father. He didn't think it would be exactly proper for me to work." Holly paused, smiled, looked squarely at Shawn. "I guess I've said the wrong thing again."

Starbuck shrugged. "Nothing wrong in that—or in your wanting to be a schoolmarm, either, far as I can see. But I reckon I know how your pa felt. Man in his position—guess it wouldn't be right for his daughter to work."

"That's the way he put it. I suppose it didn't really matter to me—and I certainly didn't want to embarrass him. Especially if he does become governor."

"The chances pretty good for that?"

"He says they are, and he's usually right. He's well known, being half owner of the bank in Vegas, and President of the Cattleman's Association, and all that."

47

"Expect he'll make it then," Shawn said, touching the chestnut lightly with his spurs. "Let's take a closer look at your Indian ruin."

They rode off the rise at an easy lope, reached the flat and drew the horses down to a walk. Starbuck felt Holly's eyes upon him and he turned to her questioningly.

"Something's wrong?"

"I was thinking about your mother. . . . What was she like?"

"I was pretty much a kid when she died. I can remember she was tall, had a quiet way of speaking. Could be firm when she wanted to be, though. My pa always said I favored her—had the same eyes and looks while Ben, my brother, took after him. . . . Always wished she'd lived a little longer. Things probably would have been different."

"It was different with me," Holly said, her gaze fixed on the still distant ruin. "My father isn't my real father, you know."

Shawn shook his head. "No, I didn't know."

"My real father was killed in the war. Mother and I moved out here after his death—there was nothing left of the family plantation in Virginia—to live with some old friends."

"And that's where he met your mother?"

Holly nodded. "He was just getting his ranch started. He'd come to see Mr. Cameron who owns the bank— they're the friends we came to live with—about buying up some property. Mr. Cameron brought him home to supper that night. Mother and he were married a month later. . . . He was good to us. Everything has turned out so well."

"A fine thing for everybody all around."

"My own father couldn't have done more for me," Holly said. "Where do you come from, Shawn? Your original home, I mean."

"Farm up in the Muskingum country of Ohio. It was sold when my pa died."

"And you've been wandering ever since?"

"Ever since." He could see no reason to tell her of Ben, although he was finding conversation and being with her very pleasant.

"Where will you go when you leave here?"

"North, I reckon. Want to take a look at Colorado. Then head on up into Wyoming, maybe Montana."

"You could stay here," she said impulsively. "I think my father likes you—and you said yourself that we have a fine ranch."

48

It would be wonderful to settle down and—he had to admit it—be near Holly Underwood. But that was not possible, unless his search for Ben came to an end with his meeting of Henry Smith. However, he could not make plans of any sort; that was a fact of life he'd learned to accept long ago. One day, perhaps—and if Henry Smith did prove to be Ben, then—

"Be fine," he said noncommittally.

"I'd like it, too, Shawn," Holly said and then quickly added, "That's a strange name. Does it have some special meaning?"

"Indian. Short for Shawnee. Ma gave it to me. She once taught some Shawnee children. Took a fancy to it, I guess."

"I like the sound of it. . . . She must have been a wonderful person. What was your father like?"

A recollection of Hiram Starbuck rolled through Shawn's mind, and unconsciously a stiffness crept into his tone. "He was a good man. Maybe a bit on the rough side, but you had to be that way back in those days when he was getting started. . . . Learned a lot from him—mostly how to look after myself."

Holly's face brightened at once. "Did he teach you to fight the way you were doing yesterday? Father said you were a boxer."

He looked at her in surprise, then recalled the faces he'd seen in the ranch-house window. "Too bad you had to see that."

"I've seen men fight before," Holly said. "In Sante Fe —even here on the ranch when nobody knew I was around. I never saw anyone fight the way you did."

"Pa was very good at it. Used to give exhibitions every Saturday back in Ohio. Men would drive in for miles just to see him put on a match."

Holly sighed heavily. "You have the most interesting family—and life. I have—well, hardly anything."

"Only a father who's probably one of the biggest and most important men in the Territory of New Mexico," Shawn said with a smile. "And on top of that—everything you want."

"That's still nothing when you come right down to it. For me, personally, I mean. Oh, I love the parties and the balls in Santa Fe and Vegas, and things like that, but I still—"

She let it hang there. Shawn gave her a sidelong glance, did not press her for a further explanation. It was best to not get involved in such matters—and besides, if she

49

wanted to unload her troubles on him, it would be not at his insistence. Holly, however, didn't realize how fortunate she was. He supposed that was normal. Most persons seemed never to understand how well off they were until something changed and it was too late to go back.

The crumbled walls of the pueblo were just ahead. Reaching the first scatter of rock and round-edged mud bricks, they slowly circled the perimeter, cut finally onto a narrow, beaten trail and made their way to the highest point. A few, half-buried wall remnants still remained to form the outline of separate rooms. There were signs of digging here and there. Shawn pointed to the nearest.

"You, or the prairie dogs?"

Holly laughed, swung off her sorrel. "Me. I spent a lot of time here—once."

Shawn guided his horse to the top ledge, a point where redskinned sentinels had, no doubt, centuries ago maintained watch for hostile invaders.

Abruptly he halted. Four riders had pulled up in the shade of a small tree in a coulee a hundred yards or so distant. He recognized Sam Underwood instantly. And then, one by one, he picked out Guy Rutter, Mysak, and Pete Brock.

They appeared to be discussing something important, with Underwood slightly apart facing his friends and using his hands to emphasize his words. The three men were merely staring at him, listening. Finally Rutter shook his head, and motioning to Brock and Mysak, wheeled about and moved off toward the definite scar of a road that ran on into the west.

"We should get back . . ."

Starbuck turned at once and swung the gelding back down the incline to where the girl was scuffing about with the toe of her boot.

"Expect so," he said glancing at the sun. "Must be getting close to dinner time."

His mind was not on what he was saying, was instead mulling over the angry scene he had just witnessed. No doubt an argument had been in progress—one Rutter and the others had won simply by riding off.

He started to mention the nearby presence of her father to Holly, thought better of it. If there was something wrong between Sam Underwood and his one-time fellow soldiers, it would be better to let him handle it. Setting the girl to worrying over the father she worshipped would be pointless.

He watched her mount, and then followed her down the

trail to the flat where they cut north, heading for the long rise beyond which lay the ranch.

Holly was quiet on the return trip, holding her horse to a steady jog that allowed small opportunity for conversation. That she had something weighty on her mind was evident, however, and when they reached the ridge and were moving toward the bottom of the slope that ended near the ranch house, she suddenly faced Shawn.

"I—I meant what I said about you staying here. I'd like it very much, Shawn."

He started to voice his regret, cushion his refusal with an explanation as to why that was impossible, but the girl veered away from him sharply, and spurring her long-legged sorrel, raced for the yard, giving him no chance to speak.

He watched her go, his thoughts suddenly dark and heavy. She couldn't realize how much he would like to stay, should Sam Underwood make him an offer; but it was out of the question unless Henry Smith—

Starbuck cast that from his mind. Too many times hope had risen, only to be dashed to earth again when a man he felt certain would be Ben was not. He'd learned not to allow such hope to arise—only to wait and see. . . . And never make far-reaching plans for the future.

Turning his horse into the yard, he angled toward the corral, seeing Manuel leading Holly's sorrel into the barn as he crossed over. She was already inside the house, he supposed.

Halting, he stepped down, and immediately began to pull his gear from the chestnut. He heard the hard thud of boot heels behind him, and then Tom Gage's voice.

"Have yourself a ride?"

Shawn nodded. "Went over to those Indian ruins."

The foreman nodded and said, "The little gal used to spend a lot of time there, digging about. Many's the time I had to go scouting after her for her ma. Reckon she had a kind of feeling for the place. Told me once—she weren't no more'n a little button then, six maybe seven—the only friends she had was the people who used to live in that old pueblo. . . . Seems to have took quite a shine to you."

"Expect she's curious, mostly. Same way folks like to look at a two-headed calf," Starbuck said, throwing his gear over the top bar of the corral.

Gage cocked his head to one side. "Maybe."

"Anyway," Shawn said quietly, "that's all it had better be. . . . Underwood come in yet?"

"Rode in a few minutes ahead of you two. Said he'd put

51

his friends to work on the north range. Set them to drifting some stock over onto new grass."

Starbuck stared off across the low hills. When he had seen the rancher he was well south of the ranch—not north. And Rutter and the others certainly were not engaged in moving cattle. Again he reminded himself that it was no business of his, but he did voice one question.

"That road near the ruins. Looks fairly well traveled. Where's it go?"

"Las Vegas. It's the main one. Cuts across Sam's land from the east. . . . Come on, best we grab ourselves a bite to eat before the cook gets all worked up."

◎ 9 ◎

The afternoon passed and Henry Smith put in no appearance. Shawn whiled away the hours helping Manuel, the hostler, in the stable, working with Sam Underwood's prize horses, currying, brushing them vigorously, cleaning their hooves and generally performing all the small tasks he took pleasure in.

The rancher had a fine string of horses for the personal use of himself and his family: a matched team of whites to draw a gleaming black surrey, Holly's sorrel, a bay for his own use, and another white that was Mrs. Underwood's but which she now, according to Manuel, seldom rode.

Shawn had an easy, natural way with animals, and he enjoyed working with them. When darkness came and the cook announced the evening meal with a loud clanging on an iron bar hanging just outside the kitchen door, Underwood's riding and driving stock never looked in better condition.

"If you can spare yourself," Tom Gage said from the doorway of the barn, "it's time to be eating again."

Starbuck grinned, washed up and went to the crew's dining quarters with the foreman. When they had seated themselves at the long table, Gage glanced around and shrugged.

"Them friends of Sam's ain't showed up yet. Was they around this afternoon while I was gone?"

Shawn said, "Didn't see them. Was in the barn most of the time, though."

He could have gone further into the matter, told how he had seen Rutter, with Brock and Mysak, riding west on the Las Vegas road after their meeting with Underwood, but again he felt it was no business of his and so remained silent. If Gage pressed the subject, however, he would be forced to tell. He owed that much to the old man.

53

But he'd drop it there, not bother him with an accounting of his meeting with the three men that previous night, and a report of the ultimatum Guy Rutter had issued. He had decided that before and he'd stick with it. His problems were his own. If Rutter intended to make something of his presence at Underwood's when they came face to face again, he'd handle it himself. Tom Gage had enough worries.

"Senor. . . ."

Starbuck, roused from his thoughts, turned to see a small Mexican boy at his elbow.

"The *patron* is send me to say he would talk with you." A smile parted the young, dark face as he swung then to Gage. "You will also come, *Senor Caporal*."

Tom squeezed the boy's arm affectionately. "All right, Juanito. We'll be there's soon as we're done."

The youngster trotted off, disappearing into a hallway that apparently led deeper into the main house. Gage studied his coffee.

"Now, I wonder what Sam's got squirming around in his mind?"

Starbuck grinned, resumed his meal. "Maybe he doesn't like drifters going riding with his daughter."

"Could be," the foreman replied laconically.

When they had finished, Gage led the way—not through the corridor, but out into the yard and along a path that circled to the front of the house.

"Sam's missus don't allow the hired hands to go traipsing across her carpets no more," he explained. "Was a time when it was fine with her, but since they got to be such biggity folks, we ain't welcome inside. Sam's even built hisself a office at the end of the front porch. That's close as we can get to being under his roof. Amy Underwood's a fine woman but she's sure changed."

"You've worked for Sam a long time?" Starbuck asked as they rounded the end of the structure and stepped up onto the wide gallery.

"Since he bought the place from Jud Higgins—right after he hit this country. Might say I sort of come with the land. Was Jud's foreman, too."

Underwood was seated behind a massive, carved desk when they entered his business quarters. It was a fairly large room and several lithographs and calendars hung on the walls in the company of the mounted head of a large mule deer. No carpet covered the floor but there were half a dozen or so comfortable cowhide chairs arranged to face the desk.

54

"Wanted to tell you," Gage began before he was even seated, "them three yahoos you hired never showed up for supper. You reckon they've gone and got themselves lost?"

The rancher stirred, laid aside the sheaf of papers through which he was leafing. "Guess I forgot to mention it. Told them they could ride in to Vegas after they got that stock moved. Seems they felt like blowing off a little steam."

"Damn it, Sam!" Gage exploded irritably. "You ought to tell a man when you do something like that. Can't run a ranch with two of us giving orders."

Starbuck listened, surprised at Underwood's words. It had appeared from the hill that Rutter and the two men with him had made their own decision about visiting Las Vegas. And there was the additional fact that they had not been working, were far from the north range. Why would the rancher lie to his own foreman?

"Understand from my daughter, Starbuck, that you're sort of taken with my place."

Shawn became aware that the rancher was speaking to him. He nodded. "It's a fine ranch, Mr. Underwood."

"Call me Sam, same as everybody else. It took a lot of hard work to build it up—on my part and Tom's, too. Owe him plenty."

Some of the anger faded from the old foreman's eyes. "Reckon we can stack the Sunrise brand up against the best of them seven days a week," he said. "There something you wanted to talk about?"

Underwood opened a desk drawer and withdrew a box of cigars. He offered the container to Gage who selected one, eyed it appreciatively. Shawn declined. When he did smoke, which wasn't often, he preferred a cigarette. The rancher chose a cigar for himself, settled back.

"Had it in mind to offer Starbuck a job," he said. "Being my foreman, I naturally wanted you to set in on the talking."

"Doing what?" Gage asked, frowning. "Sure'd like to have him around but we've got more cowhands than cows now, seems like."

"Wasn't exactly thinking of him as a cowhand."

Gage's frown deepened. He bit off the end of his stogie, searched about for a match. Shawn, mulling the rancher's words through his mind, glanced out the window. Evidently Holly had used her persuasive powers on her father. He guessed he could use a job for a while but he wasn't so sure it would be wise to accept one from Underwood—not with the girl around.

55

"Then what—"

The rancher leaned forward, features intent. "You know how things are shaping up for me, Tom. All this talk of the governor's chair, and there's a good chance I'll be buying Ira Cameron out at the bank, taking over the whole shebang as sole owner."

"Figured it'd come to that someday. Ira's getting a mite old."

"Means I've got to do a lot of running around and such. I need a good man—one I can trust to sort of be, well, my right hand. Like you are here on the ranch. I leave the running of it to you and never worry about it. Now I need the same sort of man to go with me—"

"A hired gun?" Starbuck asked quietly.

The rancher studied the still unlit end of his smoke. "I suppose you might put it that way—but you'd be more of my assistant. You'd have jobs to do, errands to run. Important at times that I get a message to certain men, maybe in Vegas, or maybe in Santa Fe. Sending it by stagecoach mail is too slow. You'd carry it personally. Be a hell of a lot faster and I'd know for sure it was getting delivered to the right party.

"I suppose there'd be some bodyguarding to it. Tom can tell you there's times when I'm carrying quite a bit of money on me—times I'm out buying stock or picking up a piece of land—things like that. I'd sure feel easier having you along with me then. . . . Seeing the way you handled yourself with Rutter and Pete and Rufe Mysak's what gave me the idea. You be interested in that kind of a job?"

Starbuck shifted in his chair. "Done it before, but I'm not exactly interested in a job—leastwise not until I've talked to Henry Smith. After that I'll know where I stand."

"What's Henry got to do with it?"

"Starbuck's a-lookin' for his brother," Gage explained. "Ain't seen him in ten year or better. Thinks maybe Henry's him."

Underwood stroked his closely shaved chin. "And if he is?"

Shawn said, "Means we've both got a long ride back to Ohio ahead of us."

"If not?"

"I start looking again."

The rancher smiled. "Then I don't see how putting you to work for me would interfere much with your plans. You could stay on for two, three months while things are busy for me and until I could find another man to take your place. Then you could move on if you like. . . . Man living the way you are probably has to stop every now and then to build up his cash, anyway."

Shawn said, "You're right." He was more or less at that point now—but with Holly close by—running into her. . . .

"Pay'd be a hundred a month and found."

Starbuck swallowed. That was good money. Even if he worked only two or three months he'd have enough cash in his pockets to carry him on through winter. It was an offer he couldn't afford to turn down; where Holly was concerned he'd just have to keep looking the other way, keep his mind on his job.

"It's a deal. You've hired yourself a messenger boy, or whatever you want to call me. Want it understood, however, that if Henry Smith turns out to be my brother, it's all off."

"Fair enough," Underwood said, slapping the top of his desk. "You can bunk down——"

"He's staying in my cabin," Gage broke in. "After that go around he had with your friends, I figured he'd best not be in the same room with them."

"Good," the rancher said, rising to show that the interview was at an end. "Don't have anything particular for you to do at present, but hang around close, keep yourself available."

Shawn extended his hand, shook that of the rancher. His thoughts flipped back to the incident near the Indian ruins.

"There anything I should know—maybe about somebody I ought to watch out for or keep an eye on?"

Sam Underwood wagged his head. "Not a soul. Guess you might say I'm everybody's friend. I make a habit of keeping it that way."

◎ 10 ◎

Starbuck and Tom Gage were standing in front of the wagonshed late the next morning when Guy Rutter, flanked by Brock and a dozing Rufe Mysak, rode in. Immediately, the old foreman, eyes burning, stepped out to meet them.

"Where the hell you been?" he demanded.

Mysak came awake with a start. Rutter, mouth set to a crooked line, shrugged. "I reckon we're a mite late."

"You're damned right you are. You're supposed to be working, same as the rest of the hands on this ranch."

Brock rested his arms on the saddlehorn. "Maybe Mr. Underwood forgot to tell you we was taking us a little ride into town."

"He told me, but you was due to go to work this morning—early, just the same. How the hell you think I can run this place if the crew comes and goes when it damn well pleases?"

"Would be a problem," Brock admitted mildly. "You aim to give us a whipping?"

"Never mind, Pete," Rutter broke in, dismounting. He shifted his eyes to Shawn. "You're not much good at taking advice."

"Depends on the advice," Starbuck replied. "I—"

Gage, red-faced, pushed forward. "We ain't talking about him! We're talking about you and that pair of—"

"I said we was sorry, old man—"

"Sorry—hell! I'm telling Sam Underwood that he can—"

"Be telling him a few things myself."

"Then you can tell him I said you was fired—the lot of you! I won't have you around giving the rest of the crew ideas, making them think they ought to be acting like you."

Rutter's gaze settled on the foreman. Behind him Brock and Mysak had dismounted and were watching quietly.

"Now, we're trying to get along with you, Gage," the

redhead said, "but you're making it mighty hard. We aim to do our work, but we just had to pay us a little visit to town, see the elephant and such."

"You ain't ever going to get along with me till you start in doing your work, like you're supposed to."

Rutter nodded. "We're going to do that, but I was just thinking . . . you hadn't ought to go jumping all over us like you're doing. It ain't being nice to Sam's friends; and I just might mention to him that he ought to fire you, 'stead of you firing us."

"He won't have to fire me," Gage said in an anger-choked voice. "Anytime it's you calling the shots on this ranch, I quit. Now, *you* tell that to Sam when you see him!"

"Just what I'll do," the redhead said calmly, and then swung to Starbuck. "You had your warning, so now it'll be the hard way."

Turning on his heel, he walked off, followed by Brock and the glowering Mysak. At the front corral they left their horses, and moved on toward the main house. Gage watched them in fuming silence for a bit, then spun to Shawn.

"What's he talking about—you getting your warning, and doing things the hard way?"

"We had a few words. Gave me notice to ride on."

Tom Gage's fury soared again. "Why, that flapping-jawed jackass—who the hell he think he is spouting off with that kind of talk? I'll set him—"

"Don't bother," Starbuck said. "Met his kind before, probably run up against plenty just like him by the time I'm ready to die— Means nothing to me."

The kitchen door opened and Holly stepped out into the yard. Rufe Mysak slowed, raked her with his eyes, whistled softly. He said something to Rutter who only shook his head and continued on his way. The girl, paying no attention to them, moved farther into the yard, seemingly unaware of Mysak's persistent stare.

"Good morning!" she said brightly, walking in front of Shawn. "I hear you're taking a job with us after all. . . . I'm glad."

She gave him a wide smile, hurried on in her light, quick step for the barn where Manuel was leading out Amy Underwood's horse. Swinging to the saddle, she looked back to Starbuck.

"Promised Mother I'd take Blanco for a run today. She doesn't ride him near enough. Be pleased to have you come along."

59

Shawn nodded, touched the brim of his hat politely. "Obliged, but I'm a working hand now. Have to hang around close."

Holly tossed her head, swept out of the yard in a hammering of hooves. Tom Gage, his temper cooled, clucked softly.

"Like I told you, that gal sure has took a shine to you. Why don't you go on with her? Sam ain't needing you."

"Neither does she—somebody who can only cause her hurt."

"Pshaw—that ain't no way to talk. You're young. Ought to be thinking about the future."

"I've got no future—not the kind you're talking about —until I find Ben. . . . Can't you figure up a chore or two for me to do?"

Tom Gage was staring past Shawn toward the house. "Maybe I ain't the one who'll be telling anybody what to do around here from now on," he murmured.

Starbuck turned. Sam Underwood, with Rutter, Brock and Mysak in tow, was advancing across the hard pack. The rancher's features were strained, contrasting sharply with the settled, satisfied expression of Guy Rutter.

"Tom," Underwood began with no preliminaries. "Rutter tells me you jumped all over him and the boys for just coming in."

"You're damn well right I did!" the old foreman shot back, anger soaring again. "First thing you know the whole crew'll be thinking they can come and go as they please."

"I told you they had my permission to go to Vegas—"

"Ain't claiming you didn't. But they was due back here in time to go to work this morning, same as everybody else."

"I didn't set any time for them to return. Told you that, too."

"The hell you did, Sam! You said—"

"Well, I sure meant to. I'm sorry, Tom. Guess it just slipped my mind. . . . Anyway, it's all right."

"How can it be?" Gage demanded, thoroughly aroused. "You telling me to treat them privileged like, let the rest of the crew think they're something special, and better'n them?"

"Not exactly. But for the time being I want to make an exception—"

"Exception, hell! I'll tell you what you can do, Sam— you can get yourself another ramrod. I ain't never run a place favoring some over others, and I ain't about to start now."

Underwood's face was white, drawn. "Now, hold on. Don't go off half-cocked."

"I'm done gone," the older man shouted. "I quit. Give me my time and I'll pull out. Then you can turn the job over to one of your special friends; let him do as he pleases."

"Sam," Mysak said, pushing forward. "I'd be real pleased to take on the job."

Underwood flashed the man an angry look, and laid his hand on Gage's shoulder. Worried lines cut deep into his features.

"Don't do this to me. I need you here. Fact is, I couldn't run this ranch without you."

"Then leave me alone, dammit! Keep your nose out of what's my business."

"What I intend to do—just like I always have. Whole thing's been a mix-up. And you won't need to worry about these fellows none. They'll work direct for me. Won't have anything to do with the rest of the hands."

Gage began to simmer down. After a moment he said, "Good enough. You keep them out of my hair, look after them yourself."

Underwood's eyes reflected his relief. Standing behind him Guy Rutter was silent, his features betraying no emotion of any sort. That he had merely wanted to put the old foreman in his place was apparent to Shawn.

"Then we've got it settled," the rancher said. "It be all right if they stay in the bunkhouse?"

"Nothing to me long as they mind their manners and keep their lips buttoned up."

"They'll do that," Underwood said with a sidelong glance at the three men.

Guy Rutter shrugged disinterestedly. Mysak winked broadly at Pete Brock. The rancher swung to face Starbuck.

"Got an errand for you. Something's come up, important that I get a letter quick to my partner in the bank, Ira Cameron. You be able to ride in an hour or so?"

"Whenever you say," Shawn replied, pleased that at last he had something to do.

Underwood deliberately turned his back to the other men, drew Starbuck aside. "Letter's more important than you might think," he said in a hushed, confidential way. "Don't be afraid to use that gun of yours getting it there —if need be."

Shawn signified his understanding. Guy Rutter was watching narrowly, he noted, a dark frown on his ruddy face.

"Be no hurry for you to return," Underwood said, his voice lifting to normal level again. "Stay the night, head home in the morning. Thing I'm interested in is that letter being put in Cameron's hands today."

Starbuck again nodded. A night in the settlement would be a welcome treat. A drink or two in one of the saloons, a few hands of cards—a man missed those things when he was on the trail day after day.

"Get my horse saddled," he said, turning for the corral.

Underwood also swung about, started for the house. "Be an hour or so. I'll sing out when I'm ready."

Rutter, with Brock and Mysak crowded up close to him, stood for a time watching the rancher move off, and then with a hard glance at Starbuck, headed for the bunkhouse. At once Tom Gage crossed to where Shawn was pulling tight a cinch.

"I ain't sure," the old foreman said, his eyes on the three men, "just what's going on around here, but you keep your eyes peeled while you're making that ride."

Shawn paused. "Meaning what?"

"Meaning I wouldn't trust them three saddlewarmers half as far as I could throw a cow barn—especially after that warning Rutter gave you."

"Way I feel about them," Starbuck said. "I'll be watching—going and coming."

Sam Underwood stood at the rear window that over-looked the yard and watched Guy Rutter, accompanied by Brock and Pete Mysak, ride off.

A feeling of satisfaction flowed through him. They were taking the bait he'd so carefully dangled in front of them, were doing exactly as he had hoped. Starbuck had been gone much less than an hour and already they were setting out to follow.

He had been certain they would. Rutter had a devious, suspicious mind and the letter—actually no more than some mortgage papers he'd brought home to read over and sign—would represent a possible double cross and a threat to the success of the bank holdup they planned.

Rutter would think he was tipping off Ira Cameron, in-structing him to call in the sheriff, set up an ambush inside the building. He'd not rest now until he got the letter in his hands, examined it and made sure.

That wouldn't be easy to accomplish. Starbuck, whom he'd impressed with the importance of the envelope and the need for delivering it at any and all costs, was not the sort to fail a trust; he'd fight. Rutter, even aided by Brock and the thick-skulled Mysak would be no match for an ex-pert gunslinger like him.

Thus it would come down to a shootout. Rutter, Brock and Mysak were bound to get the worst of it. He'd not be surprised if at least two of them ended up dead—and that was exactly what Sam Underwood wanted; two of them, or even one out of the picture, and there'd be no bank robbery. One man could not possibly pull off the job. . . . Two, perhaps, but the risk would be great, and Rutter, should he be one of those still alive, wasn't likely to take the chance.

He need not fear reprisal by way of the "girl" and the "letter" the three had mentioned, if indeed such a girl and such a letter recounting the affair at Medford's Crossing existed. According to Rutter she'd been directed to hand the confession over to the law if there proved to be a trap awaiting them when the robbery was attempted. An unfortunate encounter with a gunman on the trail during which Rutter and the others got themselves shot to hell before any robbery attempt could hardly apply to the instructions that had been given her.

And by then he'd have had time to do a little investigating himself, learn who the girl was, and if there was a letter, get it by paying her off. Women of the sort Rutter would associate with always had a price, particularly when the man she'd made a deal with and expected a bonus of cash from was dead or wounded and unable to pay.

He'd worked it out carefully, thought it through to the end. Rutter and his buckos would discover they'd underestimated him, that they'd picked the wrong man to squeeze down on, try to blackmail. Hell, he hadn't got where he was by being stupid.

He hadn't been too obvious, not with either Starbuck or Rutter. He'd shown just enough secrecy there in the yard to pique Rutter, arouse his suspicions—and just the right amount of seriousness where Starbuck was concerned to impress him with the importance of fighting for the letter, if need be.

He would have liked to bring Starbuck a bit deeper into his scheme, actually warn him about Rutter, but that might have spoiled the whole thing. It was better if it all came off unexpectedly; a sudden attack by the three men, the quick and violent reaction of Starbuck protecting a most valuable envelope entrusted to his care. That's what he counted on. . . . He did hope Starbuck came out of it all right, though. He liked the young man.

He reckoned he didn't have to worry about Shawn Starbuck, however. He could take care of himself. One look into those cool, gray eyes, or at the way he handled himself even when the odds were all wrong, gave one the idea that he'd been down the road plenty and there was damned little that could faze him. Starbuck would come out on top—maybe with a bullet hole or two—but he'd make it, and he'd get the job done.

Regardless, in Sam Underwood's mind the result justified the means. He could not, under any circumstances, permit anything to stand in the way of getting what he desired most—the governorship of the Territory. The power and prestige that came with it meant everything to him and his family, as well as to a considerable number of fellow ranchers, businessmen and certain important politicians.

Actually, when you viewed it objectively, he would be breaking faith, letting them down if he didn't take drastic steps to block off any and all threats to the fulfillment of his plans. They were depending upon him, basing their futures on what he could do for them once he attained the Governor's Palace. It would be criminal to allow a ghost out of the past to wreck their hopes.

Underwood grinned wryly. He could expect some violent repercussions from Starbuck when it was all over and done with. The tall stranger had guessed that all was not rosy between him and his army pals. His meaning had been clear when he asked if there was anyone in particular he should keep an eye open for—and he had meant Guy Rutter, Mysak and Brock. . . . He was glad he'd had the presence of mind to deny any and all enemies.

Well, he'd play it that way right through to the finish. He'd make Starbuck—assuming he survived the trap Rutter and the others were certain to lay for him once they'd swung by and gotten ahead—believe that he had no idea of their intentions; that, as far as he was concerned, they were old, trusted friends and had fooled him completely.

Starbuck would believe it—or possibly, he would not since he wasn't the kind to be fooled easily; but if he didn't swallow the explanation—what of it? There was absolutely nothing he could do about anything.

Motion at the far side of the yard drew Underwood's attention. Tom Gage, coming in from the range where he'd been looking things over, no doubt. It had been touch and go with Tom there for a bit. For a few moments he thought he'd lost him—and that would have posed a serious problem.

As long as Tom Gage was around to run Underwood, he had no worries as far as the ranch was concerned. In fact, and he had freely admitted such to everyone, he'd realized a long time ago that he couldn't have made it to the top of the heap without the help of the crusty old cowman.

He must keep Tom satisfied and happy, humor him along, no matter what it took. Only then could he feel secure and know, after he became governor, that the ranch was not going to pot for lack of management.

But he guessed things were all right with the old foreman now. He'd cooled off when it appeared he was to have his way, and that there'd be no more interference from anyone. . . . He'd not allow an explosive situation like that to arise again—that was for sure.

Underwood watched Gage ride up to the corrals, halt and sit quietly staring at the horses in the front enclosure. The old man was sharp. Damned little got by him. He was noticing now the absence of the horses Rutter, Brock and Mysak used. He wouldn't guess, though, that the three men had ridden out to follow Starbuck—and meet their doom. He'd have no reason to think of such; he'd simply assume they were off somewhere, and forget it.

Taking a deep, satisfied breath, Sam Underwood looked off across the yard to the low hills beyond and smiled contentedly while through his mind passed this thought: *Mr. Governor-to-be, you've done yourself proud, climbing out of that mess. By the time this day's done you can forget Guy Rutter and Pete Brock and Rufe Mysak and Medford's Crossing, and start figuring who you're going to favor with all those fat appointments you'll be passing out after you're sworn in. Got to hand them over to those who can do you the most good. . . . You scratch my back, I'll scratch yours. It's a good rule.*

"Samuel. . . ."

Amy Underwood's voice reached him from an adjoining room. She always used his full name although he preferred the diminutive. Her genteel Southern upbringing, he supposed. But it did sound a bit more dignified and formal. Maybe, after the inauguration, he'd sort of start using it.

"Samuel?" Amy said again.

"Right here."

"I told Holly to invite the Camerons over for dinner Sunday. She'll stay over and ride back with them."

A frown clouded Underwood's face as he pivoted on a heel slowly. "Holly—did she go to Vegas?"

"Yes. . . . Was there something you wanted?"

A great fear was blossoming within the rancher. In a long stride he crossed the room to the connecting doorway.

"When did she leave?" he asked in a breathless voice.

Amy, comfortable in her pink velour rocker, looked up from her tatting. "An hour or so ago. That new man you hired was riding in—some business of yours, Holly said, and—"

"Starbuck? Did she go with Starbuck?"

"Why, yes, that's the name she mentioned. She had some shopping to do, asked if it would be all right to go with him. I told her yes, of course."

Sam Underwood stood frozen, eyes bright with shock, lower jaw sagging. Amy, a look of concern covering her face, rose, moved anxiously to his side.

66

"Wasn't it all right? Both you and Tom seemed to think this Starbuck is a fine, young man."

"Holly—oh, my God!" Underwood muttered as visions of what awaited her on the trail rocked through his mind.

"Did I do something wrong? She's ridden to town before with the hired hands. I couldn't see why—"

"Never mind," he said, the realities and necessities of the moment grasping him harshly. "Something I've got to do. . . . Don't wait supper for me."

In the next instant he had snatched up his hat, was running through the doorway into the yard, yelling for Manuel to get his horse saddled.

◎ 12 ◎

Starbuck, no more than a half mile from the Underwood ranch, caught the sound of hoofbeats in his wake. Instantly he swung the chestnut off into a dense tamarisk windbreak. Hand resting lightly on the butt of his pistol, he waited.

Soon, Holly, dressed in her corduroy riding outfit but this time wearing a man's wide-brimmed hat instead of the usual brightly colored scarf, broke into view. Her face was intent as she looked down the road.

Shawn moved out of the thicket, the tautness slipping from his long frame. "Hunting for me?"

Reining in sharply, she whirled, startled. A smile of relief parted her lips.

"I was afraid I'd missed you."

Shawn frowned. "Missed me?"

"I thought maybe you were farther ahead than I expected, and I'd have trouble catching up. . . . I'm riding in to Vegas, too."

Starbuck's brow puckered with disapproval. He wanted no company on this journey—particularly hers.

"Your father know about this?"

"He does by now. I told Mother. . . . There's nothing wrong with it. I often ride to town with the men." She studied him soberly as they continued down the road. "Why? Don't you want me along?"

"Not that," he replied, shifting on the saddle. "Happens I'm running an errand for your father. Important one, I guess. Aimed to travel fast and hard."

"I know. It's a letter to Ira Cameron at the bank. I overheard father talking to you. . . . That's where I stay— with the Camerons."

Shawn gazed ahead, settled himself resignedly on the chestnut. He didn't like the idea but he guessed it was all

68

right—and there seemed little he could do about it, anyway. Almost curtly he bobbed his head in agreement.

"Let's go," he said and spurred the gelding to a fast lope.

She moved up beside him quickly, riding her sorrel with a flawless, natural grace. Abreast, the two horses, one only a slightly darker red than the other in the hot, afternoon sun, stretched out in a matching pace.

Some time later they were out of the trees and brush, were once again on open, grassy range. For a full hour they traveled across an almost level plain, and then the road began to rise toward the mountains in the distance. The grass thinned, became irregularly spaced clumps; the land began to break up with scatterings of rock here and there while rabbit brush, sage and groundsel became more plentiful.

Shawn glanced at Holly's sorrel and noted the lather flecking his coat. At once he began to slow, realizing he'd not given her mount thought, was gauging endurance and fitness by the standards of the powerful chestnut. Pulling into a trot, he brushed sweat from his forehead, shifted his attention to Holly. Her tanned, serene face was glistening from the heat but she had voiced no complaint, and made none now.

"Shade down there," he said, indicating a stand of small trees a quarter mile distant. "Be a good place to pull up, rest a bit."

The girl nodded, then pointed to a darker patch of green higher up on the slope above the road. "That's where we usually stop. There's a spring. We can get a cool drink, water the horses."

Shawn was not especially interested in any lengthy stop, and the chestnut was not in need of watering, but he had Holly to think of. Immediately he swung onto a narrow path that veered off the road, angled upward.

It was pleasant beneath the cottonwoods and chokecherrys. The grass was thick, a rich emerald, and the murmur of water bubbling from under a granite ledge, rushing over a bed of sand and pebbles for a dozen strides to disappear again into the dark earth, was soothing. Wild verbena lay like a purple mat on the nearby slopes and yellow crownbeard, standing in dense profusion, crowded the banks of the creek.

Under different circumstances Starbuck would have appreciated the mountain oasis, would have considered it a fine place to loaf away a summer's day, but with Sam Underwood's letter tucked inside his shirt, its sharp corners digging into his skin reminding him of its presence, dalliance must necessarily be limited.

"Best we move on," he said, getting to his feet. "Sooner I get this—"

Words died on his lips as the distant, hollow thud of running horses somewhere below came to him. Moving forward, he looked down slope. The spring lay in a fairly deep hollow and a long, rock-studded ridge shut off his view completely. He turned back to where Holly waited with the horses.

"Riders. Several, sounded like."

The girl swung to her saddle, not waiting for him to assist. "Lots of people use the road," she said. "Connects with the one that runs into Texas. Anyone going from there to Vegas or Santa Fe—any of the towns in the Rio Grande Valley, will use it."

"Don't think they were on the road. Seemed farther, below that, moving fast."

She smiled down at him, her eyes mischievous. "Taking a short cut. . . . Maybe they're anxious to get to town and see the saloon girls, too, like you."

"Not the reason I'm in a hurry," Starbuck said, stepping up onto the gelding.

Holly was probably right, he thought, and he should forget it, not become disturbed. But he found himself wondering about the riders as they worked their way back down the slope to the road. . . . It was that damned letter, he guessed. If Underwood hadn't gone so strong at impressing him of its importance and the absolute need for getting it delivered safely to Ira Cameron at the bank, he likely would not have given the passersby any consideration.

They reached the well-marked roadway, resumed the journey. Once again Starbuck set the pace at a good lope, but now his attention was on the country ahead. He should be able to glimpse the riders somewhere in the distance since the land rose and fell in a series of slopes and crests created by the higher ridges to the north.

He hoped Holly was right in her assumption—that what he had heard was only cowpunchers on their way to town for a spree, but the ingrained caution of the man would not permit him to accept such an explanation without some degree of reservation. Thus he continued to search the winding dust ribbon before him; he had to be sure.

He saw the three men a short time later. They were climbing a long grade somewhat below and parallel to the road. They were crowding their horses hard. The distance was too great to make recognition possible, but suspicion rose instantly in Starbuck's mind, and when the riders dropped over onto the far side of the ridge, he swerved in close to Holly.

"There another way to Las Vegas besides this one? A trail, maybe?"

The girl shook her head. "Not that I ever heard of. They say the country in between is very rough—all canyons and buttes. Why?"

"Would as soon get off this road," he replied, and let it drop there, not wishing to alarm her unduly.

She glanced at him, a petulant frown on her face. "I thought it would be fun riding with you, Shawn. . . . You won't even talk, much less joke and cut up like the other hands."

"Wasn't my idea, your coming along."

Her face colored and her shoulders came back. "If that's how you feel I can go on alone," she said stiffly.

"Not saying that I feel that way. Just that this letter of your pa's is important—probably a lot more than you think."

She looked at him closely. "It's those riders you're worried about, isn't it?"

"Not especially worried—just being careful."

Holly shrugged. "I still think they're just cowboys going to town for a good time."

"And I'm hoping you're right," he said, but deep within him felt that she wasn't.

Not long after that they gained the summit of the long slope on which he'd caught first sight of the men. An equally lengthy distance below, the road entered a somewhat narrow passage hemmed in on both sides with rock and brush, and then again began to climb another slanting hillside.

Starbuck gave that some thought. The riders should be in view as they made their ascent. There was no one visible anywhere. Such could only mean they had stopped in the maze of tangled growth and boulders at the foot of the grade. Once more he swung in close to the sorrel.

"There water down there in the bottom?"

Holly shook her head. "That spring where we were, it's the only place between the ranch and Vegas."

Small warning flags began to wave inside Shawn Starbuck's brain. It sounded like an ambush. Underwood's warning had not been for nothing. Someone wanted the envelope he was carrying—bad.

He studied the country before him. The road angled to

71

the left, dropped off to a fairly steep slant as it snaked its way downward to the ragged arroyo at the junction of the two slopes. Alert, he continued on its course, following the rutted tracks to a point where they whipped back in a sharp bend and he knew that Holly and he would not be visible to anyone watching from below, and there cut abruptly away, taking to the rough, open land on their right.

"Where are you going?" Holly demanded, puzzled.

"Higher up. We'll keep in the hills," he explained. "Got a hunch those men are waiting for us at the foot of the slope. Not taking any chances. We'll circle around them."

Surprisingly, she did not protest, but simply swung off the road and followed him up a steep slide covered with loose shale, to a higher level. There they broke out onto a ridge, soon dropped off into a short, shallow valley that ran east and west, as did the road.

Coming to the far side, Starbuck rode to its lower rim, looked down. The arroyo was still a considerable distance in front of them. To bypass, as he planned, he would have to keep to the higher land for another mile at least.

With painstaking care he probed the slopes and little gullies before him. There was no deep swale now in which they could ride unseen, only a series of dangerous slides backed by towering bluffs. The horses would have hard going.

Moving out in front of Holly, he said, "Keep up close. If the sorrel starts spooking, we'll walk."

The girl's presence was a complication. Alone, the chances were he'd not take such trouble to avoid what possibly was no ambush at all but merely three men resting on their way to Las Vegas. But he couldn't afford to gamble on that; if it was a trap designed to stop him and take Sam Underwood's letter, and he rode into it, there'd be gunplay, and he couldn't risk Holly getting hurt.

Better to take all precautions, better to be sure. . . . He'd have a look, though, when they reached a point where he could see down into the arroyo clearly.

Starbuck knew it was an ambush well before that moment came. As he rode near the edge of a treacherously loose-surfaced bench, his eye caught the sudden bright flash of sunlight on metal in the brush. He pulled up short.

"What is it?" Holly asked instantly.

Shawn pointed at the undergrowth below. There was no reason now to hold anything back from her.

"Keep looking," he said.

72

It came again—the metallic glint just within the fringe of the brake.

"The riders we heard—they're holed up in there, waiting for us—for me. That was sunlight shining on a gun barrel."

She showed no sign of fear, but asked, "Who are they? You have any idea?"

Starbuck had a vague hunch, but no more than that. Therefore, he said, "Three men—about all I can say."

"What can we do?"

His attention swung back to the land facing them. "Can't keep going straight across, that's for sure. Buttes up there block the way. Have to angle down slope, get back on the road."

"They'll hear us—see us, too."

Shawn nodded. "How they had it figured, I expect. Hills coming together there, like they do, makes a natural pass. Only way through is by the road." He raised his glance to meet hers. "Be a good idea for you to double back, keep clear of this."

Holly's chin set itself firmly. "I'd feel better with you—safer."

Shawn thought back to those earlier moments in the yard at Underwood's when Rufe Mysak had first seen the girl and had swept her with his hungering appraisal. Keeping her close by where he could watch out for her would be better.

"Then listen close. Want you to stay on my right, in behind my horse until we reach that flat you see about a quarter mile below us. . . . We get there, you slap your spurs to that sorrel and head for the road. Once you're on it—don't stop until you reach town. Understand?"

She signified her agreement, but there was a frown on her face. "What are you going to do?"

His plan was to keep himself between her and the men in the brush, draw fire away from her, while at the same time he tried to pin them down with his own weapon.

But he said, "Sort of curious about them. Think I know who they are, but I aim to have myself a look, be sure."

The explanation satisfied her and they moved on, letting the horses pick their way over the uncertain, steep footing. Careful as they were, there was a continual dislodging of small rocks and a steady spilling of gravel. As they drew nearer to the flat strip of almost level ground Shawn had pointed out to Holly, he drew his pistol and rode with it in his hand. When they came to the little flat they would not be far from the arroyo.

The sudden, spiteful crack of a gun brought all thought, all speculation to an end. Shawn jerked the chestnut to one side, allowed Holly to crowd by onto the flat.

"Get out of here!" he yelled, and slapped the sorrel on the rump so that the horse leaped away and plunged off the low bank to the level racing for the road some fifty yards farther on. Starbuck, wheeling the gelding, fired blindly into the brush-filled arroyo. Again a pistol cracked. The bullet splatted dully into the bluff behind Shawn.

He was in a bad position—and an easy target. Throwing a hasty glance at Holly that assured him that she had gained the road and was quickly pulling out of danger, he cut back, pivoting so sharply the chestnut came up on his hind legs, and then jumped the horse off the ledge into a narrow wash several feet below.

Shots were coming in quick succession now, but he was in back of a mound of rock and no longer in the open as before. Two more guns began to blast. Apparently only one of the trio had spotted him and Holly at the start. The others, hiding elsewhere in the undergrowth—probably on the opposite side of the arroyo—had heard and come to add their support.

Bent low over his horse, he hurried along the floor of the gully, holding his return fire. The men in the brush continued to hammer the side of the hill where they had seen him last—thinking him still in the undergrowth. Abruptly he broke into the open. Instantly the pattern of shooting changed. A bullet sang off the metal horn of his saddle; another clipped the brim of his hat, while others spurted sand around the chestnut's hooves.

Cursing, he spurred the big horse ahead in a quick surge for the road, snapped two shots into the arroyo at the point where the firing seemed to come from. At once two horses shied out of the stunted trees and brushes onto a bare strip of ground at the base of the slope. His bullets had evidently hit close, frightening them. A man appeared, racing to grab the trailing reins of the animals before they could bolt.

Anger, but no surprise, ripped through Starbuck as he recognized Brock. Surely, Guy Rutter and Mysak would be the others who had lain in wait for him.

Emptying his pistol into the brush as he reached the hard surface of the road, he veered right. A shoulder of weed-covered earth closed him off from view of the arroyo. He took a deep breath as the shooting suddenly ended.

Pointing the chestnut up the long slope, he began to rod the spent cartridges from the cylinder of his forty-five, and thumb in fresh loads. . . . Sam Underwood was going to be surprised when he learned his army pals were far from friends.

◎ 13 ◎

Holly was waiting at the top of the hill.

"What the hell are you doing here?" he shouted, furious at her. Halting the chestnut, he twisted about, threw his glance down to the arroyo. Fortunately, Rutter and the others had not yet begun a pursuit.

"I told you to ride for town," he added, his manner softening.

The worried look on her face had faded. "I—I was afraid for you. I had to know—I had to wait."

"I'm fine," he said gruffly. "Let's move out. They'll be coming."

At once they cut into the road, here another long, flowing grade. The gelding was winded after his fast climb and Starbuck did not press him too hard. Their lead on the three would last for a time. If the men did close the gap, he wanted the gelding ready for another hard run.

"Who were they?"

Shawn had expected the question, and had been unde-cided at first as to how to answer it. For her own safety she should know.

"Guy Rutter and his sidekicks—Brock and Mysak."

Holly stared at him in astonishment. "You mean those friends of my father—the ones who came to see him?"

"Friends!" Starbuck echoed the word scornfully. "Can't call them that. They wanted this letter of your pa's so bad they didn't mind killing to get it."

The girl was silent for a full minute as the horses pounded steadily on. Then, "It's hard to believe."

"The hard thing to figure is how they can be friends of your pa's. Not the kind I'd expect him to have."

"It goes back to the war. They were in the same outfit. . . . I suppose that explains it. They were all right then, but they've changed."

76

"*Somebody* sure has," Starbuck muttered, more to himself than to Holly. "Are we far from town?"

"Only an hour or so. . . . What are you going to do about them?"

"Nothing—unless they keep pushing. I figure it's up to your pa. They're *his* problem."

"The sheriff should be told about it. You could have been killed."

He shrugged. "That's up to your pa, too. Was his letter they were after. Far as I'm concerned I'll look after myself."

There was still no sign of the others when Shawn and Holly reached the outskirts of Las Vegas and turned into the main street. As they rode down the wide, dusty channel between buildings, Holly pointed out the bank to him.

"You'll find Mr. Cameron there. . . . I'm going on to his house—spend the night with them." She hesitated and added impulsively, "Later, if you feel like it you could ride out to the Cameron place. It's at the far end of the town."

Shawn was unwilling to commit himself. The three men would show up, he was certain. They would arrive too late to stop delivery of the envelope, but that didn't mean he'd seen the last of them. They'd warned him earlier to move on; now they would have to silence him before he could report the attempted ambush to Sam Underwood. With him out of the way—and since Holly had not actually seen any of them—they could deny knowledge of the incident.

"I aim to check into the hotel, take things easy."

"Go to the Exchange," she said, pointing to a building a few doors on down from the bank. "It's the best."

"Want to give myself a good scrubbing, then see the sights."

Holly nodded, understanding probably more than he gave her credit for. "If you do take the notion, you'll be welcome at the Cameron's," she said, and rode on.

He swung into the hitchrack fronting the bank, halted and dismounted. Entering the low-ceilinged, shadow-filled building, he paused just inside the doorway and glanced around. To his left a lone teller dozed in his cage; to the right an elderly man sat at a desk behind a waist-high counter.

"You Ira Cameron?" he asked, moving up to the latter.

The man with the shock of snow-white hair got to his feet, a practiced smile on his lips. "I am. What can I do for you?"

77

Shawn dug into his shirt, produced the letter and passed it over. "Take this," he said, relief in his tone. "Rode in with it from Sam Underwood."

Cameron deftly slid an opener under the envelope's flap, glanced at its contents and tossed it onto his desk.

"Thank you," he said. "Something wrong with Sam?"

"No, just wanted to get that letter to you in a hurry. Sent me with it."

The banker shrugged. "Was no need for all the rush, Mr.——"

"Starbuck."

"Mr. Starbuck. Sam could have brought it in the next time he came to town. You a new hand at his place? Can't recall seeing you before."

Shawn puzzled, ignored the question, pointed instead to the letter. "You mean there's nothing important in that?"

"Only some mortgage forms, trust deeds and such. Ordinary bank business, that's all."

Anger whipped through Starbuck. *Nothing important!* Sam Underwood had led him to believe the envelope was vital—something he should be ready and willing to protect with his life, if necessary. His temper mounted higher. What the hell was going on? Why would the rancher lie about it? Moreover, why would Guy Rutter want the letter? What good would mortgage papers be to him and his friends? None of it made any sense.

Turning back to Cameron, he said, "If there's any answer or something you want taken back to Underwood, I'll be at the Exchange Hotel. Figure to spend the night."

"I'll remember that," Cameron said, moving back to his desk. "Obliged to you again."

Burning, Starbuck returned to the street. Stopping close to the wall of the building, he swept the dusty roadway with his glance. There was no sign of the three men. Then mounting, he rode to the stable at the rear of the hotel. Instructing the hostler as to the chestnut's care, he slung his saddlebags across his shoulder, doubled back to the front of the two-storied building and entered the lobby.

At the desk he registered, asked for and received a room facing the street, made his way to it. He stepped immediately to the window, swept back the frayed curtains. He had a fairly complete view of the road. Satisfied, he moved back, threw off his clothing and washed himself down from the china bowl and pitcher. He'd planned on a soak in a tin tub at the barber's but that was out now. He was too worked up over Underwood's deceit and Guy Rutter's attempt to ambush him. He had some accounting

78

due from both; Underwood's he'd get when he returned to the ranch—Rutter when he showed up in town.

He took time to shave, and then drawing on the same clothes he was wearing when he rode in, went back to the street. For a time he lounged in the cool shade of the Exchange's gallery, idly watching the coming and going along the walks. . . . Las Vegas seemed a fairly busy town. There was hope, he'd heard someone say—Underwood, he thought—of a railroad soon.

Such would make the settlement the largest and most important city in the Territory, the rancher had said. No doubt it would be true—at least temporarily. What men like Underwood forgot and what he, personally, had noted in his wanderings, was that railroads never called a halt, had a habit of pushing their iron rails farther and farther, extending their reach to other towns, bringing to them greater size, importance and—usually—fleeting glory.

Weary of watching, waiting, Shawn moved off the hotel's porch and headed across the street for the ornate swinging doors of the Gold Dollar Saloon, easily the largest and apparently the most popular establishment of its kind in the settlement.

The last of the sun's rays were spraying a golden fan into the sky beyond the mountains to the west, tinting the windows of the shops and spreading a faint haze over the gradually cooling town. Here and there lamps had been lighted and a few storekeepers were locking their doors for the night.

A church bell was measuring off the hour—seven o'clock—in slow, mournful peals, and in the street adjacent to the saloon, a dusty mongrel was barking frantically at a buckskin-clad, bearded man entering on a starved-looking mule.

It was good to be in a town again, hear the sounds of people, smell the odors that reminded him of home, feel the presence of others bustling about at the business of everyday living. It had been some time since he'd found himself in anything larger than a ranch.

He'd make the best of it—Rutter and Underwood be damned. A few drinks to cut the dust and ease the tension that yet gripped him; then a good meal at one of the restaurants. Afterwards he'd go back to the Gold Dollar and while away the evening hours. . . . He wasn't forgetting about playing a few hands of cards, either; with the kind of money Underwood was paying him, he could afford to splurge a little.

He tried to put aside the thought of confronting Rutter

79

and the others. They hadn't put in an appearance so it would seem they were not anxious to meet him. Good enough, he'd find and settle with them later. . . . Right now live a little.

There was no need to worry about Holly. She would be with the Camerons, in good hands—not that her welfare was any concern of his, but he did feel sort of responsible for her after what had happened. . . . He could figure the night was his. He could relax, enjoy himself. Tomorrow would be soon enough to dig into the puzzle of why Underwood would send him on a useless errand that had almost gotten him killed, and why Guy Rutter had wanted so badly a letter of no value.

He reached the front of the Gold Dollar, halted, threw his glance back along the street for a final look. A half-dozen soldiers from Fort Union were coming into view at the north end of town. . . . A small boy with an apron that reached down to his shoe tops was sweeping the porch at Hayman's General Store. . . . A dozen or so persons sauntered along the sidewalks in the soft velvet twilight, soaking in the pleasant breeze drifting in from the high peaks of the Sangre de Cristos.

Satisfied and at ease, Shawn came back around, took a step toward the batwings. He halted abruptly as a man pushed hurriedly through, met him face to face.

Pete Brock. . . .

◉ 14 ◉

Starbuck's resolution to put his problems behind him vanished in a flare of anger. His hand dropped to the low-slung pistol on his hip.

"Don't move," he said harshly.

Brock's swollen, discolored features stiffened and a wild, apprehensive light came into his eyes. "Now hold on—wait a minute. . . . I—"

"Where're Rutter and Mysak?"

"Vida's room—inside—"

"Take me there—easy and quietlike."

Brock hesitated, cast a look to the right and then to his left in desperate hope of assistance. No one was watching. Starbuck's fingers tightened about the butt of his pistol and his free hand clenched into a fist.

"Now," he said softly.

Brock swallowed noisily, bobbed his head, and, turning, moved back into the saloon with Shawn crowding him. The smoke-hazed room was well filled with patrons, rocking with noise. In a far corner, barely audible above the lift and fall of the racket, a piano was being played.

Careful, alert, Starbuck followed Brock through the crowd. Several men turned, gave them brief attention during their passage, and then resumed whatever they were doing. Brock reached the foot of a stairway and slowed.

"This better not be a trick," Starbuck warned in a tight voice. "Not if you want to live."

"It ain't no trick!" Pete protested. "You said take you to Rutter. That's what I'm doing."

They mounted the steps to the second floor and entered a hall. Brock led the way down its shadowy length to a door at the extreme end, halted.

"In here. . . ."

Shawn nodded coldly. Drawing his pistol, he said: "Open it—step inside."

81

Brock hesitated uncertainly. Starbuck's balled fist came up. Instantly the outlaw reached for the knob. He gave it a twist, flung back the thin panel.

"Look out!" he shouted, and tried to duck to one side.

Starbuck's right slammed into the center of his shoulders, sent him plunging forward. Pete Mysak, almost directly in line with the door, sprang to his feet. Brock, off balance and under the force of Shawn's blow, crashed into the larger man. Both went sprawling to the floor.

In that same fragment of time Starbuck veered left and swung his gun like a club at Guy Rutter who had been sitting around a small table with the gaudily dressed Vida and Mysak. The blow caught Rutter on the side of the head as he clawed for his revolver, knocked him staggering into the wall as the woman yelled and leaped back.

Flushed with anger, breathing hard, Shawn kicked the door closed with a heel. Arms folded across his heaving chest, weapon hanging loosely in his hand, he surveyed the disorder.

The woman, a thick-waisted blonde with heavily rouged cheeks and vacant, colorless eyes, was drawn up against the back wall watching him with a fearful fascination.

Rutter, holding a hand to one side of his head, sagged against the adjacent partition, a burning hatred glowing in his stare. In the narrow space between the bed and the opposing wall, Brock and Mysak were untangling themselves, struggling to their feet.

"What the hell's this all about?" Guy Rutter demanded.

"Don't give me that!" Starbuck snarled. "Little matter of an ambush—one that didn't work. . . . I figure we ought to finish it—now."

A slyness filled the redhead's eyes. Keeping his hands well away from the pistol at his side, he drew himself erect, moved back to the chair he had so hastily vacated, and casually sat down.

"You ain't getting me to go for my gun," he said calmly. "Neither'll Pete or Rufe. You shoot, you'll be killing us in cold blood—and they hang a man in this town for that."

"Maybe. Odds are three to one, and you're all wearing guns. That might change a jury's thinking a bit." Shawn paused, swung his weapon slowly back and forth so as to cover all the men generally. "You want to stay alive, lift your pistols slowly with your left hand and drop them on the bed. . . . All of you."

Mysak swore vividly into the hot silence, did as ordered, and turned angrily to Brock.

82

"What the hell'd you bring him here for?" he shouted.

Brock rid himself of his weapon. "You think I done it a purpose?" he shot back. "Nailed me going out the front of the saloon—"

"You damned fool," Rutter snapped in a low, controlled voice. "I told you to keep out of sight."

"I was," Brock insisted. "Only going over to that store for a sack of Bull—"

"Sit down," Starbuck cut in. "On the floor—lean up against the wall," he added to Brock and Rufe Mysak.

Grumbling, the two men settled themselves on the scarred boards. Rutter slumped in his chair, one arm draped across the table. The woman—Vida—did not move. Shawn looked at her.

"You, too."

He righted the chair Mysak had occupied, shoved it up to the table with a foot. Vida pulled away from the wall, took her place next to Rutter.

Starbuck swept them all with his smoldering glance. "Now we get back to that ambush. . . . What was it all about?"

Mysak and Brock only stared. Rutter's lips drew into a scornful smile. Temper flared through Starbuck. He came away from the door against which he leaned, pistol ready in his left hand, right knotted into a big knuckled fist cocked and ready to strike. Guy Rutter jerked back, threw up both arms in fear.

"We wanted that letter you was carrying for Sam Underwood!" he cried.

"That's a goddam lie!" Starbuck replied. "Wasn't anything in that envelope but some mortgage papers."

Rutter's brows lifted as a look of incredulity crossed his face. He cast a sidelong glance at Pete and Rufe.

"That so?"

Shawn nodded. "It is. What did you think was in it?"

Again the redhead looked at his friends. "Well, uh—money. . . . A lot of money."

Starbuck swore in disgust. "A holdup," he muttered. "Robbing a man who figured you were his friends."

Mysak laughed, slapped his knee. "I guess we just ain't no-account!"

"Lower than that. . . . You could have killed Underwood's daughter, or got her hurt."

Rutter's manner was now indifferent. "Been too bad. Truth is, we weren't expecting her to be with you."

"But she was—and that didn't hold you back any. Figure I owe you for that, as well as for myself."

83

Rutter shrugged. "Up to you, but you ain't getting us into no fight. . . . What I'm thinking is you'd be smart to forget the whole thing. Tell Underwood, if you're of a mind, let him do what he likes—but you forget it. Nobody got hurt and you done the job you was hired to do. Ought to be satisfied."

"Not so sure that's all there is to it," Shawn said, thinking of Underwood. "What gave you the idea there was money in the envelope?"

"Sam did. Him telling you how important it was that it get delivered to the bank—and him sending it by you, his fancy gunslinger. Only natural we figure it was cash money. . . . You say there was nothing in it but papers, mortgages and stuff like that?"

"That's all."

Guy Rutter smiled. "Well, I'll be goddamned," he murmured. "Old Sam sure fooled us."

Fooled me, too, Starbuck thought bitterly, *almost into getting myself shot up. . . .* The rancher had better have some good reasons for what he had done.

"Reckon you can see now it was all a big mistake," Rutter said in an amiable tone. "Real sorry it happened. If you're willing, we'll just forget the whole thing."

"Seems I remember you ordering me to move on—"

"Forget that, too. Was a bit riled when I said it. I'm for letting that be bygones, too, if it's all right with you."

"Not a chance!" Starbuck rapped. "I'm getting some satisfaction, one way or another. You're all too gutless to stand up to me, so the next best thing is the law."

"The law—" Brock echoed, straightening.

"Sheriff's right here in Las Vegas. I'm filing charges against you for attempted holdup. Maybe I can even stretch it to attempted murder."

Rutter only smiled. "Best you talk that over with Sam Underwood first. How'd it look for him? A big man, head of the bank, getting all set to be the next governor—all cozy with somebody like us. Folks might start wondering just what kind of company he keeps was they to hear how his friends tried to rob him."

Pete Brock settled back. Mysak bobbed his bullet-shaped head. "That's a fact. Sure wouldn't help him none."

Shawn had a sudden impulse to give way to temper, start in on the three men, work them over good. But he knew it would accomplish nothing other than to salve the angry frustration that rankled him.

"Now, you talk to Sam about it," Rutter said in a self-assured manner. "Tell him what you're figuring to do. If he's agreeable to your going to the sheriff, you go ahead. We'll be right here. . . . We ain't planning on going nowhere."

Starbuck, choking back the rage that was boiling through him, circled Rutter and the woman, gathered up the weapons lying on the bed. Holding them in a pocket shaped by his right arm, he backed to the door, opened it and stepped into the hall. Dropping the pistols to the floor, he booted them into a far corner.

"Don't step out here until you're damned sure I've gone," he said in a taut voice. "All I need is a little nudge to start shooting. . . . Already got plenty of reason."

Reaching for the knob, he drew the panel closed and wheeled back into the corridor.

◎ 15 ◎

Fuming, upset by his inability to satisfy the sense of outrage that claimed him; puzzled more than ever now by Sam Underwood's actions, Starbuck moved down the stairs, shouldered his way through the resounding clamor in the saloon and stepped out into the clean, cool night.

Nothing jibed. There was no sense of guilt in the three men for what they had attempted to do—and being the sort they were, he could understand that; it was the absolute lack of alarm, of fear they exhibited when he threatened to bring the law into the matter.

It was as if they were under some mysterious, powerful protection that would not permit the law or anyone else to punish them regardless of their crimes. They were willing to leave everything up to Sam Underwood even though they blandly admitted they had intended to rob him of money they thought he was sending to the bank.

Something was haywire somewhere—something that tied in directly with the rancher. He was the key, and the sooner he was confronted, forced to speak up and explain, the quicker the answers would be out.

Moving off the porch of the Gold Dollar, Starbuck grimly turned toward the Exchange. He'd not stay the night; he'd get the chestnut and head back to the ranch immediately. The way he felt he'd not get any sleep anyway.

His long stride slowed. A rider had turned into the south end of the street, horse limping badly. In the almost complete darkness the man looked familiar. Shawn's head came up abruptly. It was Underwood.

Rigid, he stepped off the board sidewalk into the dust, stalked toward the rancher in a purposeful line. A dozen paces short, Underwood recognized him, pulled up. The rancher's face was pale, strained, and his movements as he dropped from the saddle were anxious.

"My daughter—Holly—she all right?" he asked, hurrying forward.

Starbuck stared at the man coldly. "She is, no thanks to you. What's going on, mister? Speak up—I want to know —quick!"

Underwood's shoulders slumped in relief. He turned, led the horse to a close-by hitchrack, wrapped the reins around the bar and came slowly about.

Resting his weight on the crosspiece, he said: "Rutter and the others—they try to stop you?"

Shawn, holding tight to anger, nodded curtly. "You know damn well they did. Just happened I spotted them first, managed to slip by. You set up that ambush for me, didn't you?"

Underwood drew his handkerchief, mopped at his sweating features. "Guess you could say I did—in a way."

"Just what the hell does that mean?"

Two men passing along the walk on the opposite side of the street slowed, glanced curiously across, and then continued on their way.

"Didn't actually set it up—that is, I didn't tell Rutter and them to do it."

"You're beating around the bush, Mr. Underwood! I want the truth—all of it!"

The rancher again swabbed his face and neck. "Idea was to make Rutter think it was—well, valuable. The letter, I mean—the one I gave you to deliver."

"Then you figured he'd take out after me, set up an ambush and gun me down for it. . . . Why, in the name of—"

"Not you—them!" Underwood said in a sudden gust of words. "I thought you'd get them, being better with a gun —faster and with a lot of experience. None of them could even match you—alone or together. I knew that. It's what I was banking on."

Starbuck was studying the rancher in astonishment. "You mean I was supposed to kill them protecting that envelope?"

Sam Underwood bobbed his head weakly. "Seemed a good idea when I first thought it up. Was sure you could take care of yourself, come out on top."

"I'd probably be laying out there now, full of holes, if Holly hadn't suggested we turn off at the spring for a drink of water."

"Didn't know she was with you," Underwood said heavily. "Not until my wife mentioned it an hour or so after you pulled out. Grabbed my horse and followed fast as I could. Damned animal pulled up lame about ten miles out,

87

or I'd been here sooner. . . . Never been so worried in my life as I was when I learned Holly was with you."

"And I was riding into a trap," Shawn finished drily. "I'll tell you this, you came close to getting us both shot."

Underwood looked up quickly. "She know who they were?"

"She does. Was for me going straight to the sheriff about it. Told her they were your friends, that I'd leave it up to you. Getting a mite sorry I decided that way. They seem to think it's all a big joke."

"You've seen Rutter since?"

Starbuck jerked his thumb at the Gold Dollar. "In there, all of them. With a woman they call Vida. Tried to force them into a fight, settle a few scores, but they flat backed down."

"They say—anything special?"

"Laughed at me when I said I was going to the law since I couldn't even up things personally. Said I ought to tell you the whole thing because it was your property they were pulling the holdup for and your daughter who almost got hurt. Thought you ought to be the one to handle it with the sheriff. . . . Plenty sure of themselves."

Underwood stirred wearily. "Guess they are."

Starbuck crossed his arms, leaned forward slightly. Anger was still tightening his voice. "Got a hunch that's the answer to what this is all about. What makes them so damned sure? I want to know because whatever it is just about got me killed—and far as I'm concerned, I'm not done with them yet."

Underwood scrubbed nervously at his chin. "You could be, if you're willing to listen. . . . I'll pay you off. You can ride out, be on your way with a full month's wages. Job I hired you for is finished anyway, and—"

Shawn was shaking his head before the rancher had finished. "I don't like somebody throwing lead at me—and I don't like getting set up like a clay pigeon in a shooting gallery. . . . I'll pull out when I know what's behind all this, and after I've done some settling."

Sam Underwood lifted his hands, nodded woodenly. "Figured as much—you don't need to go on. And I reckon you've got a right. . . . First off, however, I'd like to see Holly, be sure she's—"

"Holly's fine," Starbuck cut in crisply. "Staying with the Camerons like she always does. Been there ever since we hit town."

The rancher's eyes traveled up and down the street, his expression desperate. Night had settled over Las Vegas and the saloons were all going full tilt with the Gold Dollar by far emitting the most racket.

"My horse—lame. Ought to see to him—"

Underwood was seeking escape, a way out, some excuse for delaying his explanation. Shawn eyed the man coldly.

"There's a stable behind the hotel. We can take him there. . . . Make up your mind to this, Underwood, you're not getting out of my reach until I hear what this is all about."

Abruptly the rancher seemed to wilt, shrink as if a tremendous weight had settled upon him. "All right," he said tonelessly, pulling the horse's reins free. "Let's get this animal to the stable, then go where we won't be bothered. . . . What I've got to say has never been told to anybody —not even to my wife."

◎ 16 ◎

"They're going to rob the bank—my bank," Sam Underwood said when, a short time later, they were in Starbuck's room at the Exchange. "Forcing me to help them."

Shawn, slumped in the solitary, battered chair his quarters afforded, watched the rancher pace nervously back and forth in front of the window. Out in the street there had been no lessening in the racket emanating from the saloons.

"Hell of it is, I can't do a damned thing about it. Tried tricking them, using you—but that backfired. Now I'm caught."

Starbuck leaned back, fingers interlaced across his belly. "Force you—how?"

Underwood's pacing ceased. His head tipped forward as his eyes studied the ragged carpeting on the floor. He seemed to be considering the question, making up his mind whether to answer or ignore it.

Shawn said, "If it ties in with your trying to get me shot up—I want an answer." There was no compromise in his voice, only a hard, unrelenting insistence.

The rancher raised his eyes, studied the tall rider for several moments, and then shrugged. "Guess I've got no choice," he said resignedly. "Have to tell you the whole thing. Goes way back."

"To the war."

"To the war," Underwood said. "We—Rutter, Mysak, Brock and another fellow named Gault—Billy Gault—he's dead now—we were all in the same outfit. Rutter was the leader of our bunch—the five of us. Used to prowl around together when we weren't on duty. Things had quieted down a good bit in the part of the country where we were stationed, and we had a lot of time on our hands.

"Well, one day Rutter heard about a paymaster's wagon passing through the area on its way to another camp. He

90

came up with the idea of robbing it. I was against it myself, but the war was coming to an end and we'd all be turned loose soon—dead broke, he kept telling us, and it was only right we grab what we could. Was the war's fault we'd be in the shape we'd be in—and on top of that none of us would have a job."

Underwood turned, stared through the window at a group of riders passing slowly by, heading out of town. One had consumed far more than his capacity of liquor and the man next him was struggling to hold him to his saddle.

"Was a damned fool to listen to Guy, but you know how things are at a time like that—when you're part of a bunch, I mean. You sort of have to go along with the rest. . . . Well, we ambushed the paymaster's wagon. A couple of soldiers got killed—actually three—and we ended up with the money. Was around six thousand dollars apiece.

"We stashed the money near camp and took turns keeping an eye on it. A few months later we were all discharged. We got together, dug up the sack and split the cash, then went our own way."

"Didn't the army look into the robbery, make an investigation or anything?" Starbuck asked, frowning.

"Oh, sure. There was a hell of a ruckus over it. For a while we had more brass in camp than we had regular soldiers. Then somebody came up with the information that Rebs had been seen in the neighborhood about the time it all happened, so everybody just assumed they were the ones who did it, and it all blew over. . . . Never did know for sure but I always had a hunch it was Rutter who started that rumor about the Rebs.

"I headed out west, ended up in this country. I used my six thousand to buy up a ranch, get myself started in the cattle business. Always told myself I'd send that six thousand back to the government someday, with a letter explaining where it came from—"

"Were you signing your name to it?"

Underwood shook his head. "No, couldn't very well do that, of course. There was those men killed trying to protect the wagon—I wasn't one of them that pulled a trigger, but I was in on it just the same. . . . Thing's bothered me a lot in the last few years. Should have sent the money back—things went good for me and I could spare it easy, but somehow I just never did. Now, I sure wish—"

"Wouldn't have meant much without your name to it," Starbuck said.

"Would've had it off my conscience—"

91

"The money, maybe, but not the killing of those soldiers —or the thing itself. . . . You ever see Rutter and the others again after that?"

"Not until they rode into my place a couple of days ago. Thought they were behind me for good, but seems they heard my name mentioned somewhere. Natural, me being boosted for governor and all that, and then owning a big ranch and part owner of a bank, and so on.

"They'd run through their share of the money a long time ago and had evidently been getting more by pulling off small-time holdups and robberies. When they got a line on me, Rutter come up with one of his smart ideas. They'd blackmail me into helping them rob my own bank." He reached into his pocket, produced a thick gold watch and looked at it. He peered out the window, wiping the sweat from his brow with his handkerchief.

"Anyway, Guy's plenty sly. When he found out where I stood in the Territory, he knew he had me by the short hair. He wrote a letter confessing to the robbery of that paymaster wagon, telling all about it—naming names—the whole works. Even dug up some of the old newspaper clippings that told when and where it took place, put it all in an envelope and addressed it to the U.S. Marshal.

"Then they came to the ranch, same day you showed up, told me if I didn't string along with their plan or tried to double-cross them, the letter would be handed over to the law. . . . That would fix me for good."

"That when you got this idea of sending me up against them, using that letter to Cameron as bait?"

The rancher looked anxiously again through the window and nodded. "Was a fool thing to do, suck you into it, but I reckon I wasn't thinking straight. All I could see was what it would do to me politically—and how it would ruin my family. Felt I had to stop Rutter somehow.

"I couldn't go to the law, of course. Guy had given the confession and clippings to his woman to hold—expect she's the one you saw—told her to hand it over to the sheriff if anything goes wrong during the robbery and they don't come out of it alive."

"Could be a bluff."

"No chance. There's a letter. I know Guy Rutter—his mind works that way. If he got himself killed robbing the bank, he'd get even by dragging me down. He's that kind of a man. That's the reason why I've had to go along with him and the others. Scared not to. Like I said, they've got me right where they want me. All I can do is squirm. They figure to pull off this bank robbery, lay low on my

92

place for a time. I'm their protection. It happens somebody spots any of them pulling the job, I've got to say they're hired hands of mine, that I know for a fact they haven't been off the ranch."

Underwood moved to the bed and sank heavily upon its edge. Hands clasped, shoulders slumped, he stared at the floor in complete dejection. Shawn considered the rancher thoughtfully. He could hold no good feeling for this man, for the things he had done, yet a thread of pity stirred through him.

"When's the robbery coming off?" he asked.

"Tonight," Underwood said in a flat, helpless voice. "It's almost time now. Lot of money in the safe this part of the month. Probably near a hundred thousand dollars."

Starbuck swore under his breath. Why in heaven's name was he getting himself involved in situations like this? All he wanted to do was find Ben, clear up some problems concerning his own life. . . .

One thing was clear. He knew now why Guy Rutter and his two friends were so cocksure, why they were unafraid of repercussions from the law. They had Sam Underwood in a position where he must either go along with their plans, or else bare his past to the world and thereby commit political as well as personal suicide.

But there was more to it than that. Robbing the Las Vegas bank meant disaster to others—businessmen, ranchers, homesteaders, ordinary persons who kept their hard-earned money in its vault. To stand by and permit that to happen was to countenance a crime that would have far-reaching effects—and Shawn knew he could not have that on his conscience.

Sam Underwood had a duty to perform, an accounting to face. It would be bad, especially for Holly and Mrs. Underwood, but there was no other way out; one thing every man had to do eventually was pay for bed and board—and Underwood's time had come.

"You got only one choice," Starbuck said. "To go to the sheriff, bring him in on the deal."

The rancher's head came up slowly. "I'd have to admit —tell—"

"Yes. But down deep you knew someday you'd have to answer for that holdup."

"Yes—I guess I did. Only, there's my family—all my big plans for the Territory—"

"Be tough, not denying that, but I can't see where there's anything else you can do. Robbery was a long time ago—during wartime. That might change the way the law

93

will look at it some. . . . And you'll get credit for the good things you've done. Far as your family's concerned they'll stand by you. But you'd better forget about being governor, even if they turn you loose. Folks like to think their statesmen are without fault—and I reckon they're right."

"They won't turn me loose. You're forgetting about those men that got killed. They'd send me to prison for that—maybe hang me."

"Risk you'll have to take. Point is, you can't let Rutter and them go through with the robbery."

Underwood shifted nervously. "There must be some way of stopping them and still not ruin everything," he said in a desperate voice.

"Don't see how you're going to do anything without owning up to—"

"Wait!" the rancher exclaimed, leaping to his feet. "Just come to me—!"

Starbuck eyed the man coldly. "If you're figuring on me —don't."

"But I'll have to. Only way I can keep them from doing it!" Underwood reached into his pocket and pulled out his watch again. "Got about a half hour before they start."

Shawn was studying the rancher's flushed face. He was into Underwood's problems just about as deep as he was going to go, and the thought of how the man had used him, deliberately set him up, still irked. . . . But if there was going to be an attempt made to rob the bank within thirty minutes, he was obligated to do what he could to stop it—like it or not.

"What's this idea of yours?"

"We'll keep them from doing it," Underwood said in a sudden rush of words. "You and me. We can slip in the bank by the back door—"

Starbuck's hands came up angrily. "No! We get the sheriff—bring him in—"

"There isn't time! I don't think Abrams is even in town, and I don't want to fool with a deputy. No time to do any organizing, have an armed party waiting. The two of us will be enough, anyway. Just three of them, and we'll have surprise on our side."

Wary, Shawn said, "We catch them, then what? You're still going to have to tell the law the whole story, because Rutter sure as hell will."

The rancher nodded slowly. "Guess there's no way around that. Like you said, I'll just have to take my chances, hope everything doesn't go down a rat hole. . . . You willing to give me a hand?"

Starbuck got to his feet. "I'll help, long as you aim to square yourself. . . . Not much time left. We'd better be getting over there. Rutter'll probably be keeping an eye on the place in case you've changed your mind. There a back way to the bank?"

"He won't be watching—not Rutter," Underwood said, moving toward the door. "He's dead sure of me. Figures I'll do exactly what he told me to. . . . But we can use the side entrance to the hotel, go down the alley. Nobody'll see us."

Starbuck hitched at his gun belt. "Let's get over there."

◎ 17 ◎

Underwood led the way down the almost totally black alley to the rear of the bank. It was not difficult for Shawn to understand why the others had chosen that hour of the evening for the robbery. The noise along the street was of such volume that little else, including gunfire, would be heard.

The rancher produced a key and opened the door; they entered. The building smelled dry, and the heat trapped within its walls was stifling. Closing and locking the panel, Underwood moved forward into a small, cleared area in which were two desks and several chairs.

In the dim light filtering through the window that faced the street, Starbuck could see the teller's cage to his right; he saw that he was behind the counter where Ira Cameron had stood when he had delivered Underwood's letter.

"Where's the safe?" he asked in a low voice.

The rancher crossed to a door beyond Cameron's desk. It appeared to be the entrance to a closet but when he drew it open, the black, iron face of a vault was visible.

"They'll be using blasting powder on that," Starbuck commented.

"What they figure to do. Mysak's sort of an expert on it. Was his job in the war—blowing up bridges and houses —things like that. He'll manage it easy."

And being a man experienced with explosives it was likely no one would hear it, Shawn thought. The correct amount of powder affixed to the safe's knob, the door quickly closed and buttressed with a desk, and the noise would be so effectively muffled that no one would be aware of what was taking place.

Starbuck looked more closely at the furnishings, now becoming distinct as his eyes adjusted to the dimness. He pointed to a short counter jutting off at right angles to the teller's barred compartment.

"One of us can hide behind that. Other ought to be on the opposite side of the room. They'll gather in front of the safe. We can cover them from two sides."

"Good," Underwood said, and took up a position back of the counter.

Shawn moved to the far side of the area. There was nothing similar there to employ as cover, and dragging one of the desks around until it faced the safe closet, he crouched behind it. He could watch both front and rear entrances as well as the vault from that point.

Hunkered in the darkness, he tried to figure how the outlaws would gain entry and prepare himself accordingly. It wasn't likely they would attempt to break through the front. Although most of Las Vegas seemed to be indoors, either in the saloons or their homes, a few persons were strolling along the sidewalks, and the crash of breaking glass would certainly draw attention.

It was logical to assume Rutter and his friends would come in from the rear, prying the thick panel from its hinges, or possibly daring to use an axe. They'd run no great risk, working from the alley where they would certainly never be seen and very probably not heard.

The problem settled in his mind, Shawn drew his revolver, checked its loads. There should be no cause to use it unless the men proved to be fools, tried to fight. And they weren't likely to do that—not with two guns pinning them down from opposite sides, trapping them in what could be a murderous cross-fire.

Starbuck raised himself partly, looked toward Underwood. "When you see me stand up—do the same," he called softly. "Let them know quick they're covered by the two of us."

"I'll be ready," the rancher replied.

Keeping his weapon in hand, Shawn leaned back against the wall, taking the strain off his leg muscles which were beginning to ache from the squatting position he was forced to assume. Noise from the Gold Dollar, almost directly across the street, seeped into the darkened room in steady waves, filling it with muted shouts, laughter, the dull thump of a piano. . . .

Starbuck tensed. There was a sound at the rear door. He braced himself, planting his feet squarely that he might rise swiftly and on balance. A ripple of surprise rolled through him. A key had grated in the lock. The faint squeak of hinges sounded and then came a stir of fresh, cool air as the panel swung open.

A key!

There was only one answer for that. Underwood had given it to them—forced to, he'd claim. Disgust curled Starbuck's lips. The rancher might as well have gone all the way—opened the safe and had the money ready for them.

A faint scuffing of boots and the thud of heels reached him. Rutter, Brock and Mysak, the latter two carrying sacks of some sort, were suddenly in the center of the room. They tarried a moment there, then crossed to the door behind Cameron's desk. Rutter opened it wide, stepped back, made a sweeping motion with his arm.

"Get at it, Rufe."

The thick-bodied man dropped to a crouch before the dully gleaming iron panel with its nickeled trimming. He examined the knob and handle briefly.

"Going to be easy," he said.

"What I told you, wasn't it?" Rutter said in a quick, impatient way. "Now, we got everything straight? Soon's that safe's open, you and Pete grab all the money you can find, stuff it into the bag. I'll keep standing watch close to the window, keep an eye peeled in case somebody heard the powder going off."

"You still want to head straight for Underwood's instead of north to Denver?" Brock asked.

"Underwood's," Rutter said. "Be the smartest move. We head for Denver we could run into the law—this town's got a telegraph office. Best we do like we planned, make out we're working for Sam."

"Save your breath," Starbuck said, rising to his full height from behind the desk. "You're going nowhere. . . . Keep your hands up—high, so I can see them—"

Brock was the one to make the first wrong move. He yelled something, dodged to one side, his pistol shattering the heat-laden hush. Shawn drove a bullet at the outlaw's shifting shadow, triggered another at Mysak, leveling down at him.

"Open up!" he yelled to Underwood.

Mysak went down in a heap, and then the room was in a haze of boiling smoke. Shawn could locate neither Brock nor Rutter, but they had him placed. Two more shots blasted deafeningly in the room. Leaden slugs splintered the surface of the desk back of which he crouched.

Why the hell didn't Underwood give him some help? A cross fire would force the men to surrender immediately.

One thing certain—he couldn't stay were he was. He doubted they could see him anymore than he could locate them in the swirling murk, but they did have his position spotted and eventually one of them would get lucky. Bent low, under the thick-layered cover of smoke, he lunged across the intervening space to the counter where Sam Underwood had taken a stand. The rancher, pistol in hand, saw him, jerked back.

"No!" he cried in a hoarse wisper. "You'll draw their fire. . . . Get away—"

"What the hell's the matter with you?" Starbuck demanded in a savage voice. "Shoot—dammit! We'd had them cold if you'd shown yourself."

"I—I can't," Underwood moaned, shaking his head. "Too much at stake—to lose. . . . Can't risk it. . . . All up to you. . . ."

A dark shape loomed up in the haze directly in front of the counter. A gun blossomed bright orange in the darkness and a hot iron seared across Shawn's left wrist. He fired instinctively. Pete Brock yelled in pain and staggered. Reflex action triggered the weapon clutched in his hand twice, sent dual bullets smashing into the window of the bank. The glass fell to the floor with a loud crash.

Starbuck, belly flat, crawled clear of the counter and the cringing Sam Underwood. Rutter was somewhere in the gloom. His hand struck something yielding. . . . Brock's lifeless body. Groping about, he found the pistol. Picking it up, he tossed it into a far corner.

Instantly a gun blazed from the shelter of the closet in which stood the safe. Shawn's answering shot followed so quickly it was like an echo.

"Don't shoot—I'm hit!" Rutter's voice was high pitched, laced with fear and pain.

"Throw your gun through the window," Starbuck ordered. "Then walk out where I can see you

There was a thud as Rutter's pistol struck the wall below the opening of jagged glass, dropped to the floor. A moment later the outlaw staggered into view, one hand clutched to his side.

"I'll take care of him." Underwood's husky voice was strong at Starbuck's elbow. "Get over to the saloon and find that woman. Got to have that letter."

Several dim shapes in the street were moving cautiously toward the front of the bank, evidently not sure yet that it was safe to draw near.

"What difference does that damned letter make now?" Starbuck snarled. The rancher's courage had returned with amazing swiftness. "You're telling the whole thing to the sheriff, anyway."

"Just it," Underwood said in an urgent tone. "Want to

99

do the telling myself. Don't want him finding out that way."

Shawn was silent for a moment. Then, "Probably would be better. . . . If I see the sheriff out there, I'll send him in."

"Go out the back," Underwood said hastily as Starbuck moved toward the opening in the window. "Some fool might take you for a holdup man and shoot you."

Shawn nodded, wheeled about.

"Don't lose time," the rancher called after him. "Be like her to make a run for the sheriff's office minute she hears what happened."

Starbuck made no reply, simply turned when he stepped into the alley, and trotted for the street.

◎ 18 ◎

As Starbuck hurried along the narrow passageway that separated the bank from its adjacent neighbor, two quick gunshots echoed across the clamor of the night. He gave that brief wonder, turned into the street, and strode for the brightly lit front of the Gold Dollar.

Men were crowding past the batwings, collecting on the porch, yelling questions at those converging gingerly on the bank. Others were running up from different points along the roadway, and somewhere a voice was shouting, "Abrams! Anybody seen Abrams around?"

Shawn stepped up onto the gallery, bulled his way against the current and entered the saloon. Moving to one side, he swung his glance around the room in search of Vida. He located her at a corner table, seemingly undisturbed by the mounting excitement. A puncher, very drunk, was beside her.

Crossing the littered area in long strides, Starbuck halted before her. "Upstairs," he said gruffly, jerking his thumb toward the second floor.

Vida stared at him dully from her lifeless eyes. The puncher stirred, raised his head, attempted to focus his gaze on Shawn. Failing, he lapsed again into a state of semiconsciousness. The woman shrugged, glanced at her partner.

"Why not?" she muttered thickly. "Your money's good as his."

Rising, she led the way across the saloon dance floor, up the stairs to the corridor, and on to her room. Once inside, Starbuck closed the door, turned the key. Vida, a fixed smile on her slack lips, wheeled expectantly, faced him.

"Seen you before, cowboy," she began. "You ain't never been—"

Starbuck's hard words cut her off. "I want that letter Rutter gave you."

101

Life stirred in her eyes. A frown knotted her brow as the lines in her face cut deeper. Abruptly her mouth fell open. She drew back a step.

"You're the one that come busting in here, raising hell with—"

"Where's that letter?"

A coyness slipped into her. She was drunk but not so far gone as to have lost her slyness.

"Don't know what you're talking about. . . ."

Starbuck seized her arm, shook her roughly. A comb fell from her hair, loosening several thick strands that spilled down around her shoulders.

"The hell you don't! I'm giving you one minute to hand over that letter or I'm taking this room apart—you along with it."

Vida looked down. "I ain't got no letter," she muttered sullenly.

"Don't tell me that. Rutter said he gave it to you—told you to take it to the sheriff if he didn't make it back. He won't. He's shot up plenty bad. Brock and Mysak are dead. You want to stay out of trouble, you'll fork it over —quick."

Vida was staring at him woodenly. "Dead?"

"All but Rutter. He'll live to go to jail—maybe hang."

She pulled back further, sat down on the creaky bed, eyes fixed on the tattered, faded paper covering the wall.

"Told him it wouldn't work. . . . Told him," she mumbled.

Shawn grasped her shoulder, again shook her. "That letter—where is it?"

A hardness wiped away the slack in her face as she looked up. "How much it worth to you?"

"Not a cent. Means nothing to me. I'm here for somebody else."

There was a loud burst of cheers down in the saloon, more in the street. Horses pounded up, stopped.

"You're from that rich sonofabitch who's wanting to be the governor—that's who you're from. . . . Ought to be worth a-plenty to him, the way Guy talked."

"Maybe it is. Up to him to decide that—and you can do your horse trading with him later. Right now I want that envelope."

"And trust him to pay me later? No, sir, not me! They're the worst kind—them rich ones. Bastards are always out to skin you. You go get him—"

Shawn stepped in close, caught the woman's dress by its low neckline, drew it taut.

102

"Expect I know where you're hiding it. You want me to rip off this rag, get it myself?"

Vida glared at him angrily, shook her head. "All right," she said, pushing his hand away. "You can have the goddam thing."

Thrusting her fingers deep into the cleavage between her ample breasts, she produced a folded envelope, passed it to him. Shawn glanced at the writing on its front. It was addressed simply: U.S. Marshal or Sheriff. As Underwood had predicted, Guy Rutter had not been bluffing.

Tucking the letter inside his shirt, he turned for the door. Vida's coarse voice lashed out at him.

"You tell that bastard I'm looking for him to pay me for that—you hear?"

Starbuck jerked the door back, said, "I'll tell him," and halted. The drunk Vida had been entertaining at the table was just reaching for the knob. Off balance, he swayed forward, caught himself by clutching the door frame.

"Say—where—" he began protestingly.

"She's all yours, friend," Shawn said, and taking the man by the shoulders, spun him into the room.

He walked the length of the corridor, went down the stairs. There appeared to be more of a crowd inside the saloon now than before, most of which was clustered about a man who was speaking excitedly.

"Was three of them. . . ." Starbuck caught the words as he drew abreast the tightly packed group. "Was all set to blast the door off'n the safe. Bag of powder's laying right there."

"And Sam got them all?"

"Every cussed one of them. . . . Seems he just happened by, seen them moving around inside, so he slips in the back way and throws down on them. Well, they decided to fight it out—and they sure got themselves into a dandy. Sam nailed all of them."

Shawn had come to a full stop. . . . *Sam got all of them!* The rancher was taking credit for the whole affair, but more than that—it sounded as if Rutter also was dead. Suddenly the meaning of the two gunshots he'd heard became clear to Starbuck. Underwood had shot him. Either Rutter had attempted to escape—or had been cut down in cold blood.

Bitterness filled Shawn's mouth. If that was it, then Sam Underwood had done it for one reason only—to silence Rutter to prevent his telling of the past. He swore silently. He'd been played for a fool again—and by the same man! The rancher had never intended going to the sheriff, mak-

103

ing a clean breast of the past; he'd only wanted to get the three out of the way, and had persuaded him to help on the strength of a promise.

He'd been a fool. He should have realized why Underwood was so insistent that he leave the bank after the shooting; he'd made it appear he was anxious to get his hands on the letter Rutter had written. Undoubtedly he was, but he was more interested in being left alone with the wounded outlaw.

And the letter. . . . Starbuck reached into his shirt, felt it with his fingers as he continued on toward the doorway. Should he turn it over to the law? He stood there on the saloon porch deliberating the idea as commotion and noise continued to claim the street.

Several carriages had arrived. Spotted among the shifting throng were several soldiers. Lamps had been lighted inside the bank and Shawn could see a considerable number of persons had gathered there.

Maybe it wasn't exactly the way he'd figured; maybe he was jumping to conclusions too fast—and he should give Underwood the benefit of the doubt. It was possible Rutter had tried to escape and the rancher had been forced to kill him—just as it was also possible the man in the saloon had gotten some of his facts garbled in that he had given Sam Underwood full and solitary credit for preventing the robbery.

He reckoned he'd better hear things firsthand before he started condemning Underwood, and made any rash decisions as to the letter.

Descending the gallery, he waded through the milling crowd and worked his way toward the bank. Onlookers were ten deep in front of the shattered window, and he veered aside, moved back to the passageway he had used earlier.

Turning into it, he gained the alley. It was deserted, and cutting left he made his way to the rear entrance to the bank. A figure stepped from the shadows just within the doorway, barred his progress; a small, thin man with a rifle and wearing a deputy's star.

"Where you think you're going?" he demanded, lifting his weapon.

"Inside," Starbuck answered, faintly angered.

"Like hell you are. Ain't nobody going—"

"I'm with Sam Underwood. Name's Starbuck."

The deputy half turned, yelled, "Mr. Underwood, man back here named Starbuck. Says he's with you."

A lull in the drone of conversation settled over the

room at the lawman's call. Shawn saw the rancher look back, make an indifferent gesture.

"It's all right, Harvey. He's one of my hired hands."

The deputy pulled back. Starbuck walked toward the rancher and the group clustered around him. Holly was there, along with a younger girl and an elderly woman. The Camerons, he supposed. The banker himself was near the doorway, holding the panel open for several men who were carrying out the bodies of the outlaws.

Shawn halted behind Underwood. The rancher had resumed where he had broken off when the deputy interrupted, was talking in a steady, flowing stream. Holly, her face glowing, glanced to Starbuck and smiled proudly.

"Took a lot of nerve, Sam," someone in the crowd said, "standing up to three killers the way you did."

"Man does what he has to—when he has to," the rancher replied. "Couldn't just back off—and there wasn't time to get help."

"Well, you sure saved our hides," another commented. "Hate to think of what a robbery like that would've done to this town."

"Busted us all—that's for sure."

"We all owe Sam a lot for what he's done. . . ."

Underwood laughed, raised his hands. "You got to remember, there's money of mine in that safe, too. They'd have got it along with everybody's else's—and I didn't want that to happen."

Everyone laughed heartily except Shawn Starbuck. Silent, he listened to the comments while a wary scorn built up within him. The man in the saloon had been relating correctly; alone, Sam Underwood had come upon the outlaws, and unaided, challenged them, and when they resisted, shot them down in a gun duel.

Sam Underwood. . . . The town hero. . . . He'd be a cinch to sit in the governor's chair now. The local newspaper would plaster the Territory with a vivid, elaborate account of the incident. Underwood's niche was assured—as well as the exalted position he apparently felt was worth any cost to achieve.

Again the need to be fair and honest put a tight rein on Starbuck's thoughts. He could be wrong in this, too; Underwood was taking all the credit for himself perhaps only to enhance his reputation and prepare for the moment when he would make known the facts of his past. That could be the explanation.

The rancher could be planning, after all, to hand the letter over to the sheriff or the marshal, and being a master politician, was simply striving to improve his image and lay the groundwork for a sympathetic hearing of his crimes.

Maybe that was it, and he should give the man—fighting desperately to prevent the empire he'd built from crumbling to dust—the benefit of the doubt, at least for the time being. As far as any credit for the killing of the outlaws was concerned, Starbuck could care less. Let Sam Underwood claim it, glory in it, make the most of it if it suited his fancy. . . . All he was interested in was seeing that right was done.

Shawn became aware of a dwindling in the conversation, of the fact that the rancher, deigning now to notice him, had stepped back.

"You get the letter?" Underwood's question was low, the words coming from the corner of his mouth.

"I got it," Starbuck drawled.

The rancher edged closer. "Slip it into my side pocket. Don't want anybody seeing it. . . ."

"No, I reckon not," Shawn said. "Figured I'd better hang onto it until you're ready to talk to the law."

Sam Underwood stiffened. "Now—hold on here. I—"

"I'll be at the hotel," Starbuck said, and pushing by the rancher, past Holly, and the others in the room, he moved through the doorway into the street.

◎ 19 ◎

In less than an hour, probably the minimum time it required for him to slip away from his throng of admirers, Sam Underwood rapped on Starbuck's door.

Shawn, again slumped in the lone chair, but placed this time near the window so that he could face the entrance to the room, stirred restlessly. He thoroughly disliked the role he found himself in—that of custodian of a man's future—but it had been thrust upon him and he could not in conscience turn away.

"It's open," he called.

The scarred panel flung back and the rancher, taut and angry, stepped in. He crossed to the center of the room, halted, hands on hips.

"Well—spit it out! What's your price?"

"For the letter?"

"Hell, yes—why else would I be here? You've got a price, I expect."

Shawn nodded.

"How much?"

"Not money," Starbuck said quietly. "All you've got to do is go to the sheriff, tell him the truth."

The rancher swore wildly. "I knew I was a damned fool —letting you in on it!"

"If you hadn't," Shawn said in a dry voice, "you wouldn't be the hero everybody's talking about."

Underwood stared, then shrugged and, moving to the bed, sat down. "Can't see why you're getting so hardnosed about this. Means nothing to you. . . . I'm willing to pay for your help. Worth five hundred in gold—your help and that letter."

"Lot of money," Starbuck said. "But I'm not Rutter or the others."

The rancher groaned. "You've got a price—same as every man. This holier-than-thou act of yours isn't fooling

107

me. Let's cut it and get down to hard cases. Five hundred's not enough—all right—how much?"

"You heard the price."

Underwood rose from the bed in a sudden burst of rage. "Why, you saddletramp! You think you can blackmail me? I—I'll—"

"Expect I could," Shawn said calmly. "Be real easy to do—but I'm not figuring on it. All I want is for folks to know the truth about you. Afterwards, if they want to overlook it, forget all about what you've done, it'll be fine with me. I just think they've got a right to all the facts about the man who's wanting to be their governor."

"The facts! I'd be crazy to tell—"

"You don't know for sure how they'd take it. Could be they'd stand by you."

The rancher relaxed slightly. "You think they'd do that —stand by me?"

"Odds seem pretty fair to me. Far as I'm concerned they can go on thinking you're a hero—and I reckon you've done some good for the country."

Underwood was silent for a full minute. Finally he shook his head. "No, I just can't risk it. . . . Too much to lose."

"Heard you say that before," Shawn said, his voice hardening. "Back there in the bank when we went up against Rutter and his bunch. . . . You were to side me."

"I know, I know," Underwood murmured. "Couldn't seem to make myself do it—face those guns—"

"Takes guts to lie, too. You've got plenty of that kind."

The rancher lifted his hands, allowed them to fall. "Didn't actually plan it that way, Starbuck. You've got to believe that. Everybody just sort of latched onto the idea —me being there alone. Before I knew it the word was going around fast. . . . You know how things like that spread."

"Didn't hear you bothering to straighten anybody out on it. . . . Makes no difference. Killing a man—good or bad—is nothing to be proud of. One thing I'd like to know, however."

Underwood frowned, resumed his place on the bed. "What's that?"

"Rutter. . . . Did he try to run for it after I left, or did you shoot him down to keep him from talking? Way it's worked out, none of that bunch pulling that paymaster holdup is alive now but you."

"He was going to run for it—"

"With a bullet in his side and bleeding like a stuck hog —and you holding a gun on him?"

"He tried to get away," Underwood insisted dully. "It's the gospel truth."

Starbuck shifted his legs. "I'm hoping so. You're going to have hell living with the thought of it, if it wasn't."

"Not worried about that," the rancher said, regaining a grip on himself. "What about that letter? I've got to have it. Let's come to some kind of terms."

Shawn shrugged. "You've heard mine—and I won't track over them again. You take a walk with me to the sheriff's office—"

"Abrams isn't in town—"

"A deputy'll do. Moment you start talking, I'll hand you the letter and move on."

"I'd rather wait for Abrams—no use bringing the whole town in on it at first. Give me the letter now and you've got my word I'll wait for Abrams, tell him the whole story minute he shows up."

"Afraid that's not enough."

"My word's good to plenty of others!" Underwood exploded defensively. "You think you've got me by the short hair, don't you? Mister, you're wrong as hell! I've got a lot of friends around here—friends that owe me favors. If I want, all I need do is walk out into that street, tell a dozen men that you're setting up here trying to rawhide me into paying you off for something, and in less time than it takes to skin a snake, they'll have you swinging from a tree!"

"Maybe so," Shawn replied, "but during that time I'll get some talking done. And I'll manage to get that letter into somebody's hands who'll be curious enough or honest enough to see that it's delivered. Then what?"

"They'd give it to me first."

"Doubt that—it being addressed to the U.S. Marshal or the Sheriff."

The rancher was studying Starbuck narrowly. "You open it?"

"No. Leave that up to the law."

Sam Underwood came again to his feet, stretched forth his hand. "Mind if I take a look at it?"

"Not for you, either."

Anger again flamed in the rancher's eyes. "I can see there's no sense trying to reason with you. I'm willing to treat you right, but you won't listen. What do you aim to do next?"

"Only thing I can. If you won't go to the law, I'll take

109

the letter to the sheriff—or maybe on to the marshal in Santa Fe."

Underwood mopped at the sweat beading his forehead. "Supposing I raise the ante—say to a thousand. That's a hell of a lot of money."

"Won't argue that."

"A thousand would buy a man most anything he had a hankering for—could even get himself started in the cattle business."

"You're wasting your breath, Underwood. I'm not about to change my mind."

"Goddammit! What's the matter with you? This thing don't mean anything far as you're concerned. You don't even live in the Territory! What difference it make to you who or what—"

"Man can't turn his back on a wrong just because it's not in his own yard. Was taught that. . . . Expect you were, too."

"Ain't the point. . . . Way I see it, you're meddling in where you don't belong, mixing yourself up in business that sure ain't none of your business. . . . Fact is, nosing around like you are could get you killed."

Shawn stirred, smiled faintly. Now came the threats. Sam Underwood was trying everything in a desperate effort to get his hands on Guy Rutter's letter.

"You think I was bulling you about getting a dozen men to work you over on my say-so? Be no problem at all, and there'd be no questions asked by Sheriff Abrams —or anybody else. You're a stranger here. I'm not. This is my town, my Territory. What I'd tell them would—"

"You won't yell for help," Starbuck broke in wearily. "Too big a chance of that letter getting into the wrong hands—for you."

"Not that at all. Just don't want to cause you a lot of trouble."

"Trouble's yours, not mine."

The rancher swore angrily again. "You're a plain fool, Starbuck! Work with me and I'll make you a big man around here. A thousand dollars to start. Then when I'm governor, I'll put you in as chief of the mounted police. That's one of the promises I've made folks—that I'd organize a mounted police force, like the Texas Rangers. You'd make a good chief. . . . A thousand in gold on top of that. I'll put it in writing if you say so."

Shawn got to his feet slowly, almost lazily. "You're a hard man to convince, Underwood—and I'm tired of

110

wrangling. Nothing's changed. If you're not going along with my terms—get out."

The rancher stared. His face whitened and his lips worked convulsively as rage swept through him. "Nobody talks to me that way—"

"Could be they never had the chance, or maybe they had too big of an axe to grind. Happens you don't count with me one way or another. I'm looking for nothing— just want to see the right thing done."

"The hell! Who're you to say what's right and what's wrong?"

"Already asked myself that question. Man can only go by what he knows inside himself is right."

"According to what *he* thinks is right. . . . Could be you're wrong, Starbuck—dead wrong! Well, I'm promising you this: it's a hundred yards down the street from here to Abrams' office. You'll never get there alive."

"We'll see," Shawn said coolly. "So long, Mr. Underwood."

The rancher's eyes flared, and then wheeling stiffly, he crossed the room, yanked open the door, and disappeared into the dark hallway.

◎ 20 ◎

Starbuck gazed at the opening through which the rancher had vanished. Moving forward, he pushed the panel closed and stood for a time with his eyes on the knob.

As far as the sheriff was concerned, there was nothing he could do until morning, and possibly not even then if Abrams had not returned to the settlement. And he would not risk taking the matter to the deputy—Harvey, or whatever his name was. He appeared to be one who would succumb quickly to Sam Underwood's blandishments and persuasion.

But there was no ignoring the rancher's final threat. The man, a deceptively ruthless one, pushed to the extreme by the possibility of seeing his political ambitions collapse in personal disaster, would doubtless act quickly; and with the influence he was in a position to wield, he'd find many men to do his bidding regardless of its nature.

Thus it would be foolhardy to take Underwood's promise lightly. Brazen as it might seem, the chances were that hidden marksmen would keep him from ever reaching Sheriff Abrams' office; moreover, now that he gave it thought, the likelihood of his even getting out of the hotel was probably growing slimmer with each passing moment.

Starbuck swore impatiently. All he wanted was to find Ben; instead he'd gotten sidetracked, and the whole purpose of his being in the Territory was lost in the shuffle. Best thing he could do was climb out of the jam he was in fast, get back to his original purpose.

Take first things first. It was dangerous to hang around Las Vegas any longer; the letter was addressed primarily to the U.S. Marshal who maintained an office in Santa Fe. The solution, therefore, was to slip out of town immediately without the rancher being aware of it, swing by the ranch in the hope that Henry Smith had returned, talk with him, and then, regardless of the outcome, ride on to Santa Fe and deliver Rutter's letter. . . .

It was the only sensible way to handle the situation. Leaning down, he drew aside the curtains, looked out into the street. There were still a few persons abroad and a guard had been positioned in front of the shattered window of the bank. Business in the saloons had not slackened.

Shawn's glance paused on three men standing in a close group a short distance beyond the Gold Dollar. One of them was Underwood. He grinned tightly. The rancher was doing as expected; he was already busy recruiting those dozen men he had mentioned. . . . He was being blackmailed, he'd tell them; there was a personal letter involved, one that belonged to him despite what it said on its face. Sam Underwood, hero, would be able to convince them of anything.

Reaching up, Shawn drew the sun-stiffened shade and turned to the bed. Pulling back the patch quilt, and using one of the two pillows, he shaped the bed clothing into the semblance of a sleeping person. That done, he took up his saddlebags, pulled on his hat, and moving to the door, opened it cautiously.

There was no one in the hall. Although acting swiftly, Underwood had not yet had time to station a sentry in the hotel. Stepping out, he closed the panel silently, locked it and thrust the key into his pocket.

Making his way down the corridor, he came to a second hall crossing at right angles. He turned left into it, followed along its narrow channel to the rear of the building. A door faced him at its end, and again cautious, he cracked it slightly. A low sigh passed his lips when he saw that it led into the yard that separated the hotel from the stable.

It was what he looked for. Stepping out onto the landing, he threw his glance to all directions, saw no one. Considerable noise was coming from the street, now on the opposite side of the structure, but he felt he had nothing to worry about from that point; it was unlikely anyone could see the yard.

Holding his saddlebags, he crossed the weed-littered hard pack to the barn, slipped inside. The hostler's quarters lay to his left. Shawn eased up to the door and peered inside. The room was empty. The hostler likely was out in the street savoring the excitement.

Hurrying on down the runway he located the chestnut. His gear had been slung across a nearby rack, and grabbing up the blanket, he saddled and bridled the gelding in quick, efficient moves.

That finished, he backed the horse into the clear, again stopped at the hostler's quarters. Stepping inside, he laid a silver dollar and the key to his room on the dust-covered table and withdrew. . . . He was square now with the Exchange Hotel and the stablekeeper.

A few moments later he was astride the chestnut and making his way through the deep shadows along the edge of the yard, toward the street. The road east lay at the opposite end of town, and he would be forced to cross over. He'd do that well down, beyond the view of anyone standing near the hotel or the saloons.

He pulled up, leaned forward, searching the night-shrouded shrubbery for any indication of an alley or similar passageway that would permit him to reach that point without going all the way to the street. There seemed to be none; a rail fence ran the full depth of the adjacent property.

He started to come about, have a look at the land behind the stable, thinking perhaps to find an open field. He pulled up short as the sounds of someone approaching caught his attention, sent a warning racing through him.

"On the front, Sam said. . . ."

In the broad shadow cast by an aged cottonwood, Starbuck hung motionless and prayed the gelding also would make no move.

Two figures came from the front of the hotel. They walked with care but the gravel crunched solidly beneath their tread. Reaching the end of the walk they turned, headed for the rear entrance to the hostelry.

"We could've gone through the lobby," the smaller of the pair said in a grumbling tone. "Old Pankey'd be asleep this time of night. Always is."

"Somebody else might've seen us—and Sam said we was to be quiet, do it without no fuss."

The chestnut shifted, stamped a hoof. Instantly the men halted, wheeled.

"Who's that?" the taller one called.

Both pulled away from the wall of the building, edged deeper into the yard. Weak moonlight glinted feebly on the pistols they had drawn.

"Nobody special," Shawn replied, his hand sliding down to where it rested on the butt of his own weapon. "No need for that hardware. . . . One of you the hostler?"

"Hell, no," the tall man said in disgust. "You coming or going?"

"Little of both, depending on how you look at it. Know where the hostler'll be?"

"Probably down at Kaseman's saloon. Where he is most of the time. You're a-wanting to stable your horse, best thing you can do is see to it yourself. He ain't apt to show up till every saloon in town's closed."

"Obliged," Starbuck said, and nudging the gelding gently, doubled back over his tracks toward the wide doors of the stable.

Entering, he halted in the odorous blackness, looked over his shoulder. The men were just going into the hotel through the same door he had used earlier. He waited out a long two minutes, assuring himself the pair would not reappear, and then cut back through the stable's entrance into the yard.

He'd best waste no more time scouting for a back way out of town—there was none left, not with Underwood's friends already moving in on him. Likely there were others in the front watching the window and the lobby door. The rancher evidently had decided not to wait until morning to act; his own hunch to pull out had been a good one.

Holding the chestnut to a walk, and again in the deep shadows, he made his way to the street. Turning sharply right, he rode along the shoulder, deserted in this fringe area, until he came to the last building. Then, touching the big horse with spurs, he crossed and swung onto the road that led to Underwood's ranch.

"Gone!"

The word ripped from Sam Underwood's lips with all the suddenness of a pistol shot.

Standing in the darkness behind the bank, the tall puncher nodded his head vigorously.

"Yessir, gone. When we got inside his room all we found was the bed fixed up so's it looked like somebody was sleeping in it. . . . Only it wasn't nobody."

The rancher swore harshly. "Now, when in the hell could he have got out? Wasn't no more'n thirty minutes after I left him that I sent you two over there."

"Must've done it right after you left," the short rider said.

"You sure he ain't in one of the other rooms? Could've played it smart—changed."

"We got Pankey on his feet, asked him that. Said no.

Far as he knew that Starbuck fellow was in the room he'd rented—Number Four."

"You look in the others?"

"Sure did—them that wasn't rented, which most of them ain't. Never found nobody."

"Then he's here in town somewhere, hiding," Sam Underwood said with conviction. "Got to root him out."

"We checked all the saloons. Couldn't spot him. And I ain't about to go opening them doors on the second floor of the Gold Dollar. Man could get his head blowed off doing that."

Again the rancher swore, deeply, fiercely. He hadn't expected Starbuck to run for cover, had figured he'd wait in the hotel until morning to see Abrams. Starbuck was no fool. He'd underestimated him—had all along, he guessed.

"What you want us to do now, Sam?"

The rancher shook his head, walked slowly for the street. "Got to do some thinking. Wherever he's holed up, the place he'll be trying to get to in the morning is the sheriff's office. Got to keep him from doing that."

"Now, how you—"

"Charley, I want you to take your rifle and get up on the roof of Hayden's Feed Store. Keep hid so's nobody'll see you. . . . Tuck, you plant yourself in that empty store building down the street from Hayden's."

The tall man drew a loud breath. "You mean you're wanting us to shoot him right out there in broad daylight?"

"What an outlaw like him deserves," Underwood said. "Anyway, won't anybody see you if you're careful. He'll line out for Abrams early. Street'll probably be empty, and I'll be standing on the porch of the Exchange—"

"Why don't you just go ahead yourself, Sam, do the shooting?"

"Be better if I don't, after all that killing I did this evening. Can't have folks thinking I'm gun crazy. Like I said —I'll be on the porch of the hotel. When I see him drop, I'll run to him, get them papers he stole from me. You two can sort of fade off, come into the street farther down —like you'd just heard the shots, was wondering what they was all about—"

"I'd as soon folks knowed it was me that done it— shooting an outlaw like him," Tuck said. "Might make some around here show me a little respect instead of laughing at me and looking down on me the way they do."

"However you want it," Underwood said impatiently. "If you don't want folks knowing, I can say I saw a rider leaving town hell for leather, that I think he was the one who did it."

Charley scuffed at the dirt with the toe of his boot. "I ain't sure, Sam," he mumbled hesitantly. "Comes to shooting a man—bushwhacking him—wish we'd find him tonight so's—"

"Wish't we could've found that jasper we bumped into there at the stable," Tuck said. "I'll bet he seen that Starbuck fellow, and could've told us where he went."

Sam Underwood had come to stiff attention. "What jasper?"

"Some bird we seen back of the hotel when we first got there. Was looking for Smitty, that old soak that runs the stable. Said he—"

"You get a good look at him?"

"Hardly none. Was setting his horse under that big cottonwood."

"What about the horse—you see it?"

"Some. . . . Was big, know that. Think maybe it was a bay."

"Chestnut. Fourteen, fifteen hands high. Had white stockings and a blazed face?"

"Reckon that was the one. Where'd you see—"

"You damned fools!" Underwood snapped in disgust. "That was the man you were looking for."

Charley straightened up in surprise. Tuck pulled off his hat, scratched at his head. "It was? Well, we wasn't looking for no horse."

"Reckon it could've been at that," Charley said thoughtfully. "If I'd a guessed, I'd have taken a closer look at him. . . . Did go back to the stable later. Thought maybe he'd still be there. Aimed to ask him if he'd seen somebody—"

"And him and the horse were both gone," the rancher finished.

"Sure was. Couldn't find hide or hair of them."

"How long ago was this?"

"Hour, maybe. No more'n that."

Underwood stirred wearily. He should have known better than to line up a couple of bronc stompers like Charley and Tuck to do the job for him, but then it was a touchy situation and he didn't have much choice. They were stupid enough to do what he told them, and not smart enough to ask any questions.

Maybe it didn't matter. Maybe it was better this way. Starbuck was clever—he figured a move would be made to take Rutter's letter from him, so he ducked out, planning to lay low until his chances improved. Safest bet would be for him to get out of town. . . . He might even head for Santa Fe and the U.S. Marshal—and then get clear out of the country.

Of course—that's just what he'd done. He was on his horse, all mounted and ready to ride when Charley and Tuck ran into him. He wouldn't have saddled up and all if what he had in mind was to just change places in town.

But he wouldn't go straight to Santa Fe. He had some kind of an idea that Henry Smith was the long-lost brother he'd been hunting for. . . . Seemed mighty important that he find him. He wouldn't head for Santa Fe until he had first stopped by the ranch, had a talk with Henry. . . . That was it. That's what he was doing.

"Get your horses," Underwood said in a sudden, harsh way. "Meet me at the south end of town in thirty minutes. . . . Charley, you stop by Abrams, get yourself a deputy's badge out of his desk drawer—I'll explain to the sheriff later."

"Yessir, Sam. . . . Where we going?"

"My place," the rancher replied. "That's where we'll find Starbuck."

◎ 21 ◎

Starbuck rode into the ranch shortly after sunrise. Leaving the chestnut at one of the hitchracks, he went immediately to Tom Gage's cabin. He was under no illusion about Sam Underwood; it wouldn't take the rancher long to discover he was not in Las Vegas, and probably even less time to figure he'd head for the ranch to see Henry Smith before riding on to Santa Fe.

Thus the minutes were at a premium unless he wished to wait and have a showdown. He would as soon avoid such. He had no personal quarrel with the man—at least one serious enough to warrant bloodshed, and, too, he was thinking of Holly. Bleak moments were ahead for her when she learned the man she idolized was not all she thought, and he had no desire to add further to her heartbreak.

Smith should have returned, he thought as he pushed open the door of Gage's quarters; he'd see him, have a talk, and then if it was the usual false lead he'd come to accept as almost inevitable, he'd line out for Santa Fe. But if Smith did prove to be Ben—well, he'd decide then what to do.

The old foreman was sitting on the edge of the bed rubbing at his whiskered face as Shawn came in. He glanced up, grinned.

"Back, eh? Good to see you."

Starbuck nodded. "Smith come in?"

"Sure did. Yesterday—late. . . . Hear Sam had hisself quite a whingding in Vegas. Them stinking sidewinders. Knowed they was no good the day I first laid eyes on them."

Shawn, about to return to the yard, make his way to the bunkhouse, paused in surprise. "How'd you know about it?"

119

Gage began to pull on his clothing. "The little gal—Holly. Got in early—her and Ira Cameron's womenfolk. Was so worked up and near busting her buttons about what her pa'd done, she couldn't wait to tell her ma and us all about it. Cameron had one of his hands drive them in his surrey. . . . Sam come in, too?"

"No," Starbuck said. "Be here soon, I expect."

Gage stood up, stamped his feet into his boots, began to close his shirt. "That gal is sure proud of Sam. He really do all she says—shoot it out with them jaspers and such?"

Shawn was silent for a long minute. Finally, "Expect she's telling it the way her pa told it to her."

The old foreman paused, studied Starbuck with his shrewd eyes. After a bit he resumed dressing. "Never figured Sam had that kind of spunk in him. . . . How'd it happen you wasn't in on it?"

"What did Holly say about me?"

"That you'd gone over to the saloon for a drink, left Sam by hisself."

The corners of Shawn's mouth pulled down into a wry smile, and then he shrugged. . . . Let it pass. It didn't really matter.

"Like to see Smith soon as I can," he said, getting off the subject.

"Help yourself. He'll be in the bunkhouse with the rest of the boys. Whole bunch'll be going in for chow in a minute. You could see him, do your eating at the same time." Once more Gage hesitated, considered Starbuck thoughtfully. "Something bothering you, son? You're acting plenty spooked."

"Hard ride. Expect I'm a bit on the wore-out side. Just want to see Henry Smith, move on if it turns out he's not my brother."

"Just like that, eh? Was figuring you to hang around for a spell. Didn't you sign on with Sam—that there special job—"

"Quit last night," Starbuck said, moving to the window. Several of the punchers were in the yard, standing around sleepily, yawning, stretching, having a first smoke.

"Any of those men Henry?" he asked.

Gage crowded up to his side, scanned the hard pack. "Nope, ain't one of them. . . . There—that's Henry coming out the bunkhouse now. One wearing a red-checkered shirt."

Starbuck pivoted swiftly to the door of the cabin, stepped out into the yard, quick, hard tension building

120

within him. Henry Smith was dark and a stubble that covered his cheeks and chin looked blue.

Shawn's hopes rose. He could be Ben. . . . Built a lot like Hiram Starbuck—actually looked something like him. . . . Those big hands, that square-cut face. . . . Starbuck's pulses quickened, began to hammer as he strode toward the man. . . . Maybe he'd finally come to the end of his quest; perhaps this was the finish—here in the yard of a ranch where trouble was racing to overtake him.

He reached the front of the bunkhouse. Smith had stepped to the edge of the landing, was gazing at the hills to the east.

"Henry Smith?" Shawn said hesitantly as he pulled up a pace or two away.

The trail boss turned lazily. "That's me, I reckon."

Dark eyes—not blue. . . . But maybe the color had changed through the years.

"You want me for something?"

Shawn caught himself, said, "Yes. . . . My name's Starbuck."

Smith waited, his face quizzical. "So?"

"That name mean anything to you?"

"Nope, can't say as it does. It supposed to?"

A ponderous, weighty disappointment settled over Shawn. "Was hoping it would. I'm looking for my brother. Name's Ben. Was hoping you might be him."

"Ain't got no kin," Smith said. "I'm purely a orphan." He half smiled, looked closer at Starbuck, a suspicious glint in his eyes. "You funning me?"

"No. . . . Man up in Kansas said you sort of fit the description I gave of Ben—what I have, anyway. Rode down here to see you, thinking maybe—"

"Well, I'm real sorry you had yourself a long ride for nothing. I sure ain't your brother. I ain't nobody's brother. Like I said, I'm a orphan."

Shawn, clinging to one final strand of hope, stepped up onto the landing. Bitter as Ben had been when he ran off, it was possible he still entertained the same feelings about the family name and would refuse to admit any relationship. . . . There was that one proof he could neither hide nor deny.

"You looking for something special?" Smith asked mildly.

Shawn's eyes were on the rider's face, searching for that telltale scar over the left brow. . . . There were

121

lines, cut there by endless days in the sun and wind, but no memento of that day in the rocks now so many years in the past.

Shoulders going down, Starbuck fell back. "No, I guess you're not him. Maybe you don't even look like him, I don't know for sure."

"Well, he's a right lucky soul," Smith drawled, "not taking after a ugly critter like me. Ain't you got no idea a'tall where you can find him?"

"None," Shawn answered, staring off across the hard pack. "Don't even know what name he goes by. Doesn't call himself Ben Starbuck—sure of that."

Henry Smith whistled softly. "Mister, you've picked yourself one hell of a smoke trail to be riding! Why, a man could follow it till Kingdom Come and not find what he's looking for."

"I'll find him," Shawn said wearily. "Got to."

"If you're lucky—and he ain't dead," the rider said. "Well, I'm hoping you do. He all the kin you got?"

Starbuck nodded. "Trailing herds, you run into a lot of people. You ever remember seeing a man that might've been him? He'd probably look a lot like you—build and such. Eyes more'n likely are blue. . . . Main thing, he's got a scar over the left one."

"So that's what you was doing—looking for a scar!" the trail boss said with a wide grin. "Figured there for a bit I maybe had lice or something." He sobered, scrubbed the stubble on his chin, his glance on the rest of the crew now drifting toward the kitchen for the morning meal.

"When you first mentioned what you was after, I did recollect a fellow, but I ain't one to send no man out on a snipe hunt."

"Only way I'll ever find Ben is to ride down every prospect I hear about. Been doing it for quite a spell. Another failure won't matter—and this time it just might be him. . . . Who is this man and where'd you see him?"

"Name of Jim Ivory. Punches cows for the Box C outfit, down Arizona way—the Mogollon country. Fellow once said we looked enough alike to be twins."

Revived hope stirred within Shawn. "How long ago was this?"

"Couple, three years I reckon since I seen Jim. Reckon he's still there if he ain't gone and got hisself killed in a poker game. A plain dang fool when it come to cards. Carries a deck right in his pocket. Every time he sets down, out comes them cards. If he can't talk some of the boys into playing with him, why, he just plays by hisself."

"Box C," Starbuck murmured. "The Mogollon country. Was through there about a year ago—on my way to Tucson. Didn't stop. Remember there was a town by the name of Lynchburg."

"Your rememberer's good. Box C's about twenty miles west. Big spread. You won't have no trouble finding it."

The cook began to hammer on his iron bar, summoning the stragglers. Smith yawned, grinned, said, "Reckon he means us. I ain't even got around to washing the night off my face, but I ain't minding it if nobody else does. . . . Come on, Starbuck, we'd best be getting there."

"Go ahead," Shawn said, extending his hand to the rider. "Appreciate what you told me about this Jim Ivory, and sorry if I bothered you some."

"No bother—only wish't I did belong to somebody. Ain't you eating with us?"

"Not this morning," Shawn replied. The last thing he wanted was to sit down at Sam Underwood's table, eat his food. "So long. . . ."

"*Adios*," Henry Smith said, stepping off the landing and heading for the kitchen. "Luck."

Shawn turned, moved toward the chestnut waiting patiently at the hitchrack. *Tot up one more failure*, he thought, but the slash of disappointment was not so deep as once it was; too many other promising leads had ended this way.

He glanced over to Gage's cabin. He would have liked to see the old foreman before he rode on, to express his thanks, but he'd be with the crew now, having his breakfast. Just as well he wasn't handy. Tom's eyes had told him he wasn't swallowing the story Holly Underwood brought back from Las Vegas—not entirely, anyway. He'd ask questions, sharp and probing—and Shawn knew he couldn't lie to the old man.

And Holly. . . . He didn't want to see her again, either. Her estimation of him after what her father had told her would be at its lowest point. He regretted leaving her with that belief, but that was the way it had to be. Someday she'd know the truth and perhaps think better of him. At the present, however, he doubted if she would even speak to him, much less tell him farewell and wish him luck.

He reached the chestnut, jerked the reins loose, prepared to swing up. He froze as his eyes reached to the corner of the bunkhouse beyond the gelding.

Underwood, on a borrowed horse, flanked by two men —one of whom wore a deputy sheriff's star—was coming around the end of the building and entering the yard.

◎ 22 ◎

Momentarily startled, the rancher pulled up short, the horses of the men with him shouldering against his own at the sudden stop. Shawn recognized the pair; they were the two he'd encountered back at the Exchange Hotel. Pivoting fast, he drew his pistol, stepped in behind the chestnut so that his back was to the corral fence.

Underwood, recovered, wagged his head. "Put it away, Starbuck. You're on my land now."

Shawn cast a fleeting glance to the yard behind him. Everyone was inside the house at breakfast. Resting his arms on the gelding's saddle, holding the gun steady on the three men, he said, "Makes no difference to me."

"Should. You'll never leave here alive unless I say the word. . . . Now, all you have to do is drop that letter on the ground—then you can mount up, ride out."

"Letter stays with me. Taking it to the marshal in Santa Fe."

"Like hell you are!" Underwood shouted suddenly. "I sing out—my whole crew'll be crawling over you. Give it up. You ain't got a chance."

"Long as my first bullet's aimed at your heart, I have."

Over in the direction of the main house a door slammed. Holly's voice cried, "Papa—you're here!"

Starbuck remained rigid, not daring to turn and look around. He could hear the girl running. The door slapped again, this time with less abandon. Mrs. Underwood, probably. . . . Coming to welcome the hero.

Abruptly Holly was moving by him, her steps slowing as an expression of bewilderment crossed her face. She halted just beyond Shawn, stared first at her father, then at Starbuck, back to Underwood once more.

"What—what's the matter?"

"Just a little trouble between me and Starbuck, honey,"

the rancher replied. "You and your mother best get back in the house. Take the Camerons with you."

The girl whirled to Shawn, eyes blazing. "What's the meaning of this? How dare you point that gun at my father—right here in his own yard!"

Starbuck's face was wooden. "Ask him. Maybe he'll tell you why."

"Tell me what?"

Shawn shrugged. The girl looked to her father. "What is it? This over what happened in Vegas?"

"Part of it," Underwood said. "Go on—do what I tell you, Holly. No place for you here."

"I won't!" the girl cried stubbornly. "Not until he puts that gun away and I know what this is about. . . . Was he in with those other outlaws—the ones you had to shoot?"

"In a way—"

"I thought so!" Holly said triumphantly, moving toward Shawn. "My father had to shoot them, stop them from robbing his bank—and you're here to get even. That's it, isn't it?"

Starbuck's eyes never strayed from Underwood. "That what you want her to believe—a lie?"

The rancher, slumped on his saddle, merely stared. The two men beside him remained silent, watchful. Some of the assurance had faded from Holly's manner, however. She studied her father, a frown pulling at her brow.

"I don't understand. . . . What does he mean? What lie? You said he wasn't there, that he'd gone to the saloon for a—" Abruptly she whirled to Starbuck. "Wasn't that the truth? Didn't you go to the saloon?"

Shawn nodded.

"Then it happened just like Papa told me, didn't it?"

Starbuck remained quiet. There was movement back and around him now, hushed, careful. The crew, attracted by the sound of voices, had come out, were circling, boxing him in.

"Well, didn't it?" Holly demanded.

"You'll have to ask your pa," Starbuck said wearily.

"I'm asking you!"

"And you'll get no answer."

Holly smiled, bobbed her head in satisfaction. "Just as I thought. You're after vengeance. I knew my father wouldn't lie."

"Mr. Underwood," a voice cut in from the far left side of the yard, "I got him covered from here. Akins' drawing a bead on him from the feed shed. What you want us to do?"

125

A hard grin parted the rancher's lips. "Don't let him move. . . . I say the word—shoot."

"You're a dead man if you do," Shawn warned softly. "I don't want gunplay, but it'll come if you force my hand. Best you call them off."

Underwood considered Starbuck's set features for a long minute while the tense hush in the yard deepened. He shook his head. "Hold off, boys. Jump him and he's liable to do something crazy—and there's womenfolk around." The rancher shifted heavily on the saddle and glared at Shawn. "What's it to be? We just going to stand here all day?"

"Maybe was we to find out what this is all about we could straighten things up," Tom Gage's voice broke in from somewhere behind Starbuck.

A trickle of relief began to run through Shawn. Gage was one man in the yard he felt he could trust. Sam Underwood shifted again.

"Keep out of it, Tom."

"No, reckon not. We got a standoff here that'll probably end up with somebody dead," the old foreman said, moving up until he was directly opposite Shawn. "Sure don't want that. . . . Now, since ain't either one of you willing to talk, maybe somebody else is. How about you, Charley? Say—is that there a deputy star you're wearing? Didn't know Abrams was that hard up for help."

Charley displayed a self-conscious grin. "Aw, I ain't no real deputy, Tom. Mr. Underwood told me to get this here badge—"

"Shut up, you damned fool!" the rancher snapped.

Gage considered Sam Underwood narrowly. "Keep talking, Charley."

"About what? I don't know nothing much," the rider said. "He hired Tuck and me to sneak into that there fellow's room at the hotel. Was supposed to get a envelope with some papers in it. Something he was blackmailing Mr. Underwood with. . . . Fellow got away before we could grab the papers, so we followed him here."

The foreman shifted his attention to Shawn. "You got some papers, like Charley says?"

"Got a letter. No blackmail on my part. It was written by Rutter. He meant for it to be turned over to the U.S. Marshal if he got killed."

"And you're aiming to deliver it but Sam's against your doing it—that what this is all about?"

Starbuck said, "Covers it. Matter for the law."

Gage glanced to the rancher. "Sam, you going to say anything?"

"He was wanting us to shoot the big jasper," Tuck volunteered. "Said we wasn't to let him take that there letter he's carrying to the sheriff. Just had to have it."

A faint gasp came from Holly. She turned, started walking toward her mother. The foreman frowned. "What's that letter all about, Sam?"

Underwood's features were set, grim. His eyes hardened and filled suddenly with a wild, desperate light as he looked around the yard.

"The hell with all of you!" he shouted and drew his pistol fast. He fired point-blank at Starbuck and in the same instant jammed spurs into the horse sending the animal plunging straight at Shawn.

Starbuck leaped away and fired his weapon as the rancher got off a second shot. Underwood's first bullet was wide but the second ripped through the sleeve of Shawn's brush jacket, thudded into a corral pole behind him. Starbuck crouched, prepared to fire again. There was no need. The rancher was sagging forward on his saddle, one hand clutching his shoulder. Back near the house Holly was screaming and men were closing in from all sides.

"Everybody just hold up a minute now!"

Tom Gage's words sounded above the confusion. The thudding of boots died. Shawn relaxed gently. The foreman stepped forward, grasped the reins of Underwood's nervous horse.

"Couple of you men—help Sam down. . . . He ain't hurt bad." Gage swung about to face Starbuck, extended his hand. "I'll be taking that letter—see if it's worth all this ruckus. It is, I'll see the marshal gets—"

"No!" Underwood groaned, his head coming up with a jerk. His eyes came to a level, saw Holly and his wife running toward him, met also the wondering glances of the crew. Abruptly his head lowered again.

"Let him see it," he muttered in absolute defeat. "Let them all see it. Tell them everything—the whole damned mess. . . ."

Starbuck holstered his gun. "Nobody sees it," he said quietly. "Nobody but the U.S. Marshal. If he wants to do anything about it, it's up to him."

Holly and her mother rushed by. Together they pushed away the two punchers supporting Underwood, assumed the task themselves. The rancher, a puzzled look on his face, stared at Shawn, and then once more he dropped his eyes.

"Don't matter. . . . I'm done with thinking and worrying and sweating over things. . . . Going to the marshal myself, put it all in his hands. . . . Won't have it setting on my mind then."

"Best thing you can do—" Starbuck began.

"You get out of here!" Holly screamed at him, whirling. "You've shot him—hurt him—isn't that enough?"

Shawn lowered his head. "I'm sorry. I—"

"Sorry! What good's that? You might have killed him! If you don't leave right now, I'll get a gun myself and—"

"I'm going," Starbuck said quietly and stepped back to the chestnut.

Swinging onto the saddle, he wheeled about, rode slowly from the yard, not allowing his glance to touch any of those in the yard. There was no point in making any gesture of farewell—he knew he would get none in return.

Gaining the land swell to the south of the ranch, he paused, looked back. Sam Underwood, with his women assisting, was just entering the house. Gage and the punchers were moving off, preparing to take up the day's work. Two riders were turning into the trees west of the buildings. . . . Tuck and Charley returning to Las Vegas.

Shawn heaved a long sigh, reached into his shirt and procured Guy Rutter's letter. He read again the writing on its crumpled surface: *U.S. Marshal or Sheriff*. . . . He'd been both judge and jury where Sam Underwood was concerned, and it had been an uncomfortable and far from pleasant experience. But it was finished. The rancher had finally faced up to himself—and would now have to meet his obligations to others.

Taking the letter between his fingers, he began to tear it into small bits, allowing the light, pinon-scented breeze to scatter the scraps across the slope. Underwood had made peace with himself, would now with the law—there was no need for Rutter's denunciation.

Nor was there any necessity for him to think any more about it, or the friends he'd made and lost and would again someday, perhaps, regain when the truth was out. He needed now to put his mind on the ride ahead—a ride that would take him into the Mogollon country of Arizona where he would look up a man called Jim Ivory. . . . He just might be Ben. . . .

The
OUTLAWED

1

As the lean, coppery figure of the Apache rose suddenly from the tall brush fringing the trail—dark face contorted, black eyes glittering with hate—Shawn Starbuck reacted instinctively. Lunging to one side, he avoided the slash of the brave's knife, and reaching for the pistol on his hip, threw himself backwards off the saddle.

He struck the sandy earth hard, thorny brush raking him savagely, carving red runnels across his arms, his face. Smothering a curse, he rolled away, barely escaping the blade again as the Apache sprang upon him, bore him down. Heaving with all his strength, he partly dislodged the sweaty body, lashed out with the forty-five clamped in his hand.

The barrel connected with the brave's skull, made a dull thudding sound. The knife fell to the sand, and for a moment the muscular, crouching figure above him seemed to waver; and then Starbuck felt strong fingers close about his throat. Frantically he grabbed the Apache's wrist, pulled, seeking to break the tightening grip, while through the swirling dust he could see the brave's free arm upraised, a stone hatchet poised to strike.

Desperate, Starbuck jerked his head to one side, kneed the straddling Indian hard in the back. As the tomahawk swished by his ear, buried itself in the soil, he humped his body quickly, rocked the brave off balance, and holding tight to the pistol jammed the barrel deep into the Indian's groin, all the while sucking deep for breath.

The buck groaned in a wild sort of way, fell back. Starbuck, no longer encumbered by the fingers at his throat, struck again with the heavy weapon. The blow caught the Apache across the bridge of his plowshare nose, cracked ominously.

The brave gasped, sagged weakly. Instantly Starbuck

5

swung again, now holding the pistol by its barrel, using the butt as a deadly club . . . it would be simple to pull the trigger, blast all life from the Apache in a single fragment of time and thus end it, but such might be a mistake. Likely the brave was not alone, and a gunshot echoing across the hills and arroyos could serve to bring other copper warriors down upon him.

The blow went true, caving in the Apache's skull. He wilted soundlessly, the muscles of his lithe body relaxing, his eyes glazing as he slid quietly onto the hot sand.

Shawn lay completely motionless, muffling the sound of his labored breathing, listening into the searing heat of the August afternoon. Sweat and dust caked his body, blurred his vision. He had an overpowering urge to rise, scrub at his eyes, clear his mouth, spit, but he turned away the impulse, waited. If there were other braves nearby who had heard the struggle, they would be coming, working their way in silently, cautiously.

The minutes dragged by under the scorching sun. A quarter hour . . . a half . . . his ears had caught no sound. Slowly, carefully, he raised his head a couple of inches off the hot sand, looking first for his horse—his sole hope of getting out of the area fast if compelled to make a run for it. He breathed a little easier.

The sorrel, a horse he had recently traded his ailing chestnut gelding for, badly frightened and shying off when the Apache had risen like some fearful specter from the brush, had raced off ten yards or so and then halted in a slight depression on the plateau, was now picking disinterestedly at the scanty growth along its edges. He would not be hard to reach.

And Shawn reckoned he'd damn well better do just that —assuming the opportunity presented itself. A couple of more tussles with renegade Apaches, such as this, and there'd be a good chance he'd never make it to Lynchburg, where he planned to look up a man named Jim Ivory who, hopefully, was his long-missing brother.

He'd gotten wind of this Jim Ivory up New Mexico way from a cowhand who thought Ivory fit the description of Ben Starbuck, such as it was, that Shawn had given him. It was slim, of course; it had been a full ten years since Shawn last saw his older brother, and there wasn't much he could go on.

Actually, he had ridden all the way from Kansas to see the cowhand he'd spoken with—a man who's name was Henry Smith—in the belief that he was Ben. But as had

6

been the case in a dozen or more previous instances when he had gone chasing across the frontier on the strength of a tip, the lead had proved a false one. Henry Smith, while resembling the mind's-eye picture Shawn had of his brother, had not been him.

In the ensuing conversation, however, Smith had mentioned a man he'd worked with on a ranch in Arizona's Mogollon country—a fellow called Jim Ivory. He fit the description, Henry Smith had declared, and it might be worth Shawn's time to ride down, look the man over, and have a talk with him—if he didn't mind the hard trip.

Starbuck didn't. He never passed up the smallest lead, for until he found Ben, who had run away from home at sixteen to escape their iron-fisted father, Hiram, the Starbuck estate was in suspense and the thirty thousand dollars lying in the vault of an Ohio bank could be touched by no one. Half the money was Shawn's, but the will directed he must find his brother before claiming his share.

In the beginning it had been a sort of lark to the young farm boy, a wandering about that started first at a point on the Mexico-Texas border where he had recalled Ben once professed a wish to go. Arriving there and finding his brother had long since moved on, he then began an arduous but resolute quest directed only by rumors, the vague and unreliable memories of men he chanced to encounter—and pure hunches.

Eventually the novelty wore off and to the farm boy, still young but developed now into a tall, gray-eyed range rider of serious mien, the search became a way of life, one that ofttimes appeared to be leading nowhere and accomplishing nothing other than to store within him a wealth of experience and knowledge of the vast land he crisscrossed and the people he encountered.

And it brought to him many times, as he sat on a hilltop and gazed down upon a quiet ranch house where lamplight laid soft, yellow squares against the darkness, or watched smoke curling upward from some homesteader's simple cabin, that his was a rootless sort of existence; that he also had accumulated nothing—not even friends, since those persons, met once, were only acquaintances not likely ever to cross his path again.

One day he knew it would all come to an end, and if asked what he had to show for the lifetime a tolerant Creator had granted him on earth, he could give no answer, for he felt there was none.

Oh, there were those he'd had occasion to lend a hand and give aid to in their time of stress and trouble, but

7

Shawn Starbuck considered such unworthy of special note, since, to him, to assist another at such moment was in the nature of duty—his duty as a human being. He could see no logic in accepting acclaim when he had done only what was right—what he believed any other man would have done had he been presented with a similar set of circumstances. And to those involved who looked at it differently and sought to thank him, he had, almost shyly, turned a deaf ear and ridden on, pricked by some strange sort of embarrassment.

Just as each man is stirred by a different tune, and lives by his own set of values, Shawn, the product of an idealistic schoolteacher mother and a hard-bitten, practical, son-of-the-soil father, was no exception to that principle; he lived by a code that had been painstakingly instilled within him by that unlikely duo and saw no reason to take glory for something he considered the simple obligation of one man to another.

He glanced at the Apache. Indians were on the move again—he'd heard that as far back as Magdalena, had seen evidence of the fact as he'd ridden deeper into Arizona on a southwesterly course that led him between the landmarks of St. Peter's Dome and Green's Peak and on to Big Mountain; from there he altered course slightly, now faced directly into the sunset, came finally to the Corduroy River and the Big Butte country where he presently was.

The great, forbidding Mogollon Mountains, like a vast, dark barrier flung up against the clean sky, were to his right here—the north, and from that he knew he was drawing near journey's end. Soon he'd enter the Rockinstraw Valley, then would come Lynchburg, and twenty miles or so outside that settlement he would find the Box C Ranch where Jim Ivory worked.

He had stalled long enough. No other Apaches had appeared. It could be the buck was alone, but he still had his doubts as to that. Ordinarily they ran in parties, preferring to hunt both man and game in the company of fellow braves. Again Shawn lifted his head, swept the surrounding country with a hard, thrusting glance.

Nothing. From where he lay, however, he could not see into the broad basin on ahead. There could be others there. If so, he could take comfort from the thought that they were unaware of his presence on the little plateau, otherwise they would have closed in on him by now.

He'd be a fool to wait around any longer. The dead brave would be missed and a search instituted. Drawing his legs up beneath him, Shawn brushed sweat from his eyes and slowly came to a crouched position. Instantly he froze as motion down in the basin, now within his line of vision, caught his attention.

An Apache brave, sun gleaming on his near-naked body, was directly in front of him in the brush-and-rock-littered sink less than a hundred paces away. The buck halted, became an immobile bronze statue as he listened intently for something—or someone.

There were more. Shawn's eyes, narrowed to cut down the blinding glare, picked up movement a short distance below the first brave. He saw three more along the opposite edge of the basin. Only two carried rifles; the others had feathered lances, or, like the one who had attacked him, a stone tomahawk and a knife.

They seemed to be working toward a central point, as if closing in on some objective. The brave he had stumbled on had evidently been part of a shrinking circle.

Starbuck frowned, again swiped at the sweat clothing his face, blurring his vision. What were they after? He could see nothing, no one in that tortured welter of blistered rock and starved, shoulder-high brush. But there was a reason—there had to be.

Speculation came to a full stop. A man, dust-gray in the driving heat, head down and slightly staggering, broke into view. He was leading a starved-looking bay horse that favored its left foreleg.

The question cleared instantly for Shawn; the Apaches were after the rider with the lame horse, were allowing him to work out onto a small flat a short distance ahead where he would not have protection of the rocks and dense brush.

One of the braves with a rifle could have handled the problem at any point without difficulty, but they were wasting no bullets. Such were precious, hard to come by. It was much more practical to hold back, permit the lone white man to reach the open where a lance would be as accurate and every bit as deadly.

Starbuck hunched lower, crossed swiftly to a thick clump of cedar. From that screened position he had a much more complete view of the basin. Crouched, he took it all in—the slowly unfolding drama of violence as the solitary, unsuspecting man, in a bad way himself, leading his crippled horse over the rough, broken ground, moved deeper into the gradually tightening noose of Apache braves.

Shawn brushed at his jaw, glanced to where the sorrel

was grazing. It would be a simple matter to drop back, work his way down the slight incline to the gelding, and mount up. By keeping well away from the rim of the sink he could continue his way unseen, soon put himself well in the clear of all danger in the basin.

He brushed the thought aside. He had to consider the gaunt stranger and his horse. The man had ten, possibly fifteen more minutes of life remaining unless he was warned—and given help. The problem was how to reach him in time, stop him while he was still in the comparative shelter of the brush.

Starbuck turned away, dropped back quickly to the sorrel. Thrusting a toe into the stirrup, he sprang to the saddle. For a moment he sat there, studying the land from his elevated vantage point, and then, again brushing at the salty brine clouding his eyes, wheeled the red gelding about and doubled back up the draw, across the flinty little plateau where the dead Apache lay, and angled for the upper end of the sink.

By coming in from above he should be able to reach the doomed man without the Indians being aware of his presence. At least, he hoped that was the way it would work out.

A narrow trail led off to the right of the plateau, going down into the sink. He bypassed it, realizing it would take him down onto a level with the Apaches, and place him opposite rather than behind the man he sought to help, and so continued on.

Abruptly the flat dropped off into another fairly deep gully. He rode into it, cut right, and shortly entered the brush fringing the sink. The rider was below him now, but he could not be certain the same was true of all the Apaches; he had no idea how many braves were skulking about in the basin—how large the living noose that was tightening around its intended victim. He could only guess.

He gave thought to dismounting to improve his chances for passing unseen through the undergrowth, then dropped the idea. He would be moving slower if such a plan were followed, and time was running out for the stranger. He had to be stopped before he got beyond the protection of the rocks and brush.

Bent forward on the saddle, Shawn urged the gelding on, keeping to the narrow aisles between the rank growth and mounds of boulders. He saw no indication of additional braves, but took no confidence from that; he saw no horses either, knowing well the Apache's ponies were somewhere nearby. If they could be successfully hidden, so could several more warriors.

The sorrel's ears flicked suddenly as he paused in stride. Starbuck drew in instantly, the understanding between man and horse strong. The gelding had seen something he, himself, had missed. For a few moments he remained motionless in the heat-blasted depths of the brush-filled sink, listening, probing the undergrowth with careful eyes.

He could neither hear nor see anything suspicious. It could have been a bird veering through the shadows, or possibly a rabbit scampering out from beneath the sorrel's hooves.

11

Lifting the leathers a bit, he started the gelding forward, now at a slower gait and with more thought to silence. He couldn't be far behind the man with the lame horse, and if the Apaches had worked in, closed the loop, there was every possibility there'd be two or three of them ahead.

Starbuck saw the brave a split second before the coppery warrior, hearing the muted sound of the sorrel's tread on the loose sand, wheeled. The Indian's eyes flared in surprise and alarm; his mouth opened to yell just as Shawn, leaving the saddle in a low dive, hit him full on.

The brave went down in a flailing of arms and legs. A stifled cry escaped his lips despite Starbuck's fingers clamped about his throat, and then there was a muffled groan as Shawn, again using the forty-five, clubbed him hard on the side of the head.

Instantly Starbuck was on his feet. He'd silenced the buck—but not soon enough. That one strangled sound would have been heard by others. They would hesitate, wonder, and then one or two were certain to investigate. He had only moments left now to reach the man somewhere just ahead, voice a warning, and then quickly find a suitable place where, together, they could make a stand.

He swore silently, dashing at the sweat. If he could just yell—call out! But that was out of the question; there were the Apaches in the remainder of the circle to remember —and hopefully keep at a distance until safety was reached.

The lame horse was suddenly before him. In the same instant he saw the dusty, dejected figure of the man. They were still in the brush, only paces from the clearing where the Apaches would undoubtedly strike.

Starbuck halted, emitted a low whistle, pivoted to glance about, seeking a place where they could pull off and find some degree of protection. A butte to his right offered possibilities. It would give them something to their backs, and a fairly good-sized boulder would serve as a rampart in front.

He swung his attention again to the rider. The man had halted, studied him with dull suspicion. His worn, pinched face was florid, marked with even brighter red splotches where the pitiless sun had left its mark on skin unaccustomed to stringency; it was a face that appeared too old for a body that could be no more than ten years Shawn's senior.

"Apaches—all around us!" Starbuck called in a hoarse whisper. "This way—we'll make a stand at that bluff," he added, pointing.

Immediately he turned the sorrel for the reddish formation, urging him with a steady pressure of his rowels. Halfway he glanced at the rider. The man had not stirred. Impatience flared through Shawn.

"Come on—dammit! They're closing in on you!"

In the next breath a lance, its feathers swirling brightly in the hot sunlight, soared across the open ground, struck point down and quivering an arm's length back of the lame horse. The man delayed no longer. Pivoting, he started for the bluff at an awkward run.

Starbuck, reaching the formation, hit the ground fast as the basin came alive with the yells of Indians. He saw a brave dart from a clump of brush a few steps beyond the rider, race toward him. Sunlight glinted on the shining steel blade of the knife clutched in his hand. Taking cool, deliberate aim with his forty-five, Shawn dropped the brave in his tracks.

In the next moment man and horse were behind the rock, the rider dropping the reins as the bay sidled anxiously up to the sorrel as if seeking kindred companionship, while the haggard traveler, pistol in hand, took a place next to Starbuck at the boulder.

Shawn, eyes sweeping restlessly back and forth, taking in both sides of the area fronting the bluff, swore deeply. Suddenly there were no Apaches—not even any yells. The braves had disappeared completely; it was as if it had all been an illusion. But they were there, silent as dark shadows, reorganizing, getting themselves set and planning their next move. There were two white men now.

"Obliged to you, mister," the rider murmured in a dry, raspy voice. He swallowed noisily as if speaking was a chore.

Shawn shrugged. "Spotted you from above. Had you surrounded and I figured I'd better set in on the game. . . . My name's Starbuck—Shawn Starbuck."

"Mine's—uh, Mason. You get jumped doing it?"

Shawn's glance followed Mason's line of vision. There was a streak of blood on his forearm, more on his sleeve.

"Bumped into a couple. Keep watching the left. I'll take the right—and we'd both best keep an eye out straight ahead. They'll be hitting us again—soon as they figure out our weak spot."

"Whole damned place is a weak spot," Mason said, looking around.

"Won't argue that—and I sure didn't pick it on purpose! One thing for certain, we've got to get out of here before dark."

Mason was silent for a time, then: "How many Apaches did you spot?"

"Eight, maybe ten. Hard to tell, way they were moving in and out of the brush."

"A God's plenty of them. No way I can see that we can get away from that big a party."

The defeat in Mason's attitude and voice was evident. A man who's been through hell a couple of times, Shawn thought, and wondered if it had come about from being in the war; but the war had been over for ten years; you'd think a man could have shaken the terrible memories that possessed him in that length of time.

He slid another glance at Mason, now turned from him, eyes on the brush and patches of open ground below. He had thin, straw-colored hair badly in need of trimming. His clothing—pants and shirt—were of some sleazy material, coarse and ill-fitting. His boots were worn, although the heels appeared to have been repaired recently. The pistol in his gnarled hand was an old Colt forty-four-caliber Walker. No rifle was slung from his saddle.

"Answer's to get ourselves up and out of this sink," Starbuck said, replying to the man's resigned comment. "We make it to the flat above us, chances for slipping off are plenty good."

Mason twisted about, looked to the rim above them. "How'll we do it?"

"Trail behind us—between those two rock slabs. Saw it when I came off the plateau to warn—"

"Warn—you mean you came down from there to warn me?" Mason broke in incredulously.

"Couldn't yell. Apaches would've cracked down on you fast then—and that would have ended it."

Mason continued to stare at Starbuck in a troubled, not-understanding way. His thin lips were set and his small eyes were dark and filled with a sullen bitterness.

"Reckon I truly am obliged to you," he muttered, almost resentfully.

"Forget it. What we've got to worry about is staying alive. Next time—"

Shawn's words were cut off abruptly as the air once again was filled with yells. A half-dozen Apaches rushed into the open, breaking from the thick brush to the south and heading for a large mound of rocks and weed-covered earth a dozen strides away.

Mason rested the old Walker on his left forearm, pressed off a shot. It was a clean miss. Starbuck, wishing he had grabbed his rifle before he turned the sorrel loose,

14

steadied himself against the rock, dropped the buck in the lead as Mason thumbed back the hammer of his weapon, fired again. This time his aim was good. The brave spun, went down in a swirl of dust, feet beating a tattoo against the sun-baked soil. Those remaining, suddenly dissuaded, wheeled, rushed back for the shelter of the brush.

Hastily reloading, Starbuck turned his attention to Mason's bay. "What's wrong with your horse?"

He was calculating their chances for escape by making a run for it, assuming they could gain the plateau above.

"Hoofs are split. Left fore's in bad shape. Been leading him all day."

Mason could forget riding him—at least until the horse could rest and receive treatment. But the situation wasn't too serious. The sorrel could carry double. He was a big animal, stronger than average—and Mason didn't look to weigh much. The gelding, however, could not be expected to take on such a load for any lengthy distance. He'd had an ordinary day, covering quite a few miles in the intense heat, and was himself in need of rest. Again Shawn considered the trail leading up between the cleft in the rocks. It was their only hope.

"Apaches'll be trying something else pretty quick. We've got them in a stand-off right now, but they won't let it stay at that."

"Why don't they use their guns?"

"Saw only a couple in the bunch. Could be more but I doubt it—and they don't want to waste bullets. Big reason they're after us—they want our guns and ammunition."

Mason brushed at his eyes. "Was we to spot the ones with rifles, pick them off, maybe we could get past the others. Not too hard to dodge a lance."

"Would work only we don't know for sure how many've got guns. Spotted a couple, but I've got a hunch there're more braves out there, and that could mean more rifles."

"Then what—"

"They're trying to reach that pile of rocks. If they can get a couple of braves bedded down there, they can come at us from three directions. I figure we'd be smart, if we're lucky enough to turn them back their next try, to make a run for that trail, try to get on top."

"Horses'll slow us up—"

"I'll send the sorrel ahead. The bay'll follow if we do a little persuading. No sense trying to lead them—and we've got to have them if we do get there."

"Bay of mine won't be of any use. . . . You make a try for it—I'll hold them off long as I can."

15

"No need for that. Sorrel can carry double, leastwise until we're far enough to be fairly safe. Not long now until dark."

Mason brushed wearily at his sweaty face. "Glad of that. Be cooler. Heat's about got me down."

"Moving toward the desert. Days won't get any better."

And then once more the sink echoed with the piercing shrieks of Apaches. Three braves spurted from the brush, lunged for the rocky mound. They were not alone in the attempt. From the opposite side of the formation two more bucks appeared, running low, one carrying a rifle. The scheme was evident; they were endeavoring to split the fire of the men behind the rock, thereby increase the chances of the one with the rifle to gain protection of the mound.

Shawn, again bracing himself against the rock, once more cursing himself for not having his own long gun, leveled his weapon at the dodging figure with the Army Springfield, squeezed off the trigger. The Apache threw wide his arms as the slug caught him in the chest while the Springfield went spinning into the dust. He pivoted then to aid Mason. He had stopped the lead man of the trio; the two others had slowed.

"Keep 'em busy!" Shawn yelled, turning to the horses.

Grabbing the sorrel's leathers, he led the gelding to the mouth of the trail, pointed him upgrade, and slapped him sharply on the rump. As the big horse, startled, leaped away, Shawn seized the bay's reins, sent him into the cleft in quick pursuit.

Immediately he wheeled, dropped back to Mason's side. A rifle cracked. The bullet spanged into the wall of the butte behind him, screamed off into space. A wry grin on his lips he wiped sweat from his face, hunkered beside Mason. That had been a close one.

He looked toward the mound. Another of the braves had snatched the fallen rifle and was making use of it. He had reached the rocks, finding his opportunity while Starbuck was attending the horses and Mason was concentrating on the Apaches coming in from his side, was now firmly entrenched just below the crest. Only the top of his head and a small glint of the rifle were visible. More bucks were coming into the open now, weaving and dodging in and out, taking courage from the belief that shortly they would have the men behind the rock pinned down. That fact dawned swiftly on Shawn Starbuck also.

"Come on!" he yelled at Mason, and emptying his pistol at the Apaches, raced for the mouth of the trail.

3

Heaving for breath, sweat cutting channels in the dust clothing his face and neck, Shawn gained the summit of the trail. He glimpsed the horses off to one side on the plateau, mentally recorded their location as he thumbed cartridges into his weapon, and wheeled back to the edge of the plateau. Mason swung in beside him, gasping from the hard climb.

"They're coming!" he managed.

Starbuck dropped to his knees, looked down into the sink. A dozen Apaches were swarming across the sandy stretch of open ground that separated the mound of earth from the rock behind which he and Mason had stood, and racing for the mouth of the trail. Raising his pistol, he snapped a shot at the brave in the lead. The bullet, too hastily fired, missed its weaving target, but did have its effect; instantly the glistening, sweaty figures melted into the nearby brush.

"Take the horses—head that way," Shawn directed in a quick, hard voice and pointed to the path leading southward. "I'll be coming shortly."

Mason, recognizing the wisdom of the plan, moved off immediately, and catching up the trailing reins of the two mounts, started down the trail. Shawn wheeled again to the sink. The Indians were still in hiding, crouched low in the underbrush and behind the rocks.

He was not visible to them, he knew, and that alone was keeping them pinned down, since they were not anxious to brave guns positioned they knew not where. But they would throw off their reluctance, patience at such times not being one of their virtues; two or three of the bolder ones would work their way around, attempt to close in from the sides. It would require an hour at least

17

—and that was long enough to permit Mason and him to get clear of the area.

He should take full advantage of the situation, however; buy as much time as possible. Glancing about, he noticed a thick stand of wolfberry growing among a scatter of rocks at the edge of the flat. Bulling his way into its center, he drew several of the tallest stems into a sort of column. Holding them together, he removed his hat, perched it on the tips of the thorny uprights, then returned to the open ground.

Hunkered on his heels, he considered his handiwork, grunted in satisfaction. The hat had settled down to just the proper level when the stems had straightened. From the sides, the angle at which the Apaches would first view it, there would appear to be a man forted up in the rocks and brush. It was costing him a good hat—but better no headgear than no hair.

Such would further delay the renegades, and while they were figuring out a means for coping with this danger, he and Mason should be able to get well beyond their reach. But it would be wise to play it for all it was worth. Staying low, he returned to the rim of the plateau, and flat on his belly, peered down into the basin. At first he saw nothing, no signs whatever of the Apaches—and then the moving of a clump of sage drew his attention.

A smile pulled at his lips as he brushed away the sweat slipping into his eyes. The Apaches were up to an old trick —that of holding clumps of weeds or thickly leafed branches over themselves to mask their advance. Muffling the click with the cupped palm of his left hand, Starbuck thumbed back the hammer of his forty-five, kept his gaze on the brush-pocked ground at the foot of the butte.

A bush somewhat apart from the others stirred, moved forward a few inches. Shawn leveled his weapon at the clump, squeezed off a shot. The bush erupted instantly, coming apart into several sections. A lank figure leaped upright, spun, scurried for the more substantial cover of the nearby rocks.

Starbuck pulled back quickly. It wasn't necessary to see what the remaining braves, so painstakingly advancing under their camouflage, would do; they'd simply stall, debate with themselves, and shortly abandon the ruse, realizing the white men entrenched on the plateau above were onto their plan. Their next logical move would be to pull back, circle wide, and come in from opposing points, whereupon their attention would be focussed at once upon a man lying in wait for them in the brush.

18

Keeping low and well back from the rim of the butte, Shawn moved off down trail at a trot, being careful to plant his feet in the soft, yielding sand and deaden the sound of his retreat. He was already feeling the lack of the hat he'd left in the wolfberry; the sun's rays had slackened little in their ferocity although the afternoon was growing late. But darkness would soon prevail, and with it would come relief.

He saw Mason a short time later as he rounded a shoulder of granite. The older man halted at once, wheeled, faced him unsmiling.

"That shot—they come at you again?"

Starbuck took the sorrel's reins into his own hands, shook his head. "Just letting them know I was there. Longer they think they're pinned down, the better for us." Swinging onto the saddle, he kicked his foot free of the stirrup, extended his hand to Mason. "Let's go."

The man frowned, hesitated, and then as Shawn reached farther, more insistently toward him, he took the proffered arm, slid his toe into the wooden bow, and settled himself behind Starbuck.

"Can't go far in this country, riding double," he said, pulling the bay in behind the sorrel with the reins as a lead rope.

"Don't aim to—only until we're far enough from here to be safe. Other side of that hogback ought to be about right."

"That's Cibique Ridge," Mason said.

Starbuck, glancing back over the trail to be certain it was still empty and they were as yet not followed, touched the sorrel with his spurs and moved the big horse out. Apparently Mason was no stranger to the land, yet he seemed oddly reserved concerning the fact. There was a reason, he supposed, and further guessed that if Mason wanted him to know about it, he'd speak up.

"You lose your hat?"

Starbuck nodded. "Sort of. Planted it back there on the flat, in some brush."

"Tricking the Apaches?"

"Hoping to."

"Have to rig you up something before tomorrow. Man sure can't be out in this sun for long without covering up his head. Bake your brains."

"Got an old one in my saddlebags. I'll dig it out in the morning. Not much, but it'll do until I can get to where I can buy another."

They rode on in silence after that, and a time later, with

sunset a flaring explosion of color beyond the purple Mazatzal Mountains to the west, they pulled into a small clearing at the foot of a high palisade.

"Man never knows about Apaches," Starbuck said, staring at the dully gleaming face of the formation, all light and shadow from the cloud-reflected rays of the sun, "but I don't think they'll bother us any more tonight. If things worked like I planned, it'll be full dark by the time they learn there's nobody under that hat—and then it'll be too late to track us."

Mason nodded, slipped from his perch on the sorrel. Shawn dismounted, began to tug at the gelding's cinch buckles. Glancing at Mason, stolidly removing gear from the bay, he let his eyes run swiftly over the man's equipment. He traveled light, that was certain; no brush coat, no chaps, no slicker—only a canteen and what appeared to be totally empty saddlebags and a single wool blanket. Mason was no working cowhand, that was evident.

"That got water in it?" he asked, ducking his head at the almost new container.

"About half full," Mason replied, laying his saddle aside. The hull was old, badly cracked, with the lining of the skirt torn and missing in several patches. "Filled it this morning."

"Grub?"

"About out. Bite or two left, I reckon."

"Got plenty for the both of us," Shawn said. "Be in Lynchburg tomorrow. Can stoke up on supplies then."

"Obliged to you, but I'll get by," Mason replied, his tone making it clear he asked for no favors.

Starbuck shrugged, pulled his saddle free of the gelding, and placed it carefully on its side under a nearby clump of brush.

"Glad to share what I've got. . . . You want to work on your horse while I throw a meal together?"

Mason paused. "Not a hell of a lot I can do for him."

"Main thing you need is water—and we've got enough to get by if you use what's in your canteen."

"You mean I ought to soak his hoofs?"

"Only thing to do. Mix up some mud, then take rags, pack it around his hoofs, like a poultice. Keep things sort of wet all night and he may be in shape to ride in the morning if we take it easy."

"You think it'll help?"

"Know it will. Had the same trouble with the sorrel. Hoofs dry out, usually because some dunderheaded blacksmith gets careless with his rasp and scrapes off too much

20

of that coating—varnish, I've heard it called—when he's fitting shoes. That happens and the horse gets to traveling in country like this where it's all hot sand and never any mud, cracks open up. . . . You soak his hoofs good, then soon as you can start treating them with oil—neat's-foot or maybe linseed, whichever you can get—and you'll cure him."

Mason smiled for the first time, a brief, ragged pulling of his lips. "Guess I'd forgot that," he said, and taking the bay's reins, led him off to one side.

Shawn, staking out the sorrel, opened his saddlebags, dug out hardtack, dried beef, a can of peaches, coffee, along with a lard tin and a blackened spider. Moving to the end of the palisade, he cast a long glance to the slope, now almost wholly dark, saw no signs of the Apaches, and then crossed to the foot of the towering formation and built a small, compact fire. Placing the water-filled tin over the flames, he paused to study his companion.

Mason had given the two horses their drink, was now stirring up an amount of mud. He had produced an old undershirt, either from the flat-looking saddlebags, or perhaps utilizing the one he wore, and had ripped it into four strips.

The treatment wouldn't cure the bay's problem, but it would help. The horse should be able to make it in to Lynchburg if they took it slow and kept to soft ground. Drawing the slim-bladed Mexican knife from the sheath stitched inside his right boot, Shawn squatted, began to cut the beef into chunks, drop it into the skillet. He hesitated again as a thought came to him; he had assumed Mason was heading for Lynchburg, but in truth, he did not actually know that.

"You riding for any place in particular?" he asked, resuming his chore.

Mason was apportioning the mud onto the strip of cloth. He did not look up. "Lynchburg—then I'm going on south to the Mescal Mountain country. Got some land there."

"Was close by the Mescals once, never right down in them. Guess Lynchburg's the only town around here."

Mason nodded but made no further comment as he began to work with the bay's hooves, affixing the baglike poultices of mud, tying them securely in place while Starbuck continued his supper preparations.

The night closed in quickly and they finished the last of the coffee with only the faint glare of the fire flickering against the wall of the granite behind them to hold back

21

the shadows. Stars had broken through the flowing blackness overhead, and a pale radiance had settled over the country, softening its harshness, shrouding all things, changing them to mysterious, unfamiliar objects. Night birds began to call, timidly at first, and then more boldly; far back in the regions of the higher peaks a wolf howled, challenging one and all to dispute his dominion.

Starbuck sighed contentedly, forever moved by the matchless beauty of the night, and reaching out, picked up a handful of dry branches, tossed them into the flames.

"You born around here?" Mason wondered.

"No, Ohio's my home. Little town called Muskingum."

"What brought you west?"

"Looking for my brother. Could be you've run into him if you've done much drifting around."

"Doubt it," Mason replied listlessly.

"Be a man around twenty-five. Probably has dark hair, sharp blue eyes. Could be on the stocky side. Always sort of favored my pa in that."

"Talk like you ain't seen him in quite a spell."

"Ten years or so since he ran away from home. Pa's dead now. Need to find him so's I can clear up the estate."

"What do you call him?"

"Ben—Ben Starbuck, that's his real name, but I don't reckon he's using it. Swore he never would when he lit out that day. About all I can go on is what I think he'll look like and the fact that he's got a little scar over his left eye."

"Not much to work with."

"Found that out a long time ago. Plenty of men fit the description I give, but nobody yet has filled it."

"You think he's in Lynchburg?"

"Not exactly—maybe on a ranch nearby. I was told about a cowhand there who sort of fit the picture. Only way I ever know for sure is to do a bit of talking, have a look for that scar."

Mason was staring into the small knot of leaping flames. He opened his mouth to speak, hesitated as the wolf bayed again into the depthless night, drew this time a coyote's querulous response.

"Expect you'll maybe ride till doomsday and not find him with no more'n you've got to go on," he said finally. "This cowhand you're going to see, he got a name?"

"Jim Ivory. Ever hear of him?"

"Nope, can't say as I have. What outfit he work for?"

"Ranch called the Box C."

"Heard of it," Mason said, his tone altering. He contin-

22

ued to gaze into the fire for a time, then raising his eyes, made a motion toward the ornate, engraved belt buckle Shawn wore. "That's mighty fancy. Silver, ain't it? And that figure of a fighter on it—that ivory?"

Shawn nodded. "It was my pa's."

"He a champion fighter in that newfangled boxing style?"

"Never was a champion—a professional, but I expect he could've been, had he wanted. Nobody ever beat him."

"He learn you?"

"Taught Ben and me both. Said he wanted us to know how to take care of ourselves."

Mason stirred, wagged his head. "Sure is a wicked way for a man to fight. Once heard about a fellow mixing it up with a boxer—a professional—got himself so bad whipped folks thought somebody'd used a knife on him."

"Fists can be terrible weapons if a man knows how to use them."

"And I reckon you do."

Starbuck moved his wide shoulders slightly. "When I have to," he said, and rising, walked again to the end of the palisade where he could look back over the trail they had covered. Moon and starlight now flooded the slopes, brought all things into soft-edged focus. Nothing moved in the ethereal glow; the Apaches, he hoped, as he had hoped earlier, had given it up. Wheeling, he returned to the fire, resumed his place.

"You know," Mason said, "a thing like that could be a way to find your brother. You hear of a fighter, the boxer kind, it'd be smart to go have a look at him."

"Has brought me close a couple of times," Shawn admitted. "One of these days I'll hear about it in time, get there before the man's moved on. Need a lot of luck in what I'm trying to do."

"What you need most, seems to me," Mason said, tossing the last dregs of his coffee into the fire. "Like chasing a moonbeam. Well, reckon I'll turn in. Apaches sort of took the sand out of me. You figure we ought to stand watch?"

"No use taking chances. You go ahead, I'll take the first turn."

Mason raised no objection, simply reached for his blanket, rolled himself into it.

Starbuck's eyes were on the man curled up near the fire; he was asleep almost at once. There was something about Mason he couldn't quite fathom—something in his manner that mystified, even disturbed, him. True, he had opened up a bit during the evening, become more talkative, but thinking back Shawn realized the man had revealed little of himself—and nothing of his past.

It was Mason's own business, he decided, again coming to his feet. Drawing his rifle from its scabbard, he walked slowly toward the end of the palisade and the outcrop of rock that would provide a sentry post from which to observe the trail. A man has a right to keep his personal history to himself if so inclined. One thing sure, Mason didn't seem too pleased by the fact they would soon be in Lynchburg.

They were up well before dawn, both realizing that with the coming of light came also danger from the Apaches. The night had passed without incident, but now a new day faced them and the odds were the renegades, at that very moment, were searching out the tracks of the two horses.

In a tight silence they ate hurriedly, packed their gear, and by the time the first raw sunlight was tipping the crags of the more distant ranges and flooding down the long slopes, they were mounted and on their way—Shawn wearing the battered old hat he had dug out from the bottom of his saddlebags, Mason considerably more at ease now that he was again mounted.

The mud treatment and the night's rest had done much for the bay, and while he was, of course, far from cured, some of the lameness had disappeared and he was usable. If ridden sensibly and with care, he should last out the remainder of the journey to the settlement.

All that could change swiftly, Starbuck realized. If the Apaches were trailing them and gained rapidly, thus nullifying their lead, the bay would be unable to stand any hard running even for a short distance. The alternative to a headlong race—that of forting up or once more making a stand—would be necessary. He hoped this time a more advantageous spot could be found.

Mason seemed to have improved somewhat in spirit. While the hard-cornered bleakness of his features had not vanished, there was a breaking down in the bitterness that seemed to fill him, and for the first time since they had met, there appeared to be an appreciation for the broad, savage vistas of the country through which they were slowly making their way.

Once, near mid-morning, when they halted on a long ridge to breathe the horses and probe their back trail for

25

pursuit, he gazed out over the endless, rolling country and sighed quietly. There was a vacuity to the man, as if somewhere along the line life had dealt him a terrible blow from which he had not recovered.

"You never know how much you can miss all this—the mountains and the sky—even the heat, until it's taken away. Can miss anything, I reckon. Sounds funny maybe but a man can miss the smell of blood and death once he's grown used to it, and then puts it behind him."

Starbuck's eyes were on the distant slopes. He thought he had seen movement but wasn't certain. "Suppose so, but I wasn't in the war so I don't know. You were, I take it."

"Four years—four goddam years."

"It was hell, I'm sure of that," Starbuck said, deciding the motion he thought he saw was merely the shimmer of steadily rising heat. "I've heard others hash it over."

"Something nobody won—a man ought to remember that. Nobody ever wins a thing like that. The North came out on top but that don't mean it won. I wore a blue uniform, fought for Mr. Lincoln's idea of saving the Union. But I lost—personally. Everything except a piece of land I've got down in the Mescals. Was the same story with every man that got into it except the rich ones. They just got richer."

"Plenty of them lost, too—fortunes in cash as well as property."

"Property—land," Mason went on as if not hearing, "that's all that counts in this world. Man can lose cash, his house and furniture, cattle—things like that, and start over. But if he loses his land he's finished. He's got nothing to start from."

"This place of yours, in the Mescals. You planning to make a new start there?"

Mason turned, rubbed the bay's neck slowly. "What I aim to do. Was just getting it going when the war hit. Felt I had to go. My folks tried to talk me out of it but I was young and full of vinegar—wanted to do my part for my country. Wouldn't listen, went just the same.

"Reckon it made them kind of proud of me, being one of the few who went and volunteered from around here. Anyway, I'd just begun building my cabin—and I plain up and walked off to do my bit leaving behind five thousand acres of good grass, timber, and year-round water just standing there."

"You've never been back?"

26

Mason shook his head, lapsing again into that near sullenness that characterized him. "Not since."

Shawn moved to the sorrel, reached for the reins, and prepared to mount. Idly, he glanced once more to the trail behind them; no sign of Apaches, but his thoughts had centered on something else: the war had ended ten years ago; where had Mason been in the intervening time?

"Sounds like a fine place," he commented, going to the saddle.

"It's going to suit me," Mason said in a low voice and let the subject drop, offering no explanation as to why he had taken a decade to return to what obviously was very dear to his heart.

Starbuck waited until the man had mounted, and then led off, continuing along the ridge which lifted gradually to a higher plane where a round, thumb-like peak thrust itself bluntly into the sky.

It was all much like the land he had so recently covered in New Mexico, he thought as he swept the surrounding country with his glance. The same clean, blue sky with its batches of snowy cotton clouds; the same yellow and tan earth gashed here and there with reds and browns; the same towering hills, some clothed in green, others in barren, gray rock.

But then this had been part of New Mexico once, he recalled, before the war began. At the onset a Confederate colonel, John Baylor he thought it was, had split the territory down its center and given the western portion the name Arizona.

It had been a shrewd move on the part of the officer; those souls inhabiting that part of the sprawling domain had long sought separation and independence. For the miles that lay between them and the capital in Santa Fe were hazardous and long—so long in fact that their pleas and presence had gone practically unnoticed year after year by the politicos in power.

Mesilla, a settlement not far north of El Paso and adjacent Fort Bliss, was declared the capital of the new district, but such glory was short-lived. A victorious North, while permitting the division of the land to stand, thereby breaking up a territory that would have proved a close rival in size to Texas, voided Mesilla's claim to fame and relegated it once again to the status of irrelevancy—a small town dozing in the sun, disturbed only now and then by the noisy exploits of passing outlaws.

It was close on to noon when they reached the base of the huge peak, and there again paused to rest the horses.

Shawn took advantage of the opportunity to inspect the bay's hoofs, found them holding up well. Another night's rest and packing in soft mud, followed by applications of oil, and the horse would be on the way to recovery.

"He'll make it if we keep taking it easy," he said, moving to a rise on the rocky flat surrounding the peak. Gaining its highest point, he turned his gaze once more to the trail over which they had passed. He stiffened, his attention being drawn to a dozen or so figures crossing a sun swept flat in the valley below. Apaches. They had gained appreciably.

"There they are," he said, pointing.

Mason climbed to Shawn's side, followed his leveled arm. "Them sure enough. Dogging our tracks."

"Means we'll have to move faster. They'll try to cut us off and I don't know how far we are from Lynchburg."

"Ten, maybe twelve miles," Mason said readily, and pointed to another, somewhat higher ridge forming a horizon in the southeast. "Town's on the yonder side of that —in the middle of a big valley—the Rockinstraw they call it."

Again Shawn realized Mason was a great deal more familiar with the country than he let on.

"No need stewing over them getting close. We just move right along like we've been doing and we'll soon be in the Rockinstraw," Mason continued, turning back to where the horses waited. "Won't bother us there."

They pressed on shortly after that, a heavy silence, for some unaccountable reason, falling upon the two men— one that was broken only when around the middle of the afternoon, they reached the foot of the ridge's far side and were on a well-marked road leading to the settlement.

A while later they pulled off into a grove of sycamores where a small creek cut a clear, narrow channel, watered the horses and took advantage of the occasion to wash the caked dust from their faces and arms. Refreshed, and leaning against one of the trees, Starbuck stretched, yawned.

"Going to feel good sleeping in a real bed, eating somebody else's cooking for a change." Pulling off the old hat he'd produced from his saddlebags, he dusted himself down the front. "Reckon about the first thing I'd better do, however, is blow myself to a new lid. Seen better-looking hats on the plow horses back home."

Mason ignored the humor, merely nodded. "Man can miss the comforts or he can get used to doing without."

"Sure," Shawn agreed, "but when a man's been on the

trail for what seems like months, the change is mighty welcome."

They moved on after that and soon houses began to appear in the broad sweep of the valley; small ranches, a dirt farmer here and there, planted fields, haystacks. Still in the distance and somewhere near center, smoke was rising into the sky; Lynchburg would lie there, Starbuck guessed.

He wondered where the Box C would be, remembered then that it was to the west of the settlement some twenty miles, and shifted his attention to that direction. A faint, blue haze clung to the area and all was not as definite as it might have been. It appeared to be an area of low, rolling hills, like gray bubbles spread across a wide flat beyond which were many buttes and benches. There was no large timber visible except in the higher reaches edging the Rockinstraw to the north.

A mile short of town, which loomed up suddenly when they broke out of a thickly brushed swale onto a level flat, two men in a buggy cut in from a side road, overtook their slowly moving horses quickly, and passing by, made the customary salutary wave. Both then turned abruptly, as if startled, stared briefly, and then continued on toward the settlement at a fast clip.

Lynchburg itself looked to be slumbering in the afternoon's intense heat when Shawn and Mason turned into the single main street and proceeded slowly. Starbuck, brushing at the freshly accumulated sweat on his forehead, pointed at what evidently was the largest saloon—the Maricopa.

"Don't know about you, but a beer is the only thing that's going to cut the cotton out of my throat. What do you say we stop there first?"

"Suits me," Mason replied indifferently.

Together they swung from the street's center, rode up to the hitchrack, and dismounted. In that next moment Shawn was aware of motion directly behind them. He threw a glance over his shoulder. A man wearing the star of a town marshal pinned to the pocket of his plaid shirt and carrying a Wells-Fargo shotgun was advancing slowly. A half-dozen men, all armed, accompanied him.

Starbuck frowned, slid a look to Mason. He, also, was aware of the group, was watching them with dark, fathomless eyes. All the ease that had erased his earlier attitude had melted away, and he was again the bitter, deeply withdrawn man he had been in the blistered depths of the sink.

Stepping away from the hitchrack, Shawn pushed his

29

worn, sweat-stained old hat to the back of his head, moved along the flank of the sorrel until he stood at the gelding's hindquarters. Leaning against the horse, he considered the oncoming lawman and his supporters stoically. On the whole he respected the men who wore the star of authority and ordinarily got along well with them, but there were those who made nuisances of themselves; this one appeared to fall in that category.

"What's on your mind, Marshal?" he asked in a patient voice.

The lawman came to a halt, his eyes narrowing as his lips pulled into a tight line. He flicked Starbuck with a sharp glance, turned his attention to Mason. The other men—merchants and town elders, Shawn supposed—ranged about him, forming a half-circle. Other persons were coming now, attracted by the conflux in the street.

A tall individual standing directly behind the lawman swore, said: "By God, it *is* him!" in a strained voice, and drew his pistol. The man next him looked familiar—one of the pair who had been in the buggy.

Patient, Shawn waited in the burning sunlight while the small clouds of dust lifting from beneath the shuffling feet of the citizenry drifted aimlessly about. This was no ordinary confrontation between a small town's officialdom and unwelcome drifters being invited to move on, he realized. This was much more—and undoubtedly serious.

"Asked you a question, Marshal," he pressed firmly.

The lawman flashed him a hard glance, and cradling the shotgun, faced his companion. "All right, Mason Lynch—put your hands up!"

"Means you too, saddletramp," the tall man who had earlier drawn his pistol added, motioning at Starbuck.

The marshal threw a confirming look at Shawn, made a gesture with the shotgun. "Now—the both of you—head for jail."

5

The marshal had called his trail partner Mason Lynch. Shawn pondered that as temper stirred through him. He'd been misled, not actually lied to, perhaps, but the truth had been withheld for some reason, and that rankled him; for now he was finding himself again in the position he continually sought to avoid—that of getting involved in someone else's troubles.

Anger for this man he had helped but who had seen fit to deceive him brimmed suddenly, spilled over, spattered also the lawman.

"The hell with you, Marshal," he said in a quiet, flat voice. "I'm not going anywhere until I get some reasons."

The lawman's face colored and the shotgun in his hands came up warningly. "You being with Lynch is all the reason I need."

"For you, maybe—not for me. There some law against bumping into a man on the trail, riding with him?"

"You lay down with a dog, you'd best figure on some fleas," the marshal said, wagging the shotgun suggestively. "You coming along, or am I going to take you?"

Shawn drew himself up fully, glanced out over the threatening crowd. Half-turning, he caught Mason's eye, saw the look of helpless frustration on his bitter features, heard the plea in his voice.

"Do what he says. This whole bunch is trigger-happy. I'll try to make Huckaby believe you once we're inside."

Starbuck shrugged, moved out into the ankle-deep dust, and took his place beside Mason. One of the men in the crowd, a husky, wide-shouldered, well-dressed blond with neatly trimmed mustache and beard, stepped in behind him, shoved him roughly.

"Damned gunslinging saddlebum, coming here. We ought to—"

31

Starbuck, anger again boiling over, swung a lightning-fast right fist, caught the man full center of his belly. The blond gasped. His eyes bulged as his color changed to a pasty white. Hands clutched to his middle, he took a few faltering steps backward, sat down hard.

Huckaby whirled, shotgun once more lifted. "You try that again, I'll bend this over your head!"

The faintest smile pulled at Starbuck's lips, but there was no humor there, only a quiet self-assurance.

"Tell him, and anybody else with the same notion," he said coolly, "they'd best keep their paws off me. I don't take a roughing up from any man—including the ones who wear a star."

Huckaby kept the twin black circles of the shotgun's muzzle drifting back and forth over Starbuck and Mason Lynch.

"I'm taking that as a threat."

"Makes no difference to me. I've done nothing to get jailed for. Your reasons for doing it had better be good."

The marshal, a thin, graying man with a hook nose, full sweeping mustache, and small, black eyes that peered out from the deep sockets of a heavily veined face, nodded slowly.

"You've heard it."

"No reason far as I'm concerned."

In the tense, hot silence of the street the only sound was the retching of the man Starbuck had struck. Huckaby said: "That's because you don't know nothing. Get inside. I'll do my talking there. Rest of you people," he added, not taking his glance off his two prisoners, "clear out. I want help, I'll ask for it."

Shawn, shoulders stirring in resignation, moved on with Mason Lynch at his side. The crowd, ignoring the law-man's order, followed. As they stepped up onto the landing fronting the jail, Shawn looked back, saw several men helping the blond, still holding tight to his belly, into the Maricopa Saloon. Starbuck reckoned he shouldn't have hit the man such a punishing blow, but he'd asked for it.

"Keep your hands up," Huckaby ordered crisply, hurrying into the room behind them. "Stand over there against the wall—facing it."

Mason complied obediently. Starbuck, anger never decreasing, followed reluctantly. When he had taken his position, the lawman dropped back to the doorway.

"Homer—you and Pete Fortney, come in here. You too, Spearman. Want some witnesses." Huckaby paused, and as the men summoned thumped into the heat-packed

32

little office, he asked the crowd in general: "How about Kemmer? He hurt bad?"

"Nope," a voice replied. "Got knocked loose from his wind—and doing some puking. Said it felt like that jasper drove a knife clean through him."

The lawman grunted. "Well, you tell him if he gets to feeling right, he's to come over here. Being on the town council, he's in this, too."

Boot heels rapped on the bare floor again as the marshal turned back into the room. Shawn felt the weight on his hip lighten as his pistol was yanked from its holster.

"Turn around."

At the lawman's command Starbuck wheeled slowly, stiffly, keeping a tight grip on himself as he faced the four men standing behind the desk at the opposite end of the sweltering office. All were sweating freely, and one, a dark-bearded, elderly man, drew out a red bandanna, mopped nervously at his neck.

"Hurry this up, Virg," he said peevishly. "I got my place to look after."

Shawn took a half-step forward, words forming on his lips, checked when he felt Mason's finger press into his arm.

"Hold off. I got you into this—let me try getting you out."

"Be none of that!" Huckaby barked. "I want you to talk, I'll tell you."

Mason's shoulders stirred with indifference. "Happens this man here's my friend—only one I've got, far as I know—and I don't aim to see him hoorawed on account of me."

Huckaby laid the shotgun across the desk where it would be within quick reach, wagged his head. Pulling off his hat, he dropped it beside the gun.

"Don't try peddling that bull to me, Lynch. I know you and I figure anybody running with you's going to be the same stripe. What are you doing here?"

The arrogance of the question was like a slap in the face to Starbuck. "This is a free country. Expect he can go anyplace he likes!"

"Don't apply to him," commented the second of the men the lawman had called in—a balding, fat man with the smell of a livery stable to him.

"Applies to everybody—"

"Nope, not to him," Huckaby persisted stubbornly, verifying the other's contention. "You giving me an answer, Lynch?"

33

Mason said: "Came back for some things I've got stored away, left with some folks."

"What folks?"

"The Schmitts. A trunk of family things, keepsakes and the like."

"Heine Schmitt's place burnt down five year ago," Homer said. "Him and his missus were lost in the fire along with everything else inside the house."

Mason Lynch's head came up slowly as if in disbelief. The livery-stable man clawed at his chin. Beyond the doorway in the street a voice reported loudly: "Claims he come back to see old Heine Schmitt—"

"You'd best come up with a better answer'n that," Huckaby said drily.

"Only one I've got," Mason said in a weary tone. "The truth."

"Then there ain't no reason why you can't climb back on your horse and move on," the lawman said with finality. "The both of you."

"Don't count on me," Starbuck drawled, pushed as far as he intended to be. "I came here on some personal business, and I intend to see it through. I wind it up, I'll ride out. Now, that'd better suit you, Marshal, because that's the way it's going to be."

Huckaby's face colored darkly. Homer glanced at him, then at the pair with him. He wagged his head in dissatisfaction. "I don't like this, Virg—not a damned bit. Them two are up to something. They've got no call coming back here except to even up that score."

"Whatever that means—it's wrong," Shawn snapped. "Business I've got here is with a man working on a ranch called the Box C. Don't figure that it's any of your put-in, but a stranger seems to need a reason for coming to your town."

The room was in complete silence. Finally Huckaby spoke. "You say the Box C?"

"Got nothing to do with the Canfields and the trouble I had with them," Mason said hurriedly. "My friend here is named Starbuck, and he's looking for his brother. Thinks maybe one of the hands out there could be him."

Homer looked in scorn at the others, centered his attention on the lawman. "Man'd sure have to be mighty goddam dumb to swallow a yarn like that! Just happens to be going to see a cowboy who's working for the Canfields— the brothers of the man his partner Lynch here spent ten years in the pen for killing! Any fool can see what they've got in mind."

34

Shawn stared at Mason. The puzzling things concerning the man were making some sense now; the gap of years that had elapsed since the war's end, the deep-seated bitterness, the desperate but reluctant hopefulness overshadowed by some deep fear.

Mason felt the pressure of Starbuck's thrusting gaze. "Guess I should've told you—explained—"

"Something I'd best do—want him to get it straight," Huckaby broke in, his manner toward Shawn relenting somewhat as it became apparent to him that he was making a mistake insofar as the tall rider was concerned.

"This fellow you took up with on the trail is Mason Lynch. Born about twenty miles west of here—on the ranch you're talking about, the Box C. Only then it belonged to his folks and was just called the Lynch place. His pa and ma were the first people to settle here in the valley—that's why the town's named Lynchburg, after them. He tell you that?"

"Some of it," Starbuck replied, not wanting to make it any worse for Mason than it already was. But within him there was a smoldering resentment for the man; he had been a friend—Mason had not returned that friendship, had instead permitted him to become a part of his trouble, whatever it was.

"Before the war started everything was going along everyday like. Then Mason went off and when he came back four years later, he found his folks had died, and that they'd sold off their place to the Canfield brothers. Deal was made a few months before they passed on—a runaway accident. They'd been living right here in town, in Homer Boyd's hotel."

"Nobody'll ever make me believe they just up and sold out," Mason said in a low, dogged voice.

Virg Huckaby slapped the top of his desk in exasperation. "Goddammit—that's what got you in trouble before! They sold—and the Canfields have got the papers to show it."

"Anybody around here see my pa sign them papers? You see him do it, Marshal? Names can be forged."

"Wasn't nothing like that happened. Deal was all straight and legal, even if it wasn't made right under your nose. Anyway," Huckaby said, coming back to Shawn, "Mason here got all worked up and jumped Wade Canfield—there was three of the brothers—and they both went for their irons. Mason was a mite quicker, killed Wade. I barely got him out of town and hid before Kit

35

and Barney Canfield, and a bunch of their hired hands and friends, could get to him to string him up.

"Finally got him to a trial and the judge was right generous to him—because he'd been a soldier, I suspect. Gave him ten years in the pen instead of hanging him or putting him away for life, way most folks figured he ought've done."

Shawn Starbuck had listened in silence. It was not a new story, simply a variation of the old one; a man makes a mistake, pays for it—but there are those who will never let him forget. Unconsciously, his sympathies drifted to Mason.

"Most folks," Starbuck repeated the words carefully. "That include everybody besides the Canfields and their friends?"

Huckaby bristled slightly. "Most folks—just leave it at that," he said.

Mason stirred. "Reckon you can see now why they ain't exactly happy to see me around here."

Shawn nodded. "Think you've come back to kill off the rest of the Canfields—cause a lot of trouble for everybody."

"Only that's not it at all. I aim to move on. What I said was the truth—I left a trunk full of family belongings with the Schmitts. They say it got burned up so I've got no reason to hang around. I'm ready to ride on—"

"Except you're not going anywhere until that horse of yours gets some doctoring."

"The bay? What's the matter with him?" the livery-stable owner asked, looking through the dust-filmed window.

"Dry hoofs. Starting to split. Left front's pretty bad. I packed them in mud last night but having to ride him today sort of undid all the good. Needs more rest and doctoring."

The lawman swung to the stocky stable owner. "That right, Pete?"

"Can't tell from listening—have to look him over. Splitting sure can cripple a horse. But he was rode in and I don't recollect him being too lame. Expect, was I to work on him, he could be in shape tomorrow."

"Make it noon," Starbuck said, "and we'll both ride out. I'll have my business done with by then—and I sure don't want to hang around this town any longer'n I have to."

Huckaby's features darkened and his mouth tightened. "No need to get all het up now, friend. Only natural we'd be suspicious of Mason, showing up here like he has. And

36

you riding along with him—how was we to know you wasn't some hired gun he brought along to help out?"

"Same way that I know you're not Santy Claus," Starbuck answered, his voice sharp. "One thing the bunch of you could learn—don't go jumping to conclusions the first time you see a man. Could get yourself hurt bad one of these days." He paused, faced the lawman squarely. "It's settled?"

"It's settled," Huckaby replied. "You got till noon tomorrow. Long as you don't start trouble, you won't be bothered by me."

"Supposing somebody else starts it?"

"Don't let them. Walk off. I can't be responsible for what a lot of folks've got stuck in their craw, and if you think—"

"Virg," Homer Boyd cut in, staring through the open doorway into the street, "maybe you'd best hold up on that there agreement you're making. Here comes the Canfields. Kit and Barney both. Could be they might not go for it."

6

A splintery light came into Huckaby's black eyes and the corners of his mouth pulled down to hard lines. Mason Lynch shifted nervously.

"I'll be taking my gun back, Marshal."

"The hell you will," he said in a tightly controlled voice. "I'm the law around here—not the Canfields."

Horses pounded up to the hitchrack fronting the jail, halted. A babble of words sounded in the street and then boot heels rapped a quick, angry cadence on the pine landing. Shortly a ruddy-faced redhead with snapping blue eyes came through the doorway, followed by a larger, dark-haired man. The Canfields sure didn't look much alike, Shawn thought.

The redhead shot a hasty glance around the room, planted himself squarely before Mason Lynch. Lower jaw outthrust, hands on hips, he said: "You've got a hell of a lot of gall coming back here!"

"Ease off, Kit," Huckaby said stiffly. "Reckon he's got a right to—"

"No he ain't! Got no rights at all around here, far as I'm concerned! The sonofabitch lost them when he murdered Wade!"

"Went to the pen for that," Mason said woodenly. "Cost me ten years out of my life."

"Should've been hung!" Canfield snapped, whirling to Huckaby. "I want him out of here, Virg!"

The lawman's anger blazed instantly. "*You* want him out of here! Where do you get off giving orders like that? I'm the marshal here—not you."

The rancher's eyes squeezed down to narrow slots. "You heard me, Huckaby. I want him run out of town— clean out of the county, in fact—now!" He hesitated,

38

again swept the men in the tension-filled office with his brittle glare. "You don't—then by God, I will!"

"No," Huckaby said, plainly struggling to remain calm, suppress the anger that was ripping through him, "you won't do nothing! You hear me, Kit? I won't stand for you horning in!"

Canfield threw a glance to his closemouthed brother, Barney, looked beyond him to the crowd packed around the doorway looking in, avidly absorbing the controversy. A smirk crossed the rancher's face. He settled back on his heels in a satisfied sort of way, bucked his head at Huckaby.

"You forgetting who you're talking to?"

"No—it's you who's doing the forgetting—that I'm the law around here."

"Maybe not for much longer."

The marshal drew himself up to his full height. "Meaning you'll get my job. . . ."

Canfield's eyes shifted to the three men standing behind the desk, touched each with a warning definite as if it had been put into words: this was a matter in which they were not to meddle.

"Could say that. I recollect your appointment comes up again in a couple of months. Might just be the town could stand a change."

Huckaby's expression did not alter. "Been the law around here since before you come. Like as not I'll still be after you're gone."

"Don't bet on it," the rancher said, and, turning his back on the marshal, faced Mason. "Mount up!"

"Tomorrow," Lynch said, shaking his head. "Be gone by noon."

"Hell with that. I want you out of here now."

"He stays till noon, if he's of a mind," Huckaby said. "He has my permission."

"Permission—hell . . ."

"He can't leave, Mr. Canfield," Boyd interrupted, evidently feeling pressed to ignore the rancher's visual warning. "He's got a lame horse. Pete Fortney's aiming to work on him tonight. That's the reason Virg's letting him stay."

Kit Canfield wagged his head stubbornly. "I don't give a goddam for his reasons—his or anybody else's. I want him gone!"

Starbuck, silent through the exchange, shifted angrily, unable to restrain himself any longer. "Back off, Canfield," he said, folding his arms across his chest. "The man's paid for his mistake. You've got no call riding him."

39

Canfield shot a quick look at Shawn, his pale eyes sparking as he took in the well-worn trail clothing, the ragged, soiled hat. His lip curled back in disdain.

"Best you keep your snoot out of this—unless you're looking for trouble."

"Which maybe I am," Shawn said mildly.

Canfield's ruddy face darkened. "Who the hell are you, anyway?"

"Friend of Mason's. Like you've been told, we're pulling out tomorrow, come noon."

"Not good enough!" Canfield declared stubbornly. "I want him gone by sundown—and if he ain't—"

Barney Canfield reached out, laid a restraining hand on his brother's shoulder. "Simmer down, Kit. Tomorrow'll be all right. He ain't about to try anything."

The redhead threw the hand off impatiently. "How do you know he ain't?" He hesitated, as if struck by the thought, pivoted to Huckaby. "I'm asking you that, Mister Marshal. How do you know he ain't here to bushwhack me and Barney like he did Wade? You tell me how?"

The lawman's mouth tightened. "Man tells me he won't, I take his word."

"Word!" Kit Canfield exploded. "You mean you'd take the word of a goddam killer? What's the law coming to in this town?" he asked, turning to Fortney and the others. "I'm mighty sure we're needing a change when the man we've got wearing the star sides with a murderer against decent folks."

"I'm not taking sides," Huckaby said quietly. "You're twisting things around to suit yourself. Like Starbuck there said, Lynch's paid for that he's done, got a right to do what he likes long as he hurts nobody."

"Well, that ain't the way I see it!" Kit shouted, again knocking aside Barney's hand. "I'm serving notice on you right now, if you don't get him out of town by dark, I'm taking things into my own hands, doing it myself."

Fortney cast an alarmed look at Homer Boyd, the hotel owner. Spearman, the third man, who had stood by the entire time in stony silence, suddenly came to life.

"Now, Mr. Canfield, we can't go doing something that'll upset—"

"Upset—hell! What if it'd been your brother he shot down?"

"That was ten years ago," Huckaby said, gaining confidence from the support he appeared to be getting. "About time you forgot it. I gave Lynch and his friend permission to hang around until noon tomorrow—mostly because there's

40

not much else they can do. I'm standing by it—and you're not to come busting into town later with a bunch of your hired hands and trying to change it. You do and I'll get word to the United States Marshal in Tucson."

"He's right, Kit," Barney Canfield murmured. "We don't want no more killings. If Huckaby's willing to stick his neck out, guarantee we'll have no trouble from Lynch, I don't see nothing wrong with letting things slide till tomorrow noon. If he ain't gone by then—well, I figure we've got us a call coming."

"Be smarter to do something about it right now," Kit Canfield muttered. Sullen, he faced Huckaby. "All right, go ahead and do it your way, but you damn well better keep them locked up tight until its time for them to travel—"

"Not much you don't lock us up!" Starbuck said, coming into the conversation. "We've done nothing to get jailed for—and we're sure not sitting out the next eighteen hours in a cell just to please you."

The rancher spun to Shawn. "Goddam you—told you to keep your nose out of things that ain't none of your business!"

"Getting locked up in a cell for nothing is my business, and it'll take more than you—"

Canfield's hand swept down to the gun at his hip, checked abruptly as Huckaby caught up the double-barreled shotgun from his desk, brought it to bear on him.

"Figured it'd come to that," the lawman said in a low voice. "When you don't get your way, you try taking it. Now, best thing for everybody is for you to get out of town, and stay out. Forget about Lynch and Starbuck. I'll see to them."

Kit Canfield swore angrily, glared at Mason, who returned his stare with unblinking eyes.

"Huckaby's right," Barney said, taking a firm grip on his brother's arm this time. "Be smart to pull out, leave it up to him. It goes wrong, it'll be him we'll blame."

The redhead nodded slowly, seemingly calm now. "I'll do more than blame him," he said in a promising sort of tone, "I'll make him sorry he ever pinned on that badge!" Wheeling, he strode to the doorway, a rigid, outraged figure teetering on the edge of total violence, and halting, leveled a finger at the marshal.

"I'm not agreeing to this—want you to remember that. I'm just going along with you and them gutless bleeding hearts there behind you because Barney wants me to. Either one of us gets bushwhacked, I—"

41

"Ain't nobody going to get hurt—"

"You willing to guarantee that?"

The lawman, with the hating look of a man pushed to the wall, nodded impatiently. "All right, I'm guaranteeing it!"

Kit Canfield spat into the dust beyond the doorway, nodded abruptly, and with Barney at his heels, stepped out onto the landing. Immediately there was a flurry of questions from the bystanders in the street, all of which were ignored, and then the Canfields were mounted and spurring away.

For a time the men in the lawman's cramped quarters were still, and there were only the sounds from the street —the muffled words of those loafing about the front of the building, the more distant noises of the town's normal activities. Finally Pete Fortney heaved his bulk away from the wall against which he had been leaning, and rubbing his sweaty palms together in a nervous way, started for the door.

"Expect I'd better get that horse over to my place, start working on him. Sure don't want that to be the reason you can't leave tomorrow, Mason."

Boyd scratched at his beard, equally shaken. "God, no! Don't let nothing mess things up. If I know Kit, he'll do what he's threatening to."

Turned edgy by the words Canfield had whipped him with, Huckaby spun to the hotel man. "You saying I can't keep him or anybody else in line around here?"

"Not saying no such a damn thing! Only—"

Starbuck stepped into the sudden breech that could lead to more wrangling. "Be obliged if you'll take my sorrel along with the bay," he said to Fortney. "Give him a measure of grain along with the hay. Better watch the water—and I'd be obliged if you could find time to rub him down."

"Got the time," the stableman rumbled. "Two hostlers laying around the place most of the day, doing pure nothing. What about your gear?"

"Leave my saddlebags at the hotel when you go by. Aim to put up there for the night."

The tension in the heat-filled room had cleared. Fortney went through the doorway, muttered something to the crowd outside, crossed the street and took charge of the two horses. Homer Boyd and the tight-mouthed Spearman followed immediately, separating as they stepped into the open. Shawn looked questioningly at the lawman.

"We free to go?"

42

For a reply Virg Huckaby, his expression blank, slid Starbuck's pistol across the desk to him. Mason extended his hand. The marshal shook his head.

"Be getting yours back when you're ready to ride out. And I'm putting Starbuck in charge of you."

"Now, hold on!" Lynch protested. "That ain't right, you loading me onto his back. Doubt he'll want to be bothered anyhow."

"Said he was your friend, didn't you?"

"Sure, but that was before—"

Shawn stirred, wiped at the sweat on his face. "It's all right. I'm owning up to being considerable put-out at the way you kept me in the dark, but it's over and done with. Best thing we can do is forget it."

"Reckon I did look at it wrong, but I couldn't see no reason for telling you my troubles—not after what you done for me back there in that sink."

"What was that?" Huckaby asked, watching the two move for the doorway.

"Apaches. Had me cold. Starbuck saved my hide."

Huckaby nodded, thought for a moment. "Good. Then you ain't likely to cross him up, do something foolish."

"Not about to," Lynch replied soberly. "I ain't so stocked up with friends that I can afford to lose even one."

Again the lawman signified his approval. "See that you keep thinking that way. And watch your step, the both of you. Where you headed now?"

"After that beer we were thirsting for when you and that reception committee stopped us," Shawn said.

"Then you're going to the hotel—"

"Going to find ourselves a square meal first. Both a might gaunt."

"Try Ma Chuckson's. Grub's real good there. What about that personal business you mentioned? When you taking care of it?"

"Figured to ride out to the Box C first thing in the morning."

"And get your head blowed off," the lawman said sarcastically. "You loco or something?"

Starbuck scratched at the stubble on his jaw. He hadn't given that side of it much thought, being anxious to meet with Jim Ivory, but since the Canfields seemed to think he was a close friend of Mason Lynch's, possibly even a hired gun, it would be stupid just to go riding in. But it was an errand that had to be completed—the reason, in fact, that he was there. He shrugged.

"Have to manage it somehow."

43

"Best thing'll be for me to ride with you," Huckaby said. "Me and the Canfields don't see eye to eye on much of anything, but they ain't apt to try nothing with me along."

Starbuck agreed. "Be obliged to you. How about a beer with us?"

"Maybe later, thanks," the marshal said, and then as Shawn and Mason Lynch stepped out into the street, added, "You watch yourselves. Don't want no trouble."

"No trouble," Starbuck assured him, and with Mason at his side, walked through the few remaining onlookers yet gathered in front of the jail and crossed to the saloon.

7

Hostility, like a dark and solid mass, met them as they pushed through the saloon's swinging doors and halted in the smoke-filtered lamplight. The silence was abrupt, and as Shawn and Mason angled for the bar extending along the opposite wall, two men lounging against it took up their drinks, sauntered off into the scatter of tables and chairs to their right.

Starbuck, his sardonic eyes probing the large room, settled his attention on what appeared to be a congregation near center. He saw it was the man who had earlier pushed him and that he had subsequently dissuaded from further participation in the affair with a blow to the belly. Kemmer, Virg Huckaby had called him. Shawn remembered then: THE MARICOPA SALOON . . . FRED KEMMER, PROP., the sign outside had proclaimed. The man he'd slugged was the owner of the place. He gave Mason Lynch a wry grin.

"Seems I flattened the proprietor. You reckon our money'll be any good here?"

"Maybe not," Lynch replied as they halted at the long counter. "Not the only place in town."

But a moment later a balding man wearing an apron separated from a knot of sympathizers gathered around Kemmer, and moved in behind the bar.

"Beer," Shawn said, holding up two fingers.

The bartender drew two large mugs of the foaming brew, slid them across the counter. Starbuck passed a coin to the man, said, "Hold the change. We'll be wanting more," and followed Mason to a nearby table, where both sat down.

"Feels good," he said, sighing gratefully. "Tail of mine was beginning to grow to the saddle."

"Same here," Mason replied in a preoccupied sort of

45

way. He took a long swallow of his drink, set the glass back on the table. "Don't blame you for getting riled some at me. Reckon you'd like to hear some explaining now."

Starbuck shrugged, swished the amber liquid about in the container he was holding. "Little late," he said indifferently. "No surprises left. Don't bother if you're not of a mind."

Lynch bobbed his head. "Expect that's it—I want to. Nobody ever much listened to my side of the thing."

"That judge must have. Man's usually hung or sent to the pen for life when he kills somebody. Was something in your favor or it wouldn't have worked out that way. . . . You did kill Wade Canfield, didn't you?"

"Never denied that. Plenty of witnesses saw me. We were talking—was right out there in the street, in front of Gabaldon's Feed Store—about this thing of my pa selling out the place to him and his brothers.

"I was just back from the war feeling plenty busted down and out of everything. Then I was hit with the news of my folks being dead and the ranch being sold only a little while to the Canfields. Didn't make sense to me, and I told Canfield that. He didn't like the way I said it, I guess, and real quick got all fired up. He was a hotheaded one, like Kit. Next thing I knew I'd called him a liar. He went for his gun—I beat him to it. Was a dozen men who saw it."

"Long as he drew, seems more a fair fight to me."

"Only Wade Canfield was big shucks around here. Him and his brothers had brought a lot of money into the country and the town was doing right well from Canfield business. Me, the way they looked at it, brought nothing but trouble. Only natural they stood by the Canfields."

"Huckaby—seems I remember him saying he was the marshal here then, that right?"

"Virg's been marshal ever since I can recollect. Why?"

"He side with the townspeople and the Canfields?"

"About all I can say is that he seen to it that I didn't get lynched and that I got a trial."

Starbuck stared into his glass. The animosity that existed between the lawman and the Canfields was a definite force. It evidently had a basis other than Mason's trouble with the three brothers.

"But that judge was a squareshooter," Lynch went on. "Guess he sort of figured I had a break coming, sentenced me to only ten years." He hesitated thoughtfully, added: "Ten years—that's a hell of a long time."

Shawn took another swallow of beer. Some of the weariness had slipped from his long frame now as he sat in the cool depths of the shadowy saloon talking with Mason Lynch, hearing the voices of other men, savoring the odors of spilled liquor, sweat and dust, that were somehow agreeable.

"Your coming back here—it for the reason you say?"

"That's it. Wanted to pick up the stuff I'd left with the Schmitts." Lynch straightened slowly, eyes fixed upon Shawn. "You think I'm lying?"

"Not that, but since we're hashing this out I just want to get it all straight."

"You've got the truth. If my horse was able, I'd ride on right now. Got no more use for this bastard of a town than it has for me."

"Seen friendlier places," Starbuck murmured. "You still think the Canfields crooked your folks out of their ranch?"

"Thought about it a lot when I was laying it out in the pen. Still not convinced they sold—willingly, anyway—and I never will be."

"But you had a place of your own down in the Mescals and they knew you wouldn't be taking over their land when you came back. Makes sense to me they'd sell when they got the chance."

"Told myself that, and maybe down deep I believe it. But something won't let me admit it."

Shawn stirred. "You figure you're right, you ought to fight about it—only not with a gun. Get yourself a lawyer, let him dig into it. If there's been some crooking done, he'll find it."

"Mighty sure he would. Like—for one thing—where'd the money go? If the Canfield's paid the folks in cash, what happened to it? Nobody's ever been able to answer that, and there was so much dust got kicked up when I got hauled in for shooting Wade that it was lost in the shuffle."

Lynch settled back in his chair, moved his shoulders indifferently. "What the hell—I don't care now, anyway. It's all over and done with. The Canfields can have the damned place—and if I never set foot in this town again it'll still be too soon."

"Grew up here, didn't you?"

"Sure—"

"Little hard to forget that."

"Not for me—not when everybody figures you for a sonofabitch."

47

"Such a thing as a man coming back, facing up to what he's brought on himself, and living it down."

"Not worth it, far as I'm concerned. I'm going to crawl into my place in the Mescals and stay there. Be damned few times when I'll be visiting what folks call civilization because I aim to go only when starvation or something like that forces me to. I'm plumb sick of people and what they think and the million stinking laws they want a man to live by."

"There's only ten—the Commandments," Starbuck murmured. "Once heard a preacher point that out. All the rest, he said, were just little two-bit rules that men have added to the book and could be forgotten if a fellow would stick to the others."

Mason Lynch was silent for a time, then spoke again. "Reckon he's right, but it don't matter much to me now. All I want is to get off to myself, be left alone—see if I can learn to live again like a human's supposed to. In ten years a man can get out of practice."

Starbuck picked up the empty glasses, stepped to the bar and obtained refills. Setting them on the table, he resumed his chair, noting as he did that the crowd in the saloon was increasing steadily as the evening wore on.

"Being alone's not going to help much," he said after a bit. "There nobody waiting for you—a girl, maybe?"

"Was one," Mason said heavily. "If I hadn't of wound up in the pen we'd likely have married. Doubt if she's around now—and if she is, she'd be married and have herself a passel of kids."

"Never know about women. Wouldn't hurt to look her up."

A frown drew Mason's brows together. "You think—after ten years she might—"

"Like I said, women are hard to figure."

Lynch dropped his eyes. "No, not much chance of that," he said disconsolately. "But I reckon it wouldn't hurt to ask about her. Aim to go out to Ma and Pa's graves, too. Can do it all in the morning when you're seeing this Jim Ivory fellow. Good thing you've got the marshal going with you. Them Canfields'd never let you get off the place alive."

"Not so sure the marshal will get any better welcome than I will. Seems to be plenty of fire between him and Kit."

"Got the same idea. Canfields are pretty strong around here now, got the say-so, more or less, as to who'll wear

that star, and they figure Virg Huckaby ought to be kow-
towing to them."

"Only he doesn't see it that way. Look on his face when
Kit made that threat was pure hate. Speaking of looks, Kit
and Barney sure don't favor each other. This Wade, the
one you tangled with, he look like either one of them or
was he something different yet?"

"Him and Kit are alike—both redheads. Barney's no
blood kin—a stepbrother."

"What about those three the marshal called in?" Shawn
continued. "You know them from away back or are they
johnny-come-latelys?"

"Pete—Pete Forney, he's the stable owner, I know him.
And Homer Boyd, the one with the black beard. He runs
the hotel—the Mogollon. One he called Spearman is a
stranger to me. Sign down the street says he runs a saddle
and gun shop."

"How about Kemmer, owner of this place?"

"He was the bartender when I was last in here—ten
years or so ago. Don't know what happened to Tom
Keuhne. Like my folks and the Schmitts, he was one of
the old bunch. Some've died off and there's a few I guess
who've moved on where they can maybe make a better
living. Why?"

"Always like to get things squared away in my head so
if trouble pops up I sort of know who I can figure will do
what."

"If it does, don't look for help from anybody around
here. Whole bunch'll be looking out for themselves."

"Reckon that's normal," Shawn drawled, stretching his
long legs and sighing comfortably. "Folks sort of lean to
looking out for themselves, especially if they've invested a
lifetime getting where they are."

"You think Virg Huckaby's that way, too?"

"Can't quite make up my mind about him. Got a tough
job trying to keep the peace and still make everybody
happy. Always somebody with an ax to grind putting the
heat on a lawman."

"Like Canfield was doing today."

"Yeh . . . and all the time he was standing there bucking Kit Canfield he knew the merchants would probably
line up with him and his brother if it ever comes to a real
showdown."

"Kind of surprised me—him bellying up to Kit the way
he done."

"Didn't have a choice if that star means anything to
him. Figured once he let the Canfields grab the hoe han-

49

dle, he'd be walking on his knees to them from that minute on."

"Lot of hate inside Virg Huckaby for Kit," Mason said thoughtfully. "Like to know what caused it—but then Kit's the kind that's easy to hate, always causing trouble—"

"Which I reckon's on the way now," Starbuck cut in lazily and nodded at the Maricopa's entrance.

The Canfield brothers had just entered and halted in front of the batwings. Kit, jaw outthrust, swept the saloon with his arrogant glance. Locating Shawn and Mason Lynch, he said something over his shoulder to Barney, and then the two started forward.

Both Canfields had been drinking, Starbuck observed, but they were far from drunk as the pair swaggered up to the table. Kit stopped in front of Mason Lynch. Barney Canfield was a stride or so behind him.

"Get out, jailbird," the redhead said, jerking his thumb at the doorway. "You're leaving town."

Mason did not stir as the racket inside the saloon died rapidly. Shawn, tension building suddenly within him, drew himself up in his chair, draped one arm over the back.

"Move on, Canfield," he said softly. "We don't want trouble."

"Asked for it the minute you rode into town," the rancher countered. Swinging half around, he touched the saloon patrons with his glance as if inviting all present to hear and bear witness. "Changed my mind about the two of you—you're pulling out."

"No, I reckon not," Starbuck said. "We made a deal with the marshal, and you agreed to it—"

"Huckaby made you a deal, not me! Told everybody plain I thought it was a fool thing to do."

"You agreed, just the same—"

"The hell I did!" he shouted, wiping flecks of saliva from his mouth. "Was Huckaby and you in on it. I just went along. Got to studying on it, knew I was right, so I come back to straighten it out."

Canfield's raised voice was a powerful magnet drawing the crowd in nearer. Men began to line up along the polished counter; others continued the string into a half-circle that enclosed the Canfields and the two men at the table. The bartender, joined now by a recovered Fred Kemmer, had changed his position, stood now at the near end where he would miss nothing.

51

Shawn wagged his head slowly. There was a coolness to him, a quiet, unruffled veneer on the surface, but underneath all was boiling turbulence, crystallizing steadily into the hard-core anger men such as Kit Canfield always created within him.

"No matter how you brand it," he said, "you're backing out—welching—not standing by your word."

Canfield's red-lidded eyes flared. "Don't you go lecturing me, you goddam saddlebum!"

"Somebody ought to. Leastwise, somebody ought to teach you that a man's only as good as his word. Now Mason couldn't leave here if he was willing. Horse of his can't be ridden. You know that."

"You're goddam right I know it—and I fixed it! I'm giving you a horse. Lynch. Trading you a sound animal for that bonerack you're forking. No reason now why you can't move on."

A rueful smile crossed Mason's face. "Expect that's just what you're hoping I'll do—light out on a Box C horse. Wouldn't get five miles before you'd be coming to string me up for a horse thief."

"You'll get a bill of sale," Barney Canfield said, breaking his silence. "It's an honest offer—and better'n you deserve."

Starbuck came up stiff in his chair, irritated by the statement. "Why's that? Why is it more than he deserves? Way I see it his debt to you has been wiped out. He paid what the law said he owed for doing what he did. Come to think about it, maybe it's the other way around—maybe you owe him something. So why would trading him horse for horse be more than he deserves?"

The Canfields stared at Shawn, a puzzled look on their slack faces. His words were over their heads and completely beyond understanding. A man at the bar said something in a low breath and the one next him laughed. Kit Canfield's eyes flashed with anger and his face darkened. He flung a furious glance in that direction, rocked forward toward Shawn, began to jab at him with a forefinger.

"I don't know what the hell you're talking about, buddy," he snarled, "but whatever it is, I don't like it! Now, you and that yellow-bellied killer sidekick of yours harness yourself up and be on your way inside thirty minutes or, by God, I'll—"

The anger within Shawn Starbuck surfaced. He came to his feet in a smooth, deceptively fast motion, knocked the rancher's hand aside. The points of his jaw showed white

52

through his short stubble of beard and a hard glitter filled his eyes. He had tried to avoid trouble—but a man can take only so much.

"No need waiting, Canfield—you can start the ball right now. We're not leaving until tomorrow."

"The hell you ain't!" Canfield yelled, and swung a looping right at Starbuck's head.

Shawn blocked the blow easily with his left forearm—remembered suddenly that he had in plain words promised Virg Huckaby that he'd sidestep trouble—and catching the rancher by the shoulders, threw him back into the crowd.

"Go on home, Canfield," he said. "I don't want to fight you."

"You're sure as hell going to anyway!" Canfield shouted, beside himself with rage, and lunged.

Starbuck stepped quickly away from the table and chairs, wanting no encumbrances underfoot. He could hear the crowd yelling encouragement to the rancher, and there was a steady swishing of the batwings as more onlookers poured in from the street.

"Give him a lick or two for me, Kit!" Fred Kemmer called from behind the bar. "I'm owing him."

Canfield rushed in. Wheeling fast, Shawn halted him with a stiff left that spun the man half around. As Canfield struggled to regain his balance, Starbuck stung him sharply with several jabs to the face, crossed with a right that smacked loudly, and then danced away.

The rancher, hands dangling loosely at his sides, looked about stupidly as if not certain what had happened. The hard blows had fallen swiftly, seemingly from nowhere. He continued to hang motionless, as if listening to the yelling of the crowd, and then Barney Canfield stepped in, swung him around to where he could see Starbuck waiting patiently.

Shaking his head to clear away the webs, Canfield shuffled forward, his boots making dry, scraping sounds on the bare floor. Abruptly he swore, lowered his shoulders, charged.

"Goddam you!" he shouted, boring in with both arms flailing.

Shawn gave way before the furious rush, taking several retreating steps. He felt hands against his shoulders, realized he had backed into the crowd—into someone.

"Here he is, Kit!" Barney Canfield said, and pushed.

Starbuck stumbled forward, went head-on into a hail of rocklike fists. He weathered the onslaught, danced aside, feeling the sting and throb where the rancher's knuckles

53

had smashed into him. He tossed a side glance to Barney Canfield, regarded him with a grim, promising smile, and then squared away to meet the encouraged redhead rushing in once more.

"One of them fancy dans!" a voice cried as Shawn dropped into a stance. "Look at the way he's holding his fists!"

"Show him how a real man fights, Kit!" another added.

Canfield slowed, shuffled to a halt, smirking broadly as he regarded Starbuck. "One of them show kind, eh? Always did want to try my luck."

"Now's your chance," Shawn murmured, and flicked the rancher lightly across the eyes.

Canfield bellowed, plunged forward. Starbuck feinted, shifted fast, crossed with a right that brought Kit to a flat-footed halt. Smooth and quick, Starbuck cut back, stabbed a straight left into the rancher's face. A trickle of red began to flow from Canfield's nose. Not delaying, Shawn struck again, this time with a right that thudded.

The blow was too high on Canfield's head to do any great amount of damage, only caused him to blink, take a staggering step sideways. Starbuck, weaving, dodging, shifted to the man's right watching for another opening.

From the tail of his eye he saw motion, ducked away, spun. Barney Canfield was stepping in behind him once again. At the same instant Mason Lynch yelled a warning to that effect, Shawn came full around, unleashed a cocked fist. It caught the dark-haired Canfield on the ear, sent him sprawling to the floor.

"Stay there, damn you," Starbuck muttered through clenched teeth and wheeled to face the brother.

The rancher had taken advantage of the interruption. He was closing in fast. Shawn rocked back on his heels as a fist drove into his midsection, winced when a knotted fist grazed his jaw. Sucking for wind, he instinctively dropped low, getting beneath the pistonlike action of the man's arms, pivoted on a heel and spun away. Before Canfield could adjust to the swift change, Starbuck wheeled again, bobbed to the side, and came in, his left jabbing viciously, right shaped into a lump hard as granite, poised like a rattlesnake waiting to strike. Abruptly he found the opening.

The streaking blow found the point of Canfield's jaw. The rancher's head flew back, his arms dropped limply to his sides. Eyes rolling wildly, he staggered to one side, halted. Strength deserted him. He sank to his knees, braced himself with extended arms to prevent complete collapse.

Shouts came from the crowd, urgent cries to get up, to finish the fight, show the fancy dan. Shawn, sweat pouring off his face, waited. He slid a glance to Barney Canfield, half expecting him to make some sort of move. The younger Canfield, hand clapped to his ear, seemed content only to watch.

Kit Canfield shook his head, pulled himself laboriously to an unsteady, upright position. Rubbing at his eyes, he turned about, faced Shawn. As their glances locked, the rancher's slack jaw tightened, his arms came up with great effort, and he stumbled forward, game but almost out on his feet.

Starbuck dropped his guard, moved away, permitted the rancher to reel by. Commotion in the crowd drew his attention. Looking up, he saw Virg Huckaby pushing into the center of the cleared area. As Kit Canfield righted himself, wheeled awkwardly, and started again for Shawn, the lawman caught him by the arms, pushed him back.

"Be enough of this!" the marshal snapped.

"Leave me be—damn you—" Canfield mumbled thickly. Wrenching free, he threw himself at Starbuck.

Shawn avoided the wildly swinging fists, maneuvered about to where he was behind the dazed rancher, and again taking him by the shoulders, propelled him toward one of the chairs and shoved him into it. Turning, Shawn motioned to Barney Canfield.

"He's your kin—look after him."

The younger brother's eyes flashed. "He's full growed —let him look after himself."

Continuing on, Starbuck returned to the table where Mason Lynch waited. He was breathing hard and several places in his body ached dully from the blows he'd taken from Kit Canfield. Picking up his mug of beer, he slaked the dryness in his throat, nodded crisply to Mason.

"Let's get out of here—get something to eat." His voice was taut, reflected the anger that still rolled through him.

Mason, smiling broadly, unable to hide his admiration, said, "Sure, sure—any time you're ready. Man, what a trimming you gave Kit! He'll be healing up from that one for a long time."

"Expect he'll live through—"

"What started this?"

At Huckaby's harshly put question, Shawn turned. He was expecting to be crawled by the lawman for becoming involved in the fight—but he was in no mood to take a tongue lashing for it.

"Kit—ordering us to ride out tonight," Lynch said, replying for Starbuck.

"I told you to stay out of trouble—"

"You should have told Canfield that!" Starbuck countered.

The lawman's lips pulled into a thin line and his small eyes sparked. Shifting his glance, he looked to where Kemmer's bartender was pouring a tumbler full of whiskey for the battered rancher. A subtle expression of satisfaction stole across Huckaby's features—and Shawn had a fleeting wonder as to his inner feelings—wondered, too, how long the marshal might have stood outside, beyond the swinging doors, and observed the fight before putting in his official appearance.

"Reckon Kit got more'n he bargained for," Huckaby said. "You're a real handy-andy with them fists of yours."

"His pa was a sort of champion," Mason volunteered. "Shawn learned from him."

A glass crashed to the floor, shattered, as Kit Canfield swept the table before him clean, struggled to his feet. Eyes blazing, he glared at the men surrounding him.

"Leave me alone! Don't need none of you—hear?"

His brother, Barney, the side of his face now swollen and discolored, moved in closer as the bystanders fell back. "Let's be getting back to the ranch, Kit. Supper'll be waiting, and we've got to—"

"The hell with the ranch—the hell with you!" the redhead shouted, stepping back. Colliding with a chair, he kicked it aside savagely. "The hell with every goddam one of you!" he added, and crossing to the doorway, knocked the batwings aside and disappeared into the street.

9

Silent and chagrined, Barney Canfield followed his brother into the falling darkness. Huckaby shook his head. "He ought to take Kit home. Be trouble around here to-night sure as hell, if he don't."

"Lock him up," Starbuck suggested indifferently.

The lawman brought his attention back to Shawn, squinted at him narrowly. "Just might do that, if it gets needful. Was a mighty fierce working-over you gave him. Did I hear Mason say you were some kind of a champion?"

"No, it was my pa—and he wasn't a champion, just plenty good at it."

"That buckle you're wearing, it yours or his?"

"His." Shawn glanced at Lynch. "We going after something to eat?"

Mason started to rise, hesitated as the marshal laid a hand on his shoulder, pressed him back.

"Was a man killed down in Las Cruces, over New Mexico way, about a year ago. Was by a fellow fighting the way you were doing—boxing as you call it."

Starbuck came to attention, not sure of what the lawman was getting at but instantly alerted, as always, when someone with training in scientific fisticuffs was mentioned; there was always the possibility that the person involved could be Ben.

"So?"

"Seeing you at it there set me to wondering—you ever in Las Cruces?"

Shawn laughed, the blunt accusation showing through the question. "Wasn't me, Marshal. Been through the town a couple of times but I never got in any fights. This man you're looking for, he charged with murder?"

"That's what it is—murder."

"How'd you hear about it?" Starbuck asked, sitting down and shoving a chair at Huckaby. "You get a wanted dodger on the man?"

Ordinarily such a poster would carry a picture of the sought-for criminal, or if none was available, a description would be given. Evidently the latter was true, otherwise Huckaby wouldn't have asked his question; but a detail of the boxer's appearance, and a name, could prove of great value in providing a lead on Ben.

"Nope, nothing like that," Huckaby said, settling onto the chair. "Sheriff of that county rode through asking about such a man. Asked me to keep my eyes peeled."

Shawn's hopes withered. "Well, sure wasn't me."

He let it drop there, not wishing to mention the name of Jim Ivory and the possibility of him being Ben. He was not certain if the lawman was acquainted with Ivory and he would as soon not point suspicion in that direction until he had met and talked with the man.

Huckaby said, "Didn't much think you were. Seems the fellow he was talking about was short, and he'd be older'n you, by several years, if I recollect rightly. You're sure going to need some helping going out to the Canfield's now. What time in the morning you want to leave?"

Shawn was only half listening, was already laying plans to visit the old settlement of The Crosses and make inquiries as to the boxer being sought for murder—should his meeting with Jim Ivory prove unproductive. It was not a comforting thought that Ben could be wanted by the law, but there was that possibility, since skilled boxers were not plentiful along the frontier.

"You hear me?"

Shawn became aware of the lawman's raised voice, said: "Sorry, Marshal, guess I was thinking hard. You ask me something?"

"Want to know what time we're riding out to the Box C."

"Any time suits me. How about nine o'clock? Feel like I'm going to be real lazy once I crawl into a bed."

"All right, nine o'clock," Huckaby said, and got to his feet. "Be seeing you then—"

"Marshal," Lynch broke in, "something I'd like to ask before you go."

Huckaby frowned, rested both hands on the back of his chair. "Let's hear it."

"The Hope family—they had that little place down by the creek—they still around?"

A stillness came into the lawman's features. "No, they moved away a long time back—leastwise, Tom and his missus did."

"The girl—Marie. What became of her?"

The lawman shrugged. "Reckon I'd forgot about Marie and you." He studied the backs of his weathered hands. "She's one of the women at Frisco's—bawdy house at the edge of town."

Mason's eyes closed slightly as if he had been struck with sudden and intense pain. He lowered his head. "How —what happened?"

"Same thing that usually happens to a lone woman. Her folks were around here for six, seven year after you left. Marie lived with them, had herself a job table-waiting at the old Elite Café, and then later on at Ma Chuckson's. Then she up and got herself married, and right after that her folks pulled out. Went back to Nebraska, somebody said."

"Who'd she marry?" Lynch asked with no great interest.

"Don't recollect his name now—didn't know him, actually. Was a cowhand working on a ranch east of here. Decent sort of fellow, I reckon, but he went and got himself killed—gored by a steer. Well, they didn't have no money, of course, so Marie came back here after it was all over, got herself a job in Newt Duckworth's saloon. Was all she could find.

"Then she up and quit there, sort of, well—dropped out of sight for a time. Next thing I knew she was at the Frisco House—and I didn't know that until she come in one day to bail out some drummer she'd been laying up with."

"God—I never thought . . ."

"Don't you go faulting her none!" Huckaby said sharply. "Was what she had to do, I reckon."

"Not blaming her," Lynch replied in a lifeless tone.

"Well, you want to see her, she'll be at the Frisco House. You know where it is."

"I know," Mason said.

The lawman nodded his head at Starbuck, turned away, and moved for the swinging doors. Shawn studied his friend's dark, bitter features for a long minute, and then realizing the man's trend of thought should best be changed, pushed back his chair.

"We were heading for a square meal," he said, "one that won't have a cupful of sand mixed in it. You know where this Ma Chuckson place is?"

Lynch stirred, got to his feet. "Next to the hotel."

Starbuck said, "Lead the way," and throwing a glance at the men still in the saloon, trailed Mason to the batwings and out onto the gallery that fronted the building. Again he looked over the room; no one had made a move to follow. He sighed gratefully, guessed the affray with Kit Canfield had generated no other challengers honing to try their skill, as was quite often the case; he was dog-tired and he had enough aches and bruises to last for a while.

"There it is," Lynch said, pointing to a low-roofed structure squatting alongside the Mogollon Hotel.

They crossed over, entered a clean, well-lit room where a dozen or so small tables with complementing quartettes of hard-backed chairs were distributed in a precise arrangement that made the most of all available space. Three were occupied, and Shawn and Mason selected a vacant one near the window. The street was quiet now as darkness had settled over the town, dispelling some of the heat and bringing a softness to the hardlined structures along the dusty way.

An elderly woman appeared, gave them an impersonal appraisal, took their orders for steak, potatoes, biscuits, and coffee without unnecessary comment, then returned to the rear of the establishment where the kitchen evidently lay, walking with the heavy-footedness of one sick to death of her work.

The meal was excellent in Starbuck's estimation, and Mason, now more silent and withdrawn than ever, laconically agreed. Finished, they went back to the street, stood for a time in the cool shadows, enjoying the break in the heat as the settlement gradually awoke to the night. But the day had been a long, hard one, and Starbuck began to consider the comforts of a soft bed. He glanced at the hotel.

"I'm about to get myself caught up with, so I think I'll turn in. You ready?"

Mason was staring off down the street toward a small, white church where a bell was tolling the members to evening prayer meeting.

"No—you go ahead. I'm kind of jumpy. Don't think I could go to sleep was I to try."

"You got something special in mind to do?"

Mason shook his head. "Thought maybe I'd mosey around a bit, just looking. Might visit Ma and Pa's graves, do a little listening to the church services."

"Go ahead. I'll get a room for the both of us. The clerk'll tell you which one."

"Fine," Lynch said and moved off into the soft darkness. "See you later."

Starbuck turned to the steps leading up onto the Mogollon's porch. "Good night," he answered.

10

Mason Lynch slowed, watched Shawn cross the hotel's narrow gallery and disappear through the doorway into the lobby. He moved on then, the irony of the situation striking hard at him in that moment; he was in his own home town, among persons he knew, perhaps had even grown up with, yet his only friend was an outsider—a stranger he had encountered on the trail.

But he guessed no one was to blame but himself, even for the way things had turned out for Marie Hope. If he hadn't lost his head that day and cut down Wade Canfield, like as not he and Marie would be happily raising a family and building a ranch—in that order—down in the Mescal Mountain country.

He strolled on, noting idly the storefronts—some familiar, some new: Dr. Amos Hewlett . . . Cornman's Hardware Store . . . Mrs. Broadwell, Ladies & Childrens Ready-to-Wear . . . Pete Gabaldon, Feed & Seed . . . Sam Lingle, Gen'l. Mdse. . . . His wandering gaze stopped on that long, narrow building with its warped, paint-scaled false front. Did Sam Lingle still own what evidently was still Lynchburg's largest store? Sam had been an old man fourteen years ago.

Traffic along the street was light, and he saw only a few persons along the plank sidewalks—none he recognized or that acknowledged him. Several men lounged around the front of the Maricopa, and as he passed, aware of the tinkling of the piano, the muffled drone of voices and smells of beer and whiskey, something was said and there was a cautious laugh among the loafers.

Mason dismissed it without second thought. In the decade that had passed under the most trying and degrading of circumstances, he had learned the futility of taking offense at every disparaging remark cast his way as well as

62

acquiring a philosophy for survival—accept the cards dealt you, play them as best you can. There was actually little in life worth fighting for.

He drew abreast the Rawhide Saloon—Newt Duckworth's place—and slackened his step. Marie had been forced to work there for a time, he recalled Huckaby saying, and for several minutes he stood quietly in the warm night staring past the open doorway into the murky, smoke-filled depths of the small building.

It was hard to think of her working there—a third-rate establishment with no tables, no music, no gambling or dancing. What use would Duckworth have for a girl employee? His was the sort of place that catered to men seeking to get thoroughly and quietly drunk at the cheapest rates.

A yellow-wheeled surrey rolled into the north end of the street, its iron tires making a grating sound as they sliced through the sandy soil, the sleek-looking matched grays stepping proudly on their way to some destination at the opposite end of the settlement. A man and a woman occupied the front seat—two small children were in the rear. Strangers, too—newcomers to the area. Mason reconsidered that thought, corrected himself; after ten years' absence he reckoned he was the newcomer.

The strains of "Onward Christian Soldiers," sung with fervor and abetted by the solid thump of a piano, drifted to him from the open doorway of the church, now just ahead. With the hymn ringing in his ears, he entered the yard, circled the narrow, white structure with its steep, gable roof, came to the small cemetery lying behind it.

Weeds had made good progress with the two graves, and he spent a quarter-hour policing the mounds and re-setting the wooden markers which time and the elements had conspired to tilt. The lettering, skillfully carved into the pine by the church sexton, was still legible, but just barely. Now that he had returned maybe he could replace the wood with stone or marble. It would take a little money, something he was plenty shy of at the moment, but later, perhaps—if things went well.

His thoughts halted as his eyes reached down the darkened street, moving past the squat adobe huts occupied by the Mexican people, and settled on the two-storied bulk of the Frisco House, standing silent and apart from all others.

Instantly Marie Hope was again in his mind, provoking memory, and giving rise to a vague, lonely aching. He was remembering her as he last saw her—dark eyes, smooth face sober, hair gathered in a bun on her neck as she stood in the crowd and watched him, cuffed and shackled, climb into the stagecoach with the U.S. Marshal who was taking him to prison.

He never saw or heard from her after that final moment. No letter writer himself, he would have found little opportunity in those first two years behind the grim walls of the penitentiary, even had he been so inclined, as brutal punishment details, designed to break the will and spirit, were a daily fare.

And after that, when matters eased off more or less into a dreary, monotonous routine, it was too late. Marie would certainly have forgotten him, for no word had ever arrived from her—not that such was proof she had never written; letters from home, more often than prison officials would admit, somehow failed to get delivered. But it was better to assume that she had forgotten him, had simply given him up; it was the only practical thing for her to do.

Now he wondered about her; had she changed? Would she be thinking of him, too, when word of his return reached the Frisco House—which it probably had by that hour? He shrugged. Likely Marie would give him no thought at all. He was a closed chapter in her life—meant nothing. Unquestionably the years of bitter tribulations had marked her appearance; as to her heart and soul, there could be no doubt of it.

Crossing to a log bench someone had thoughtfully placed beneath the spreading trees at the edge of the fenced plot, Mason sat down. The lilacs strung along the back of the area had bloomed and were now without fragrance; but wafting in from some close-by location was the odor of honeysuckle, and he sat for a time enjoying its sweetness and remembering how his mother had coddled and coaxed a vine to grow above the kitchen window of the old place.

The singing inside the church had ended and he could hear the deep-throated voice of a man—the minister, he assumed—exhorting his flock to walk the path of righteousness. The words were mostly unintelligible to Lynch but their urgency was undeniable, and he thought back to long ago when he, too, at the inflexible insistence of his parents, had regularly taken his place on one of the hard-bottomed pews and been fed a diet of salvation.

Those had been good times, and recalling them awakened pleasant memories; but there was no profit in thinking of days gone—for there was no method of changing what had happened. He had come to realize that just as no

64

man had ever yet found a place where he could hide from himself, so also was it equally impossible for him to undo the mistakes he had made. It was a fact of life of which he had always been aware, but it had taken a decade for him to fully comprehend the meaning.

Head down, Mason sat in the darkness of the sweetly scented night, only partly conscious of the singing again pouring from the throat of the little church, of the black, star-spangled canopy above him, of the gradually decreasing activity along the street as the hour grew late. He knew only a nagging, persistent longing that throbbed deep in his mind to see Marie, perhaps even talk to her. What she was now did not matter, nor was there any desire within him to avail himself of her talents; it was senseless, useless, but the need simply to look at her once more was pushing at him with irresistible force.

Rising, he started back through the cemetery, following the path that wound among the graves and led finally to the churchyard. The congregation had departed, and glancing through the still-open doorway into the lighted sanctuary, he could see the minister, a tall, lonely figure, standing off to one side reading from a book.

Continuing, Mason turned into the narrow side street and made his way along the darkened huts toward the distant, taller structure of the Frisco House. Now and then a dog barked at his passage, and once he heard a child crying as if frightened by something in the dark.

Arriving there, he halted in the shadow of the long-abandoned stable that stood directly across from the large building. Once the place had been a stopping point for stage-coaches, with the depot on the ground floor, the upper level arranged in a series of rooms available to travelers who wished to lay over, rest briefly from whatever rigorous journey they were making. The stable where the teams were fed and sheltered had been erected conveniently near, with the holding corral—now a square of staggering, rotting posts—to the south.

All had been abandoned for newer quarters in the settlement at some time during the years when he was away fighting the war, and a minor boom was taking place in Lynchburg. It had been called the Frisco House then, and as is quite often the way, the name stuck, was never dropped regardless of the change in the nature of the tenantry.

It now appeared to be in total darkness, but it was a deceptive impression. Light streaks lay along the edge of shades not completely drawn or that ill fitted their window

65

frames, and from the squares of different-colored glass panes making up the front door—once a solid slab of thick wood—there issued a muted glow.

Abruptly that door opened and a slash of lamplight broke through the night, illuminating a rectangle of the weedy yard momentarily and offering a quick glimpse into the garishly furnished entry hall before it swung closed again.

The man who had emerged made his way unsteadily along the well-beaten walk, veering sharply once when his faltering legs carried him into a thorny bush of wild roses, came finally to the street. He pulled to a wavering halt there, got his bearings firmly established, and then began the trek back to the settlement.

Lynch stood for a time contemplating the weaving shadow, seemingly ricocheting from one side of the roadway to the other, and when it had at last vanished into the darkness, brought his eyes back to the building before him.

Uncertainty again possessed him. There was no sensible reason to see Marie, much less talk with her. It could result only in the reopening of old wounds, raking fresh the thinly healed scars. Yet . . .

On impulse he stepped from the doorway of the stable, crossed the street, and started up the path leading to the front steps. Reaching there he once more paused, torn again by indecision. He swore silently at himself; once such irresolution had been no part of his character—but after ten years during which all thinking, all decisions had been done for him, it had become a way of life.

Still vacillating, he turned from the path, moved to the window immediately to his left, where a strip of light separated the shade's lower edge and the sill. It would be better, perhaps, first to have a look inside. Standing close to the wall, he peered through the narrow opening. This had been the main room of the depot, he recalled. Now it was the Frisco House's parlor, replete with plush chairs and couches, a massive table with fancy, scrolled legs, carpeting on the floor and framed prints on the papered walls.

A thick-bodied woman was in one of the larger chairs. Her hair was a startling yellow, like the goldpoppys that cover the slopes in spring, and as she knitted at some sort of garment, face tipped down, she was talking steadily.

Mason shifted to the opposite side of the window, where he had a different view of the room. Two younger women were seated on a couch placed against the near

66

wall, one leafing through an old, well-handled magazine, the other staring absently at one of the pictures on the wall. He felt his throat tighten as he recognized the latter. It was Marie.

In silence he stood there, leaning against the cool stone of the old building, eyes riveted to the girl. She had changed, of course. Thinner by considerable, her face almost gaunt and now turned ugly by the rouge and rice powder so generously applied. But her eyes were the same —or so he thought. A moment later she turned and looked directly toward the window as if suspecting someone's presence.

There was change. No longer did they have the soft, doelike quality that had made of her, a girl of only ordinary attractiveness, one of quiet, stirring beauty. Her eyes now were dull, sunken, filled with a listlessness that bespoke the desperation that filled her.

Mason Lynch drew back, a sickness gripping him. He had made her that way. He had been the cause of it—him and his anger and his unwillingness to accept what he did not want to face. Now it was too late to make amends, to try and right the wrong he had done. Or was it? Should he talk to her, tell her of his plans for the place in the Mescals—ask her to become a part of it, of his future? Would she listen—or would she laugh in his face?

The light running sound of an approaching horse reached him. He glanced to the street. A rider was coming up from town. Stepping into the tangle of unkempt shrubbery growing along the wall, he watched the horseman, vaguely familiar, swing into the stable, reappear shortly on foot. Entering the yard, he crossed to the porch in purposeful steps and halted before the door.

The night suddenly echoed with his impatient pounding as he demanded entry. The door flung back. Mason's lips curled as light fell upon the now easily recognizable figure of Kit Canfield. Then all was again plunged into darkness as the rancher entered and the multicolored panel closed behind him.

For several moments Mason Lynch did not stir, and then drawn by some irresistible force, he returned to his place at the window. Canfield, a bottle of whiskey in one hand, had entered the room, was standing before the two girls on the couch. His face was swollen, dark with bruises from the beating Shawn Starbuck had given him, and as he reached down, grasped Marie by the wrist, and pulled her upright, there was a brutish anticipation in the slackness of his hard grin.

Pushing her toward the stairway, he followed, saying something to the woman with the yellow hair as he passed, laughed. The woman joined in, dutifully it seemed, and thoughtfully watched the rancher climb the steps; then shaking her head, she resumed her knitting.

Mason continued to stand at the window, staring into the room but seeing nothing while an unreasoning, towering rage hammered at him. Kit Canfield and Marie—his Marie! Goddam the man to hell! If he had a gun he'd . . . he'd . . .

Town Marshal Virgil Huckaby stood in the dark passageway separating Spearman's and the widow Broadwell's establishments, and there wholly unnoticed by the few persons wandering along the street soaking in the evening coolness, maintained his watch on the side door of Duckworth's saloon, into which Kit Canfield had disappeared an hour or so earlier.

There was no mystery as to what lay behind the door; it was the living quarters of the new girl Duckworth had brought in from Prescott to work for him. By rights she should be in the saloon now, helping Newt behind the counter. He had discovered, more or less by accident, that such was good for business—a well-rounded, skimpily clad female bartender—but Kit, in his usual loud and despotic manner, had claimed her services and Duckworth was being forced to cope with customers alone. Kit, however, would have his fill of her shortly, permitting her to return to regular duties—and thus turn Canfield loose on the town again.

For this Virg Huckaby waited hopefully. Not that the rancher's insatiable hunger for women, so strong as to often require the services of several during a single night, was of particular interest to the lawman; likely, fired with liquor, goaded into a searing fury by the licking he had so publicly taken in the Maricopa, it was only logical to expect this would be just such a night—and God pity the whores he bedded down! The man was a sadist at heart and he'd be taking out his rage and frustration on each of them.

All of which was nothing new to Huckaby; he'd seen Canfield in similar moods before, had on occasion seen fit to step in, cover for the man's actions, all in the interests of the town—but that was over now. Kit had drawn a sharp and definite line, making it clear where he stood and what his intentions were. Now, as far as Virgil Huckaby was concerned, all the bars were down and Kit Canfield

68

had best look to his hindquarters—for one slip on his part and the wolves would close in.

Lock him up! Starbuck had said earlier that evening when he had mentioned the possibility of trouble from Kit after he had gone storming out of the Maricopa. *Lock him up!* Why not? If he could nail Canfield for doing something that was a clear violation of the law—why not? He could expect no mercy from the rancher—why not simply beat him to the punch?

He guessed he hadn't ever really understood how deep his hatred for the swaggering, loud-mouthed rancher was until that afternoon late when Kit had voiced his threats. Of course there had never been any cordiality between them, the lawman having categorized and pegged Kit Canfield for what he was the first day they met. And then when the Mason Lynch murder thing had been settled and much later, after Marie Hope had married, lived for a time with a husband, and become widowed, the feeling toward the rancher had intensified even more.

Virg had thought a lot about Marie, had not only felt sorry for her because of the turn fate had given her, but had known a genuine affection, entertaining thoughts of asking her to marry him despite the fact he was old enough to be her father. And it seemed to him he was making progress along such lines, too.

Then Kit Canfield became aware of Marie's obvious charms—a young widow in the full bloom of early womanhood—and moved in. In a short time he had completely overcome her, swung her to his way of thinking, and if she had ever seriously considered wedding the lawman, it was blasted to the winds by the rancher's swashbuckling, free-spending manner.

He'd had some rough moments there in the Maricopa when Mason Lynch had asked about Marie, and what he had been forced to say had ripped open all of the old sores, set them to festering again. He owed Kit Canfield plenty, not only for Marie, who, tired of within a few months by the rancher who kept her in lonely splendor and solitude in a cottage at the edge of town, eventually ended up in the Frisco House, but for all the insults, the humiliation, and the sly, steady undermining of his position in the town as well. . . .

His morose thinking came to a halt, as down the street he saw Mason Lynch emerge from the churchyard, where he had evidently been visiting his folks' graves. Mason paused, then moved off through Mexicantown—on his way, no doubt, to pay a call on Marie Hope.

Mason was a fool to do that, he thought. He would find nothing but disappointment and disillusionment; things can never be put back in proper order once a change has been made. Physically, perhaps; in all other ways, no. Mason Lynch would be better off to turn around, come back—forget about the girl he had once planned to make his wife.

He watched Lynch's slight figure dissolve into the shadows, listened idly to the dogs tracing the man's passage with their successive barks, brought his eyes back to Duckworth's. Homer Boyd, in company with Doc Hewlett, strolled along the street on the opposite side, bearing for a final nightcap at the Maricopa.

If he could manage to get something on Kit Canfield, could he expect Boyd and the rest of the merchants to stand by him? Or would they think only of their pocketbooks and back the rancher?

He didn't like the answer that came so readily to mind; a marshal would be easy to replace—a successful rancher pouring thousands of dollars into a town's business firms each year would not. It would take something really serious to turn people from Kit. Fighting, drunkenness—such simple infractions as that were out; it would require a coldblooded killing, or the rape of a decent woman—preferably a young girl—to bring him down. And while he was capable of both he was much too clever to get caught at it.

But he had to find an answer. Canfield had thrown his cards face up on the table, made it plain what he intended to do; Huckaby had accepted the challenge, declared it a fight to the finish. He was only sorry that Kit's encounter with Starbuck had ended as it had, wished instead, with no qualms, that it had gone a step farther, and the rancher, completely losing his head, had reached for his pistol. Starbuck, who undoubtedly was a gunman, would have shot him dead. That would have settled things once and for all.

He drew to quiet attention as Duckworth's side door opened. The girl appeared, circled to the front of the saloon, and entered. She was back shortly, carrying a quart bottle of whiskey, and re-entered her quarters. She did not remain, however, simply left the liquor with Kit, and retracing her steps to the saloon, took her place behind the bar.

Kit evidently liked what he found in the girl, planned to spend the remainder of the night with her. She would probably be going off duty in another hour or two. Huckaby, disappointed, rubbed at his jaw, shrugged. He might as well give it up until morning. Maybe it would be smart to get with Duckworth's new girl, see if something could be set up.

The door opened again. Canfield, bottle clutched in his hand, stepped out into the shadows lying alongside the saloon. He stalled for the space of time required to take a drink of the liquor, and then wheeling, circled back behind the building to the rack where his horse waited.

Shortly he was again in view, slumped in the saddle, the black he was riding moving at a tired walk as he turned into the street and headed south—for the Frisco House.

Virg Huckaby delayed until the rancher had been swallowed by the darkness beyond the church, and then, careful not to be seen by any of the few persons remaining abroad, he doubled back to the alley, and followed.

Starbuck sat up, roused from a sound slumber by a pounding on his door. Reaching instinctively for the pistol hanging in its belt from the back of a nearby chair, he glanced to his left. That side of the bed was empty. Mason Lynch had not returned.

Frowning, he threw his legs over the edge, drew on his britches, and moved to the door, wondering, dully, if the hotel clerk had forgotten to give Mason the key left at the desk for him, wondering, also, what time of the night it was; somewhere around two or three o'clock, he guessed.

The insistent hammering came again. Shawn, now fully awake and cautious, stepped to the left of the panel.

"Who's there?"

"Huckaby." The lawman's answer was quick, blunt. "Open up, Starbuck!"

Shawn thrust his forty-five under the waistband of his pants, picked up the extra key he had obtained, and turned the lock. In the dim glow of the hallway's bracketed lamp, he saw the marshal, Fred Kemmer, and three or four other men. Their faces were grim.

"What's the trouble?" he asked, but a deep worry was beginning to move through him; this had something to do with Mason. Turning, he halted beside the table, struck a match to the lamp's wick, and as the yellow glow spread over the room, came about. He saw then that Huckaby had his pistol in his hand, ready.

"Where's Lynch?" the lawman demanded, eyes prowling the room.

Starbuck shook his head. "Not here yet. Wasn't ready for sleeping when I was. Left him standing out there on the street."

Kemmer, his fleshy face sallow in the weak light, nodded to the marshal. "That proves it. It was him that did it."

"Did what?" Starbuck asked patiently. "Let's have it, Huckaby—what's this all about?"

The lawman leaned against the washstand, folded his arms across his chest. "You certain you don't know?"

"How the hell would I know anything? Been in this bed since first part of the evening."

"You prove that?"

"Say!" Kemmer exclaimed, a brightness coming into his eyes. "You maybe've got something there, Virg! Why couldn't it've been him? He had trouble with Kit in my place. Could have hunted him up, finished him off."

Huckaby, head cocked to one side, impassively studied Shawn. "You got an answer for that?"

Shawn stirred indifferently. "Might—if I knew what you're getting at." His hunch had been right, apparently. Something had occurred and they were suspecting Mason —even him—of doing it.

The lawman continued to stare for a long breath and then said, "Kit Canfield got killed tonight. Murdered."

Starbuck came up slowly, but it was no big surprise; men such as Canfield never live to a ripe age. In that next moment the full implication of the lawman's words and presence came to him.

"And you think Mason Lynch did it?"

"Or maybe you," Kemmer said slyly.

Shawn favored the saloonman with a withering look, "You're a damned fool, mister." He put his attention on Huckaby. "You're wrong, Marshal, if that's what you're thinking. Mason wouldn't have done it—I'm sure of that."

"Why not? He still hated the Canfields—still packed that big grudge."

"And Kit was killed with his own gun," one of the other men said. "Means the man who shot him didn't have no iron of his own. Virg has got Lynch's over to his office."

"That proves nothing," Starbuck said, drawing on the remainder of his clothing, "except that Canfield knew whoever it was, figured him for a friend and let him get up close. Where'd it happen?"

"Out in front of the Frisco House," Huckaby said. "Seems Kit was there late—stayed on quite a spell. Mason must've been there, too, waiting in the old stable across the road."

The Frisco House . . . the girl named Marie Hope . . . Shawn was thinking back, remembering what had been said about her. Once she had meant a great deal to Mason

73

—it was possible she still did; in fact, he himself had suggested Mason should see her. And Virg Huckaby was aware of the connection, too, would be remembering.

"Anybody see Mason around there?" he asked casually.

Huckaby nodded slowly. "One of the women seen a man standing in the dark inside the stable. Claims she didn't know him but she'd recognize him again, was she to see him."

"Standing in the dark?"

"Expect there was a little light."

Starbuck finished his dressing. "Somebody—but not exactly Mason Lynch. Way you're all putting it, sounds like you're sure it was him."

"Mighty hard to believe it wasn't," Kemmer said. "I'll lay you odds that Lynch came back here with that in his mind all the time—to square up with the Canfields like he started out to do ten years ago."

Shawn strapped on his pistol. "That's a bet I'd win. Mason's had enough punishment. He's not going to let something he no longer cares a whit about get him in trouble again." Glancing up to Huckaby, he added, "What about me? Decided whether I'm guilty or not?"

The lawman shrugged. "I'll tell you this—you ain't out of the woods yet."

"Well, if there's any doubt, you might ask the clerk downstairs. He'll tell you I never left the place after I turned in. Knew I'd be sleeping hard so I left the extra key for Mason at the desk."

"Which he never come back and used," Kemmer said pointedly. "Means he's skipped out."

"Not for sure," Starbuck replied, stubbornly.

"Then where the hell is he?" Huckaby shouted, suddenly angered. "He ain't here and we've looked all over town."

"What about his horse? It gone?"

"Going there next," the marshal said after a long breath during which he and Kemmer exchanged glances. Evidently they had overlooked that possibility, were trying now to make it appear no oversight. "Figured to come here first."

Starbuck grunted, pulled on the old hat he still had not found time to replace, and turned to the door. It was a bit strange that the lawman had searched the town for Mason Lynch before coming to the most logical place to seek him —in his hotel room. And the part about his horse; that, too, would seem to be one of the things that would be checked on at the very beginning.

"You seem plenty sure it was Mason," he said again. "Looks like you could've done more about it than just hunt for him."

"He's the one with the reason—"

"You telling me Kit Canfield didn't have any enemies?" Shawn asked, eyeing the lawman narrowly as they moved down the hall and began to descend the stairs. "I got the idea he was a man with more'n his share. Pretty plain you're included in that bunch, too."

Huckaby's expression did not alter. "Ain't denying it. Never did like Kit. Always throwing his weight around. But I managed to get along with him."

"Hell," Kemmer said deprecatingly, "like to see the man who doesn't have a few enemies. But Kit's weren't the murdering kind, just soreheads."

"Any man with a grudge can turn into the murdering kind," Starbuck said as they started across the lobby. "And you're claiming Mason Lynch wasn't carrying one?"

"I am. Whole thing was a lost cause far as he was concerned. Same as told me he wouldn't have his folk's old place back as a gift."

Kemmer laughed. "And you believed that?"

"Yes," Shawn said quietly as they stepped out onto the porch of the Mogollon, "I believed him." He pulled up short, anger and disgust stirring through him. Several men had gathered in the street, were waiting in the cool darkness. One, a coiled rope hooked over his left shoulder, was fashioning a hangman's noose. Abruptly he wheeled to Huckaby.

"What kind of law is this?"

The marshal shook his head. "Not my idea. These men have got their minds pretty well made up." Moving to the edge of the gallery, he motioned to the man with the rope. "Put that away, Harry. Ain't going to be no lynching around here."

Harry did not cease his methodic shaping of the knot. "Nothing wrong with being ready."

Starbuck spat, dropped off the porch, and turned toward Fortney's livery stable. No lights burned along the silent street, not even in the saloons, and the only sounds to be heard were those made by the men trooping along through the dust. Huckaby forged up to a position ahead of Shawn.

"Never mind," he said drily, "I'll take charge."

"Then do it!" Starbuck snapped. "We find Mason at the

stable, that bunch of vigilantes back there had better keep calm or I'll use my gun!"

"You'll do what I tell you—same as they will," Huckaby said stiffly. "Thing I'm looking out for here is that you don't get in the way, let him make a run for it if he's holed up."

"If I knew where he was, I sure wouldn't be leading you and that crowd to him—"

"Didn't figure you would, but was we to bump into him accidental-like, could be you'd try making it easy for him."

Shawn made no reply not certain in his own mind how he would react if they did encounter Lynch. He felt sure the man was not guilty of Kit Canfield's death, yet he could not forget Mason had practiced deceit on him after they had met. Even so, if it did develop that Lynch was guilty, he'd still be unable simply to draw back, see him pay for the crime at the hands of a hanging party.

Ahead of him the lawman halted. The wide, double doors of Fortney's were open, as was customary on summer nights, but the lantern ordinarily hanging in the runway was missing.

Huckaby drew his pistol, glanced at Shawn. "Pretty sure he's hiding in there. You want to try some talking, see if you can get him to give up without a fuss?"

Starbuck stepped into the opening. "Mason!" he called. "It's Shawn. You in there?"

A muffled answer of some sort came from the tack room on the left. Instantly Huckaby whirled and hurried to it, the men behind him following quickly. Starbuck, off to one side, drew his pistol, waited. A match flared in the gloom, and shortly a lantern's glow spread through the area.

"It's Ernie!" a voice shouted. "He's been tied up!"

Starbuck slid his weapon back into its holster; he had been certain it would be someone other than Mason Lynch, but he was taking no chance. Jaw set, he crossed the runway, shouldered his way through the men crowded around the door that led into the small anteroom. For the first time since Virg Huckaby and the others had appeared in his hotel quarters, he was having doubts. The answer would lie with the hostler; he wanted to hear it first hand.

Huckaby was slicing through the light rope that bound the elderly man's wrists, Kemmer was tugging at the gag. It came loose and the oldster hawked, spat angrily.

"Consarned stinking rag—"

"Who was it, Ernie?" Huckaby asked, closing his knife as the cotton strands parted. "You get a look at him?"

"Look—hell, I was talking to him!"

"Was it Mason Lynch?"

"That's who it was—Mason Lynch! Come bustin' in here all in a hurry for his horse. Tried to tell him that nag of his'n wasn't in no shape to travel, but he wouldn't listen. Saddled up and *then*, before he left, tied me good. Took my gun, too."

Huckaby, a smugness spread across his features, glanced at Starbuck, turned back to the hostler.

"How long ago was this?"

"Couple—no, I reckon it was about three hours."

Shawn felt Kemmer's eyes upon him, heard the man say: "Reckon that ought to prove who did it. You satisfied?"

"Only proves that he's gone—not that he did it," Starbuck said. He realized he sounded thick-skulled and arbitrary but it was difficult to believe that Mason Lynch could have undergone so drastic a change in mind and outlook.

He swung to Huckaby. "Marshal, have you stopped to think that Mason might've heard about the killing, and knowing he'd be blamed first off, got scared and left town fast as he could? He hasn't forgot that you had to keep a lynch mob off him ten years ago."

"No, I reckon I haven't," the lawman drawled, "but I expect, was I to set my mind to it, I could come up with a whole bunch of fancy tales like that."

"Could have been the way of it," Shawn insisted, hanging on to his temper.

"If so, then he'd a been smart to come right to me, not make things worse by hightailing it out of town."

"Time like that it's not easy for a man to think straight."

"Can't see as it bales hay one way or another what we think," Kemmer said. "Point is he's gone—and while we're standing here jawing, he's putting miles between us."

"That's right," one of the men in the crowd said. "Let's get mounted up and a-going after him."

"You see in the dark, Ike?" Huckaby asked in a mild voice. "That's what it'll take." He came about to where the hostler was now sitting, chafing his ankles ruefully. "You got any idea what direction he rode off in, Ernie?"

"Nope. Throwed back there in the corner like I was, I couldn't see nothing."

Huckaby rubbed at his chin. "Well, he won't be traveling fast. We can start tracking him soon's it's daylight." He glanced toward the street. A half-dozen riders were wheeling in from the west, slowing, and then pounding on for the stable when they caught sight of the gathering.

"It's Barney," the rider called Harry, still fiddling with his rope, said. "Got some of the Box C boys with him. Somebody must've sent word to him."

"I did," the lawman said. "Right after Kit was found."

"He won't be much for waiting around for morning," Kemmer said. "He'll decide quick it was Lynch who done it when he hears he's lit out. He'll want to do something about it right now."

"You figure he can see in the dark like Ike?" Huckaby demanded sarcastically. "We'll go after him, but there ain't no use starting—"

"You got him?" Barney Canfield's hard voice shouted from the runway.

"Who?" the marshal asked.

"Lynch—who the hell you think? Was him that did it, wasn't it?"

"Way it looks," Ike said before Huckaby could speak. "He's long gone."

The rancher strode angrily into the crowd of men. "Gone?"

"Sure is. Come and got his horse and run for it. Tied up Ernie so's he couldn't set up a holler."

"Then let's get a posse mounted and start beating the brush," Canfield snapped. "Sooner we get after him, sooner we can nail him down."

"Posse won't be necessary," Starbuck said, raising his voice above the hubbub. Moving through the gathering, he halted in front of Huckaby. "Marshal, I want you to deputize me. I'll go after Mason by myself. Like to see him brought in alive."

12

The silence following Starbuck's words was long and complete. Barney Canfield broke it. "The hell you will!"

A welter of words broke out, some angry, all frankly skeptical. Shawn waited until the racket had died off.

"I'll tell you this, Marshal," he said, "you let this mob find him and you'll have a dead man on your hands—an innocent dead man."

The rancher spat. "Your job was to keep an eye on Lynch. If you'd've done the job, we wouldn't be here now."

"Not exactly the way I understood it," Shawn replied.

"Was the way I meant it!" Huckaby snapped.

Starbuck shrugged. He guessed he should have taken the lawman's words more seriously; he doubted, however, if it would have made any difference. Likely Mason Lynch would have done what he pleased. But perhaps the thought could be turned to his advantage.

"Good reason why it ought to be me that runs him down," he said.

A slyness came into Virgil Huckaby's eyes. "Maybe so. You got some idea where he'll go?"

"Nothing for sure. He mentioned a few things that might help."

"Like what?" Barney Canfield asked quickly.

Starbuck gave the rancher a dry smile. "I'm not about to tell you—or anybody else—not the way things are around here."

"I'm the law," Huckaby said. "You'll tell me, or I'm slapping you in jail."

Shawn hadn't considered that possibility. Now he studied the marshal narrowly. Huckaby was bluffing, he concluded.

"Suit yourself," he said. "I figure I can find him, but it'll

79

have to be on my terms. You don't go for that, then forget it."

"Just what we're going to do," Canfield stated, loud and flat. "Like as not the two of you are working together, anyway. Maybe you'd find him, but it'd be to join up so's the both of you could keep riding. Boys, I'm calling for a posse. Everyone of you willing to—"

"Back up, now, Barney," Huckaby cut in, stepping into the center of the room. "Posse comes under the heading of my business, and it'll take its orders from me."

The rancher bobbed his head, smiled. " 'Scuse me, Virg. I know that, but I want to get things started. I don't aim to let my brother's killer get away. Want to say right now, I'll pay a hundred dollars gold to the man who gets him."

"Dead or alive?" a voice asked.

"Makes no difference to me—"

"It damn well does to me!" Huckaby said, raising his hands for silence. "Any of you aiming to ride along is going to take my orders. That don't suit your fancy, then pull out now, go home, don't mix in. That clear?"

There was no direct reply, only a murmur and a shuffling of booted feet on the dusty floor.

"All right, then," the lawman continued. "Let's get this thing organized. Couple of you trot over to Yaqui Joe's, roust him out. Bring him to Kemmer's place. We'll start from there soon's it's light."

"What do we have to wait for?" Canfield protested. "Why ain't we leaving now?"

"Nobody knows what direction he took off in," Kemmer explained.

"Would've rode south—for the border," Canfield said. "That'd be my guess."

Shawn felt a twinge of alarm. In his judgment also, Mason would have taken that route, not for the border however, but for the Mescals, where he could hide out and rest the bay until the horse was better able to travel. Fortunately, no one in the crowd seemed to remember Lynch's place.

"New Mexico line's closer," a hooknosed puncher commented. "Was it me, I'd take my chances that way. 'Specially was I forking a lame horse."

"Yeh, reckon you could be right," the rancher said. He sucked at his lips, glanced over the crowd. "Virg's right. It'll be smart to wait for daylight, then put the Indian on his trail. Meanwhile, we can do our congregating at Kemmer's, sort of get set."

"Want everybody on a fresh horse," Huckaby said. "Ain't no telling how far we'll be riding."

"Till we catch him, that's how far," Canfield said. "Want that understood. Nobody quits and goes home till we've got him caught—and took care of." He paused, looked around, and then pointed at Starbuck. "What about him?"

"He's coming with us," the lawman said promptly. "Claims he's got some idea of where Mason might've gone. Fine. I figure if the trail Yaqui Joe digs up heads off in the direction Starbuck's thinking of—then we can make a straight run for whatever it is he's got in mind, save ourselves a lot of time that'd be lost in tracking."

Canfield nodded slowly. "Sounds good but maybe you're overlooking one thing—how do you know he'll tell us?"

Huckaby smiled grimly. "Oh, he'll talk up, all right. Don't worry about it."

Shawn looked closely at the lawman, also smiled. "That mean I'm being arrested?"

"More or less," the marshal replied. "Main thing, I want you handy so's we can find Lynch, get this thing squared away. Play it smart and everything'll work out fine for you." Huckaby hesitated, eyes on the men clustered around Barney Canfield and shifting toward the doorway. "Now, you get your horse, meet us at the saloon."

Starbuck watched the marshal turn away, become a part of the general exodus. Riding with Huckaby and his posse was the last thing he had in mind to do; what must be done was find Mason Lynch, warn him, and get him safely to some other town until the matter of Kit Canfield's death could be straightened out.

It could be possible that Mason, in a fit of anger, had killed the rancher, although Shawn still found the idea hard to accept. But if it did turn out to be a fact, then Lynch was entitled to a trial before a judge and jury and not deserving of rope justice—which was what he would get if the posse caught up with him. Perhaps Virg Huckaby sincerely believed he could control Canfield and those who would be riding with him, but there was every doubt in Starbuck's mind.

The last of the men had gone. Wheeling, Shawn stepped out into the runway. It was best he act quickly, gain all the time he could. Moving along the row of stalls until he came to the one in which the sorrel stood, he entered, began to throw his gear into place. Finished, he took the gelding's headstall in his hand, backed him into the runway.

Allowing the reins to trail on the littered floor, Starbuck turned, trotted to the yet open double doors, peered into the street. Lights were now on in the Maricopa and a few horses were tied at the hitchrack; the posse was beginning to assemble. He probed the surrounding area carefully. No one was in sight.

But it would be smart to take no chances—use the stable's rear entrance; in so doing he could be certain that his riding off alone rather than joining with the others forming the posse at the Maricopa—as he had been ordered by Huckaby to do—would not be noticed. Returning to the sorrel, he took up the reins and moved into the gloom filling the rear of the barn.

Starbuck reached the end of the runway, cut right into an aisle angling in from that point. The rear door was directly ahead. He halted. It was too easy. It didn't seem likely that Marshal Virg Huckaby would put him under arrest, more or less, order him to report later at the place where the posse was to assemble—and then simply walk away and let him do as he wished.

He considered that improbability for a full minute, and then deciding that, if so, two could play at the game of cleverness, and moved on, stopping again a half stride in the open. Poised there, he cocked his ear into the night. There was only the calm silence of the early hour. Still leading the sorrel, he stepped farther into the clear, away from the barn, paused. The hush persisted and his searching glance found nothing suspicious. He guessed he had misjudged the lawman; there appeared to be no one watching the livery stable after all.

Turning, he swung onto the saddle, kneed the gelding gently, sent him walking briskly down the lane between the wagon yard and a corral. Fortunately he was moving away from the buildings and the town itself, thus would run no risk of being spotted from the street. All he need do was proceed on a direct line and he would soon be in the low, brush-covered hills to the west of the settlement. Once there he would be free to move as he wished without fear of being observed.

Cigarette smoke . . .

At the first pungent whiff borne to him in the slight breeze, Starbuck drew up short. He'd been right. Huckaby was keeping an eye on him—undoubtedly had a man watching the front of Fortney's, too. He smiled grimly into the darkness. Huckaby was not about to let him slip off and find Mason Lynch on his own; he was permitting him to go but he and the posse would be following at a discreet distance.

Silent, Shawn hunched over the saddle, pulled his feet free of the stirrups, and dropped to the ground, thus eliminating the silhouette his sitting high on the gelding afforded. Standing in the cool semi-darkness behind the stable, he tried to locate the source of the tobacco smoke, reasoning that since it came in to him on the breeze, the man would be somewhere directly ahead—to the west.

Cautious, he started forward, halted as not one but a pair of small, red eyes glowing in the night appeared on his left. The eyes brightened and dulled with pulsing regularity. Huckaby had put two men on the job.

Shawn considered that. One could be to hurry with the word of his so-called escape to the lawman, waiting with the remainder of the posse at Kemmer's saloon; the second could have been directed to follow, leaving suitable trail markings and signs for them to go by.

Virg Huckaby had him, Shawn recognized the fact. The lay of the land was such that he was forced to pass directly in front of the men if he intended to reach the hills. Nor was there an alternative; he could expect the street side of Fortney's to be under surveillance, also. All he could do was play out the hand, endeavor to outsmart the lawman in some way.

Mounting, Starbuck again moved forward. Instantly the twin glows disappeared. They had seen him, had rid themselves of their smokes. Keeping his eyes straight ahead, Starbuck rode on.

Shortly he came to the first of the sand hills, turned into a narrow draw crowded with sage and other rank growth, pressed on, resisting the almost overpowering urge to look back, see if Huckaby's men were following the plan he had assumed.

A hundred yards later he swung left, and urging the gelding to an easy trot, continued due south until he was well below the town. There, once again he altered direction, aiming deliberately for the rugged, rock-studded butte area sprawling like a great, ugly scar east of the settlement.

Once inside the welter of boulders, overhanging ledges, and tall mesquite, he ventured his first glance to the rear —almost instantly located a lone pursuer. The man was following his trail patiently in the pale light of the stars. There was no sign of a second tracker; it evidently had been as he suspected, and likely at that very moment Huckaby and his posse were preparing to get underway.

The country turned rougher, grew steadily wilder. On all sides now were ragged-faced buttes, arroyos that were deep-cut and twisting, filled with mesquite, greasewood, and hedges of tough Apache plume. It was all somewhat of a surprise to Shawn Starbuck; he did not expect to see so much desert growth this far in. It was as if a section of that harsh, burning country miles to the south and west had been lifted bodily by some gigantic hand and arbitrarily set down in an area given over primarily to forested, grassy hills.

He should be changing course again, not get too deep into the brake before he put into effect his plan for finding Mason Lynch. But the maneuver would require skill; he must be certain the rider dogging his tracks did not suspect. He glanced about, eyes straining in the half-light to see clearly his surroundings. He was presently following a fairly well-defined path that wound in and out of the rocks and brush as it gradually ascended to a mesa, dimly visible farther on.

Abruptly the path veered into a narrow aisle lying between almost perpendicular walls of reddish earth. Shawn halted, eyes on the ground. Hoofprints were plentiful in the space between the formations, indicating that the passage was undoubtedly the sole route for reaching the plateau on beyond the brake.

He rode the sorrel into the passageway for a short distance, then backed him out. Once again in the wider area he swung the gelding off into the thick brush, and there, well concealed, waited. Within few minutes Huckaby's man came into view, a hunched shape on his saddle, patiently working out the path.

Shawn delayed until he was certain the rider had entered the narrow pass, and then not wanting to take any chances of running head-on into the posse, hastily backtracked to where he could cut away and there pointed the sorrel south. He was reasonably sure that his activities would keep Huckaby and his posse puzzling over the trail for some time and thus leave him free to search the Mescal country for Lynch.

Free. The word evoked a strange feeling within him. This breaking away, this eluding of Virgil Huckaby and the law he represented, placed him in the same category as Mason Lynch; now they were both outlawed. He shrugged. It was a situation that had been forced upon him, and with a man's life at stake, he had no regrets.

He had not noticed but it had grown lighter. A pale flare filled the heavens to the east and the stars were beginning to fade. Not long until sunrise. He would be reaching the country where he could expect to find Mason at about the right time.

Mason would not have covered much ground despite the several hours start that he had. His horse was in no condition for a hard, fast ride, and thinking it over, Shawn concluded his best bet was to move south as quickly as possible, get near the Mescals, and then backtrack, work his way north. In so doing. and assuming he had figured right and Mason was heading for his ranch, he could expect to encounter the man.

He wondered what Mason would find at his ranch. Apparently he had only begun its building when the war came and he rode out to fight. Those four years, plus the succeeding ten he had spent in prison, added up to a period that could have nullified and completely erased all the effort he had put into the property.

Starbuck hoped it would prove otherwise. Lynch was a man desperately seeking haven, a refuge from a life that had not been kind. And now he was opening a new and tragic chapter. Whether he had been the one who murdered Kit Canfield or not was a situation that should be faced squarely and settled.

Mason must be made to realize that. There was no future whatsoever for him if he elected to avoid the confrontation, decided to run, hide from the law and those pseudo-lawmen, the bounty hunters who would come swarming in as soon as the reward Barney Canfield most certainly would post, was noised about.

No man could find fulfillment in a life forever peopled by threatening shadows; Mason Lynch should understand that, and if innocent, take steps to clear his name. But if he were guilty, if he had been the one who killed Canfield, then—Starbuck shrugged, not liking the question that thought raised.

The law declared a man must be made to face up to his crimes; could he, by force if necessary, capture and take Mason Lynch in for that purpose? Must he personally assume what would be a most disagreeable obligation? Mason was a beaten man, one scarred cruelly by life, but the law was the guideline to which all must adhere and to which there can be no exceptions. He hoped he would not be forced to make any such decision.

An hour later he broke out into a land of rolling ridges covered with gently waving grass, sage-filled draws, and small oases of cottonwoods and other trees. A stream sparkled along the floor of a vast, far-flung valley, and at its far end he saw the rambling formations he assumed to be the Mescal Mountains.

Dismounting, he picketed the sorrel in a small clearing and made his way to a shoulder of rock thrusting itself, like a thick shelf, into the swale and affording a lofty and excellent vantage point from which to observe. He was about midway of the basin, he judged, looking to both directions, and should be well below the slower-traveling Mason—between him and the Mescals—*if he had been right*. He had only guessed that Lynch would choose this route; he could be wrong.

But he was confident that he had read the man's mind correctly. Mason, in reality, had no choice when you came right down to it; a slow horse and caught near dead center of the territory, the logical answer would be the Mescals, where, on his own land, he could lie low until the horse had recovered and it was safe to move on.

Fixing his eyes on the southernmost point of the valley visible to him, Shawn began a methodic search along the stream until he found the trail he knew would be there. In this land, not too great a distance now from the desert, travelers, both man and beast, never strayed far from water in their migrations. To do so invited hardship, occasionally even death.

Slowly, painstakingly, Starbuck began to trace the course of the creek with its complementing path, following it with his eyes as it wound in and out of the trees, through the brush, now and again in the open where it became a silver ribbon glinting brightly in the sunlight.

Halfway across a narrow flat, movement arrested his attention. He came to his feet slowly, squinting to concentrate his vision as well as cut down the glare—and then settled back as a doe mule deer walked leisurely out of the brush, paused to survey the surrounding area for possible enemies while testing the breeze with her nostrils. Reassured, she meandered on down to the water, head bobbing rhythmically with each graceful step.

Suddenly the doe came to a rigid alert. A shift in the light breeze had apparently carried a warning to her. Starbuck edged farther out on the ledge, probed the country above the poised animal with a careful gaze.

He saw then what had startled the animal. It was Mason Lynch, again on foot and leading his horse, making his way along the stream.

87

For a considerable length of time Starbuck studied Lynch's slow progress along the trail. Then, fixing in his mind the location of a rock bench well ahead of the man where an interception could be made, he returned to the sorrel, mounted and rode down the slope.

He reached the foot of the long grade without incident. Keeping above and back from the creek, he made his way to the overhanging slab of granite he had selected and halted. There again picketing the gelding but this time with greater care, he crawled to the extreme lip of the ledge. From that elevated position he could look down upon the stream and its adjacent trail as well as observe anyone approaching from all directions.

He would be above Mason's line of vision, and that assured him. There was no way of anticipating the man's reaction, now that he was a fugitive, faced possibly with a death sentence or at the least the promise of spending the remainder of his life behind prison walls. And a man once considered a friend could now be an enemy in his eyes; therefore, it was only prudent to proceed with caution.

Flat on the gray-streaked rock bench, Shawn held his gaze to the upper end of the trail, awaited the initial appearance of Mason Lynch. The sun was out and well on its way across the clean sky by that moment, and already was making its searing presence felt. Jays flitted about in the scrubby pinons and cedars, their crests lifting and falling as they scolded lesser birds, warning them from their asserted territory; high overhead a Mexican eagle soared in ever-extending circles as it hunted from an exalted level.

Insects buzzed noisily in the weedy growth struggling for life from the crevices in the rock, and a gopher, frightened into hiding by the arrival of the sorrel and his rider, satisfied finally that all now was well since he could detect no more sound or movement, reappeared, scurried up onto the lower lip of the shelf, where he rose to a rigid, military stance while he studied the land below with bright, sharp eyes.

Shawn stirred restlessly, loosened the bandanna around his neck. The heat was beginning to drill into him, reach the inner depths of his body. Mason should be close, he thought, but judging distance from an overhead position can be difficult and quite often unreliable. Lynch might have been farther away than he figured.

Impatiently, Starbuck brushed at the sweat accumulating on his face. He'd be glad when this was all over and done with, settled one way or another. Then he could go on about his business—that of looking up a rider named Ivory at Canfield's Box C and determining whether he was his missing brother, Ben, or not. That was what had brought him down into Arizona Territory in the first place, but it seemed he was always getting sidetracked—involved. . . .

The minutes dragged by. Another quarter-hour—a half. Again Shawn stirred, the direct, blazing shafts of sunlight bearing down mercilessly. The gopher, startled for the third time, darted away, disappeared into the loose rocks. The eagle had drifted on seeking more productive hunting, but the jays were still there—quarrelsome, noisy, and impertinent.

A blur of motion up-trail—Starbuck's attention focused on the point instantly. It was Lynch. He was rounding a clump of brush, hat in hand, the bay following and not limping to any great extent. Apparently Mason was permitting the horse to take it easy, saving him in the event sudden and hard use should become necessary. A pistol was thrust under Lynch's waistband, the butt sticking out at a handy angle.

Shawn remained motionless, ignoring the pesky, buzzing flies that circled his head, seeking to light on his sweaty skin. Motion, however small, could catch Mason's eyes, tip him off and seriously complicate the situation.

Looking close, Starbuck endeavored to judge the frame of mind dominating the man. He was running a great personal risk, he realized, no matter how he made his presence known. At the first sound of a voice or the small move of anything, Mason likely would react violently. His nerves would be at hair-trigger keenness and likely he would shoot blindly and without thought.

It would be wise to act when the man was still in front

89

of him and not after he had passed the ledge, Shawn decided. There was at least a chance that Lynch would recognize him in that split second before he pulled the trigger of his weapon.

Mason drew near, became definite. Sweat lay thick on his forehead and cheeks, glistened in his neck and arms. His shirt was soaked, long, dark streaks running down from his armpits, extending across his shoulders. Weariness lined his face and rode him like a leaden pack that threatened to bring him to his knees. There was no spring in his step, only a mechanical trudging, a placing of one foot ahead of the other. He'd had a hard time of it during the night and there was little strength remaining in his tortured body.

He came to a listless, sliding halt. Ground-reining the bay, he looked ahead to the now hazy tumble of the Mescals, then turned, walked slowly down to the stream. Kneeling, he dashed water over his head, against his burned face, and then dripping, sat for a time hunched on his heels, resting. But it was for only brief minutes. Rising, he glanced to the sky as if searching for relief from the pitiless heat, and finding no hope, moved back to the bay. Catching up the trailing leathers, he resumed his jaded march.

Off behind Starbuck the sorrel, annoyed by the hordes of ravenous insects, shook itself violently. Instantly Mason Lynch stopped, hand going straight to the pistol at his waist.

Shawn, flattened upon the ledge as much as possible, felt rather than saw the man's sharp eyes digging at the rocks, the slope beyond him. If the sorrel moved again the moment of resolution was at hand; if not, likely Mason, seeing nothing and hearing no more, would assume it had been some animal frightened by his approach, and move on.

The charged, blistering moments crawled by filled with the dry clacking of insects, the drone of flies hovering above his sweaty skin. He dared not raise his head to see if Mason had dismissed the alarm and was continuing his passage, feared to stir at all since Lynch could still be scanning the rock ledges and slopes for the source of the noise.

A full, interminable minute . . . two . . . three. Shawn heard the click of metal against stone, swallowed hard. Mason was again on his way—almost directly below him if he could judge by the nearness of the sound. With great care he lifted his head a few inches. Lynch was a dozen steps away.

Starbuck reached for his pistol, drew it slowly, carefully, making certain it did not scrape against the rock. Second thoughts entered his mind. He decided against the procedure, slid the weapon back into its holster. Best to face Mason with both hands clearly visible—and empty.

Drawing his legs up beneath him, balancing himself with palms flat against the blistering granite, he waited until Lynch was coming straight toward him. Then, taking a deep breath, he rose to his full height.

"Mason—"

Lynch jolted as if struck bodily by the solitary word. He threw himself back against his horse, fingers clawing for the gun in the waistband of his pants.

"It's me—Starbuck!"

At the mention of the name Lynch froze. His hand drifted away from his weapon as he saw none in Shawn's grasp. Slowly he straightened, brushing at the sweat clothing his eyes with a forearm.

"You stood a damn good chance of getting your head blowed off."

"I know that. A risk I had to take," Starbuck said, keeping his arms away from his sides.

Mason considered him suspiciously. "You come after me?"

Shawn moved nearer to the edge of the shelf. "Not exactly—not after you."

Lynch shook his head. "Wasted your time. How'd you know to come this way?"

"Remembered what you said about the Mescals—that you'd once started to build yourself a ranch there. Sort of guessed that was where you'd make for."

The tautness still held Mason Lynch in a viselike grip. "I can forget that, I reckon," he said in a low, disconsolate voice. "They'd never leave me be. Was aiming to rest my horse till morning, then hit for the border. Ain't too far from here."

"One night won't do him much good for that kind of a trip. Must be a hundred miles across there. You sure that's what you want to do?"

Mason shrugged indifferently. "Nothing else left."

"Could be. You shoot Kit Canfield?"

Lynch laughed, a harsh, grating sound. "There anybody thinks I didn't?"

Far back up the slope above Starbuck a rock clattered hollowly, set up a thumping sound as it started downgrade.

Instantly Mason's mouth snapped shut. His hand reached again for the pistol in his waistband. Starbuck spun, threw his glance to the outcropping on the crest where he had earlier stopped and shortly thereafter spotted Mason.

A dozen riders were outlined against the sky. One man, on foot, was crouched at the extreme edge of the rocky shoulder, staring down the long slope into the valley. That would be the Indian, Yaqui Joe—the tracker. He hadn't succeeded in throwing the posse off for long, Shawn realized.

He came back around, met Mason Lynch's hard, accusing eyes, saw the leveled pistol pointing at him.

"Something I never figured from you—leading them to where I'd be."

"That's not the way of it," Shawn said quietly. "They're following me—not you. Thought I'd shaken them, but they've got themselves a tracker—Yaqui Joe they called him. He must've figured what I was doing first off. Hoped I'd have a couple hours' start on them at least."

Mason Lynch only stared, his red-lidded eyes sunk deep in his pinched face.

"It's the truth. If I was leading them I would've stuck with them. Makes more sense. Fact is, I was supposed to do just that but I ducked out, came on alone."

"So's you could escort me across the border, that it?"

Shawn ignored the thick sarcasm. "Nope, to get you out of the way before that posse could catch up. Huckaby's at the head of it but they're mostly Canfield lovers, and I don't figure the marshal will be able to hold them back if they ever get their hands on you. There's only one thing on their minds—string you up."

"Them wanting to do that is nothing new."

Starbuck looked up slope again. "Well, it's what you can figure on if we keep standing here. They'll find where I came off the rim, follow my tracks—and the next thing you know they'll be right in our laps."

Mason did not lower his weapon, simply continued to stand rigidly in the blazing sun. "Could all be a double-cross . . . a trick. Maybe there's more of them circling around us. For all I know you're working right with Huckaby and Canfield."

Starbuck swore in disgust. "I'm working for nobody but myself—and, I guess, sort of for you. And why I'm doing that even I'm not sure! It's your trouble, not mine—your neck they're wanting to stretch. Hell, if I had a lick of sense I'd climb on my horse and ride out, let you handle your own problems."

"You're not about to—not with me holding this gun on you!"

"I don't think you'd shoot me, Mason—and if you did pull that trigger you'd have Huckaby and his bunch down on you before you could get a half-mile. Use your head. I'm trying to help you—trying to be your friend!"

Mason continued to stare at Shawn for another long, silent minute, and then his arm began to lower. Shifting wearily, he thrust the weapon into his waistband.

"All right," he said in a resigned voice. "I'm leaving it up to you. What'll I do now?"

15

Relief flooded through Starbuck, broke the iron-hard tension that gripped him. He wiped at the sweat on his forehead, cast another glance to the rim above them. Huckaby's riders were still there but he could no longer see Yaqui Joe. That could only mean the canny old Indian was back somewhere on the plateau, nosing about for prints that would tell him where the sorrel started down. He would locate them with little difficulty, and soon the posse would come racing down the grade.

"Got to pull out of here quick," he said, wheeling toward the thicket where the sorrel waited. "Be smart, I think, to double back upstream."

Mason made no reply, held off until Starbuck had led his horse off the bench and down to the level of the trail.

"The way I just come?" he said. "Why not keep going for the border?"

"Be what they'll figure you'd do. We cut north, stay in the stream so's there'll be no tracks, and it ought to throw them off us in a hurry. Even that Indian can't pick up hoofprints there. Got to be careful, however. Couple of places where the water's out in the open. See us easy, if they're looking."

"They're starting down now," Mason said.

That would mean that Yaqui Joe had found the point where he'd begun the descent from the plateau. He'd hoped to have time in which to brush out the tracks both he and Lynch had made in the immediate area, but it was too late now.

Leading the way, he waded into the shin-deep stream at a fast walk with the sorrel slogging in behind him, sending up sprays of water from his hoofs at each step. He could hear Mason Lynch and the bay keeping pace.

For a good quarter-mile he maintained a steady gait,

94

working up a sweat despite the cool surroundings. Finally, with breath coming hard from the sheer labor of not only bucking the current but from the continually lifting grade as well, he halted in a wide bend of the creek. There a thick covering of cottonwood branches completely sheltered them from any possibility of being seen.

Climbing out onto the bank, water dripping from his soaked pant legs where the sorrel had splashed him, he tied the horse to a clump of birch and sat down upon a rotting log. Pulling off his boots, he poured the collected water from them, then, stripping off his socks, he wrung them dry and hung them on a nearby bush. A short distance away, Mason Lynch, close-mouthed and morose, was following the same procedure.

When those necessary creature-comfort chores were completed and both had settled back to regain spent breath and ease their aching muscles, Lynch finally turned to Starbuck. The dark void of bitterness, of utter hopelessness in the man's eyes Shawn had noticed at their first meeting, had returned, and there was a conspicuous drag to his voice.

"Now what? Got them between me and the border—and I'd be a fool to keep riding north. Thinking on it, seems I've been herded around to where I'm between a high fence and a tall place."

Angered, Starbuck shook his head. "If you figure me for some kind of a Judas-goat, then climb on my horse and head out. He'll get you away from here fast—"

"I'm not saying—"

"Then quit thinking it. Just be damned glad you're hid. That's a lynch mob back there."

Mason shrugged. "I expected it to be. You say Huckaby's running it?"

"Supposed to be, but the way Barney Canfield's got the men all fired up—offering a hundred dollars gold for you, dead or alive—I don't think the marshal can stop them if they ever get a hold of you, start in."

"Doubt if he'll even try."

Shawn nodded slowly. "Got to admit that I'm not so sure of him either. Thought all along he was trying to do a job, now I'm wondering about it. You've never got around to answering my question."

"What was that?"

"Kit Canfield—you shoot him? Tell the truth, Mason. A lie will only make it harder to help."

Lynch's eyes locked with those of Starbuck, held. "It wasn't me," he said soberly. "That's the God's truth. I was

95

there—I'm admitting that—but I didn't have anything to do with the shooting."

Starbuck leaned forward. "You saw it?"

"I was about as far from Kit as we are from that big rock—fifteen, maybe twenty strides."

"Then you recognized the man who did it?"

"Seen a man—that's about all. Never got a clear look at him."

Shawn settled back despondently. "Not much there that'll help."

"What I told myself when it was all over and I was standing there in the dark. Who'd believe a yarn like that from me? Everybody knows how things stood between me and the Canfields—and a lot of them are dead sure I came back to square up with the other two. You saw that."

Starbuck's eyes were thoughtful. "How was it that you just happened to be right there?"

Mason's eyes spread slightly and then his head came forward as his shoulders sagged. "You're proving my point. You don't believe a goddam word I'm saying. It's a cinch Huckaby and everybody else'll look at it the same way."

"Not saying I don't. Let's hear the rest of it."

Mason lifted his hands, allowed them to drop to his sides in a gesture of hopelessness. "What for? Won't do no good. Either you believe me—or you don't."

"Wrong!" Shawn snapped. "You've got to convince folks and the best way to do that is start with me—a friend. Then we can work together at making somebody like Huckaby listen—maybe even Barney Canfield, if we can get close enough to him."

"Not sure there's any use trying to talk to any of them."

"We'll go to Tucson, then, lay it out for him. But the thing now is let me hear all of it—everything that went on. Just give up, keep feeling sorry for yourself and how you're going to have to spend the rest of your life dodging the law—and there'll be nothing for me to do but move on, tend to my own business."

Mason's gaunt face had tipped down. His eyes were set, staring, reflected his hopelessness. "Probably be best anyway, Shawn. All I can do is cause you grief—maybe even get you shot."

"Something for me to decide."

"You standing by me, being a friend—that's the best thing that's happened to me in a lot of years. Thinking you'd changed, brought that posse down on me, sort of

96

jolted something inside me—and then if you don't believe—"

"The rest of it," Starbuck broke in gently. "Let me hear it."

Mason shifted, brushed at his lips. He sighed deeply, picked up a twig lying at his feet, began to snap it into small lengths.

"Went down to the graveyard after I left you last night," he began. "Had a look at the folks' graves, done some weed pulling and straightening up, then I got to thinking about Marie—she's the one I told you about."

Shawn nodded. "The one you'd figured to marry."

"I was remembering what you said," Lynch went on in a wooden voice as if not hearing, "and decided I would like to see her, maybe talk to her. Thought she might have some feeling for me—that maybe there was still a chance we could sort of get together, team up.

"Her being what the marshal said she was and all that don't make no difference to me. When I studied on it I could see it was my fault she ended up that way. Besides, I ain't got much to offer either—a busted-down convict with nothing more'n a piece of land.

"Well, I went down to the Frisco House and was standing there looking through the window at her and a couple others, trying to get up enough guts to go in, when Kit Canfield came along. I watched him go inside, like he owned the place, and got right after Marie. He took her upstairs—and I know I've got no right, but it riled me plenty."

"You go in then, make something of that?" Starbuck asked hurriedly. There had been some remark to the effect that Lynch had been seen; he wasn't exactly certain of the details.

"Nope—just stood around outside. Wasn't sure what I wanted to do—or could do, not knowing how Marie would feel. I was still hanging around when Kit came out, couple hours later."

"Anybody else show up around there?"

"Not that I saw. Once I thought I heard somebody walking in the road, coming from town, but I never did see who it was. Anyway, Kit came out, started across the street for the old stable where he'd left his horse."

"That was when the man you say killed him showed up?"

Mason smiled tiredly, wagged his head. Starbuck, catching the unfortunate way he had phrased the words, said:

"Don't take that as meaning I don't believe you—it was just how it sounded."

"Sure, sure," Lynch murmured. "Fellow came out of the stable. Guess he must've been in there all the time, or maybe he was who I heard on the road. He walked out into the middle of the street and met Kit. They just seemed to be talking. Then I hear a shot, all sort of muffled, like when you cover a gun with a blanket or something and pull the trigger. Kit just stood there for a few seconds, then fell.

"The man turned and ducked back into the stable. I guess I was a little surprised or something, and I wasn't hankering to get mixed up in it, so I didn't do anything, just stood there for a little bit. Then I finally went out to where Kit was laying. He was dead."

"Shot with his own pistol," Shawn said. "They found it under him."

Lynch swore, recognizing the implication immediately. "Guess that's the cincher for a lot of folks—them that knew I wasn't carrying a gun."

Shawn made no reply. Mason, head bowed, tossed the broken bits of the twig aside one by one, said: "Came to me right then that people'd all figure it was me who did it because of the trouble I've had with the Canfields, and that I might as well forget trying to start over again."

"Didn't you go into the stable looking for the man who did it?"

"No point. Heard him riding off about the time I was looking at Kit. Headed west, it seemed."

"West?" Starbuck asked, frowning. "What's in that direction?"

"Not much—leastwise there didn't use to be. Things could've changed since I was there last but once there was only the folks' place—Canfield's now—and the road that hooks up with the one going to California."

"Somebody figuring to head out that way would've had to get himself all set—grub, water and the like. No towns for a lot of miles. You get any look at all at the killer?"

Mason shook his head. "Too dark. Couldn't see his face at all."

"Was he dressed any special way?"

"Regular cowhand clothes, I reckon. Did notice he wore some kind of a checked vest."

"Was it a plaid shirt?" Starbuck asked quickly, remembering that Marshal Virgil Huckaby had been wearing such a garment.

"Could've been," Lynch said, not making the connection. "Like I told you, it was hard to tell much about anything."

Shawn considered what Mason had said. There was indeed very little to go on; only one thing could have meaning—the checked vest or shirt being worn by the killer. Such were common but not necessarily plentiful. They had that and the belief that the man had ridden west after the murder.

"What happened then?"

"Somebody yelled in the street. The shot had been heard inside the house, too. I looked, saw a man bending over Kit, and another one coming through the yard. Right then I decided the best thing I could do was get my horse and leave town fast—try to make it across the border into Mexico. Was plain to me I'd have a hell of a time getting anybody to believe it wasn't me who done the shooting."

"Probably be harder than you think," Starbuck said. "You were seen standing there in the doorway of the stable. One of the women from the house. Says she didn't know the man she saw but that she could recognize him if she ever saw him again."

Mason swore raggedly. "You see? What's the use? Man can't buck a stacked deck!" He looked up, faced Shawn squarely. "One thing I'd like to know—you've heard my side of it, where do you stand? You believing me or not?"

"I believe you," Starbuck said without hesitation. "Thought all along that killing was something you'd not let yourself in for—not after spending ten years behind prison walls for one. Kept thinking, too, about the way you felt over being free and having your own place."

Lynch sighed. "Makes a difference to me. I'm obliged to you. Wish there was more I could tell you about that killer. Ain't much there to go on."

"Enough—maybe. A man in a plaid shirt or vest, and the fact that he rode out of town, going west—that's a little something. Thing we've got to decide is what we ought to do next."

"Plenty clear what I'd best do," Lynch said glumly. "Only way I can keep my neck from getting stretched is leave the country, like I was planning to do."

"Give up everything you want—your place in the Mescals? That girl—Marie?"

"Not much chance of seeing either one again, way things are lined up. Barney Canfield, big as he is and pushing Huckaby around like he does—and that woman seeing me there—hell, I'd be a fool to risk staying around. If you're honest with me, you'll admit I'm right."

99

"Maybe, but I don't like to see you just up and quit. If we could get some kind of an idea who the killer was, by tracking maybe, could be we could come up with something we could tell the law."

"Not Huckaby—be a waste of time. I don't trust him."

Starbuck was silent for a while, then: "Not sure I do either. Few things about him that's got me wondering, but we'll not bother with him—not yet anyway. If we can turn up something, we can ride to Tucson, talk to the sheriff there."

"I don't know," Mason said slowly, growing colder to the idea. "Lawmen sort of hang together. Nothing says he wouldn't clap me in a cell and send for Huckaby."

"Not if we had something solid to tell him, give him to work on."

Mason frowned, interest picking up. "You think we can make something of what I told you?"

"Have to. It's all we've got."

Lynch reached for his now dry socks, began to pull them on. There was a briskness to his movements that bespoke the hope stirring within him.

"Know that country west of town. Grew up roaming all through it—hunting and such. I'm remembering a few places where a man could hole up for a spell."

Shawn studied Mason Lynch for a few moments as he began to draw on his footwear. He had built up that hope in the man, was now wondering if he could deliver; there was so little to go on!

"No doubt in your mind the killer rode west?"

"Sure as I know my name," Lynch replied. "You figure there'd be any use looking for tracks?"

"Doubt it," Starbuck said, rising and stamping into his boots. "Never find the right ones along the edge of town. Too many riders coming and going. Might get lucky but I sure would hate to bank on it."

"Expect that's going to be the whole story," Mason said soberly. He was standing off to the side, his features bleak, voice lifeless. "Could all be for nothing—like shooting at the moon. With my kind of luck, we'll likely come up with a flat nothing."

"Maybe so," Shawn murmured, "but we've got to try."

Mason Lynch raised his head, glanced at Starbuck. A grudging smile parted his lips. "I reckon we do," he said, and moved toward his horse.

16

Keeping to the creek until they reached a wider, well-graveled area, Shawn guided the sorrel out into the shallows, halted. Mason drew up beside him.

"Something wrong?"

"Looking for the tracks you made when you came down this way."

Lynch raised himself in his stirrups, gazed around thoughtfully. "Be over there—by that gooseberry patch. Recollect walking by it."

Starbuck scrubbed at the sweat on his face. "Like to get over there to them without making any new ones. That Indian Huckaby's got will be hard to fool. More we mix things up, the better."

Mason glanced downstream. "We've been in the water for quite a ways. He sure won't find tracks there."

"That's how we want to keep it," Shawn said, and touching the sorrel with his spurs, angled for the trail.

"Could go right through them gooseberries," Lynch said as they broke out onto dry ground. "He won't find no tracks in them."

"No tracks but there'd be plenty of broken branches and mashed leaves that we couldn't fix. No job to cut a switch and brush out the prints we're leaving now."

Mason nodded. "Guess you're right . . . What are you aiming to do, backtrack my trail?"

"Best thing. The Indian may never get upstream this far, but if he does, I want everything plenty confused."

"He'll puzzle it out—see how I came down alone, then went back up with somebody else—and they'll guess that somebody else's you."

"Maybe, but it'll take time—and that's something we need a lot of."

They reached the berry thicket, swung onto the faint path bordering its east side, halted.

"Stay in the saddle," Shawn directed, dropping to the ground. "This'll only take a couple of minutes, and the fewer tracks we have to cover, the better."

Thrusting a hand into a boot, he drew the keen-bladed knife he carried in a stitched-in leather sheath, cut a thickly leafed branch from the back side of a gooseberry clump. Doubling back to the edge of the shallow water, he carefully swept out the prints the horses had made, pausing now and then to sift a bit of loose dirt and litter over the places that appeared to have been disturbed.

Then, once again on the gelding, he resumed the trail, keeping exactly to the line taken by Lynch when he came down into the valley. One good thing, he noted, was that the soil was firm on the long grade, being a type of solidly packed sod in which a tough, narrow-bladed glass grew. Trailing them, if the Yaqui managed to get to this point, would not be easy.

But he knew better than to sell the tracker short, and as they wound their way toward the plateau lying north of the valley, he was continually taking precautions, doing everything possible to cover signs of their passage.

Sometime before noon, with the sun blazing down in unabated strength, they climbed out of the basin and found themselves on fairly level ground. Pulling into the shade of a scatter of pines, they dismounted, easing their own sweaty bodies as well as resting the sorrel and the ailing bay, whose condition was steadily worsening. But there was no time to spare and within a half-hour they were again in the saddle, riding due west, challenging the hot wind that now was blowing in from the distant desert.

Little conversation passed between them, only an occasional and necessary comment as each man, wrapped in his own thoughts, felt inclined to keep his peace. Starbuck, for himself, was again thinking of his purpose for being in the Rockinstraw Valley country—that of looking up the man called Jim Ivory, and discussing, hopefully, the possibility of him being his long absent brother Ben.

It irritated him to become sidetracked when following out a good and definite lead, not only because of time lost but because it brought about another complication, money. The small amount of cash granted him by the lawyer handling old Hiram Starbuck's estate had long since run out, and it was now a matter of halting the quest at intervals while he took a job—one of cowhand, deputy marshal, stagecoach driver, or shotgun guard—anything

102

available if it paid hard cash—long enough for him to accumulate sufficient funds to see him through a few more months.

He was about to that low point now where the necessity for finding temporary work would be the next thing in order. If Jim Ivory proved to be Ben, then there would be no problem; if not, he'd ride on—to Las Cruces, perhaps. There was a sheriff there, according to Virg Huckaby, who was looking for a man trained as a boxer—a boxer who might be Ben. As well look for a job there and find out more about—

"That cabin—in the clearing—"

Mason Lynch's voice cut into his thoughts. He roused, looked to the direction in which the man pointed.

"It's one of the places I figured the killer might use as a hideout."

Starbuck, a little surprised at having reached the area so quickly, swung in behind a clump of oak, eyed the sagging, weathered structure.

"Old prospector, name of Tait, used to live there. Was a friend of my folks, more or less—his kind don't ever get too friendly. Apaches killed him."

"Raid?" Shawn asked, wondering why the structure had not been burned to its rock foundation.

"Nope, wasn't that. Tait caught himself a young Apache gal, somehow, kept her tied up inside the place so's he'd have a woman for himself. Got by with it for a whole winter, then a party of braves, still hunting for her, I reckon, found her.

"They hid out in the cabin and when Tait come in that evening about dark from working his claim, they jumped him. Spread-eagled him to the wall, then stood back and threw knives and tomahawks at him. Finished him off by shooting him full of arrows.

"Killed the squaw, too, only they done it quick, didn't make her suffer like they did him. Took me a long time to understand why they killed her—her being their own kind and all. Pa said it was because she'd been a white man's woman—it not making any difference whether she wanted to be or not."

"Probably the answer," Starbuck said. "But it could've been that Tait had come to mean something to her, and she tried to help him. They'd lived together for a whole winter. Seems kind of strange she couldn't have got away from him during all that time."

"Is sort of funny," Mason said. "My pa was the one who found them. Buried them back there in those trees.

Can't remember all the details—only what Pa told me—and that was in private. Ma wouldn't stand for such being talked about in front of her. They were both heathens, according to the way she looked at it."

Shawn continued to study the weathered structure. After a bit he shook his head. "Don't think there's anybody using that place. Ground's not chopped up like it would be if there was a horse coming and going. Best we be sure, though. You stay here, keep me covered. I'll circle around, come in from the hind side."

Swinging away, Starbuck followed the thick brush that fringed the clearing, pulled up shortly in a small grove directly behind the cabin. It was in worse condition, at closer range, than it had appeared at first look. That someone could be living inside seemed most unlikely.

Tying the gelding to a stout cedar, he drew his forty-five, moved quietly around the north side of the hut, and came in to the front. There were a few hoof indentations in the grass-covered sod, but all were old. Nowhere did he see any droppings.

Crossing to the partly open door, he stopped, looked down. Dust had accumulated thick on the sill; it was unsullied except for the tracks of packrats and field mice. Holstering his weapon, he placed a hand against the ax-fashioned slab, shoved it aside, and stepped into the gloomy, stale-smelling room.

A double-width bunk had been built against the wall directly in front of him. Gray ashes in the rock fireplace was proof of occupancy by some drifter or possibly working cowhand, seeking shelter from a winter storm—but they were months old, perhaps over a year. Turning, Shawn stepped out into the open, signaled to Mason Lynch, and retraced his steps to the sorrel.

"Been a long time since anybody was in there," he said as they rode on. "Any other old cabins or line shacks around?"

"Not that I remember," Mason said, his voice reflecting the disappointment he felt in not finding any evidence that could lead to the killer. "Some caves over in the next canyon."

"Big enough for a man to camp in?"

Mason nodded. "Indians once did. Sort of like cliff dwellings."

Shawn remembered such an area up in northern New Mexico, and a larger settlement farther to the west on the Colorado border; sheer embankments with living quarters gouged out of the face.

"A whole village?"

"No, nothing like that. Just a couple of caves. Probably one family driven off by the tribe, crawled in and stayed a while. Or it could've been a small party hiding from others."

The caves, no more extensive than Mason had indicated, proved as fruitless as the prospector's old cabin. The sole tenants, according to all evidence, were a pair of coyotes.

The effect it had upon Mason Lynch was immediately apparent. The bitterness in his eyes became more pronounced and a sort of surly indifference possessed him. Squatting on his haunches, toying with a palm full of sand, he muttered a curse, said: "Reckon that lays it out plain."

Shawn considered the man quietly, fully aware of the change. "Meaning what?"

"I'd be a damned fool to hang around now. I'd best be lining out for the border."

"What about the plan we set up—that of us trying to run down the rider you heard heading west?"

"Figured we'd find some trace of him—but I should've known there'd be no trace. Hell, what's the use!"

Mason raised his arm, slammed the grains of sand he held to the ground. "Nothing—never a goddam thing—works out right for me! You got to admit it."

"Only thing I'll admit is that we haven't given it a chance—our searching around, I mean. Now, if you'll feel better about it, why not hole up somewhere for a spell and let me do the looking. Or, if you'll willing to trust Huckaby, I'll wait until the posse goes back to town, slip in and have a talk with him. Maybe, after I tell him what you saw—"

"Forget it," Mason said flatly. "He'd not believe you, and about the first thing he'd do would be to lock you up for tricking him. One answer, far as I can see, and that's for me to get the hell out of this goddam country. Been nothing but a jinx to me!"

"Be a mistake to quit now, Mason—and I can't let you do it."

"You've got nothing to say about it," Lynch snapped, coming to his feet abruptly, pistol in his hand. Pain filled his eyes and there was almost apology in his voice. "Hell of a note when a man has to throw down on the best friend he's got—but it's the only thing I can do."

Starbuck stared, wagged his head slowly. "Never figured you'd turn on me—"

"For your own good. You hang around with me and my kind of luck'll rub off on you. That sorrel of yours, reckon I'll have to borrow him. Bay'll never make it—but don't worry, I'll treat him right and you'll get him back. I'll leave him in the stable at San Miguel—town just across the border. You'll be fine on the bay. Just ride straight on. The Box C's just over that ridge ahead."

Taut, angry, Shawn faced Mason Lynch. "Happens this is all your trouble, not mine," he said, rising slowly. "I'm trying to help you—not myself. Can't you get that in your head?"

"Wasting your time. You ought to've realized that by now. Thing for me to do is cross the border, lose myself in Mexico."

"You won't ever lose the bounty hunters that'll be dogging your tracks. Canfield'll put up a big reward and it'll say dead or alive. You won't stand a chance."

"Sure as hell don't stand one around here!"

"How do you know? You keep blowing up every time things don't suit you—"

"It's more'n that," Lynch said hopelessly. "It's the way things always work out for me. Nothing ever pans out right, no matter what. Just seems I can't win."

"The hell you can't!" Shawn yelled, suddenly out of patience with the man. "The sooner you quit feeling sorry for yourself, the quicker we can get things straightened up! You've got a good chance of clearing your name, starting a new life, if you'll show some guts!"

"Sounds easy enough, coming from you, but I'm the one looking at a noose. Fact is, I'm the only one—"

"No, not the only one, maybe," Starbuck broke in. "I can name another one."

Mason stared. "Who?"

"Virg Huckaby."

Lynch's jaw sagged, then closed firmly. A frown narrowed his eyes. "You handing me a line of bull? You saying that just to—"

"Stop and think. Huckaby hated Kit Canfield plenty, maybe more than anybody around—even you. Big reason is that he stands to lose his job as marshal, and that means a lot to him—everything, I'd say. He could quit worrying about it if Canfield was dead. Now, what was it you said about the shirt the killer was wearing?"

"It was checked . . ."

"Now think back to Huckaby—when you last saw him. What kind of a shirt was he wearing?"

"By God!" Lynch exclaimed, jamming his pistol back

into its place. "Virg was wearing a checked shirt!" Opening a hand, he smashed his fist into the palm. "Dammit—I wish't I could remember for sure what that killer had on. Ain't sure if it was a vest or a shirt. But checked, I know that. Maybe black and white—or it could've been red and white."

"It's something we've got to go on—and maybe even gives us a good suspect," Starbuck said. "Whole thing it proves is that you'd be a fool to run."

"Maybe," Lynch murmured, again wavering.

"No maybe to it. You do what you are thinking and it'll be worse than the ten years you spent in the pen. Man doesn't need high walls to be in prison; he can build one for himself simply by trying to hide—dodge the lawmen, the bounty hunters—the friends that hear about the reward—"

Shawn broke off suddenly, lifted his hand as the hard pound of a fast-running horse cut through the hush lying over the heated land. Rising, he crossed to where Mason stood, and together they looked down into the shallow basin where the trail continued on westward.

A lone rider—apparently heading for the Box C. The man rounded a bend, for a brief time was faced toward them. Mason swore softly as surprise rocked Shawn Starbuck. It was Barney Canfield.

17

Starbuck considered the rancher in puzzled silence. Why had he pulled out, forsaken the posse at a time when it undoubtedly appeared to all they were closing in on their objective? Thinking back, he recalled that it had been Canfield himself who had forcefully made it clear to the men that no one was to quit until Mason Lynch had been brought down.

"Thought you said he was with Huckaby and that posse," Lynch murmured.

"He was—and I'm wondering why he pulled out. Him being here doesn't make sense."

"Heading for the ranch, that's for sure."

"Could be the posse's following," Shawn said, and glanced off toward the valley. "Nobody in sight, however."

"If they were coming, wouldn't he have waited, rode with them?"

"Seems—unless he had some special reason for wanting to be alone. Any way we can get to the Box C without taking the road he's on?"

Mason pointed to the ridge he had earlier indicated. "That's a bluff. You can look down on the place from there."

Immediately Starbuck turned to the sorrel, swung up, and moved off at a good clip. Lynch, on the bay, now showing a pronounced limp, fell in behind. By the time he reached the ridge, Shawn was already off his horse, and squatted on his heels, looked down from the crest of the steep butte at the Box C. Barney Canfield, sticking to the longer, more circuitous road that curved around the north end of the formation, was just coming into view.

"Not changed much," Lynch commented, hunkering next to Starbuck and scanning the scatter of buildings.

"They've built a few more sheds—a bigger barn—and added on to the bunkhouse. More corrals."

Starbuck's eyes noted the changes as Mason pointed them out, noticed, also, the thread of regret in the man's voice and wondered if the place meant as little to him as he professed. But it could be no more than memory; a man looking back on the old days, his early life, always recalls the good and the pleasant and experiences a twinge of longing.

"Biggest house, there in front—that's where we lived. Kitchen was at the end. Looks like the Canfields have put up a new one. My room was at the south end. I remember I'd get up early when I was a kid—earlier than I had to for chores—and stand by the window and watch the quail come down from the foothills going to water in our stock pond.

"Coveys would come regular as night follows day. Sometimes it would be a big bunch—maybe a hundred birds. Other times there'd be only twenty or thirty. Always tickled me when it was the time of year for chicks. I'd see the mother hen come along, running fast, looking like a fat old lady hurrying to church. The chicks would be strung out behind her in a line, their legs pumping like hell to keep up. Used to think of that a lot when I was laying out the nights in the pen. Sort of kept me from going out of my mind.

"That—that ironwood tree there by the corner of the house—planted it myself when I was hardly big enough to dig the hole. Brought it back one day from the desert. I'd gone there with Pa. Saw the big trees all covered with purple flowers, so I dug up a little one, brought it back as a present for Ma. Took a few years before it had any blossoms, but she liked it."

Shawn, listening to Mason Lynch, once again felt a prickle of doubt. That his folks' place did mean a great deal to the man was apparent now, despite his declarations to the contrary; it was evident in his voice, his manner, in the way his eyes were glowing. And the Canfields—the fact that he still refused to accept proof that a legitimate deal had been consummated between his parents and the three brothers—unquestionably were still the object of a fierce and burning hate on his part.

Starbuck stirred, deeply disturbed by his thoughts. He had been sure Mason was innocent, basing those convictions on his knowledge of the man and his own intuition. But he had been wrong before, he realized, and he could be again. Still . . .

He shifted his attention to the flat north of the ranch. Barney Canfield was just entering the high, square gate frame, his horse approaching the yard at a steady lope. The sound of thudding hooves brought the cook from the kitchen. An old man, he stood on the landing outside his work quarters, wiping his hands on what had once been a white apron but now was a darkly streaked gray, and awaited the rancher's arrival.

Another of the help, a Mexican, moved lazily out of the barn, and leaning on the hayfork with which he had evidently been working, also watched and waited.

Canfield pounded onto the hardpack, angled toward the cook. "George, got about a dozen men riding in for a bite to eat. It's that posse that's hunting Kit's killer. Ought to be here in maybe a half-hour, could be less. Get something ready for them."

"Sure thing, Mr. Canfield."

The rancher pulled away, rode on a short distance, and stopped again, this time at one of the corrals. The Mexican propped his fork against the side of the barn, ambled forward to look after the *patron's* horse. Dismounting, Barney asked a question of some sort of the man, who replied by pointing at the bunkhouse.

Something was happening—something that was important. Shawn could feel it. Canfield, it would seem, had ridden in ahead of Huckaby and the posse, which, unaccountably, was taking time out for lunch despite the rancher's previous insistence that there be no let-up in the search for Mason.

But, assuming hunger did get the best of the men and the break became necessary—why did Barney Canfield feel it necessary to leave the party himself on such a trivial errand as notifying the cook of their coming when he could have dispatched one of the hired hands accompanying him? And the need for such forewarning to the cook was hardly necessary, anyway; with a large crew such as the Box C would run, men would be coming and going at all hours. There would be plenty of food and hot coffee available at most any time.

A deep dissatisfaction possessed Shawn Starbuck. Too many things didn't add up. He turned to Lynch.

"There a way to get down there from here?"

"Trail over there to the left," Mason replied. "You can make it on foot—not with horses." He paused, stared at Shawn. "You aiming to go down?"

Shawn nodded.

"Don't see as how that can help any," Mason said,

doubt riding his voice. "With Huckaby and that posse about due, could be kind of a fool thing to try."

"Maybe, but we're looking for answers and it could be we'll find them there."

"And maybe I'll just be helping them put that rope around my neck——"

"No need for you to come. Wait here—just show me where that trail is."

Starbuck pulled back from the lip of the butte, came to his feet. More slowly, Mason took a place beside him, features drawn into a dark frown. Abruptly he shrugged.

"Hell—if you can keep from getting caught, reckon I can, too."

Starbuck nodded. "Hoped you'd come along. Likely be some things I'll need explained to me."

Lynch gave Shawn a quizzical look, cut off to his left, and kneeing his way into a stand of stiffly resisting snakeweed, bulled a path to where the rim of the bluff had broken off and slid into a steep draw.

Unhesitating, Mason dropped into it, began to descend, steadying and bracing himself on the slant by grasping the clumps of tough groundsel and rabbitbrush that grew out of the near-vertical sides. Shortly they were at the foot of the formation. The south end of the main house was no more than two dozen strides distant.

It was the blind side of the structure; a blanket had been hung over the window in the end—the same from which Mason had often watched the quail—and Shawn, hunched low, sprinted across the open ground to the forward corner of the building. Halting there, brushing at the sweat again covering his face, he waited until Lynch joined him.

He started to ask Mason about the arrangement of the remaining structures in relation to the yard, realized he would probably know very little about it; a number of new buildings and pens had been erected since he had last seen the place. Best find out for himself.

Quickly, he crossed to the opposite corner of the house, stopped, peered cautiously around the weather-smoothed stones toward the yard. He found little advantage as the new kitchen had been built only a few feet from the main structure, leaving only a narrow, separating breezeway which severally restricted any view of the hardpack and other buildings.

Taking a hurried survey of the cooking quarters, he saw the window in the wall facing him was high, served only for purposes of ventilation, and again bent low, ran forward until he had gained the opposite side of that more recently acquired structure.

A grunt of satisfaction came from him. An old corral, no longer in use, lay adjacent. To its right was the yard with all other buildings clearly visible. Still cautious, Shawn moved to the corral, crawled through a gap in the sagging crosspoles, and took up a position inside and to the front. He now had a complete view of the yard, could watch all activity with ease as well as hear any normal conversation that took place in the open without fear of being seen.

Lynch, lying beside him, brushed at his eyes nervously. "Somebody spots us—we'll be like trapped coyotes—"

"Stay low—nobody'll see us."

"You hope. Way my luck runs, we could get caught first thing. What're you looking for?"

Starbuck shrugged. "Anything—everything. I don't know. Just that I've got a feeling. May be a waste of time, but we've got to work from somewhere. One thing, when Virg Huckaby shows up, take a good look at that shirt he's wearing."

Shawn checked his whispered words, attention drawn to the Mexican hired hand coming from the interior of the barn again. Canfield had disappeared, going into the house, Starbuck supposed, and wondered if it would have been smarter to have found a place nearer that structure. He decided he was likely in as good a position as possible.

The hired hand circled the barn at an indifferent shuffle, returned shortly leading a chunky black gelding. Tethering him with a neck rope to the hitchrack fronting the bulky building, he went inside, reappeared dragging a saddle and other gear. With no effort at haste, he began to throw the equipment onto the black, all the while softly crooning some low-pitched south-of-the-border lament on love.

A door slammed loudly. The screen of the bunkhouse. A man appeared, saddlebags slung across one shoulder, a blanket roll trapped under an arm. Shawn felt Mason claw at his hand, turned. Lynch was staring at the rider.

"That's him—that's him! He's the one I seen shoot Kit!"

Starbuck came up instantly, swiveled his eyes to the man. He was stockily built, dark, walked with an easy swing. He was dressed much the same as any cowhand except that he sported a black-and-white-checked vest of the type designed for men with the less robust occupation of gambler; it was now much the worse for the hard, everyday use it was being subjected to.

112

"You sure?"

"Sure's I can be," Mason responded tensely. "It was dark but I ain't forgetting that fancy vest."

Shawn watched the man halt beside the black, hang his saddlebags over the skirt of the hull, anchor them, then affix the blanket roll atop the pouches. The Mexican lazed against the crossbar of the hitchrack.

"You ride, eh, *señor?*"

The squat man nodded. "Tired of this place, *amigo.*"

"You here for a long time. Where you go?"

"Mexico—maybe. You want to come along?"

"*Por Dios—no!* The *Federales,* they have look often for me. I do not wish for them to find me."

The rider laughed. "What'd you do—stick a *cuchillo* in one of those *señoritas* you're always singing about?"

"Maybe. It is a thing one does not speak of."

If this was the man who had slain Kit Canfield, what was he doing on the Canfield ranch? It appeared he was a regular hand and no stranger.

"Heading for Mexico—that proves it," Mason said in a low voice. "He's running."

"Looks like it. Any chance you're mistaken? Doesn't make much sense he'd be here—one of the hired help."

"Maybe it don't—but he's the one. Couldn't be wrong about that vest."

"Other men around wearing about the same thing. Huckaby's got a checked shirt on right now—"

"Shirt maybe—but this is a vest. And there's something about the way he stands."

Shawn scrubbed at the sweat clouding his eyes, shifted to ease the muscles of his doubled under legs. "What reason would he have for killing Canfield? Got to have a reason."

Mason shook himself impatiently. "How the hell would I know? Just know he was the one who done it. Maybe he was paid to do it."

"Who'd hate Canfield enough to hire him killed?"

"You called the turn on one—Huckaby."

"He's got reasons, all right—but so have you."

There was a stiffness in Lynch's voice when he replied. "Well, it wasn't me—and that leaves Huckaby. Can't see as it's anything for us to be sweating over anyway. We nab him, turn him over to—"

Lynch's words ended as again a door slammed, this time at the main house. Boot heels rapped sharply on the hardpack. Barney Canfield appeared, coming across the yard,

113

pointing for the man standing beside the black and the hitchrack.

Starbuck crouched lower, pressed forward against the poles of the corral. "Maybe here's where we get some answers," he murmured.

18

Canfield, a fresh cigar clamped between his teeth, passed in front of the unused corral in which Shawn and Mason Lynch huddled, so near he was almost within reach. There was a slackness to the rancher's face, a look of relief, as that of a man coming to the end of a long and tedious journey.

"Ready, eh?" he said, halting beside the man with the black. Turning his head, he threw a glance to the Mexican yard-hand, made a gesture toward the barn. "Vamoose, *hombre*. Go find yourself a job somewheres."

The Mexican shrugged, ambled off in the direction of the barn.

"Ready as I'll ever be," the man in the checked vest said.

"Best thing," Canfield said in a confidential way. "You ain't around—you ain't apt to get in no trouble. Where'll you be—just in case I want you?"

"Across the border—little town called San Plomo. Been there a couple of times before. Plenty of *señoritas* and plenty of that Mex brandy."

"Maybe too much. Stuff can loosen a man's tongue"

"Never got that much yet. Wouldn't make no difference, anyhow. Most of the Mexes there are friends of mine, and what's not don't savvy anything but their own lingo. Don't work up a sweat over it."

"I won't," Barney Canfield said. "Some place special in this San Plomo burg you'll be living?"

"Corrasco's—just ask anybody for him. Sounds like maybe you are figuring on paying me a call, asking things like that."

"Nothing for sure—just never know what might turn up. I—"

The cook came from his kitchen, glanced about, and lo-

115

cating Canfield, started toward him at the painful, halting gait of an old bronc-stomper, crippled by his trade, now compelled to follow a less rigorous way of life.

"Mr. Canfield, when's them fellows coming? Got everything all set."

Conversation between the rancher and the rider had ceased at the cook's appearance. Canfield removed the cigar from his mouth, spat.

"They'll be along, George. You in a hurry?"

"Nope—sure ain't going nowheres. Sort of like to keep my vittles tasty, howsomever."

"They'll eat them, no matter what."

The cook, head cocked to one side, was staring at the departing rider. "You leaving?"

"Sending him out to look over some new range," Canfield replied quickly before the other man could speak. "Aim to be adding to the herd. Got to have more grass."

The cook jutted his chin at the blanket roll cinched tight behind the rider's cantle. "If you'll be gone for a spell, you'll be needing grub."

Checked-vest shrugged. "Figured to swing by on my way out."

George nodded, sucked at his colorless lips. "How long'll you be gone?"

"Couple, maybe three days."

The older man bobbed his head. "It'll be in a sack, laying on the table, if it happens I ain't handy," he said and turning, hobbled off toward his kitchen.

Canfield watched him briefly, until he was out of earshot, then came back to the rider. "Best you forget that. Pick yourself up some supplies next town you hit. Huckaby and the others'll be here in a few minutes."

"I'm ready to pull out soon's I've got my money."

Canfield shifted his cigar to the opposite corner of his mouth, flicked a glance at the kitchen, then to the bunkhouse. No one was in sight, and apparently reassured, he dug inside his shirt front, withdrew a leather pouch. Shielding his movements with his body, he passed the bag to the man in the checked vest.

"Thousand there—gold and bills."

The rider hefted the pouch in his left hand as if calculating its weight. "How much gold? Don't cotton to paper money. Some places just plain won't take it."

"About half. Be no trouble if you work it right. Stop in the first bank you come to on your way south, swap it for gold. Don't be a damned fool and try changing it all in the

116

same place—they might get the idea you'd pulled a hold-up somewhere. Go to three or four different banks."

"Lot of trouble. Would've been better if it was all gold."

"Scraped up what I could. Didn't have much time."

The rider shrugged, tucked the pouch inside his shirt, leisurely rebuttoned it. "You and me are all square now for what I borrowed?"

"Every nickel," Canfield said. "You don't owe me nothing. All them advance wages, all them loans I gave you to pay off your debts are wiped out. We're even."

Shawn Starbuck had listened to the conversation in grim silence, aware that Mason also was equally shocked. It was evident that the man in the checked vest was the one Lynch had seen shoot down Kit Canfield—and it was just as clear that Barney had hired him to do it. One brother murdering another . . . Cain and Abel. To Shawn, spending his life searching for a brother, it was hard to understand how such could come to pass.

Everything that Barney had said and done in town had been pure play-acting, designed to cover over the crime he had planned and brought to be. Whether he had long schemed to rid himself of his brother—stepbrother, in reality—in order to have the Box C all for himself, or had simply taken advantage of Mason Lynch's return to strike, there was no way of knowing. The timely appearance of Lynch—a convicted killer of one Canfield, and a known hater of all—unquestionably fit perfectly into whatever he had in mind.

It had worked out well for him. Kit had been murdered and Mason Lynch had fled. Townspeople, the merchants, his own hired hands, Marshal Virg Huckaby himself had accepted what appeared to be strong evidence—actual proof in the eyes of some—that Mason was the killer, and the posse had taken to the saddle at once determined to run him to earth.

It wouldn't have mattered to Barney Canfield, Shawn realized, whether Mason Lynch was caught and hanged on the spot, or brought in alive to face justice. Mason, with the stain of one Canfield killing already upon his brow, would stand no chance when it was pointed out he still felt his family had been swindled by the three brothers, had declared so publicly. A judge and jury would fall for such simple, straightforward logic and Mason would again pay a stiff price—perhaps with his life this time.

But something had happened that morning to disturb the web Barney Canfield had woven, and set up an uneasiness in the man. It could have been something as simple and ordinary as hunger. Huckaby, perhaps noting that his posse members had been given no opportunity for taking breakfast, and, understandably, in need of food, suggested that time out should be taken to repair that oversight. And as the Box C was the nearest source for food, the men should go there.

Canfield would have had no choice except to agree, but the knowledge that the man he'd hired to kill his brother was still on the premises, and as yet unpaid for his sanguinary labors, dawned upon him. Such opened up any number of dire possibilities—chief among them being a slip of the tongue on the part of the murderer after which the truth would find its way out.

He had then hurried on ahead on the pretext of advising his cook of their coming and seeing to it that all would be in readiness so no undue loss of time would occur. His real purpose had been one of a wholly different nature, however—that of paying off the killer and getting him off the ranch before the posse could arrive.

That, likely, was as close to the true story of what and how it had happened as he could guess, Shawn concluded. And now that he had it squared away in his mind to his conscience's satisfaction, he felt he could make a move, do what must be done. The killer could not be allowed to ride off—that was certain. In some way he must be delayed, held until Virg Huckaby arrived.

"That sonofabitch," he heard Mason Lynch mutter. "Was him all the time—Barney. Had Kit shot down, then unloaded the blame on me. I'm going to—"

"Easy," Shawn cautioned, laying his hand on Mason's arm. "Anything that's done now we want the marshal in on. Only way we can be sure you won't be faulted again."

Lynch drew back. "You mean we ought to just set here, wait for that posse? Hell, that killer'll be long gone by then. It's what Barney came back for—get him out of the way."

"We can't let him get away but the minute we make a move, we'll have all hell on our hands. Canfield gives one yell and all the hired hands on the place come boiling out to help him. Far as they know, you're the killer and it'll look to them like you're here to put a bullet in Barney—with me siding you. They've all got me pegged for a gunslinger hired to help."

Mason relaxed. "Guess you're right, but I ain't seen nobody else around but the cook and that Mex yard hand."

"What about the night crew? Won't they be in the bunkhouse?"

Mason nodded. "Forgot about them. Been so long since I was around a ranch, sort of slipped my mind. Yeh, they'll be there. Probably a half-dozen men—maybe more. Makes the odds plenty bad."

"If we had some way to keep Barney and the killer quiet. Expect we'll need to hold them for only a few minutes. Huckaby and that posse can't be far off." Shawn paused, aware of Mason's probing gaze. "Something bothering you?"

Lynch smiled in a strange, wry manner. "You talking about holding them—maybe having to step out there and pin down eight, even ten guns, just the pair of us—that's what. It'll be one hell of a long shot with the odds all wrong—and you sure don't owe me nothing, not after the way I've done. Best thing you can do is sit tight, not go risking your hide. I made this trouble for myself. Up to me to handle it."

"I'll own up there's lots of places I'd rather be right now than here," Starbuck said wryly. "But a man's bound to help when he has to—and wrong's wrong no matter who it happens to."

"Stay out of town—I want you to be damn sure of that!"

Barney Canfield's voice lifted suddenly as if spurred by anger. Shawn tensed, watched the man in the checked vest reach for the rope linking the black to the hitchrack. He and Mason would have to act; the posse would not be arriving in time.

"Quit fretting about it. I'll be lining out due south. First town I'll hit will be Rock Crossing—then it'll be Tucson. What about old George? Ain't he liable to fuss about me not coming by for that sack of grub?"

"I'll get in there, hide it. He'll think you came in when he wasn't around. *Adios.*"

"*Adios,*" the rider said, and started to mount.

Starbuck touched Mason's arm lightly, drew his pistol and sprang upright.

"Forget it," he said in a hard, low-pitched voice and vaulted over the top bar of the old corral. "You're both standing where you are until the marshal gets here."

19

Barney Canfield's jaw sagged. His eyes flared in surprise. The man with him fell back a step, arm going down smoothly, fingers reaching for the pistol on his hip.

"Don't—" Shawn warned softly.

The rider froze. Starbuck risked a side glance at Lynch. Mason was crouched beside him, weapon steady and leveled. There had been a bad moment when he thought the man, out of pure hate, was going to lose control, start shooting and arouse the others on the ranch; but he had not and now seemed to be all right.

"Keep your hands where I can see them," Starbuck said, adding quickly, "No—not up!" when Canfield started to extend his arms above his head. Anyone looking toward them from the bunkhouse, or elsewhere in the yard, would simply think they were four men in conversation; with arms raised they would immediately realize something else was taking place.

Canfield, fists clenching and releasing at his sides nervously, glared at Shawn. "You must be loco! You think you can hold a gun on me right here in my own yard and get away with it?"

"We're doing it," Mason said laconically.

"Not for long!" the rancher countered. "Right about now I'd say three, maybe four of my boys have got you lined up in their sights. All I've got to do is give them the signal—"

"And you're a dead man—right along with us," Starbuck finished coldly.

Sweat was standing out in large beads on Canfield's forehead. He slid a look at the man in the checked vest, shook his head.

"What's this all about?" he demanded, striving to make

120

his voice carry a note of indignation. "You here to finish me off—kill off the last of the Canfields?"

Shawn laughed humorlessly. "You're too late with that crock of bull, friend. Mason saw your hired gun there shoot down your brother. We both watched you pay him off and heard you tell him to get out of the country. We're holding the pair of you until Huckaby gets here. So what's it sound like to you?"

"A pack of goddam lies—that's what! Me—have my own brother bushwhacked? You're worse than plain loco!"

"Maybe so, but it tots to something that's pure sense and easy to figure, and I reckon it will to the marshal and his posse when they get here, too."

The rider with Canfield shifted gently on his feet. "Well, I ain't in the notion to hang around and find out," he drawled. "And the way things are, I guess I'll just climb onto my horse and ride on."

Starbuck's jaw hardened. "Be a mistake to try."

"Misdoubt that. There's two of us and two of you. I figure that jailbird ain't much good with a gun, him not having much to do with one for a long time. On top of that I can see a couple of the boys a-watching us. Way I see it, odds are all in my favor."

"And far as Huckaby's concerned," Barney Canfield put in, "it's going to be maybe another half-hour before he shows up—and you sure ain't going to be able to hold us here like this for that long."

"You think we can't?" Shawn asked quietly. "Make your move—find out."

But he knew Canfield was right. Standing in the open, in full view of anyone on the ranch, they were in a desperate situation. It was only necessary for some of the Box C men to grow suspicious, circle the buildings, and come in on them from the rear. He and Mason were then as good as dead.

Shawn centered his attention on the rider with Canfield. If trouble came now it would come from him; he had the look of wildness in his eyes, the offhanded way of a man not afraid to dare the risks.

"Got to move them out of here," he said to Mason. "Need to get under cover—fast."

"We could back them into the barn, hold them in one of the stalls."

"How about that hostler? He in there?"

"I see him working in one of the corrals, out back."

Starbuck bobbed his head at the rancher and his hired

121

gun. "Start walking," he ordered, motioning with his weapon.

The two came away from the rack slowly. Sweat was glistening on their faces, and they carried themselves loosely, arms hung forward. Immediately Starbuck stepped to the side, endeavoring to block the view of anyone looking from the upper yard.

"Get there at the door," Shawn said to Mason. "I'll herd them by—you take their guns—"

Lynch nodded his understanding, started to cross over, going in between the two men and the horse standing at the rack.

"Watch out!" Starbuck warned suddenly, seeing the danger.

In that same instant the man in the checked vest lunged backwards, smashed hard into Mason. Spinning, he drew his pistol, made a dive for the shelter of the small shed a long stride away.

Shawn fired as he saw the rider whip up his gun, lay a shot at him. He couldn't see Barney Canfield, knew only that the rancher had flung himself to the opposite direction, where Lynch, caught against the black gelding, was struggling to regain his balance.

Guns blasted from behind him. He heard a groan but there was no time to wheel, see if it was Mason or Canfield who'd been hit. The man behind the shed was firing at him now and someone near the bunkhouse was opening up. The shots had brought the rest of the Box C crew into the fight.

Ducking low, he lunged for protection of the log water trough a short distance to his right. Bullets dug into the hard-packed soil around his feet, whirred by him, thudded dully into the wall of the barn beyond him. He heard someone yelling and then the rider behind the shed stepped fully into the open. His pistol was leveled. The big, round O of the weapon's muzzle seemed only an arm's length away.

Shawn dipped low, threw himself forward, fired as he went down. The man buckled, clutched at his chest. He staggered back, fell behind the shed.

Shawn rolled frantically, gained the protection of the trough. His pistol was empty, he was sure. Heaving for breath, he lay full length, began to rod the spent casings from the forty-five's cylinder, glanced to his left. Mason, prone in the dust, one arm bloodied and tight against his side, was endeavoring to crawl to the barn. Bullets were stabbing into the ground about him.

Shawn, his weapon reloaded, came to a crouch, and keeping low, broke clear of the water trough and ran toward Lynch. He reached the man's side, bent swiftly, caught him under the arms. Ignoring the crackling guns, he started for the barn, eyes only absently noticing Barney Canfield's crumpled shape near the hitchrack.

Shocking pain in his leg, hot and numbing, brought him to a halt. Taking a firmer grasp of Mason, he tried to continue, discovered his leg would not respond.

"Get away from me!"

He became aware of Mason's voice, yelling at him through the dust and drifting smoke.

"Leave me be—ain't a chance of me making it!"

Shawn shook his head stubbornly, released his grip on the man's arms. If he stayed low, he'd not be so easy a target. Flat on his belly, he extended his hand to Lynch.

"Hang on—I'll drag you—"

"No—dammit—you go on—"

Starbuck seized Lynch by the wrist, began to work his way toward the open doorway of the now close-by structure. Another bullet ripped into him, catching him high in the shoulder, paralyzing his muscles, causing him to drop his weapon. Releasing his hold on Mason, he twisted around, tried to recover the forty-five—recoiled as a booted foot stamped down upon it.

Grim, he looked up. Barney Canfield, pistol clutched so tightly in his hand the knuckles showed white, blood streaking his face where a bullet had stunned him—but only temporarily—was standing over him.

"Damn the both of you!" he yelled in a trembling voice. "You ain't telling nobody—nothing!"

Starbuck jerked back, attempted to get his hand upon the weapon trapped beneath the rancher's foot—winced as the deafening report of a pistol slammed against his eardrums. But there was no shocking impact of a bullet, no pain. He brushed at the sweat and dust blinding him. Canfield had twisted half about, was staring with unseeing eyes at Mason Lynch. Smoke trickled from the barrel of the weapon in his hand. His glance caught Shawn's and he smiled grimly as Canfield stumbled off to one side, fell heavily.

"Wasn't as dead—as he figured," he mumbled.

Starbuck lay back, probed the dust for his pistol, found it. Men were running toward them . . . several men. Shawn pulled himself to a sitting position, wondering at the absence of gunshots. The Box C crew wouldn't let it end there. Ignoring the woodenness of his arm, the dull

123

burning in his leg, he squared himself around, prepared to make a fight of it.

The first man he saw was Huckaby. Behind him came Kemmer, and the one they'd called Ike. On beyond them others of the posse were mingling with Canfield's men. The old cook, hands wrapped in his apron, was standing nearby watching it all in a dazed sort of way.

Starbuck, throwing everything he had into it, worked himself to his knees, managed then to get on his feet. He saw a look of concern cross Mason's face.

"It's all right. It's done with," he said. "The posse's here."

"Thank God," Lynch murmured, letting himself go limp.

"Drop that gun, Starbuck!"

At the sound of Huckaby's harsh command, a bleakness settled over Shawn. He allowed his weapon to fall, watched as the lawman turned, looked to the upper end of the yard.

"Hayman—over here! Want these two patched up. They've got some answering to do."

Huckaby moved in, scooped up Mason's pistol and then Starbuck's, held them in one hand by the barrels. Near by Fred Kemmer was bending over the man lying behind the shed, while beyond Ike and another member of the posse were crouched beside Barney Canfield.

"Finished it, I see," the marshal said in a dry, angry way to Mason Lynch. "You killed him—the last one of them—just like you aimed to."

Starbuck stirred impatiently as an understanding of the lawman's attitude and words filtered into his wearied and numbed brain.

"Can see there never was any doubt in your mind," he said. "You had it pegged as Mason all the time."

"Not hard figuring it out."

"And you're a man who's never wrong—"

"That mean something?"

"Only that you think you're so damned right that you'll nail Mason and me to the cross without even trying to find out what happened."

"I got eyes—I can see," Huckaby said stubbornly.

"The hell with what you can see, you'd best be hunting for the truth! Looks don't mean a thing, most of the time. You want to know something—I figured you for the killer because it seemed to me you had the best reason."

Huckaby straightened in outrage. "Me! Why would I—"

"Anybody could see Kit Canfield was riding you raw. Hate you had in your eyes yesterday said you'd as soon kill him as draw a breath."

"Well, it wasn't me—and you can mark that down in red chalk! And if this is all because you're trying to cover over for your friend there, start something—forget it. I've got you both cold-turkey."

"You've got nothing, Marshal, far as we're concerned. Man laying over there behind that shed is the one who killed Kit. Barney hired him. Mason was there, saw it happen."

The lawman frowned, clawed at his chin as he turned to Lynch, now sitting up and being attended to by the man called Hayman. "You seen it?"

Mason moved his head slowly, weakly. The loss of blood was telling on him. "At the Frisco House. Fellow walked up to Kit, shot him. Then got away."

Huckaby glanced at the men drifting in from the opposite end of the yard. "Damned funny you didn't come tell me about it," he said in a suspicious voice. "Why didn't you?"

Mason managed a tired smile. "You know the answer to that—I'd never have got the chance to talk. Some of your good citizens would've strung me up before I got my mouth open."

Fred Kemmer moved in to stand beside Huckaby. "Still no proof you're telling the truth. Everybody's dead that was mixed up in it except you two—and a dead man sure can't tell his side of the story."

"It's the truth, just the same," Starbuck said angrily. Hayman, who seemed to have some rudimentary skills in medicine, or possibly was a veterinarian, was working on his arm now. "If it wasn't he'd never come back with me. He was headed for Mexico. I caught up, talked him into forgetting that, trying instead to clear his name."

"A good yarn," Huckaby said, indifferently. "Makes more sense, however, to think you both came here for one thing—kill Barney, finish what you started."

"Barney ain't dead yet, Marshal," one of the men hunched over the rancher called, looking up. "He can talk, maybe."

"Make him," Starbuck said bluntly, and then recalled something that had slipped his mind—something that should help convince Huckaby and the others of the truth. "Money he paid off with is inside the dead man's shirt. Leather pouch. There'll be a thousand dollars in it—gold and paper. We heard them talking about it."

Huckaby, flashing a look at Shawn, wheeled away, crossed to where Barney Canfield lay sprawled face up. Starbuck watched the lawman kneel, slip a hand under the rancher's head, raise it slightly. Kemmer had returned to the shed, was rummaging about on the rider's body for the pouch. He found it.

"Reckon he's got hisself an answer," Mason said as Huckaby lowered Canfield's head to the ground, stood up. "Be like that bastard to say it was me, no matter if he was dying," he added bitterly.

The lawman remained motionless, staring down at the rancher for several moments, and then slowly he turned, came back to where Starbuck and Mason Lynch waited.

"Guess you were telling the truth," he said in a begrudging voice as he handed them back their pistols. "Barney wanted Kit out of the way so's the ranch would be his. Hired the killing done. All there was to it."

A surge of resentment shook Shawn Starbuck. *All there was to it!* That was a hell of a thing for a lawman to say! The affair had almost cost Mason and him their lives— and it would have meant a lynching for Mason if the posse had been able to catch him during those past few hours. Perhaps for him, too, if Canfield had been able to convince the men that he was Lynch's hired gun.

But it was over now. Mason could go his way—either on to the Mescals or remain and see if he did have some claim on the Box C; and likely he could square things with the girl, Marie, go ahead with plans interrupted over ten years ago.

As for himself he could continue with his reason for being in the Rockinstraw Valley country. He turned to Kemmer, standing nervously by, looking down in that self-conscious way of a man caught in a bad mistake, pointed to the group of Canfield riders loitering in the yard.

"Which one is Jim Ivory?"

Kemmer's brows drew together. He shook his head. "Ivory? He ain't one of them—he's the one laying dead there behind the shed."

20

Starbuck stood absolutely motionless, transfixed. Somewhere deep inside him his breath had locked and he felt as if he had been struck a powerful blow to the midsection. The man in the checked vest—the killer—he was Jim Ivory. His own brother, perhaps. . . .

Vaguely he heard Huckaby's voice calling to several of the men to hitch up a surrey, a team and wagon. The words jarred him, stirred him from the paralytic lethargy that gripped him. He turned, moved slowly to the shed, halted. Jim Ivory lay on his back, face bared to the streaming sunlight, eyes half closed. His hat had come off, revealing a thick shock of dark hair. Lying under him, partly visible, was a scattered pack of worn cards, apparently having spilled from his pocket when he fell. A deuce of hearts . . . nine of clubs . . . an ace . . .

A man always with a deck of cards on him.

Shawn recalled again what he had been told about Jim Ivory. Continually ready for a game . . . would play himself if no one else was willing or handy. Gambling had been his curse, it would seem; the debts Barney Canfield had mentioned had likely come from his losses. But the man was Jim Ivory, and Ivory—possibly—was Ben Starbuck, and if true, he had shot down his own brother.

Abruptly Shawn's jaw came to a hard line. The cool, practical streak that ordinarily governed him shook off all the speculating, all the conjecture, the weighing of probabilities. Ignoring the throbbing pain in his arm, favoring his stiffening leg, he stepped up to the lifeless body, knelt beside it, looked more closely at the flaccid features.

The hooded eyes were blue. The hair was dark, and there was a blockiness to the face. Taut, Starbuck reached out, placed his fingers on the left brow, pushed aside the thick growth.

There was no scar. No scar where Ben had one.

Relief shot through him. He hesitated a long moment, looked again, knowing that he must be absolutely certain or forever have his doubts. There was no telltale, identifying mark. Slowly he pulled back, painfully got to his feet, sweat clothing him in a solid sheet as a mountainous worry slid from his shoulders. He wheeled then to face the curious stares of the men gathered around.

"Is it him?" Mason Lynch's voice was anxious.

Shawn moved his head. "No—it's not him."

He saw Mason's shoulders go down in a relieved, exhausted sort of way, heard him murmur once more: "Thank God . . ."

Starbuck echoed the words silently. For the first time in his life he was glad the man he had hoped would be his brother—was not. A spring wagon rattled up from the rear of the barn, halted beside Barney Canfield's body. As several men, directed by Huckaby, bent to lift the rancher into the bed, a second vehicle, a black surrey, came from the same direction, stopped near Mason.

Two members of the posse stepped up to Lynch, helped him aboard. Another beckoned to Shawn. Suddenly very tired, he moved toward the two-seater, idly listening to Lynch give instructions as to where their horses could be found, and directing they be taken to Pete Fortney's livery stable for care. The voices responding to Mason were friendly, sounded pleased to be of help. Mason Lynch was home again, Starbuck realized; he had been taken back into the fold.

As for himself—he stared off into the hot blue of the empty sky to the east. Las Cruces lay in that general direction. He'd have to take it easy for a few days, allow his wounds to heal, then he'd head out. Maybe next time—next time he'd find Ben.